THIRTY-ONE SELECTED TALES

THIRTY-ONE
SELECTED TALES

by

H. E. BATES

JONATHAN CAPE
THIRTY BEDFORD SQUARE
LONDON

These Tales are selected from
the following volumes

The Woman Who Had Imagination
FIRST PUBLISHED 1934

Cut and Come Again
FIRST PUBLISHED 1935

Something Short and Sweet
FIRST PUBLISHED 1937

The Flying Goat
FIRST PUBLISHED 1939

The Beauty of the Dead
FIRST PUBLISHED 1940

———————————————

Thirty-One Selected Tales
FIRST PUBLISHED JUNE 1947
SECOND IMPRESSION OCTOBER 1949
THIRD IMPRESSION 1951

PRINTED IN GREAT BRITAIN IN THE CITY OF OXFORD
AT THE ALDEN PRESS
BOUND BY A. W. BAIN & CO. LTD., LONDON

CONTENTS

THIRTY-ONE SELECTED TALES

THE OX

THE Thurlows lived on a small hill. As though it were not high enough, the house was raised up, as on invisible stilts, with a wooden flight of steps to the front door. Exposed and isolated, the wind striking at it from all quarters, it seemed to have no part with the surrounding landscape. Empty ploughed lands, in winter-time, stretched away on all sides in wet steel curves.

At half-past seven every morning Mrs. Thurlow pushed her great rusty bicycle down the hill; at six every evening she pushed it back. Loaded, always, with grey bundles of washing, oilcans, sacks, cabbages, bundles of old newspaper, boughs of wind-blown wood, and bags of chicken food, the bicycle could never be ridden. It was a vehicle of necessity. Her relationship to it was that of a beast to a cart. Slopping along beside it, flat heavy feet pounding painfully along under mud-stained skirts, her face and body ugly with lumpy angles of bone, she was like a beast of burden.

Coming out of the house, raised up even above the level of the small hill, she stepped into a country of wide horizons. This fact meant nothing to her. The world into which she moved was very small: from six to nine she cleaned for the two retired sisters, nine to twelve for the retired photographer, twelve-thirty to three for the poultry farm, four to six for the middle-aged bachelor. She did not think of going beyond the four lines which made up the square of her life. She thought of other people going beyond them, but this was different. Staring down at a succession of wet floors, working always for other people, against time, she had somehow got into the habit of not thinking about herself.

She thought much, in the same stolid pounding way as she pushed the bicycle, of other people: in particular of Thurlow, more particularly of her two sons. She had married late; the boys were nine and thirteen. She saw them realizing refined ambitions, making their way as assistants in shops, as clerks in offices, even as butlers. Heavily built, with faces having her own angular boniness, they moved with eyes on the ground. She had saved money for them. For fifteen years she had hoarded the scrubbing-and-washing money, keeping it in a bran bag under a mattress in the back bedroom. They did not know of it; she felt that no one, not even Thurlow, knew of it.

Thurlow had a silver plate in his head. In his own eyes it set him apart from other men. 'I got a plate in me head. Solid silver. Enough silver to make a dozen spoons and a bit over. Solid. Beat that!' Wounded on the Marne, and now walking about with the silver plate in his head, Thurlow was a martyr. 'I didn't ought to stoop. I didn't ought to do nothing. By rights. By rights I didn't ought to lift a finger.' He was a hedge cutter. 'Lucky I'm tall, else that job wouldn't be no good to me.' He had bad days and good days, even days of genuine pain. 'Me plate's hurting me! It's me plate. By God, it'll drive me so's I don't know what I'm doing! It's me plate again.' And he would stand wild and vacant, rubbing his hands through his thin black hair, clawing his scalp as though to wrench out the plate and the pain.

Once a week, on Saturdays or Sundays, he came home a little tipsy, in a good mood, laughing to himself, riding his bicycle up the hill like some comic rider in a circus. 'Eh? Too much be damned. I can ride me bike, can't I? S' long as I can ride me bike I'm all right.' In the pubs he had only one theme, 'I got a plate in me head. Solid silver,' recited in a voice challenging the world to prove it otherwise.

All the time Mrs. Thurlow saved money. It was her creed. Sometimes people went away and there was no cleaning. She then made up the gap in her life by other work: picking potatoes, planting potatoes, dibbing cabbages, spudding roots, pea picking, more washing. In the fields she pinned up her skirt so that it stuck out behind her like a thick stiff tail, making her look like some bony ox. She did washing from five to six in the morning, and again from seven to nine in the evening. Taking in more washing, she tried to wash more quickly, against time. Somehow she succeeded, so that from nine to ten she had time for ironing. She worked by candlelight. Her movements were largely instinctive. She had washed and ironed for so long, in the same way, at the same time and place, that she could have worked in darkness.

There were some things, even, which could be done in darkness; and so at ten, with Thurlow and the sons in bed, she blew out the candle, broke up the fire, and sat folding the clothes or cleaning boots, and thinking. Her thoughts, like her work, went always along the same lines, towards the future, out into the resplendent avenues of ambitions, always for the two sons. There was a division in herself, the one part stolid and un-complaining in perpetual labour, the other fretful and almost desperate in an anxiety to establish a world beyond her own. She had saved fifty-four pounds. She would make it a hundred. How it was to be done she could not think. The boys were growing, the cost of keeping them was growing. She trusted in some obscure providential power as tireless and indomitable as herself.

At eleven she went to bed, going up the wooden stairs in darkness, in her stockinged feet. She undressed in darkness, her clothes falling away to be replaced by a heavy grey nightgown that made her body seem still larger and more ponderous. She fell asleep almost at once, but throughout the night her mind, propelled by some inherent anxiety, seemed to work on. She dreamed she was pushing the bicycle down the hill, and then that she was pushing it up again; she dreamed she was scrubbing floors; she felt the hot stab of the iron on her spittled finger and then the frozen bite of icy swedes as she picked them off unthawed earth on bitter mornings. She counted her money, her mind going back over the years throughout which she had saved it, and then counted it again, in fear, to make sure, as though in terror that it might be gone in the morning.

II

She had one relaxation. On Sunday afternoons she sat in the kitchen alone, and read the newspapers. They were not the newspapers of the day, but of all the previous week and perhaps of the week before that. She had collected them from the houses where she scrubbed, bearing them home on the bicycle. Through them and by them she broke the boundaries of her world. She made excursions into the lives of other people: tragic lovers, cabinet ministers, Atlantic flyers, suicides, society beauties, murderers, kings. It was all very wonderful. But emotionally, as she read, her face showed no impression. It remained ox-like in its impassivity. It looked in some way indomitably strong, as though little things like beauties and suicides, murderers and kings, could have no possible effect on her. About three o'clock as she sat reading, Thurlow would come in, lumber upstairs, and sleep until about half-past four.

One Sunday he did not come in at three o'clock. It was after four when she heard the bicycle tinkle against the woodshed outside. She raised her head from the newspaper and listened for him to come in. Nothing happened. Then after about five minutes Thurlow came in, went upstairs, remained for some minutes, and then came down again. She heard him go out into the yard. There was a stir among the chickens as he lumbered about the woodshed.

Mrs. Thurlow got up and went outside, and there, at the door of the woodshed, Thurlow was just hiding something under his coat. She thought it seemed like his billhook. She was not sure. Something made her say:

'Your saw don't need sharpening again a'ready, does it?'

'That it does,' he said. 'That's just what it does. Joe Woods is going to sharp it.' Thurlow looked upset and slightly wild, as he did when the plate in his head was hurting him. His eyes were a little drink-fired, dangerous. 'I gonna take it down now, so's I can git it back to-night.'

All the time she could see the saw itself hanging in the darkness of the woodshed behind him. She was certain then that he was lying, almost certain that it was the billhook he had under his coat.

She did not say anything else. Thurlow got on his bicycle and rode off, down the hill, his coat bunched up, the bicycle slightly crazy as he drove with one tipsy hand.

Something, as soon as he had gone, made her rush upstairs. She went into the back bedroom and flung the clothes off the mattress of the small iron bed that was never slept in. The money: it was all right. It was quite all right. She sat down heavily on the bed. And after a moment's anxiety her colour returned again — the solid, immeasurably passive calm with which she scrubbed, read the newspapers, and pushed the bicycle.

In the evening, the boys at church, she worked again. She darned socks, the cuffs of jackets, cleaned boots, sorted the washing for the following day. The boys must look well, respectable. Under the new scheme they went, now, to a secondary school in the town. She was proud of this, the first real stepping-stone to the higher things of the future. Outside, the night was windy, and she heard the now brief, now very prolonged moan of wind over the dark winter-ploughed land. She worked by candlelight. When the boys came in she lighted the lamp. In their hearts, having now some standard by which to judge her, they despised her a little. They hated the cheapness of the candlelight. When they had eaten and gone lumbering up to bed, like two colts, she blew out the lamp and worked by candlelight again. Thurlow had not come in.

He came in a little before ten. She was startled, not hearing the bicycle.

'You want something t' eat?'

'No,' he said. He went straight into the scullery. She heard him washing his hands, swilling the sink, washing, swilling again.

'You want the light?' she called.

'No!'

He came into the kitchen. She saw his still-wet hands in the candlelight. He gave her one look and went upstairs without speaking. For some time she pondered on the memory of this look, not understanding it. She saw in it the wildness of the afternoon, as though the plate were hurting him, but now it had in addition fear, and, above fear, defiance.

She got the candle and went to the door. The wind tore the candle flame down to a minute blue bubble which broke, and she went across the yard, to the woodshed, in darkness. In the woodshed she put a match to the candle again, held the candle up at eye level, and looked at the walls. The saw hung on its nail, but there was no billhook. She made a circle with the candle, looking for the bicycle with dumb eyes. It was not there. She went into the house again. Candleless, very faintly perturbed, she went up to bed. She wanted to say something to Thurlow, but he was dead still, as though asleep, and she lay down herself, hearing nothing but the sound of Thurlow's breathing and, outside, the sound of the wind blowing across the bare land.

Asleep, she dreamed, as nearly always, about the bicycle, but this time it was Thurlow's bicycle and there was something strange about it. It had no handles, but only Thurlow's billhook where the handles should have been. She grasped the billhook, and in her dream she felt the pain of the blood rushing out of her hands, and she was terrified and woke up.

Immediately she put out her hands, to touch Thurlow. The bed was empty. That scared her. She got out of bed. 'Thurlow! Bill! Thurlow! Thurlow!'

The wind had dropped, and it was quiet everywhere. She went downstairs. There, in the kitchen, she lighted the candle again and looked round. She tried the back door; it was unlocked and she opened it and looked out, feeling the small ground wind icy on her bare feet.

'Thurlow!' she said. 'Bill! Thurlow!'

She could hear nothing, and after about a minute she went back upstairs. She looked in at the boys' bedroom. The boys were asleep, and the vast candle shadow of herself stood behind her and listened, as it were, while she listened. She went into her own bedroom: nothing. Thurlow was not there — nothing. Then she went into the back bedroom.

The mattress lay on the floor. And she knew, even before she began to look for it, that the money was gone. She knew that Thurlow had taken it.

Since there was nothing else she could do, she went back to bed, not to sleep, but to lie there, oppressed but never in despondency, thinking. The money had gone, Thurlow had gone, but it would be all right. Just before five she got up, fired the copper, and began the washing. At seven she hung it out in long grey lines in the wintry grey light, holding the pegs like a bit in her teeth. A little after seven the boys came down to wash in the scullery.

'Here, here! Mum! There's blood all over the sink!'

'Your dad killed a rabbit,' she said. 'That's all.'

She lumbered out into the garden, to cut cabbages. She cut three large cabbages, put them in a sack, and, as though nothing had happened, began to prepare the bicycle for the day. She tied the cabbages on the carrier, two oilcans on the handlebars, and then on the crossbar a small bundle of washing, clean, which she had finished on Saturday. That was all: nothing much for a Monday.

At half-past seven the boys went across the fields, by footpath, to catch the bus for school. She locked the house, and then, huge, imperturbable, planting down great feet in the mud, she pushed the bicycle down the hill. She had not gone a hundred yards before, out of the hedge, two policemen stepped into the road to meet her.

'We was wondering if Mr. Thurlow was in?'

'No,' she said, 'he ain't in.'

'You ain't seen him?'

'No, I ain't seen him.'

'Since when?'

'Since last night.'

'You mind,' they said, 'if we look round your place?'

'No,' she said, 'you go on up. I got to git down to Miss Hanley's.' She began to push the bicycle forward, to go.

'No,' they said. 'You must come back with us.'

So she turned the bicycle round and pushed it back up the hill again. 'You could leave your bike,' one of the policemen said. 'No,' she said, 'I'd better bring it. You can never tell nowadays what folk are going to be up to.'

Up at the house she stood impassively by while the two policemen searched the woodshed, the garden, and finally the house itself. Her expression did not change as they looked at the blood in the sink. 'He washed his hands there last night,' she said.

'Don't touch it,' the policeman said. 'Don't touch it.' And then suspiciously, almost in implied accusation: 'You ain't touched nothing — not since last night?'

'I got something else to do,' she said.

'We'd like you to come along with us, Mrs. Thurlow,' they said, 'and answer a few questions.'

'All right.' She went outside and took hold of her bicycle.

'You can leave your bicycle.'

'No,' she said. 'I'll take it. It's no naughty way, up here, from that village.'

'We got a car down the road. You don't want a bike.'

'I better take it,' she said.

She wheeled the bicycle down the hill. When one policeman had gone in the car she walked on with the other. Ponderous, flat-footed, unhurried, she looked as though she could have gone on pushing the bicycle in the same direction, at the same pace, for ever.

They kept her four hours at the station. She told them about the billhook, the blood, the way Thurlow had come home and gone again, her waking in the night, Thurlow not being there, the money not being there.

'The money. How much was there?'

'Fifty-four pounds, sixteen and fourpence. And twenty-eight of that in sovereigns.'

In return they told her something else.

'You know that Thurlow was in the Black Horse from eleven to two yesterday?'

'Yes, I dare say that's where he'd be. That's where he always is, Sundays.'

'He was in the Black Horse, and for about two hours he was arguing with a man stopping down here from London. Arguing about that plate in his head. The man said he knew the plate was aluminium and Thurlow said he knew it was silver. Thurlow got very threatening. Did you know that?'

'No. But that's just like him.'

'This man hasn't been seen since, and Thurlow hasn't been seen since. Except by you last night.'

'Do you want me any more?' she said. 'I ought to have been at Miss Hanley's hours ago.'

18

'You realize this is very important, very serious?'

'I know. But how am I going to get Miss Hanley in, and Mrs. Acott, and then the poultry farm and then Mr. George?'

'We'll telephone Miss Hanley and tell her you can't go.'

'The money,' she said. 'That's what I can't understand. The money.'

III

It was the money which brought her, without showing it, to the edge of distress. She thought of it all day. She thought of it as hard cash, coin, gold and silver, hard-earned and hard-saved. But it was also something much more. It symbolized the future, another life, two lives. It was the future itself. If, as seemed possible, something terrible had happened and a life had been destroyed, it did not seem to her more terrible than the fact that the money had gone and that the future had been destroyed.

As she scrubbed the floors at the poultry farm in the late afternoon, the police telephoned for her again. 'We can send the car for her,' they said.

'I got my bike,' she said. 'I'll walk.'

With the oilcans filled, and cabbages and clean washing now replaced by newspapers and dirty washing, she went back to the police station. She wheeled her bicycle into the lobby and they then told her how, that afternoon, the body of the man from London had been found, in a spinney, killed by blows from some sharp instrument like an axe. 'We have issued a warrant for Thurlow's arrest,' they said.

'You never found the money?' she said.

'No,' they said. 'No doubt that'll come all right when we find Thurlow.'

That evening, when she got home, she fully expected Thurlow to be there, as usual, splitting kindling wood with the billhook, in the outhouse, by candlelight. The same refusal to believe that life could change made her go upstairs to look for the money. The absence of both Thurlow and the money moved her to no sign of emotion. But she was moved to a decision.

She got out her bicycle and walked four miles, into the next village, to see her brother. Though she did not ride the bicycle, it seemed to her as essential as ever that she should take it with her. Grasping its handles, she felt a sense of security and fortitude. The notion of walking without it, helplessly, in the darkness, was unthinkable.

Her brother was a master carpenter, a chapel-going man of straight-grained thinking and purpose, who had no patience with slovenliness. He lived with his wife and his mother in a white-painted electrically-lighted house whose floors were covered with scrubbed coco-matting. His mother was a small woman with shrill eyes and ironed-out mouth who could not hear well.

Mrs. Thurlow knocked on the door of the house as though these people, her mother and brother, were strangers to her. Her brother came to the door and she said:

'It's Lil. I come to see if you'd seen anything o' Thurlow?'

'No, we ain't seen him. Summat up?'

'Who is it?' the old woman called.

'It's Lil,' the brother said, in a louder voice. 'She says have we seen anything o' Thurlow?'

'No, an' don't want!'

Mrs. Thurlow went in. For fifteen years her family

had openly disapproved of Thurlow. She sat down on the edge of the chair nearest the door. Her large lace-up boots made large black mud prints on the virgin coco-matting. She saw her sister-in-law look first at her boots and then at her hat. She had worn the same boots and the same hat for longer than she herself could remember. But her sister-in-law remembered.

She sat untroubled, her eyes sullen, as though not fully conscious in the bright electric light. The light showed up the mud on her skirt, her straggling grey hair under the shapeless hat, the edges of her black coat weather-faded to a purplish grey.

'So you ain't heard nothing about Thurlow?' she said.

'No,' her brother said. 'Be funny if we had, wouldn't it? He ain't set foot in this house since dad died.' He looked at her hard. 'Why? What's up?'

She raised her eyes to him. Then she lowered them again. It was almost a minute before she spoke.

'Ain't you heard?' she said. 'They reckon he's done a murder.'

'What's she say?' the old lady said. 'I never heard her.'

Mrs. Thurlow looked dully at her boots, at the surrounding expanse of coco-matting. For some reason the fissured pattern of the coco-matting, so clean and regular, fascinated her. She said: 'He took all the money. He took it all and they can't find him.'

'Eh? What's she say? What's she mumbling about?'

The brother, his face white, went over to the old woman. He said into her ear: 'One of the boys is won a scholarship. She come over to tell us.'

'Want summat to do, I should think, don't she? Traipsing over here to tell us that.'

The man sat down at the table. He was very white, his hands shaking. His wife sat with the same dumb, shaking expression of shock. Mrs. Thurlow raised her eyes from the floor. It was as though she had placed on them the onus of some terrible responsibility.

'For God's sake,' the man said, 'when did it happen?'

All Mrs. Thurlow could think of was the money. 'Over fifty pounds. I got it hid under the mattress. I don't know how he could have found out about it. I don't know. I can't think. It's all I got. I got it for the boys.' She paused, pursing her lips together, squeezing back emotion. 'It's about the boys I come.'

'The boys?' The brother looked up, scared afresh. 'He ain't — they — '

'I didn't know whether you'd have them here,' she said. 'Till it's blowed over. Till they find Thurlow. Till things are straightened out.'

'Then they ain't found him?'

'No. He's done a bunk. They say as soon as they find him I shall git the money.'

'Yes,' the brother said. 'We'll have them here.'

She stayed a little longer, telling the story dully, flatly, to the two scared pairs of eyes across the table and to the old shrill eyes, enraged because they could not understand, regarding her from the fireplace. An hour after she had arrived, she got up to go. Her brother said: 'Let me run you back in the car. I got a car now. Had it three or four months. I'll run you back.'

'No, I got my bike,' she said.

She pushed the bicycle home in the darkness. At home, in the kitchen, the two boys were making a rabbit hutch. She saw that they had something of her brother's zeal for handling wood. She saw that their going to him would be a good thing. He was a man

22

who had got on in the world: she judged him by the car, the white-painted house, the electric light, the spotless coco-matting. She saw the boys, with deep but inexpressible pride, going to the same height, beyond it.

'Dad ain't been home,' they said.

She told them there had been a little trouble. 'They think your dad took some money.' She explained how it would be better for them, and for her, if they went to stay with her brother. 'Git to bed now and I'll get your things packed.'

'You mean we gotta go and live there?'

'For a bit,' she said.

They were excited. 'We could plane the wood for the rabbit hutch!' they said. 'Make a proper job of it.'

IV

That night, and again on the following morning, she looked under the mattress for the money. In the morning the boys departed. She was slightly depressed, slightly relieved by their excitement. When they had gone she bundled the day's washing together and tied it on the bicycle. She noticed, then, that the back tyre had a slow puncture, that it was already almost flat. This worried her. She pumped up the tyre and felt a little more confident.

Then, as she prepared to push the bicycle down the hill, she saw the police car coming along the road at the bottom. Two policemen hurried up the track to meet her.

'We got Thurlow,' they said. 'We'd like you to come to the station.'

'Is he got the money?' she said.

'There hasn't been time,' they said, 'to go into that.'

As on the previous morning she pushed her bicycle to the village, walking with one policeman while the other drove on in the car. Of Thurlow she said very little. Now and then she stopped and stooped to pinch the back tyre of the bicycle. 'Like I thought. I got a slow puncture,' she would say. 'Yes, it's gone down since I blowed it up. I s'll have to leave it at the bike shop as we go by.'

Once she asked the policeman if he thought that Thurlow had the money. He said, 'I'm afraid he's done something more serious than taking money.'

She pondered over this statement with dull astonishment. More serious? She knew that nothing could be more serious. To her the money was like a huge and irreplaceable section of her life. It was part of herself, bone and flesh, blood and sweat. Nothing could replace it. Nothing, she knew with absolute finality, could mean so much.

In the village she left the bicycle at the cycle shop. Walking on without it, she lumbered dully from side to side, huge and unsteady, as though lost. From the cycle-shop window the repairer squinted after her, excited. Other people looked from other windows as she lumbered past, always a pace or two behind the policeman, her ill-shaped feet painfully set down. At the entrance to the police station there was a small crowd. She went heavily into the station. Policemen were standing about in a room. An inspector, many papers in his hand, spoke to her. She listened heavily. She looked about for a sign of Thurlow. The inspector said, with kindness, 'Your husband is not here.' She felt a sense of having been cheated. 'They are detaining him at Metford. We are going over there now.'

'You know anything about the money?' she said.

Five minutes later she drove away, with the inspector and two other policemen, in a large black car. Travelling fast, she felt herself hurled, as it were, beyond herself. Mind and body seemed separated, her thoughts nullified. As the car entered the town, slowing down, she looked out of the side windows, saw posters: 'Metford Murder Arrest.' People, seeing policemen in the car, gaped. 'Murder Sensation Man Detained.'

Her mind registered impressions gravely and confusedly. People and posters were swept away from her and she was conscious of their being replaced by other people, the police station, corridors in the station, walls of brown glazed brick, fresh faces, a room, desks covered with many papers, eyes looking at her, box files in white rows appearing also to look at her, voices talking to her, an arm touching her, a voice asking her to sit down.

'I have to tell you, Mrs. Thurlow, that we have detained your husband on a charge of murder.'

'He say anything about the money?'

'He has made a statement. In a few minutes he will be charged and then probably remanded for further inquiries. You are at liberty to see him for a few moments if you would like to do so.'

In a few moments she was standing in a cell, looking at Thurlow. He looked at her as though he did not know what had happened. His eyes were lumps of impressionless glass. He stood with long arms loose at his sides. For some reason he looked strange, foreign, not himself. It was more than a minute before she realized why this was. Then she saw that he was wearing a new suit. It was a grey suit, thick, ready-made, and the sleeves were too short for him. They hung several inches above his thick protuberant wrist bones, giving his hands a look of inert defeat.

'You got the money, ain't you?' she said. 'You got it?'

He looked at her. 'Money?'

'The money you took. The money under the mattress.'

He stared at her. Money? He looked at her with a faint expression of appeal. Money. He continued to stare at her with complete blankness. Money?

'You remember,' she said. 'The money under the mattress.'

'Eh?'

'The money. That money. Don't you remember?'

He shook his head.

After some moments she went out of the cell. She carried out with her the sense of Thurlow's defeat as she saw it expressed in the inert hands, the dead, stupefied face, and his vacant inability to remember anything. She heard the court proceedings without interest or emotion. She was oppressed by a sense of increasing bewilderment, a feeling that she was lost. She was stormed by impressions she did not understand. 'I do not propose to put in a statement at this juncture. I ask for a remand until the sixteenth.' 'Remand granted. Clear the court.'

This effect of being stormed by impressions continued outside the court, as she drove away again in the car. People. Many faces. Cameras. More faces. Posters. The old sensation of mind severed from body, of thoughts nullified. In the village, when the car stopped, there were more impressions: more voices, more people, a feeling of suppressed excitement. 'We will run you home,' the policemen said.

'No,' she said. 'I got my cleaning to do. I got to pick up my bicycle.'

She fetched the bicycle and wheeled it slowly through the village. People looked at her, seemed surprised to see her in broad daylight, made gestures as though they wished to speak, and then went on. Grasping the handles of the bicycle, she felt a return of security, almost of comfort. The familiar smooth handlebars hard against her hands had the living response of other hands. They brought back her sense of reality: Miss Hanley, the cleaning, the poultry farm, the time she had lost, the boys, the money, the fact that something terrible had happened, the monumental fact of Thurlow's face, inert and dead, with its lost sense of remembrance.

Oppressed by a sense of duty, she did her cleaning as though nothing had happened. People were very kind to her. Miss Hanley made tea, the retired photographer would have run her home in his car. She was met everywhere by tender, remote words of comfort.

She pushed home her bicycle in the darkness. At Miss Hanley's, at the poultry farm, at the various places where she worked, the thought of the money had been partially set aside. Now, alone again, she felt the force of its importance more strongly, with the beginnings of bitterness. In the empty house she worked for several hours by candlelight, washing, folding, ironing. About the house the vague noises of wind periodically resolved themselves into what she believed for a moment were the voices of the two boys. She thought of the boys with calm unhappiness, and the thought of them brought back with renewed force the thought of the money. This thought hung over her with the huge preponderance of her own shadow projected on the ceiling above her.

On the following Sunday afternoon she sat in the

empty kitchen, as usual, and read the stale newspapers. But now they recorded, not the unreal lives of other people, but the life of Thurlow and herself. She saw Thurlow's photograph. She read the same story told in different words in different papers. In all the stories there was an absence of all mention of the only thing that mattered. There was no single word about the money.

During the next few weeks much happened, but she did not lose the belief that the money was coming back to her. Nothing could touch the hard central core of her optimism. She saw the slow evolution of circumstances about Thurlow as things of subsidiary importance, the loss of the life he had taken and the loss of his own life as things which, terrible in themselves, seemed less terrible than the loss of ideals built up by her sweat and blood.

She knew, gradually, that Thurlow was doomed, that it was all over. She did not know what to do. Her terror seemed remote, muffled, in some way incoherent. She pushed the bicycle back and forth each day in the same ponderous manner as ever, her heavy feet slopping dully beside it.

When she saw Thurlow for the last time his face had not changed, one way or the other, from its fixed expression of defeat. Defeat was cemented into it with imperishable finality. She asked him about the money for the last time.

'Eh?'

'The money. You took it. What you do with it? That money. Under the mattress.' For the first time she showed some sign of desperation. 'Please, what you done with it? That money. My money?'

'Eh?' And she knew that he could not remember.

A day later it was all over. Two days later she pushed the bicycle the four miles to the next village, to see her brother. It was springtime, time for the boys to come back to her. Pushing the bicycle in the twilight, she felt she was pushing forward into the future. She had some dim idea, heavily dulled by the sense of Thurlow's death, that the loss of the money was not now so great. Money is money; death is death; the living are the living. The living were the future. The thought of the boys' return filled her with hopes for the future, unelated hopes, but quite real, strong enough to surmount the loss of both Thurlow and money.

At her brother's they had nothing to say. They sat, the brother, the mother, and the sister-in-law, and looked at her with eyes over which, as it were, the blinds had been drawn.

'The boys here?' she said.

'They're in the workshop,' her brother said. 'They're making a bit of a wheelbarrow.'

'They all right?'

'Yes.' He wetted his lips. His clean-planned mind had been scarred by events as though by a mishandled tool. 'They don't know nothing. We kept it from 'em. They ain't been to school and they ain't seen no papers. They think he's in jail for stealing money.'

She looked at him, dully. 'Stealing money? That's what he did do. That money I told you about. That money I had under the mattress.'

'Well,' he said slowly, 'it's done now.'

'What did he do with it?' she said. 'What d'ye reckon he done with it?'

He looked at her quickly, unable suddenly to restrain his anger. 'Done with it? What d'ye suppose he done with it? Spent it. Threw it away. Boozed it. What else? You know what he was like. You knew! You had your eyes open. You knew what — '

'Will, Will,' his wife said.

He was silent. The old lady said: 'Eh? What's that? What's the matter now?'

The brother said, in a loud voice, 'Nothing.' Then more softly: 'She don't know everything.'

'I came to take the boys back,' Mrs. Thurlow said.

He was silent again. He wetted his lips. He struck a match on the warm fire-hob. It spurted into a sudden explosion, igniting of its own volition. He seemed startled. He put the match to his pipe, let it go out.

He looked at Mrs. Thurlow, the dead match in his hands. 'The boys ain't coming back no more,' he said.

'Eh?' she said. She was stunned. 'They ain't what?'

'They don't want to come back,' he said.

She did not understand. She could not speak. Very slowly he said:

'It's natural they don't want to come back. I know it's hard. But it's natural. They're getting on well here. They want to stop here. They're good boys. I could take 'em into the business.'

She heard him go on without hearing the individual words. He broke off, his face relieved — like a man who has liquidated some awful obligation.

'They're my boys,' she said. 'They got a right to say what they shall do and what they shan't do.'

She spoke heavily, without bitterness.

'I know that,' he said. 'That's right. They got a right to speak. You want to hear what they got to say?'

'Yes, I want to,' she said.

Her sister-in-law went out into the yard at the back

of the house. Soon voices drew nearer out of the darkness and the two boys came in.

'Hullo,' she said.

'Hello, Mum,' they said.

'Your Mum's come,' the carpenter said, 'to see if you want to go back with her.'

The two boys stood silent, awkward, eyes glancing past her.

'You want to go?' the carpenter said. 'Or do you want to stay here?'

'Here,' the elder boy said. 'We want to stop here.'

'You're sure o' that?'

'Yes,' the other said.

Mrs. Thurlow stood silent. She could think of nothing to say in protest or argument or persuasion. Nothing she could say would, she felt, give expression to the inner part of herself, the crushed core of optimism and faith.

She stood at the door, looking back at the boys. 'You made up your minds, then?' she said. They did not speak.

'I'll run you home,' her brother said.

'No,' she said. 'I got my bike.'

She went out of the house and began to push the bicycle slowly home in the darkness. She walked with head down, lumbering painfully, as though direction did not matter. Whereas, coming, she had seemed to be pushing forward into the future, she now felt as if she were pushing forward into nowhere.

After a mile or so she heard a faint hissing from the back tyre. She stopped, pressing the tyre with her hand. 'It's slow,' she thought; 'it'll last me.' She pushed forward. A little later it seemed to her that the hissing got worse. She stopped again, and again felt the tyre with her hand. It was softer now, almost flat.

She unscrewed the pump and put a little air in the tyre and went on. 'I better stop at the shop,' she thought, 'and have it done.'

In the village the cycle-shop was already in darkness. She pushed past it. As she came to the hill leading up to the house she lifted her head a little. It seemed to her suddenly that the house, outlined darkly above the dark hill, was a long way off. She had for one moment an impression that she would never reach it.

She struggled up the hill. The mud of the track seemed to suck at her great boots and hold her down. The wheels of the bicycle seemed as if they would not turn, and she could hear the noise of the air dying once again in the tyre.

CHATEAU BOUGAINVILLAEA

The headland was like a dry purple island scorched by the flat heat of afternoon, cut off from the mainland by a sand-coloured tributary of road which went down past the estaminet and then, half a mile beyond, to the one-line, one-eyed railway station. Down below, on a small plateau between upper headland and sea, peasants were mowing white rectangles of corn. The tide was fully out, leaving many bare black rocks and then a great sun-phosphorescent pavement of sand, with the white teeth of small breakers slowly nibbling in. Far out, the Atlantic was waveless, a shade darker than the sky, which was the fierce blue seen on unbelievable posters. Farther out still, making a faint mist, sun and sea had completely washed out the line of sky.

From time to time a puff of white steam, followed by a peeped whistle, struck comically at the dead silence inland. It was the small one-line train, half-tram, making one way or the other its hourly journey between town-terminus and coast. By means of it the engaged couple measured out the afternoon.

'There goes the little train,' he would say.

'Yes,' she would say, 'there goes the little train.'

Each time she resolved not to say this stupid thing and then, dulled with sleepiness and the heat of earth and sky and the heather in which they lay, she forgot herself and said it, automatically. Her faint annoyance with herself at these times had gradually begun to make itself felt, as the expression of some much deeper discontent.

'Je parle Français un tout petit peu, m'sieu.' In a voice which seemed somehow like velvet rubbed the wrong way, the man was talking. 'I was all right as far as that. Then I said, "Mais, dites-moi, m'sieu, pour-quoi are all the knives put left-handed dans ce restaur-ant?" By God it must have been awfully funny. And then he said — '

'He said because, m'sieu, the people who use them are all left-handed.'

'And that's really what he said? It wasn't a mistake? All the people in that place were left-handed?'

'Apparently,' she said, 'they were all left-handed.'

'It's the funniest thing I ever heard,' he said. 'I can't believe it.'

Yes, she thought, perhaps it was a funny thing. Many left-handed people staying at one restaurant. A family, perhaps. But then there were many left-handed people in the world, and perhaps, for all you knew, their left was really right, and it was we, the right, who were wrong.

She took her mind back to the restaurant down in the town. There was another restaurant there, set in a sort of alley-way under two fig trees, where artisans filled most of the tables between noon and two o'clock, and where a fat white-smocked woman served all the dishes and still found time to try her three words of English on the engaged couple. From here they could see the lace-crowned Breton women clacking in the shade of the street trees and the small one-eyed train starting or ending its journey between the sea and the terminus that was simply the middle of the street. They liked this restaurant, but that day, wanting a change, they had climbed the steps into the upper town, to the level of the viaduct, and had found this small family restaurant where, at one table, all the knives were laid left-handed. For some reason she now sought to define, this left-handedness did not seem funny to her. Arthur had also eaten too many olives, picking them up with his fingers and gnawing them as she herself, as a child, would have gnawed an uncooked prune, and this did not seem very funny either. Somewhere between olives and left-handedness lay the source of her curious discontent. Perhaps she was left-handed herself? Left-handed people were, she had read somewhere, right-brained. Perhaps Arthur was left-handed?

She turned over in the heather, small brown-eyed face to the sun. 'Don't you do anything left-handed?'

'Good gracious, no.' He turned over too and lay face upwards, dark with sun, his mouth small-lipped under the stiff moustache she had not wanted him to grow. 'You don't either?'

For the first time in her life she considered it. How many people, she thought, ever considered it? Thinking, she seemed to roll down a great slope, semi-swooning in the heat, before coming up again. Surprisingly, she had thought of several things.

'Now I come to think of it, I comb my hair left-handed. I always pick flowers left-handed. And I wear my watch on my left wrist.'

He lifted steady, mocking eyes. 'You sure you don't kiss left-handed?'

'That's not very funny!' she flashed.

It seemed to her that the moment of temper flashed up sky high, like a rocket, and fell far out to sea, soundless, dead by then, in the heat of the unruffled afternoon. She at once regretted it. For five days now they had lived on the Breton coast, and they now had five days more. Every morning, for five days, he had questioned her: 'All right? Happy?' and every morning she had responded with automatic affirmations, believing it at first, then aware of doubt, then bewildered.

Happiness, she wanted to say, was not something you could fetch out every morning after breakfast, like a clean handkerchief, or more still like a rabbit conjured out of the hat of everyday circumstances.

The hot, crushed-down sense of security she had felt all afternoon began suddenly to evaporate, burnt away from her by the first explosion of discontent and then by small restless flames of inward anger. She felt the growing sense of insecurity physically, feeling that at any moment she might slip off the solid headland into the sea. She suddenly felt a tremendous urge, impelled for some reason by fear, to walk as far back inland as she could go. The thought of the Atlantic far below, passive and yet magnetic, filled her with a sudden cold breath of vertigo.

'Let's walk,' she said.

'Oh! no, it's too hot.'

She turned her face into the dark sun-brittled heather. She caught the ticking of small insects, like infinitesimal watches. Far off, inland, the little train cut off, with its comic shriek, another section of afternoon.

In England he was a draper's assistant: chief assistant, sure to become manager. In imagination she saw the shop, sun-blinds down, August remnant sale now on, the dead little town now so foreign and far off and yet so intensely real to her, shown up by the disenchantment of distance. They had been engaged six months. She had been very thrilled about it at first, showing the ring all round, standing on a small pinnacle of joy, ready to leap into the tremendous spaces of marriage. Now she had suddenly the feeling that she was about to be sewn up in a blanket.

'Isn't there a castle,' she said, 'somewhere up the road past the estaminet?'

'Big house. Not castle.'

'I thought I saw a notice,' she said, 'to the château.'

'Big house,' he said. 'Did you see that film, "The Big House"? All about men in prison.'

What about women in prison? she wanted to say. In England she was a school-teacher, and there had been times when she felt that the pale green walls of the class-room had imprisoned her and that marriage, as it always did, would mean escape. Now left-handedness and olives and blankets and the stabbing heat of the Atlantic afternoon had succeeded, together, in inducing some queer stupor of semi-crazy melancholy that was far worse than this. Perhaps it was the wine, the sour red stuff of the *vin compris* notice down at the left-handed café? Perhaps, after all, it was only some large dose of self-pity induced by sun and the emptiness of the day?

She got to her feet. 'Come on, m'sieu. We're going to the castle.' She made a great effort to wrench herself up to the normal plane. 'Castle, my beautiful. Two francs. All the way up to the castle, two francs.' She held out her hand to pull him to his feet.

'I'll come,' he said, 'if we can stop at the estaminet and have a drink.'

'We'll stop when we come down,' she said.

'Now.'

'When we come down.'

'Now. I'm so thirsty. It was the olives.'

Not speaking, she held out her hand. Instinctively, he put out his left.

'You see,' she said, 'you don't know what's what or which's which or anything. You don't know when you're left-handed or right.'

He laughed. She felt suddenly like laughing too, and they began to walk down the hill. The fierce heat

37

seemed itself to force them down the slope, and she felt driven by it past the blistered white tables of the estaminet with the fowls asleep underneath them, and then up the hill on the far side, into the sparse shade of small wind-levelled oaks and, at one place, a group of fruitless fig trees. It was some place like this, she thought, just about as hot and arid, where the Gadarene swine had stampeded down. What made her think of that? Her mind had some urge towards inconsequence, some inexplicable desire towards irresponsibility that she could not restrain or control, and she was glad to see the château at last, shining with sea-blue jalousies through a break in the mass of metallic summer-hard leaves of acacia and bay that surrounded it. She felt it to be something concrete, a barrier against which all the crazy irresponsibilities of the mind could hurl themselves and split.

At the corner, a hundred yards before the entrance gates, a notice, of which one end had been cracked off by a passing lorry, pointed upwards like a tilted telescope. They read the word 'château', the rest of the name gone.

'You see,' she said, 'château.'

'What château?'

'Just château.'

'You think we'll have to pay to go in?'

'I'll pay,' she said.

She walked on in silence, far away from him. The little insistences on money had become, in five days, like the action of many iron files on the soft tissues of her mind: first small and fine, then larger, then still larger, now large and coarse, brutal as stone. He kept a small note-book and in it, with painful system, entered up the expenditure of every centime.

At the entrance gates stood a lodge, very much

dilapidated, the paintwork of the walls grey and sea-eroded like the sides of a derelict battleship. A small notice was nailed to the fence by the gate, and the girl stopped to read it.

'What does it say?' he said. 'Do we pay to go in?'

'Just says it's an eighteenth-century château,' she said. 'Admission a franc. Shall we go in?'

'A franc?'

'One franc,' she said. 'Each.'

'You go,' he said. 'I don't know that I'm keen. I'll stop outside.'

She did not answer, but went to the gate and pulled the porter's bell. From the lodge door a woman without a blouse on put her head out, there was a smell of onions, and the woman turned on the machine of her French like a high pressure steam-pipe, scrawny neck dilating.

The girl pushed open the gate and paid the woman the two francs admission fee, holding a brief conversation with her. The high pressure pipe finally cut itself off and withdrew, and the girl came back to the gates and said: 'She's supposed to show us round but she's just washing. She says nobody else ever comes up at this hour of the afternoon, and we must show ourselves round.'

They walked up the gravel road between sea-stunted trees towards the château. In the sun, against the blue sky above the Atlantic, the stone and slate of it was burning.

'Well,' she said, 'what do you think of it?'

'Looks a bit like the bank at home,' he said. 'The one opposite our shop.'

Château and sky and trees spun in the sunlight, whirling down to a momentary black vortex in which the girl found herself powerless to utter a word. She walked blindly on in silence. It was not until they stood under the château walls, and she looked up to see a great grape vine mapped out all across the south side, that she recovered herself and could speak.

'It's just like the châteaux you see on wine-bottles,' she said. 'I like it.'

'It doesn't look much to me,' he said. 'Where do we get in?'

'Let's look round the outside first.'

As they walked round the walls on the sun-bleached grass she could not speak or gather her impressions, but was struck only by the barren solitude of it all, the arid, typically French surroundings, with an air of fly-blownness and sun-weariness. To her amazement the place had no grandeur, and there were no flowers.

'There ought to be at least a bougainvillaea,' she said.

'What's a bougainvillaea?'

Questioned, she found she did not know. She felt only that there ought to be a bougainvillaea. The word stood in her mind for the exotic, the south, white afternoons, the sea as seen from the top of just such châteaux as this. How this came to be she could not explain. The conscious part of herself stretched out arms and reached back, into time, and linked itself with some former incarnation of her present self, Louise Bowen, school-teacher, certificated, Standard V girls, engaged to Arthur Keller, chief assistant Moore's Drapery, sure to become manager, pin-stripe trousers, remnants madam, the voice like ruffled velvet, seventy-three pounds fifteen standing to credit at the post office, and in reaching back so far she felt suddenly that she could cry for the lost self, for the enviable incarnation so extraordinarily real and yet impossible, and for the yet not impossible existence, far back, in eternal bougainvillaea afternoons.

'Let's go inside,' she said.

'How they make it pay,' he said, 'God only knows.'

'It has long since,' she said mysteriously, 'paid for itself.'

They found the main door and went in, stepping into the under-sea coldness of a large entrance hall. Now think that out, now think that out, now think that out. Her mind bubbling with bitterness, she looked up the great staircase, and all of a sudden the foreignness of her conscious self as against the familiarity of the self that had been was asserted again, but now with the sharp contrast of shadow and light. She put her hand on the staircase, the iron cool and familiar, and then began to walk up it, slowly but lightly, her hand drawn up easily, as though from some invisible iron pulley, far above her. She kept her eyes on the ceiling, feeling, without effort of thought, that she did not like and never had liked its mournful collection of cherubim painted in the gold wheel about the chandelier. For the first time that day, as she mounted the staircase and then went on beyond into the upstairs corridor, and into the panelled music-room with its air of having been imported as a complete back-cloth from some pink-and-gold theatre of the 'seventies, her body moved with its natural quietness, accustomed, infinitely light, and with a sense of the purest happiness. All this she could not explain and, as they went from music-room to other rooms, ceased to attempt to explain. Her bitterness evaporated in the confined coolness just as her security, outside on the hot headland, had evaporated in the blaze of afternoon. Now she seemed incontestably sure of herself, content in what she knew, without fuss, was an unrepeatable moment of time.

She did not like the music-room but, as she expected, Arthur did. This pre-awareness of hers saved her from fresh bitterness. As part of her contentment, making it complete, she thought of him with momentary tenderness, quietly regretting what she had said and done, ready now to make up for it.

'Shall we go up higher,' she said, 'or down to the ground-floor again?'

'Let's do the climb first,' he said.

To her, it did not matter, and climbing a second staircase they came, eventually, to a small turret room, unfurnished, with two jalousied windows looking across to the two worlds of France and the Atlantic.

She stood at the window overlooking the sea and looked out, as from a lighthouse, down on to the intense expanse of sea-light. Her mind had the profound placidity of the sea itself, a beautiful vacancy, milkily restful.

'Funny,' Arthur said. 'No ships. The Atlantic, and not a ship in sight.'

'You wouldn't expect to see ships,' she said, and knew that she was right.

Looking down from the other window they saw the headland, the brown-lilac expanse of heather, the minute peasants scribbled on the yellow rectangle of corn, the estaminet, the one-eyed station. And suddenly also, there was the white pop of steam inland, and the small comic shriek, now more than ever toy-like, pricking the dead silence of afternoon.

'Look,' he said, 'there's the little train.'

'Yes,' she said, 'there's the little train.'

Her mind had the pure loftiness of the tower itself, above all irritation. She felt, as not before in her life, that she was herself. The knowledge of this re-incarnation was something she could not communicate, and half afraid that time or a word would break it up, she suggested suddenly that they should go down.

Arthur remained at the window a moment longer, admiring points of distance. 'You'd never think,' he said, 'you could see so far.'

'Yes you would,' she called back.

Now think that out, now think that out, now think that out. Her mind, as she went downstairs, sprang contrarily upwards, on a scale of otherwise inexpressible delight. Arthur engaged her in conversation as they went downstairs, she on one flight, he on one above, calling down: 'It may be all right, but the rates must be colossal. Besides, you'd burn a ton of coal a day in winter, trying to keep warm. A six-roomed house is bad enough, but think of this,' but nothing could break, suppress or even touch her mood.

Downstairs she went straight into the great reception hall, and stood dumb. At that moment she suddenly felt that she had come as far as she must. Time had brought her to this split second of itself simply in order to pin her down. She stood like an insect transfixed.

Arthur came in: 'What are you looking at?'

'The yellow cloth. Don't do anything. Just look at it. It's wonderful.'

'I don't see anything very wonderful,' he said.

At the end of the room, thrown over a chair, a large length of brocade, the colour of a half-ripe lemon, was like spilled honey against the grey French-coldness of walls and furniture. Instantaneously the girl saw it with eyes of familiarity, feeling it somehow to be the expression of herself, mood, past and future. She stood occupied with the entrancement of the moment, her eyes excluding the room, the day, Arthur and everything, her self drowned out of existence by the pure wash of watered fabric.

Suddenly Arthur moved into the room, and ten

seconds later had the brocade in his hands. She saw him hold it up, measure it without knowing he measured it, feel its weight, thickness, value. She saw him suddenly as the eternal shopkeeper measuring out the eternal remnants of time: the small tape-measure of his mind like a white worm in the precious expanse of her own existence.

'If you bought it to-day,' Arthur called, 'it would cost you every penny of thirty-five bob a yard.'

'Let's go,' she said.

Half a minute later she turned and walked out of the door, Arthur following, and then past the wind-stunted trees and on down the road, past the estaminet. It was now herself who walked, Louise Bowen, Standard V girls, certificated, deduct so much for superannuation scheme, tired as after a long day in the crowded chalk-smelling class-room. As they passed the estaminet, the place looked more fly-blown and deserted than ever, and they decided to go on to the station, and get a drink there while waiting for the train. As they passed the fig trees her mind tried to grasp again at the thought of the Gadarene swine, her mood blasted into the same barrenness as the tree in the parable.

'Well, you can have your château,' Arthur said. 'But I've got my mind on one of those houses Sparkes is putting up on Park Avenue. Sixteen and fourpence a week, no deposit, over twenty years. That's in front of any château.'

She saw the houses as he spoke, red and white, white and red, millions of them, one like another, sixteen and fourpence a week, no deposit, stretching out to the ends of the earth. She saw herself in them, the constant and never-changing material of her life cut up by a pair of draper's scissors, the days ticketed, the years fretted by the counting up of farthings and all the endlessly incalculable moods of boredom.

'Two coffees please.'

At the little station café they sat at one of the outside tables and waited for the train.

'Well, we've been to the château and never found out its name,' he said.

'It ought to be Château Bougainvillaea.'

'That's silly,' he said. 'You don't even know what a bougainvillaea is.'

She sat stirring the grey coffee. She could feel the sun burning the white iron table and her hands. She looked up at the château, seeing the windows of the turret above the trees.

'Now we can see the château,' she said, 'as we should have seen ourselves if we'd been sitting down here when — '

It was beyond her, and she broke off.

'What?' he said.

'I didn't mean that,' she said.

'What did you mean?'

'I don't know.'

'Well, in future,' he said, 'mind you say what you mean.'

The future? She sat silent. Inland the approaching train made its comic little whistle, cutting off another section of the afternoon.

And hearing it, she knew suddenly that the future was already a thing of the past.

A GERMAN IDYLL

A WHITE river steamer was travelling smoothly up the
Rhine in the heat of an August afternoon. The sky
was very blue and brilliant and far away, and the sun
was burning like a flaming ball of brass over the hills
on the southern bank of the stream. The steamer, like
a comet, left behind it a white tail of foam, but the
smooth water was coloured a soft green, very clear and
beautiful, as though stained to its depths with the reflected green of the vineyards terracing the high slopes
on either side. As the slopes went smoothly past an
occasional solitary peasant working high up among the
vines would appear and wave his arm at the steamer
and the passengers would wave their hands languidly
in reply. Sometimes the steamer would overtake a
slower steamer or would meet another advancing tran-
quilly downstream. The trembling white reflections of
the boats, the threshed white foam on the water, the
laughter and the waving of hands among the passengers
all produced a sensation of great excitement when one
boat passed another. Travelling up and down the river
also were long chains of barges, often as many as ten
in a chain, black and sluggish in the water with their
merchandise. The foremost barge was often a family
affair; there would be a big woman in a dirty blouse and
kerchief, and a string of children hanging over the side
watching the steamer out of sight. The children and
the women and the bargees themselves would all wave
their hands and smile shyly and rather sweetly as
though having their portraits taken. Sometimes there
appeared narrow beaches of white sand peopled with

colonies of holiday-makers lying half-naked and very brown in the hot sun. Groups of brown swimmers would race each other almost to within the path of the steamer, and occasionally light canoes, each propelled by a man and a girl, extremely serious and brown and beautiful, would dart alongside or bob across the white wake of foam. The paddlers seemed to regard the steamer with indifference and contempt, for they never turned their heads to look at it and never waved their hands. The bodies of the girls were marvellously tanned and slender and they had short yellow hair and fine breasts that hung loose in their white singlets as they leaned forward over the paddles.

A young man was sitting in the bows of the steamer. He was not more than twenty-two or three and he had brown, very English-looking hair, a thin sunburnt face and sensitive blue eyes that looked a little tired. He was travelling on the Rhine for the first time in his life. The broad hills reminded him of the hills of Derbyshire, but there was something quite foreign and dreamlike to him about the peasants, the endless vineyards and the immensity of the Rhine itself. He felt drowsy with the heat of the afternoon, the stream flowing sleepily past and the sunlight blinking like quicksilver on the green water.

Presently he closed his eyes and sat for what seemed a long time in a sort of half-sleep, conscious of nothing but the motion of the steamer, the voices about him on the deck and the jingling of a gramophone playing somewhere in the stern. He was aroused by a sudden commotion. The passengers were thronging to the taffrail and he heard a sudden clicking of many cameras. He sat up. At that moment a pair of prismatic glasses was put into his hands and an excited voice with a faint German accent exclaimed:

'Richardson, the Lorelei, quick, quick, the Lorelei.'

He automatically raised the glasses to his eyes. He had a sleepy impression of rocky slopes and afterwards of terraces of vineyards which seemed to come down to within touching distance until he could see the sunlight fretting the under-branches of the trees with soft shapes of gold and the green clusters of grapes standing out from among the vine leaves. The vines had been sprayed, so that the leaves were clouded over with a delicate vitriol-blue, like a lovely vapour. He had an impression also that the horizon was blurred with the haze of a thunderstorm. He lowered the glasses at last and looked up at the man who had thrust them into his hands. He was leaning on the taffrail, turning over the leaves of a Baedeker. The young man touched his arm with the glasses.

'Look at the storm,' he said.

The other took the glasses and became engrossed in the Rhine unfolding itself ahead and the blue haze of the gathering storm beyond. There was a brief silence and at last the young man spoke.

'What time shall we be in Iben?' he said.

The other did not answer and presently the young man repeated:

'Karl, what time shall we be in Iben?'

'Soon.'

'Before night?'

'Naturally.'

'You think so? No humbug this time?'

'Naturally.'

The tone of the answers was nonchalant and evasive, and the young man regarded his friend in silence. He was a man of thirty-five or six, tall, dark, angular, with a large arresting head covered with a crop of thick black hair that strayed over his ears and neck in tiny black curls. His broad heavy nose, his deep forehead and the large angle of his chin, all created an impression of great strength. By contrast his eyes were soft and timid and at moments he resembled strikingly some picture of the traditional Christ.

Karl had run away from Germany in order to go to London twenty years before. He was going back to his native village for the first time and the young man was going with him. He was a bookseller, carrying on his trade in a little shop like a rabbit-hutch in a street off Lincoln's Inn. He spoke English fluently and by a half-fierce, half-gentle personality, an extremely blasphemous and entertaining speech and a gift for friendship he had made friends with every kind of person in every quarter of London. He lived with a fierce, tireless energy, rushing from place to place without rest, existing on nothing but his books, occasional ham sandwiches and snatched cups of tea. Every day he bicycled about the streets of London in order to buy his stock; the bicycle was rusty and broken and had cost him eighteenpence in an East End market; Karl rode it furiously, with a kind of half-athletic, half-religious diligence, using his feet for brakes. He was never tired and he never rested. On the night-boat from Gravesend to Rotterdam he had kept the young man awake with wild stories and readings from strange poets and fantastic blasphemies whenever the ship rolled. After leaving Holland, where fields of scarlet dahlias and the first asters were coming into bloom, he had insisted on travelling long distances by train into the heart of Germany, so that the young man had grown too tired and too hungry even to look at the passing forest or the fields of harvesters, gay in scarlet skirts and embroidered blouses, working among the ripe corn in the blazing sunshine. Sometimes it happened that they changed trains at a country station; there would be a red-roofed village set among wooded hills rising on either side, and the platform would be thronged with fat, gentle-eyed peasant women dressed in countless snow-white petticoats and black velvet bodices, carrying baskets of cheeses wrapped in muslin, and live geese and eggs and wine. It would have been a sublime relief to have left the train and rested there. But the sight of his native land had filled Karl with the inexhaustible eagerness of a tourist. In four days they had travelled over half the country, riding third and fourth class in trains that crawled like caterpillars. They had seen all the towns where Karl had been apprenticed or where he had run a race or where he had fallen in love. The young man was stiff with sitting for long hours in trains and tired from running after trains and spending nights in strange beds from which Karl aroused him too early, so that they might catch other trains before breakfast. At first he had tried to protest but later he had no strength to protest. As he sat on the deck of the steamer he was utterly weary of travelling and there was only one thing to which he felt he could look forward. They were going into the country.

The steamer turned a bend in the river and slowly the Rhine straightened itself out again. The sky was dark and heavy with thunder over the distant breadth of the river. The steamer and the storm seemed to be floating towards each other at the same smooth, inevitable pace. Richardson tried to establish the point where the storm and the steamer would meet, but his thoughts wandered off to Iben, the place where Karl had been born. He imagined a sleepy village lying in a fertile valley in the shelter of a forest of pines, the valley set with orchards and tobacco-fields and vineyards, and crops of wheat and rye turning white in the hot sun.

A short German dressed in a white pink-striped flannel suit staggered on deck with his baggage and his wife. The woman, who was eating sausage sandwiches, seemed afraid of the approaching storm. She breathed like a broken-winded horse and there were beads of yellow sweat on her large moonlike face. As she ate the sausage she picked off the circle of red skin and threw it into the Rhine and the skin floating on the greenish water had a strange scarlet brilliance in the thunderlight.

The roofs of Bingen appeared, sharply outlined beneath the immense blue cloud of the thunderstorm. Afar off there had been a mutter of thunder and suddenly there was a louder peal which seemed to hesitate and hover in the sky before taking an angry leap into the distance, travelling away over the hills like a growl of artillery. The air was stifling. The German asked Karl if he thought they would be in Bingen before the storm came and Karl said 'Yes', in a tone as though the storm were a hundred miles away. The light was queer and brilliant. The vines were a wonderfully bright emerald and the river itself looked leaden and sombre under the darkening sky. The steamer slowed down its engines and drifted towards the red roofs and the storm. There was a strange stillness in the air, a hush that seemed to exist apart from the voices of the passengers, the tune of the gramophone still playing, and the quiet wash of water in the steamer's wake. The German stood ready with his baggage and his wife had ceased eating. Suddenly the white thunder rain came racing down the river and whipped across the deck. The passengers herded themselves below and Richardson and Karl went down into the saloon. The sun was still shining as the rain came down and the air was like a curtain of silver. Karl ordered some beer and while he was drinking it the rain ceased with a jerk and the storm-cloud seemed to split apart and let in the light again.

Karl and Richardson went on deck again. There was a marvellous stillness in the air, and up in the black sky hung a magnificent rainbow. It made a span between the town and the hills like a vivid, exquisite bridge. There was a soft reflection of it on the water and another reflection of it higher up in the sky. Everyone came on deck to look at it and the stout German and his frau forgot to eat their sandwiches at the sight of it. Its loveliness was unearthly and transcendent.

The steamer swung across the river and came to rest at the landing-stage. The sun was shining brilliantly again and the rainbow had begun to fade.

Karl and Richardson went up into the town. Great pools of rain lay among the cobbles of the streets and the town looked washed and bright. Karl went into a shop for some cigars and made inquiries about a bus to Iben. There was no bus to Iben but there was a bus in fifteen minutes that would drop them within three miles of it. They hurried across the town and through some public gardens. There was no time to eat. In the gardens some children under a mulberry tree were searching among the grass for the mulberries that the storm had beaten down. Richardson felt famished. He went across to a child and held out his hand. He could not speak a word of German. The child put a mulberry into his hand. He ate it and held out his hand again and the child gave him four mulberries more.

The mulberries tasted of rain and the taste of them was still in his mouth as he climbed into the bus and sat down.

Finally, when the bus started and they drove away out of the town, he turned and looked back. He could see the children and the mulberry tree and the hills beyond the Rhine, but the rainbow had vanished from the sky.

II

It was late afternoon when they left the bus and began to walk along the road to Iben. The road travelled along for a mile in the shelter of a wooded rise and curved at last into an expanse of open country. There were fruit trees growing among the patches of wheat and rye and sometimes copses of birch broke up the line of the land gently rising and falling away to the horizon where the forest began. Where the corn was ripe and heavy the thunderstorm had flattened it to the earth in broad waves. The sun was hot and brilliant again but the air was fresh and sweetly scented after the storm, and the roadside was gay with beds of wild yellow snapdragon and scarlet poppies and stars of chicory washed very pure and shining by the rain.

The road turned sharply and mounted another spur of rising ground and beyond lay another valley, and in the valley there were the red roofs and the spire of Iben.

They walked down into the village without speaking. The road was lined with trees of apple and pear and the rain had battered the ripe fruit to the earth. Richardson picked up a pear and ate it and Karl fixed his eyes on the village ahead. A solitary old woman in a white kerchief working on a patch of maize lifted her head and shaded her eyes in wonder and suspicion and watched them out of sight. They came down into Iben without seeing another soul. The street was steep and long and the houses rose up immense and gaunt on either side, rather forbidding and gloomy except for the bright green jalousies thrown back against the walls of dark stone and the little painted white balconies at the bedroom windows. The street was shadowy and deserted and the high wooden doors of the courtyards were shut. A stream of water flowed down the street, washing the cobbles a pale yellow. Nothing else moved. They came to a halt before a tall house with a great courtyard and high doors and a grape-vine spreading massive branches over the walls.

Richardson felt a sense of relief and he turned to look back as Karl walked towards the doors of the courtyard. He was astonished to find that the silence and solitude of the street had vanished. Every door and window was crowded with gaping peasants and the street was suddenly all life and curiosity and excitement. He took one look at the chattering heads and turned to speak to Karl, but Karl had already opened the wicket of the house with the grape-vine.

He walked after him and stepped into the courtyard. The peasants came hurrying down the street to take a last look at him. Karl shut the door. The courtyard was flanked on one side by the south face of the house and on the other by stone cow-barns and open sheds under which a litter of sandy-coloured pigs were feeding. A big manure heap stood steaming in the centre of the yard and red and white hens were pecking about it in the sunshine. On the steps of the house a fair-haired girl of thirteen or fourteen was stirring something in a big brown bowl. She looked up with a start. She stared at Karl and Richardson with an expression of absolute wonderment, momentarily petrified. Then suddenly she dropped the bowl on the steps and ran like a wild creature into the house.

'They don't expect me,' said Karl. 'I didn't trouble to write.'

54

They heard the girl talking excitedly in the house and they walked a few paces forward. Suddenly she returned. A thin, deep-eyed peasant woman, sixty or so, was coming after her, timid and bewildered as a child, and behind her two other women of thirty or thirty-five, stout and moonfaced and astonished. The old woman hesitated for one moment at the sight of Karl and then ran forward and began kissing him. She cried and laughed a little together and the other women came forward and kissed him and laughed too. The young girl hung back and stared with wide eyes, and the wicket gate was pushed open and a little group of peasants came and stood in the courtyard and looked timidly on at it all.

'My mother,' said Karl. 'My sister Maria and my sister Elsa.'

Richardson shook hands with the three women. They looked at him shyly and worshipfully. The young girl ran like wildfire across the courtyard and scattered the peasants and vanished into the street, slamming the wicket behind her. Everyone talked excitedly. There was a light of joyful astonishment on the faces of the three women as they led the way into the house and made Karl and Richardson sit on an old horsehair sofa in the kitchen, while they themselves ran hither and thither and clattered crockery and ground coffee and broke eggs and chattered as though the sight of Karl after twenty years had driven them mad.

The kitchen was large and dim, with a long scrubbed wooden table in the centre of it, a life-sized picture of Hindenburg on one wall and a fireplace raised up, like a blacksmith's forge, in one corner. The old woman brought a great blue bowl to the table and broke eggs into it while she gazed and chattered at Karl like a child. He returned her gaze with absolute bewilderment, as though like her unable to believe in his presence there. The old woman seemed to break eggs enough for an army, and at every egg she made a long excited speech. Richardson sat still, not understanding a word. The kitchen was fragrant with coffee. The young girl came back and talked excitedly and took the bowl from the old woman and finished beating the eggs. When Richardson looked at her she flushed crimson and bent her head over the bowl. The two sisters ran backwards and forwards as though lost, coming to snatch away the bowl of eggs and lay the cloth on the table and set out cups and plates and wine glasses. Maria ran in with a bottle of wine. Finally the wine was poured out, a soft rose-coloured wine, clouding the glasses, and the old woman and Karl and Richardson stood up and drank. The wine was strong and sharp and as cold as snow. Richardson, glad of it, drank quickly and Maria pounced on the bottle and filled his glass immediately.

Elsa ran in with a dish filled with a single enormous omelette big enough for ten men, and Maria with a tall green-patterned coffee-pot and long loaves of wheat and rye bread. Richardson sat at the table with Karl and ate. The three women hovered about them and talked inexhaustibly. The omelette was good. He had never tasted an omelette like it, very delicate and rich after the icy sharpness of the wine.

While they were eating there was a commotion in the yard outside. The women began fluttering and Karl stood up. A man of fifty-five or sixty appeared at the doorway and after him two boys of eighteen and twenty. The man was dark and moustached, with the same soft grey eyes as Karl, the same broad forehead, and the same impression of gentleness and strength. He was dressed in working clothes and a full peaked cap. He looked like any small English tenant-farmer who has worked and struggled. The sun had dried his face into a thousand wrinkles and the soil seemed to have eaten eternally into the wrinkles, as though it could never wear away again.

He came into the kitchen and Karl went forward to meet him. The son and the father shook hands. The man smiled in the shy soft peasant-fashion, but there was no demonstration. They conveyed a feeling of gladness by a dumb unblinking look at each other.

The two boys came forward. They had the same brown wondrous-eyed peasant faces as the women, but they looked wilder and darker. Their boots and leggings were plastered with yellow mud and they brought with them a smell of earth and cows and ripened corn.

They stared at Karl and he stared at them. They were his brothers and they had been born after he had run away and he did not know them. They looked guilty and hesitant, as though they had heard and be-lieved all the tales about him, the prodigal, who had run away and would never come back. But at last they came to him and shook hands. They tried to throw off their shyness and shake hands as brothers, but they seemed like strangers, and there was suddenly a queer silence in the kitchen and finally the old woman began weeping and hurried away.

The man and the sons shook hands with Richardson and gradually the old air of gaiety returned. Maria hurried in with wine again and the young girl began to break fresh eggs into the blue bowl. Soon another omelette appeared and plates of *kuchen* and cheese. The man and the boys sat down and ate too. There was a noisy confusion of eating and laughter, of popping corks and frizzling eggs and strange peasants rushing in from the courtyard to ask about the strangers, and women rushing upstairs and down again as though madly chasing each other.

Soon afterwards the old woman appeared again. Her tears were dry but she looked round the room in consternation, and Richardson saw her whispering with Elsa and Maria. A moment later Elsa and the young girl hurried off across the courtyard.

He was feeling muddled and talkative and very happy when they returned. He had a vague impression of another conversation among the women, many looks of relief and joy, and of the mother whispering hurriedly with Karl.

Finally Karl turned to him and said:

'They were worried because they haven't a bed for you here. There is room for me but they would like it if you would sleep at the inn.'

'All right.'

'They want us to go down there to-night and celebrate. They'll take your things down and we needn't go until later. You'll be all right at the inn.'

'I don't care where I sleep as long as I do sleep.'

'You'll sleep all right.'

Karl turned to speak to his mother, and Richardson became suddenly aware of a fresh face at the doorway. His bag was standing on the steps where he had left it, and he had a hasty impression of Maria and Elsa talking to someone who in turn picked up his bag and took it away.

He saw a moment later a young girl crossing the courtyard. She was dressed in a loose white blouse and black skirt and bodice. She was very fair and slender. He did not see her face and she had crossed the courtyard with his bag and vanished before he could look at her again.

They went down to the inn as darkness was falling. Maria and Elsa and Karl's mother had dolled themselves up in white blouses and thick black skirts and had scrubbed their faces until they looked rather like prim, pink-and-white dolls in half-mourning. The men were wearing dark, ill-fitting best suits and awkward white collars, and Karl's father a green waistcoat with florets of canary-yellow and rose. It was like an English Sunday preparation for church, with a smell of camphor and lavender and a rustling of skirts, an air of suppressed excitement, a never-ending hunt for things in chests of drawers and a feeling that someone would never be ready. The dresses of the women were long and old-fashioned and they looked a little as if they had stepped out of a German engraving of the last century. Upstairs Richardson washed himself and the young girl cleaned his shoes and brought them up to him. When he came down into the kitchen again the womenfolk all smiled and half-bowed to him, with a sort of obsequious delight, obviously because he was young and English and Karl's friend. Just before they were ready to start for the inn he went and stood on the steps of the house and looked at the courtyard in the half-darkness. The air was quiet and warm. There was an odour of cows and straw, the scent of what he thought were some evening primroses and the smell of the summer night itself. He felt a curious sense of peace and silence come over him and all the hurry and weariness of the journey behind him seemed to slip away.

The inn was down in the centre of the village. The whole household trooped down. The green shutters were bolted over the windows, making little ladders of yellow light in the darkness. Karl and Richardson came down the street with a string of peasants trailing behind, and another group of peasants had gathered outside the inn to wait for them. People came up and shook hands with Karl and laughed and asked if he remembered them. The entrance to the inn was through a little courtyard, where there were wooden tables set out under an old mulberry tree, making a tiny beer-garden. As Richardson went under the mulberry tree and up the steps to the inn he felt himself treading the fallen mulberries under his feet.

A long passage led down to the main room of the inn. The room was filled with extra chairs and tables for the guests. There was a smell of wine and lager and tobacco smoke, and the room was brilliantly lighted.

Maria and Elsa were walking first. They were passing into the lighted room when Elsa uttered a piercing shriek and began scolding someone in a rapid patois. Everyone stopped. Richardson looked over Karl's shoulder and someone began laughing. A little brown monkey dressed in a scarlet waistcoat and a yellow bonnet sat perched on the open door. Its neck was collared and the thin chain hanging from the collar scratched against the door as the monkey quivered and waved its hands at Elsa. Suddenly the monkey began dancing and darting forward at Elsa's head. Four or five voices shouted at once:

'Jakob!'

Everyone burst out laughing and a very excited falsetto voice giggled from behind the door. The monkey vanished and suddenly an enormous fat face peeped round the door, very jovial and beaming and excited, and after it the gigantic figure of a man. He was holding up the dried skin of the monkey on his fingers; he worked his fingers and made the monkey dance and wave its hands. He stood in the doorway like a caricature of a man, enormous, droll, powerful, giggling with excitement like a girl. His face was glorious and round and his head went back with the shape and surface of an egg, absolutely bald and shining. His left eye was missing but the right had a wonderful blue vitality. He was wearing a kind of Norfolk jacket which would not meet across his chest and a pair of pale coffee-coloured trousers of some thin material which stretched like a tight bladder over the curve of his belly.

He towered above the guests like some huge clown. He waved the monkey and rattled the chain and giggled and joked and panted. When Karl arrived he seized his hand and half-embraced him and tried to kiss him. Karl introduced Richardson and then said:

'This is the innkeeper himself. Herr Jakob Müller.'

Richardson shook hands and the honour of meeting a young Englishman seemed to overwhelm the innkeeper. He half-bowed and smiled a shy, beatific almost frightened smile. And then he spoke volubly to Karl and Karl translated:

'He says perhaps you would like to see your room. He will take you up.'

Richardson said he would like to see the room and he followed the innkeeper upstairs. Above the first landing another set of stairs went up and beyond was his room, among the rafters. The innkeeper switched on the electric light and Richardson had an impression of a clean white room, a big German bed draped in dark crimson and above the bed a picture of Christ wearing the crown of thorns. There was a smell of clean linen and old, dark wood that filled him with pleasure.

He answered all the innkeeper's questions with 'Ja, ja!' and followed him downstairs again. As they were coming down the last flight of stairs Richardson looked over Müller's shoulder and saw someone standing at the foot, as though waiting to come up. It was a young girl of twenty-one or two. She was fair-skinned and slender and her hair was as pale as ripened wheat-straw and her eyes were vividly blue and candid and shining. She carried herself in a straight, alert fashion, but she looked ready to bound away up the stairs and vanish out of sheer timidity. She was dressed in a cream-coloured dress and white stockings, with a girdle of pale blue silk about her waist.

Richardson regarded her steadily and she returned his look at first furtively but a second later with a flash of something quite bold and almost wild, as though she were trying desperately to conquer her shyness. He reached the foot of the stairs and the innkeeper turned to him and made a long excited speech, patting the girl's shoulder. Richardson stood looking at her with timid solemnity, until at last she shook his outstretched hand and hurried upstairs.

As he went back with Herr Müller into the room where the guests had gathered it suddenly came to him that she was the girl who had hurried across the courtyard with his bag. He had caught only one word of all her father had said. It was her name: Anna. He went along the passage and into the brilliantly lighted room and joined Karl and the family. He was introduced to Frau Müller and another daughter, whose name he did not catch, a girl of twenty-nine or thirty. The woman and the girl were very blonde and a little frowzy. There was a priest there also, rather muscular and heavy-faced, his dark hair cropped very close, the colour of his grey eyes faded and dissipated. There was a great deal of handshaking. The priest kept looking at Frau Müller from the corners of his eyes. He drank a glass

of hock with Karl and Richardson and then shook
hands again and bowed himself away.

Herr Müller began to run in and out with bottles of
wine and glasses of lager, panting and giggling with
delight. He saw with consternation that Richardson
was still standing. He humbled himself at once and
escorted Richardson to a seat by the piano and brought
him a glass of hock. It was all very charming and
courteous. The piano was a sacred thing. The walnut
was beautifully polished and the lid was locked and it
was evidently an honour to sit there. Everyone stared
at Richardson until he felt odd and isolated. As soon
as he had drunk half of the hock Herr Müller ran forward with the bottle and filled up his glass. Everyone
stood up and drank a toast to something. He did not
understand until afterwards that the toast was for himself. The wine made him feel strange and elated and
happy. A peasant came in with an accordion, a fair-
haired, elegant young man in a suit of large brown
checks and squeaky, tea-coloured shoes. He shook
hands with excessive politeness and unrolled a great
deal of music. The party seemed to grow suddenly
vivacious, everyone laughing and chatting and drinking, the air thick with the smoke of cigars and the smell
of wine, the young peasant playing a tune on the
accordion and all the guests stamping their feet and
singing to the tune.

The peasant had finished playing and Richardson
was drinking a glass of cherry brandy when he saw
over the edge of his glass the figure of Anna. She had
come into the room with her father and they were
coming towards the piano. Beside the immense droll
figure of Müller she looked extremely delicate and
more than ever shy and naive and slender. She was
carrying some music in her hands. Her father, like a

man performing a religious ceremony, unlocked the
piano and dusted the yellow keys and the pale rose
fabric behind the fretted woodwork.

When he had finished dusting he turned to Richardson and made a long speech, evidently about the girl.
Richardson listened, bewildered, until Karl came up.

'What does he say?' asked Richardson.

'He is telling you all about the girl. She went to
school in Kreuznach and now she goes down there
once a week to take music lessons.'

'Tell him he may well be proud of her.'

Karl spoke to Müller and Müller said something
and Karl translated.

'He is very honoured. He wants to know if you can
sing.'

'I can't sing. But tell him I am very honoured too.'

Karl spoke to Müller again and while he was speaking Richardson looked at the girl. She was standing with
her hip against the piano and she returned his look with
a quick, embarrassed flash of her eyes and then lowered
her lids quickly again. He thought she had about her
in that moment, with her downcast eyes and the electric
light very gold on her fine thick hair, a loveliness that
was inexplicably impressive and thrilling. He had an
extraordinary feeling also that she was not a stranger
to him, like the peasants, and that it was not strange
for him to stand and gaze at her while she found some
music and arranged it on the piano and sat down to
play.

He sat down at last also and she began to play. He
saw at once that she did not play brilliantly, but rather
methodically and timidly, and he felt quite relieved.
Her fingers were very long and delicate and she struck
the keys very softly and the piano sounded thin and
reedy. She played something that Richardson did not

know, a simple, rather formal air with variations, which he thought might have been written about springtime by a ghost of Schumann. The peasants were quiet, with a kind of reverence, as though it were a great honour to listen to Anna Müller, who had been well-educated and went every week to take music lessons in Kreuznach. When she had finished they applauded and smiled on her with the same sort of deference, plainly looking up to her as someone above them. She half-turned on the piano stool and smiled and Richardson gazed straight into her face and without thinking what he was doing shouted:

'Bravo! Bravo!'

He let the pleasure she had given him come unmistakably into his voice. He felt that he wanted to impress her and he smiled too. She flashed him a single look half of fear, half of delight, and at once lowered her head over the piano and her music again.

After that she played several other pieces and the peasants sang. Müller kept bringing Richardson cherry brandies, which he drank straight off, and he began to feel strange and dreamy.

A little later Herr Müller came running in and spoke to Karl in great excitement. Karl translated for Richardson:

'The village choir are outside and they want to sing for us. He says they are very good singers and we ought to treat them.'

'Tell him we're very honoured.'

Karl spoke to Müller.

'He says everyone will be very amused if we have the beer brought in one big glass.'

Richardson thought it would be amusing too, and Karl told Müller, who ran out of the room and came back a moment later leading the choir. There were ten or twelve brown, fair smiling young peasants, who looked like a group of English country labourers. They grinned and made a line at the end of the room and were ready to sing when Herr Müller rushed in with an enormous boot-shaped glass running over with pale-gold beer. All the singers laughed and took long drinks and were very boisterous. Karl and Richardson drank also. Karl took a mighty drink that left the peasants gasping and at last applauding with delight. Finally the singers were ready. They began to sing, very low and in unison, a kind of ballad with a long string of verses. They sang magnificently, their voices soft and rich and humorous, the song itself something like a mountain stream, bright and gentle at first and then faster and stronger and finally deep and gorgeous and abandoned, like a torrent plunging splendidly down to a deep ravine. They ended the song on a shout and the guests laughed and applauded, and Müller ran hastily in with another boot of beer.

A little later Müller was pouring Richardson another cherry brandy. He was called suddenly away and forgot the bottle. Richardson seized another glass and filled it and then leaned over and held out the glass to Anna.

She had been looking at some music. She raised her head and looked at him with a startled expression, and then very slowly stretched out her hand and took the glass from him. He looked straight into her face with an expression of unmistakable delight. She looked irresistible and he wanted suddenly to reach out and touch her. He sat there for a moment in a sort of faintness, overcome by his own delight and the sensation of being so near to her. He watched her without a flicker of his eyes.

Suddenly someone switched out the electric light and

put the room in darkness. For a moment or two he was conscious of nothing but blackness and of people laughing and groping about the room. But a second later he was aware also of something soft and warm moving very close to him and, lastly, of someone kissing him. The lips were warm and sensitive and the kiss itself was tremulous and eager, with a brief, unmistakable hint of tenderness. He had not time to move his hands and a second or two later the lights were on again and the lips had been drawn away.

He came to himself like a man in another world. He felt queer and intoxicated in a way that was different from the intoxication brought about by the wine. He looked straight at Anna. She was sitting half-turned to him and he thought her eyes were fixed as with a kind of tremulous, almost painful admiration.

He did not know what to do. He felt dazzled and his hands were trembling, and he felt his heart beating in a foolish, unaccountable way. He felt almost glad that he could not speak to her or make any other sign than a long, intent look at her. And they sat absolutely motionless, gazing at each other softly and steadfastly, like two people playing a strange game of endurance with each other. A long time seemed to pass. He was vaguely conscious of the choir singing again and drinking another boot of beer and finally bowing themselves through the doorway.

At last, very suddenly, the girl got up and walked out of the room. He sat back and very slowly finished his brandy and thought in astonishment of the darkness, the soft movement of Anna's arms and lastly the kiss itself.

He finished another brandy and another hock. The elegant young man played the accordion again and five or six peasants danced across the floor. The rhythmical swirling figures made him feel sleepier than ever. The girl did not come back. He recalled over and over again the moment of the kiss with her.

Finally the party began to break up. He shook hands with everyone, and Karl, who was a little drunk, promised to call at the inn for him in the morning.

'We'll go up into the forest,' he said. 'Like to see the forest, wouldn't you? The forest is lovely — lovely! My God it's lovely!'

As the guests were trooping out Müller sprang from behind the door and terrified the women with the monkey again. There was a great deal of shrieking and shouting and laughter as the party trailed away up the dark street.

Richardson went back into the inn. Herr Müller and his wife shook hands with him and smiled on him with great broad smiles. He did not see Anna. He lingered about in the guest-room pretending to look for something, but she did not come, and finally he went slowly upstairs and into his room and shut the door.

IV

He awoke between seven and eight o'clock and got out of bed and went to the window. He knew at once from the look of the sky, very soft, cloudless and tranquil, that the day would be hot again. The sun was already brilliant on the painted white walls of the inn and the flags of the courtyard beyond the shade of the mulberry tree. The shadows of the tall houses zigzagged across the street and up the white walls of the houses opposite with dark, sharp angles, as though cut out with scissors. He leaned out of the window and saw on the flags the red smears of the mulberries that the guests had crushed under their feet the night before. He remembered Anna. The courtyard and the street were deserted, but voices were talking downstairs and there was a fragrance of fresh bread and coffee.

He went downstairs and Frau Müller gave him his coffee in a little room adorned with yellowing family portraits and big oleographs of battle-scenes and bright coloured paintings on glass. While he was drinking his coffee Herr Müller came in and smiled on him and shook hands. He looked more jovial and droll and pot-bellied than ever.

He finished his breakfast and went out into the courtyard. There was no sign of Anna. He lingered about in the sunshine, hoping she would come out, but she did not come. Once or twice he thought he could hear her voice but he was never sure and at last he walked slowly away up the street to look for Karl. He met no one but a few children and an old peasant woman and a youth with a reaping-machine drawn by an old bony red cow. They all said 'Guten morgen' and the youth raised his hat to him.

He recognized the house with the grape-vine and went into the courtyard and up the steps to the kitchen door. The young girl and Maria were in the kitchen, scraping a big earthenware bowl of potatoes. Maria got up at once and wiped her hands on her skirt and smiled. He smiled at her in return and said in a questioning tone:

'Karl?'

She nodded and ran at once to the stairs and shouted 'Karl! Karl!' but there was no answer, and finally she beckoned him and led him upstairs and showed him into the bedroom.

Karl was lying in a huge wooden bed. His dark head was just visible. The pillows had fallen to the floor and the great covering bolster was lying askew and crumpled and the rest of the bedclothes were tangled about his body. He looked as though he had spent the night struggling and wrestling with something. When Richardson bent down and shook his shoulder he groaned and buried his face in the sheets and told him to go away.

'What about the forest?' said Richardson.

'God, what about it?'

'What's the matter with you? You didn't drink very much at the inn.'

'We had another party here afterwards.'

'You look like ten parties.'

His hair was tangled and matted over his forehead and his eyes looked swollen and unhappy. 'How far is the forest? I'll go myself.'

'Two miles.'

'I'll go and be back for you soon. Is that all right?'

'God, I don't care what you do.'

He groaned again and struggled with the sheets and turned away.

Richardson went downstairs and through the courtyard and down the street again. The crimson mattresses hanging out of the bedroom windows looked brilliant in the sunshine. The sky was wonderfully blue and cloudless and the sun itself was hot and dazzling on his face.

When he reached the inn again a door in the wall of the courtyard was standing open and beyond he could see an orchard and a patch of flower-garden. He thought he could hear voices also and out of curiosity he walked in. The orchard was very small and the trees were old and strangely shaped and stooping. In the flower-garden nothing but a few ragged crimson dahlias were growing and a scarlet salvia or two, very handsome

and brilliant by the wall in the sunshine. The dahlias
had been staked and tied and the stakes were hooded
with flower-pots for earwigs. He touched the heavy
heads of the dahlias as he passed along the path into the
orchard itself. The grass under the trees, very long and
thick, was scattered with fallen plums and pears. The
air was full of a smell of the dank grass and a heavy
scent, like wine, of the fruit that lay rotting everywhere
in the bright sunshine.

As he went forward under the trees he heard voices
again, and coming suddenly to an open space he found
Anna and her sister gathering the fruit of a giant pear
tree. They were standing on a ladder, the elder girl
just under the lowest branches and Anna at the ladder
head, only her blue-striped skirt and stockings visible
among the leaves.

He stood still and watched them. He had come up
quite noiselessly and for a minute or two they chattered
to each other among the branches without knowing he
was there. But suddenly he moved and the elder girl
turned and saw him and uttered a little cry.

A moment later she was climbing hastily down the
ladder. He gave her one quick smile and then looked
up at Anna. She was climbing down also, step by step,
very slowly, with her back against the ladder, the basket
of pears half-resting against her knees. She had to
come down a step or two before the leaves had swung
clear of her face and the first sight of Richardson at the
foot of the ladder was so sudden that she stopped involuntarily and stared at him in shy astonishment
before breaking into a little smile. He smiled also.
Against the curtain of dark shining pear-leaves she
looked pale, fair and curiously far away. He thought
she looked very happy and entrancing too. He felt a
strange sensation of pleasure surge up in him at the

mere sight of her, a faint, delicious feeling of the most perfect joy.

A moment later he remembered something. He wanted to take her photograph. He would take her standing on the ladder, among the pear-leaves, with the basket held just below her breast. He turned at once and called involuntarily, 'Wait a moment', and hurried out of the orchard into the house.

When he returned with the camera they were trying to move the ladder. They wanted it to reach the branches where the pears were growing thickest, in the crown of the tree. He helped them move the ladder and made it firm against a branch, and when Anna took the basket and climbed up he picked up the camera and focused her. The elder girl uttered a little shriek of delight. Anna turned and saw the camera facing her. She blushed furiously, and he motioned her to come down a little and she turned and sat on a rung of the ladder, smoothing her hands quickly across her breast and skirt and hair until he was ready.

He took a long time over the photograph. It gave him the greatest pleasure to see the clear, pale image of her in the camera and then to look up at her, sitting like an image also, watching him with an attentive half-smile, like someone listening to something very lovely and illuminating.

He remained for a long time in the orchard with them. He took photographs of them sitting together on the ladder and another of Anna alone, half-lying in the grass among the fallen pears. After taking the photographs he climbed up into the highest branches of the tree, where the girls were a little afraid of venturing, and helped them to gather the pears. He liked the sensation of being far up in the tree, moving precariously from branch to branch in the sunlight, swaying the branches so that the pears swung back into his hands. He liked the stillness of the garden also, the scent of the ripe fruit, the voices of the girls breaking up the stillness, the face of Anna looking furtively up at him through the lacework of leaves.

Somewhere about eleven o'clock Herr Müller himself came into the orchard and called them into the courtyard for a glass of wine. In the courtyard was a young peasant who had come in to see Richardson. He had been a prisoner in England and could speak a little English and it would be a great honour to meet an Englishman again.

The wine was red and very cold and sharp. They drank it sitting at the tables or lounging in the shade of the mulberry tree. The young peasant was very shy and began protesting:

'I cannot the English no more speak — not now.'

'But that's very good,' said Richardson.

'I forget.'

'But it will come back.'

'For ten years I do not say.'

'But you remember it perfectly.'

'Ja?' He was delighted. 'You think?'

Gradually he lost his shyness and they talked of England, and Richardson asked him to have some beer. 'Ein bier, Herr Müller,' he called and everyone laughed.

They talked English over the beer and the wine while the Müllers stood listening. The peasant had come straight from the fields. He and his mother were harvesting their wheat; he had mown enough for her to rake and band, but she was very quick and he must soon go back to her. Richardson said that he would like to go into the fields that afternoon to see him mowing and to take photographs of him and his mother among the sheaves.

The peasant was overjoyed and began trying to explain the way Richardson must take in order to reach his land. He tried to explain in English but failed, and, blushing and laughing at himself, he finally appealed to Anna. They talked together for a moment or two, and Anna nodded her head and Richardson felt his heart begin to beat excitedly even before the peasant said to him:

'Anna will come with you.'

He saw her look at him as soon as the words had been spoken. It was the same tremulous, almost frightened look he had seen on her face once or twice the night before.

Finally they went back into the orchard. The dahlias were beginning to droop their heads in the heat of the day and the sun was fiercely hot on his head up in the branches of the tree. This time Anna did not come up into the tree. She walked about in the grass and filled her basket with fallen pears and hardly looked up into the branches.

Whenever he looked forward to the afternoon, and when finally the afternoon came, and he was sitting about in the courtyard for Anna to appear he experienced a wonderful, inarticulate happiness.

It was still early when Anna came. She had changed her dress, as though it were something extremely important to escort him into the fields, and she was wearing a silky, cream-coloured frock which looked spotlessly preserved, as though she only wore it on great occasions.

They smiled at each other and in silence went off through the village and soon they were in the country beyond. The road wound on through patches of wheat and rye and sometimes there were vineyards and strips of maize and tobacco, the leaves of the maize drooping and glossy in the hot sun. A little distance away the forest stood, the pines like a black, silent, gloomy barricade against the sky. On the roadside the wild yellow snapdragon was growing again, with poppies and purple knapweed and solitary blossoms of chicory. The peasants were beginning to work again after the midday rest, the men mowing, the women tying and shocking the sheaves. They paused and lifted their hands and stared as Anna and Richardson passed along the road.

The young peasant and his mother were working a patch of red-eared wheat not far from the edge of the forest. The woman had a thin, dark-brown face with fine, deep-sunken peasant's eyes, very shrewd and quick and watchful, but with a wonderful shining tranquillity of the sunlight in them too. Her face seemed to burn with an inexhaustible life under her white kerchief. She seemed both curiously proud and shy and was overcome with shame at the idea of being photographed in her black working skirt, with her sleeves rolled up and a sheaf in her arms. Finally she consented to stand with Anna, without the sheaf, against the corn that was still uncut. She looked very dark and awkward and embarrassed. Anna by contrast seemed to Richardson filled with a lovely composure and light.

Afterwards he photographed the peasant and his mother and then Anna with them. At every click of the camera they laughed with relief and delight. Richardson, laughing too, promised to send them the photographs when he returned to England.

Finally as he was folding up his camera he said to the peasant:

'Is that where the forest begins — over there?'

'The forest — yes.'

'I should like to see it. You understand? I have never been in the forest.'

'No?'

'No. Will you ask Anna if she will take me? I should like to see the forest once.'

The peasant spoke with Anna, and Anna nodded her head, looking at Richardson quickly and softly, but without a trace of apprehension or timidity.

Richardson shook hands with the peasant and his mother and then followed Anna along the path to the road again. A little later they struck away from the road and took the path to the forest.

Eventually they came upon the forest path itself and walked a little distance under the trees and stood still. There was a strange deathly stillness and silence everywhere, and overhead the pines made a thick dark screen which shut out the sunlight. The earth was strewn with pine-needles, faintly scented and soundless to walk upon, making a brown floor that went on infinitely without a trace of green, into the gloomy distance of slumbering trees. Overawed by the silence, the grandeur and the primeval force of it, Richardson stood in a solemn contemplation of it until he became aware of Anna moving on again.

He did not follow her until she was some distance ahead of him. He walked behind her at last very slowly, listening to the forest and watching her at the same time. Sometimes the sunlight filtered down through a break in the pines and she walked through the shaft of it, the flash of her light hair very rich and lovely. Walking behind her he noticed consciously for the first time how she did her hair; it was plaited into one thick coil and twisted about the back of her head in the shape of a figure eight.

She walked on ahead until they came to an opening

in the pines. The sunlight suddenly poured down upon them again, burning through the light leaves of some overhanging birches. The silver trunks of the birches gleamed like satin in the sunshine and the earth was covered with a short soft grass and the leaves of wild strawberries.

As they came to the birch trees she stopped and turned and waited for him. He stopped also. She looked up at the sunlight and the birches and then at Richardson and then back to the trees again. He slipped his arm very lightly across her shoulder. He felt her body trembling and saw her breast rising and falling quickly with emotion. He looked at her uplifted face steadfastly and quietly. She seemed irresistibly lovely, her eyes marvellously blue and candid and soft, and suddenly he stooped and kissed her lightly, but with profound tenderness. The soft caressing line of her lips was familiar immediately. She uttered a little sound of pleasure, half-sighing, half-laughing, and he felt a sensation of intolerable happiness at the sound of her voice expressing her joy.

Afterwards he kissed her again and they went on through the forest. Sometimes she stopped him and clasped him by the shoulders and began speaking slowly and hesitantly in German. There was something she longed to tell him and could not express in gestures and glances. Finally she would shake her head and laugh and give it up and let him kiss her again.

'Anna, Anna,' he would say to her softly.

They turned and came slowly back along the forest-path. He did not want to speak to her. He was overjoyed simply by the thrilling nearness of her body, the touch of her breasts against him through her soft dress, the marvellously radiant expression on her face and the sensation of sweet, tormenting happiness in his heart.

Finally they came out of the forest and walked down the hot road to Iben again. As they approached the village they saw someone hurrying up the road to meet them. It was Karl. Richardson involuntarily waved his hand and Karl waved back in reply.

A moment later Richardson turned his head and discovered Anna looking at him dumbly, with a kind of timid anxiety. It was only then he remembered they were leaving Iben in the morning and were going on to Berlin.

V

They were ready to depart at noon on the following day. Richardson had packed his bag and carried it up to the farm and Karl's brothers had loaded it into a low spring cart in readiness to drive to the station. These was a station two miles away and a train there at three o'clock. Richardson and Karl had spent the morning saying farewell to everyone who remembered Karl as a child. Everyone smiled a great deal and was very charming to them and they drank wine at every house. Over the wine the peasants would ask them about England and about the war. The talk was always the same. No one had wanted a war and why had it happened? After war they would talk of money. A peasant would talk of the days when he had taken a wagon load of plums to market and had brought back a wagon load of marks and how the next day the marks had become worthless. Sometimes the old people would unlock a drawer and give Richardson a note for ten million marks and ask him to keep it in memory of them. They would let him see the drawer stuffed full of money and then shrug their shoulders as if to say, 'Of course it isn't worth a pfennig. We just keep it out of curiosity, but he felt that he sometimes detected a look in their faces as though they secretly believed that everything would be changed, and that one day they would be suddenly wealthy.

Afterwards there was a big farewell lunch at the farm, with great helpings of heavy food and bottles of hock. Richardson felt sick of wine and tried to keep up the level of his glass by pretending to drink. The day was very hot again and the food seemed sickening too.

From his place at the table he could see across the courtyard and he remembered how he had first seen Anna hurrying across there with his bag. He had not seen Anna all day, and during the morning he had wondered where she was and if he would see her again. He had not seen her since the night before, when he had returned late to the inn and had been startled by the sound of her hurrying across the courtyard. She had rested her hands on his shoulders, and had whispered to him very earnestly. From the tone of her voice he had known it was something important but he had not understood a word.

After the lunch was over they were to go down to the inn and say farewell to the Müllers. Richardson felt that he would like to take photographs of them standing under the mulberry tree.

At the inn Herr Müller greeted them with shouts and giggles of joy. Frau Müller and the elder sister came out, straightening their skirts and smoothing their hair. There was no sign of Anna. Richardson unfolded his camera, wondering desperately if she would come. At the sight of the camera the two women fled to change their dresses and came out again wearing frowsy white Sunday frocks with high collars. Herr

Müller fetched his monkey and stood with the two women under the mulberry tree. Anna did not come. Richardson felt a kind of sickening desperation in his heart and finally he could bear it no longer and said to Karl:

'Why isn't Anna here?'

He heard Karl speak to Müller. He bent his head over the camera and waited for the reply and presently he heard Karl say:

'It is the day for her music lesson in Kreuznach.'

He felt suddenly sick, overcome by despair. He lowered his head and focused the camera on the Müllers. The sunlight was shining full on their faces and he knew the photograph would be very poor, but he did not care. He simply held up his hand and the camera clicked and it was all over.

'Auf Wiedersehen, Auf Wiedersehen!' said the Müllers. 'Auf Wiedersehen!'

'Good-bye!' said Karl.

'Goot-bye!'

Back at the farm everyone was ready and the carts were waiting. Maria had packed up sandwiches of rye bread and sausage, enough for the whole journey to Berlin. Elsa was weeping and Karl's mother was trying not to weep. They all crowded into the carts and drove away out of the village and along the hot white road to the station, and the peasants ran out of the houses to wave at them as they passed.

There was an oppressive stillness about the heat of the afternoon and a tremulous dark haze over the distant patches of wheat and rye. Richardson looked at everything, the peasants working among the corn, the chicory-flowers in the parched grass, the burning sky and the dark edge of the forest, with a memory of Anna. The sickening sensation in his heart had been replaced by a soft, intolerable ache, half sweet and half unhappy.

The train was waiting in the station, hissing quietly. Karl and Richardson found a carriage and Karl's relatives crowded about the doorway, talking and weeping and shaking hands. At the last moment Karl's father handed Richardson a bottle of hock and made a little speech, which Karl translated.

'They have been very honoured to meet you. The wine is very old and good and they would like you to have it and not forget them.'

'Thank them very much,' Richardson said. 'I shan't forget.'

A moment or two later the train began to move. Everyone waved hands and shouted farewell, and Karl and Richardson leaned out of the window and waved too. The platform receded quickly, and finally the station and the waving figures vanished from sight.

Richardson sat down in the corner of the carriage without a word. The train began to pass through the forest and the sunlight came flickering into the windows between the dark shadows of the pines. Sometimes there were stretches of birch trees and the sunlight was dappled and quivering as it fell on the glass. In the forest itself there was no sunlight, but only the still, sombre gloom through which he had walked with Anna the previous day. He remembered Anna perfectly as he looked at it, her shy, tremulous face, her sensitive lips, the irresistibly lovely look of joy which she had sometimes given him. She seemed more than ever lovely in recollection and because he would never see her again.

The train gathered speed and the forest flashed past in a dark, bewildering panorama. Richardson tried to give up thinking of Anna but she remained with him persistently, like the forest running side by side with the train. Sometimes on the edge of the forest he saw patches of pink flowers like willow-herb and tall drooping flowers like evening primroses. Once he caught sight of a deer running away at the sound of the train. He thought of Anna for a long time. He had never even spoken with her and sometimes it seemed as if he had hardly known her. She had appeared briefly and wonderfully and had vanished, like a rainbow. He knew he would never see her again and he wondered if he would remember her.

There was a break in the forest and the train stopped at a station, and then the train and the forest ran on together again.

He wondered also if she would remember him.

FOR THE DEAD

A LITTLE pink-faced man, wearing a bowler hat and a mackintosh over a black suit, was hurrying towards the cemetery carrying a bunch of white chrysanthemums wrapped in newspaper and smoking a stump of cigarette that was half hidden by his greyish yellow moustache. A gentle rain was falling, a drizzling misty November rain that clung like dew to the chrysanthemums and like tiniest beads of quicksilver to the man's moustache and his bowler hat. The afternoon would be dark early. The sky was a single vast leaden cloud; the rain was coming a little faster each moment. As the rain came faster the man increased his pace. He carried the chrysanthemums close to his side, furtively, flowers downward, uneasily conscious of them.

The cemetery was deserted. In the distance the rain made a faint vapour, dissolving the white tombstones. The cypress trees drooped heavily and the branches of the leafless almond trees stood black against the sky, delicately laced with odd jewels of rain.

Hurrying, the man went past the public water-tap and the watering-cans and along the wet devious paths among the graves. He walked as though it were all very distasteful to him — the rain, the deserted cemetery, the very thought of placing the flowers on the grave of his dead wife. Yet there was a kind of indifference also in his very irritation, as though he hardly cared whether the flowers were put there or not. He began to walk even faster, anxious to have done with it all.

He came at last to his wife's grave, a rectangle of white marble enclosing a mound of neglected grass, and without taking off his hat and still sucking the cigarette through his wet moustache he took the chrysanthemums from their wrapping of newspaper, shook them and dropped them carelessly on the wet grass. On the grass, in a half-rusty green tin vase, stood the chrysanthemums he had put there a fortnight before. Once white, they were now shrivelled and blackened by frost and rain. Straddling the grave he seized the tin, wrenched out the old flowers and dropped them too on the wet grass.

Picking up the new chrysanthemums, he hesitated. The tin was empty of water. He stood for a moment wondering if he should walk back across the cemetery to the water-tap. And then, impatiently, he decided against it. It was a long way in the rain. What did it matter? A lot of trouble, a lot of trouble for nothing. The flowers would die in any case. He wanted to get it over.

He hastily picked up the new white bunch of chrysanthemums. But stooping with them he again hesitated.

Down the path, also at a grave, was another man. He was a thin stooping figure and with his black bowler hat and his black overcoat he had the almost ascetic respectability of a tired shopwalker. Like the small man he was middle-aged, and like him also he was arranging a bunch of white chrysanthemums hastily, as though it were distasteful and he wanted to escape from the cemetery and the rain.

They noticed each other simultaneously and could not avoid speaking.

'Good afternoon.'

'Ah, good afternoon.'

They were slightly acquainted and they spoke deferentially, their voices a little embarrassed, and they stood for a moment hesitant, not knowing what to do or what also to say.

Then casually the smaller man glanced up at the sky. 'I shouldn't wonder if it rained all night,' he remarked.

Then, as he lowered his eyes, he saw that the other man had removed his hat and was staring dismally at the rain, as though in thought.

'Ah!' he said heavily. 'I shouldn't wonder.' The small man glanced at the other man with secret annoyance for having removed his hat.

There was a silence, then, after a moment, the small man unobtrusively took off his hat also. His head, very bald, like a bladder of pink lard, seemed to stand out strangely large in the colourless rainy air. Then, as he stood with his head half-bowed, the little man remembered his cigarette. It seemed suddenly disrespectful and he let it fall from his mouth and it dropped on the wet grass, hissing faintly until he put his foot on it.

They stood there with their hats in their hands and with the rain drizzling on their bare heads until the tall man spoke again.

'You haven't a drop of water to spare,' he said, 'have you?'

The little man shook his head. 'But I was just going to the tap,' he said. 'I'll bring a can.'

'Oh no, I was going myself.'

'It seems a pity for us both to go.'

The tall man smiled and shook his head with a heavy and deliberate pretence of mournfulness.

'One day we shall have to go,' he said.

The little man nodded. 'I suppose so,' he said, heavily also.

Almost before they were aware of it they were walking down the path together, leaving their flowers on the wet grass. They walked at a slow almost solemn pace, with their hats still in their hands, as though to a funeral. Now and then they shot furtive glances of secret impatience at each other, each irritably wondering when the other would put on his hat. But neither made a sign, and they walked to the water-tap and back to the graves again without a change of pace, each with a can of water in one hand and his hat still in the other.

Stooping over the graves they arranged their flowers with a kind of deliberate reverence, filling the tin vases carefully, touching the flower petals with a perceptible show of tenderness. At intervals they half glanced up at each other, each as though wondering if the other were looking and what he were thinking.

At last they were finished and they stood upright. The thin man had been kneeling and he brushed his hands across his wet knees. The little man could feel the rain falling in larger drops on his bald head and collecting into even larger drops that rolled suddenly, like little balls of ice, down his neck.

They stood in silence, a pace or two back from the graves, their heads a trifle bowed in a pretence of grief. They stood there for what seemed to both of them a long time, secretly impatient, staring heavily into space, as though reflecting regretfully on the past and the dead. They had no longer any need to pretend wretchedness. The rain was coming down each moment faster and colder, dripping swiftly down from the wintry branches to the glistening marble tombs and the yellowish muddy paths. Once or twice the tall man ran his hand in concern across his damp knees and the other shook his head slightly, shivering miserably under the cold rain.

At last the tall man gave a sigh as though reluctant to depart, and picked up his watering-can.

'Well, it's no use standing here,' he said mournfully.

He shook his head as he spoke. 'No use standing here.'

The little man shook his head in melancholy agreement, sighing also.

A moment later, with secret relief, they were walking away together down the path. Unobtrusively the tall man put on his hat and then the small man put on his too. They walked deferentially, in silence, until they reached the water-tap, where they left their watering-cans.

At the gates they stood for a moment and then parted. The rain was falling heavily, the mist and the darkness together hid the farthest tombs and trees from sight, and the two men hurried away from each other with angry relief and impatience, as though they never wished to see each other again.

EVERY BULLET HAS ITS BILLET

IRMA HARRIS was eighteen when, in 1915, Lieutenant Bronson and his wife came to be billeted on her mother. Just out of High School, a pale arch-eyed girl with great masses of reddish gold hair scrolled up behind like the twists of a golden loaf, she had got to the age when she liked sitting for long hours in her own room, alone, thinking inexpressibly sad thoughts, with her hands spread out on her lap like two pink self-conscious flowers, waiting for the dew of all sorts of confused dreams to fall on them. Lieutenant Bronson and his wife had been married six weeks, and were very happy.

Mrs. Harris was a woman whose mind was done up in curling-rags: a plain, common mind which, for forty years, she had tried to frill into superiority. On a level above the neighbours, to whom she never spoke, she thanked God for Irma: thanked God that Irma's hair was rich and beautiful, that she had the aristocratic richness of a name like Irma and not the common poverty of a name like May or Flo; that Irma had been educated, was superior, had kept pure and would, by the Grace of God, still keep pure for a long time to come. Earlier, some years before the death of Harris, who had peddled hosiery on a basket bicycle from door to door and had somehow cheese-pared his way to saving money, she had shut Irma down under a glass case, and had then gone on polishing the glass until she could see in it not only Irma but her own face. Even then it was not her own plain, ordinary curl-ragged face, but a face with a great mass of loaf-gold hair and soft pure skin as pale as bread. She saw Irma: Irma

88

was herself. The girl was the lost self of the woman, unrecapturable except through the glass dome of imagination. Whatever might happen to Irma would happen also to herself.

In a podgy kind of way, Lieutenant Bronson was handsome, heavily built, with aristocratically tender feet which suffered terribly on the route marches. He came from the real aristocracy: estates in Cornwall, a house in Grosvenor Square, and at the outbreak of the war had been toying away time, on a pretence of working at oil, in Mexico. Yet he had a quality of self-effacement about him, a retreating charm of manner that was quite humble. The men liked him. He had a way of hushing up, as it were, his aristocratic identity. His wife was a little thing, a woman of whipped cream, delicate and sweet, all pretty froth and hardly tangible. An aristocrat also, she had not quite come to her senses after the tremendous crash of war and marriage coming almost at the same time, and she painted water-colours in the Harris's front room, in the real pre-war aristocratic mode, still nursing the idea that painting was a necessary accomplishment. Bronson adored her, and she was only bored when route marches and parades and mess duty claimed him too long. Then she painted hard, or wrote letters, or, on desperate days, went into the kitchen and prepared the anchovies or mayonnaise. On still more desperate days she invited Irma into the front room, to talk to her, while she painted.

The two girls liked each other. Only the thinnest veil of breeding and self-consciousness kept them apart, sometimes miles apart. Virginal, under the glass-case, Irma looked up to the older girl, envying the strange state of marriage, in which freedom and stability were so miraculously combined. Whirling

89

round on an axis which marriage and war had sent crazy, Mrs. Bronson looked down, with slight envy, on what she felt to be Irma's state of emotional rest.

Mrs. Bronson painted with timid accurate talent, creating nothing. The delicate water-colours cost her no emotion. She copied flowers, did a bowl of Gloire de Dijon roses that Irma brought in from the garden, and another of white lilies. She was always washing her hands. She used a strange soap, after which her hands gave off a remotely exotic scent. To Irma, gradually, this scent began to stand for Mrs. Bronson: her frothy prettiness, her painting, the miraculous marital state.

In this way the natural heroine-worship sprang up. Just as Mrs. Harris saw herself in Irma, so Irma began to wish that she could see herself in Mrs. Bronson. She wanted to be able to do the things Mrs. Bronson did: to paint water-colours, to mix extraordinary oils for salad, to speak with her accent, to wash with that same remarkable soap. She did her best to dress a little like Mrs. Bronson. Instead of sitting with her hands outspread, like flowers, she began to sit with her arms crossed and her hands on their opposite shoulders, in the same bemused pretty attitude as Mrs. Bronson did.

All the time Mrs. Harris was watching. Years of financial alertness, of swift concentration against the remote chance of mistaking sixpence for a farthing, had left her eyes virtually lidless. She missed nothing. Her concentration on money was part instinctive, part habitual, part a fear of Harris's memory. Built up on farthings, Harris's financial success, by which he had been able to invest in the rows of working-class houses from which Irma and she now drew income, reproached her. Inspired in this way, she missed less than Harris himself. Her concentration on money had become a creed.

Similarly her concentration on Irma was becoming a disease. For years it had been a kind of nervousness, some sort of chronic palsied illusion. As she saw Irma begin to model herself on Mrs. Bronson, it began to grow infinitely worse, more vicious, aggravated by the fact that, for once in her life, Irma was doing something outside the rule of the glass case. Having worshipped Irma all her life, it seemed beyond her comprehension that Irma could be guilty of worship in turn.

Mrs. Harris could not understand. She saw any affection between the two girls as beyond and without reason. She saw Irma captured by someone else, taken away from her. There was something unusual, fishy, not straight about it. In a fit of jealousy she tried to stop it.

'If I were you, I shouldn't bother Mrs. Bronson so much. You see, well, people like to be private. I don't think she wants you in there from morning to night.'

In meek obedience, Irma stopped going into Mrs. Bronson's room. Mrs. Bronson at once noticed it.

'Why doesn't Irma come in to see me?'

Mrs. Harris was in a quandary. No use offending Mrs. Bronson. She didn't want to lose the Bronsons. An officer and his wife were better than three privates. It would pay her to be nice to Mrs. Bronson.

So Irma went back, and the natural friendship seemed if anything a little stronger, more easy, so that Irma tried aping Mrs. Bronson not only in things like soap and dresses, but in thought and mannerisms. They naturally talked about Bronson, and once or twice Irma went in to have supper with them, and once Bronson teased her about her hair.

'You've got so much hair you ought to dish it out to the officers. One lock, one officer. You know, to put in his Bible next to his heart. It's not fair, one girl having enough hair for a regiment and keeping it.'

It was just Bronson's joke, and they all enjoyed it.

Then, once or twice, Bronson and his wife took Irma for a walk after supper. They felt a little sorry for her, sensing the situation, seeing her under the domination of the mother, the scrubbed house, the fusty passages. 'The poor kid's never had a chance. I feel a bit sorry for her,' Mrs. Bronson said. And the three of them would walk out as far as the park, in the summer dusk, under the limes, and once Mrs. Bronson, who wore no hat, said she could feel the honey-dew falling from the lime leaves down on her hair. 'Just trying to make it curl like Irma's,' Bronson teased.

To Mrs. Harris it was all incomprehensible. Fretted by jealousy, her mind could not rest. It remained nervous, discontented, without power to do anything.

Then she saw what she took to be an extraordinary thing. Irma and the Bronsons had been for an evening walk. Five minutes after they were back, she saw Irma's straw hat and Bronson's cap lying in the same chair in the hall.

Not hung up, but thrown down, and together. Not Mrs. Bronson's hat. Irma's hat. With Bronson's thrown down in a hurry. At night, under cover of darkness.

Her mind gathered the nervous power and the direction it had lacked and shot off, before she could do anything, straight to Bronson. It seemed to hit Bronson with its extraordinary charge of suspicion, and then recoil back, leaving Mrs. Harris with the hot shell of staggered conviction in her hands.

It was Mr. Bronson. Not Mrs. Bronson. Mr. Bronson. Bronson! Her mind juggled with the red-hot conviction as a man juggles with the potato too hot to hold. Tossing it up and down, lacking the nerve to hold it, she was too distraught, that night, to do anything about it, and she kept up her distressed juggling performance all night, not knowing whether to be ashamed for Irma or enraged with Bronson, or both.

In the morning she had decided. For various reasons she would speak to Irma. There was the reason of money, the necessity of not offending the Bronsons. Then there was the reason that was much nearer Irma. Something had happened to Irma and it was very likely that Irma, a young girl, did not fully understand it.

'Irma,' she said. 'I want to speak to you.' Then at the moment of crisis she felt her courage crumble. She felt that she could not say what she had to say in bare words, all pat, like a speech.

At this moment she remembered Harris. He, like the Lord, had had a weakness for speaking in parables. She would speak in a parable, and her idea of a parable was to say:

'Irma, you want to keep yourself to yourself.'

Distress unexpectedly charged her voice with passion. The girl was wide-eyed, not understanding. She did not speak.

Mrs. Harris took silence for guilt. Her mind seized the hot charge of conviction and held it painfully but in spite of pain.

'Irma! Irma!'

'But mother, what's the matter?'

'What's the matter! That's a nice thing. As if you don't know. Oh! Irma, Irma. After all I've done for you, after the way I've brought you up.' And then suddenly the plain accusation, final and incontrovertible, as if she needed nothing more than the two hats, Irma's and Bronson's, on a chair, and the girl's silence.

'Irma, you're running after Lieutenant Bronson! I won't have it. I've seen it! I know. I won't have it!'

The girl was still silent. To Mrs. Harris it seemed only like a confession, and in a way she was glad that it was all over so simply.

'That's all I've got to say — now. But I'd be ashamed of myself, Irma Harris. I would. I'd be utterly ashamed of myself.'

Irma began to go about vaguely, for the first time in her life caught up by a dream of substantial reality. Up to that time she had not thought of Bronson. It was only Mrs. Bronson. She felt excitably affectionate towards Mrs. Bronson, virginally, tenderly, longing to be like her. Bronson had not touched her.

She began now to think of Bronson. What had her mother seen? She must have seen something. Knowing that she had never looked at Bronson, the girl could only wonder if Bronson had looked at her.

She began to try to figure it out for herself, in bed at night. She took the false premise of her mother, the accusation, and built up about it the arguments for one side and another, singling out the moments when she felt that there might have been something in Bronson's way of looking at her. She tried to argue it out impartially with herself, trying to prove there was nothing in it. And gradually, all the time, she was aware of an increasing feeling that it would be nice if it could be proved the other way. Then she wanted it proved the other way. She wanted to feel that Bronson had looked at her. She wanted to know, and even if necessary against all reason, that there was something in it after all.

Then all at once she thought of the things Bronson

had said about her hair. Said jokingly, they suddenly took on the weight of great importance. She was staggered by them. Where they had seemed very trivial, not to be taken seriously, they now began to seem not only extraordinarily important, but very beautiful. As she lay stretched out in bed, she felt that all argument had ceased to have meaning. There was now no argument, no complexity. It was all different. The street lamp was still shining on the ceiling from outside, and, looking up at it, she felt herself flooded by waves and waves of incandescent beauty. Borne on light, they were at the same time like intransient cadences of prolonged music. Sentimentally and passively she let them wash over her, and then recede, leaving her mind as clear-washed as a shore after a tide, smoothed and quiet, animated only by the faint phosphorescence of an absurd sort of rapture.

Subsequently she became almost awfully aware of Bronson's nearness. She went upstairs and met him coming down; took in the Bronsons' meals and stood while he took the dishes from her, almost touching her. She was aware on those occasions of flashes of extraordinarily electric emotion, part pleasure, part pain, and at nights she put on, in her mind, the gramophone record of things he had said to her or about her, letting herself be passively swirled away from the eternal revolutions of repeated thought.

Then Mrs. Harris noticed something else: the soap. Irma's soap was the same, she suddenly discovered, as Mrs. Bronson's soap.

That could only mean one thing.

It was an awful, outrageous thing. Soap, scent, the scent of hands and body and face: together they drove her to the edge of impossible conjecture.

She rushed straight up to Irma's bedroom, only to

find the girl standing there by the window, looking at Bronson, drilling No. 3 Platoon farther down the street. For a moment Mrs. Harris could not speak. It was a moment of both humiliation and triumph. She felt enraged and yet quite strengthless. Then, before she could speak, Irma turned away from the window, lifted up her head and walked out of the room. She was a little flushed, but quite calm, and she did not speak.

Irma's look of unsubmissive tranquillity, her air of touch-me-not complacency, so beautiful and self-conscious and infuriating, aroused in Mrs. Harris a curious sort of enmity. Her synonymity with Irma was shattered. Irma had become another being, separate, unacknowledgeable, behaving with a self-confessed awful immorality that was a condemnation of Mrs. Harris herself.

Going downstairs, she followed Irma about, arguing, basing everything on that point. 'What about me? What do you think I feel? After all I've done for you. Don't you see how I must feel? Don't you ever think of me? Don't you see how it affects me?'

The girl could not say anything. In so intangible an affair, where so much was only the fiction of the mind, there was nothing much she could do except be silent.

It was in silence that Mrs. Harris saw guilt. She blamed Irma bitterly, but only Irma, seeing her part in the affair as active, not passive. Irma was committing — staring out of the window, aping Mrs. Bronson, using the same soap — a wilful and stupid folly, a slight against parental decency. 'Your father would have been *ashamed* of you.' But it had not occurred to her that the lieutenant might be condoning it.

Pushed farther into secrecy, Irma enlarged in her mind the small fiction of herself and Bronson. She was pushed back into an inward loneliness, in which she made a structure of one improbability built on another. These improbabilities, as they grew up pagoda-fashion, she began to see as solid truths, lighting them up with the shimmering adolescent light of her own fancy. In this beautiful abstract fashion, she persuaded herself into an intense belief in the reality of Bronson's affection for her, suffering with a certain pleasure, believing in the aspects of its tragedy as readily as she believed in its extraordinary ecstasy.

In the Bronsons' room downstairs there was a large black tin case. Here Bronson kept his full-dress uniform, sword and various accoutrements. One night Irma cut off some of her hair and went downstairs, intending to put the hair into the breast-pocket of one of Bronson's tunics. In the darkness the lid of the box slipped out of her hands and crashed.

The Bronsons' bedroom was immediately above, and Bronson heard the crash and came downstairs. He switched on the electric light and saw Irma standing beside the box, in her nightgown. He had come down hurriedly, without a dressing-gown, and for a moment he was too embarrassed to speak. Irma stood trembling. Then just as he was going to speak he heard a door open upstairs, and he knew Mrs. Harris was coming down.

Something made him put out the light. In complete silence, he and the girl stood in the darkness, trying to deny each other's existence. They heard Mrs. Harris shuffle downstairs in her carpet slippers, and after about thirty seconds Bronson felt her hand stab at the light.

The words were ready on Mrs. Harris's lips, like bullets waiting to be fired. They exploded straight at Bronson, rapid-firing: 'I got you, I caught you. I got you, I caught you.'

Neither Bronson nor Irma could speak. Mrs. Harris took silence for guilt. She swivelled round and fired a double shot upstairs:

'Mrs. Bronson! Mrs. Bronson!'

Bronson stood white, tragically silent. He heard his wife's voice in reply and her movements as she came downstairs. He stood quiet, more nervous than Irma, still not saying anything, aware of his predicament and yet doing nothing, seeing himself only as the victim of some unhappy and apparently unchaste circumstance over which he had no control.

Mrs. Harris fired a fusillade of bitter triumph as Mrs. Bronson came and stood in the light of the door way:

'They ain't moved, they ain't said nothing. That's how I found 'em. In their nightgowns. That's how I found 'em. I knew it had been going on for a long time, but not like this, not like this!'

Irma began to cry. Bronson and his wife stood with a kind of pasteboard rigidity, stiffened by some inherent aristocratic impulse not to give way before people out of their class. They knew they had nothing to fear, yet they saw themselves confronted by the iron suspicion of Mrs. Harris as by a firing squad. In Mrs. Harris's small distracted grey eyes there was a touch of madness, inspired by triumph. She spoke with the rapid incoherence of someone sent slightly insane by a terrible discovery. 'I don't know what you're going to do, but I know what I'm going to do. I know and I'm going to do it. If you're not ashamed, I am. I'm ashamed. I'm —'

At this moment Irma fainted.

'No wonder! No wonder! Gettin' her down here in her nightgown, on the sly. Gettin' her down here —'

The insane dangerous stupidity of it all only struck

the Bronsons into dead silence. And in silence, as never before, Mrs. Harris saw guilt.

The next afternoon the Bronsons moved to other quarters. Irma, shut up in her room, heard Lieutenant Bronson's large tin box go clanking out of the hall like a coffin.

In less than a month there was hardly a soldier left in the town. In the papers Irma read about the regiment going to the Dardanelles, and read Bronson's name, a little later, among the killed.

More than two years later she read how Mrs. Bronson too had been killed. In Mexico, where she had gone to clear up some of Bronson's affairs, she had been hit, while sitting in a café, by a stray bullet in a local revolution.

Irma envied Mr. and Mrs. Bronson, the dead. She began to feel that she was going about with a bullet in her own heart, and was only gradually beginning to understand, by the pain of longer silences between herself and her mother, who had fired it.

THE IRISHMAN

WE were sitting under the cart-hovel one winter afternoon, my grandfather and I, listening to the cold rain
swirling at the bramble-roof and watching it sweep in
smoky gusts and toss the stray seagulls across the bare
land, when the Spriv walked into the stackyard, as
usual, to borrow the gun. He was a large, florid,
purplish-faced man, with the arrogant strut of a cock
pheasant and a big straw-chewing mouth that never
opened except to lie and boast of his own doings with
the gun and the trombone or to sneer at the littleness of
other people. He was notorious in a score of parishes
round us as a belcher, a lazy boozer, a man who
poached all the week and played in the chapel band on
Sundays and sponged all the year round on his old
aunt, playing her periodic solos from hymns and
operas on his trombone in the expectation of a legacy.
He swaggered into the stackyard once or twice a week
with his hands stuck in his belt and his cap defiantly
over his right ear, spitting every ten yards or so with
a sort of boastful ferocity; our miserable stables and
carts and pigs and stacks and the hen that ducked out
of his path filling him with majestic scorn.

He swaggered across the yard that afternoon in the
cold sweeping rain without haste, as though he were
too big to be rained upon.

'Goin' to lend us th' old pop-gun for five minutes?'
he said to my grandfather.

'You're never goin' shootin' in this?' my grandfather
said.

'What d'ye think I'm made on?' the Spriv said.
'Sugar?'

'You'll never see,' my grandfather said.

'See? I could stand under this hovel o' yourn and hit all the weathercocks on Lowick church, all the thirteen on 'em,' he boasted.

And before my grandfather had time to speak again the Spriv had walked from under the hovel and across the yard to the tool-barn where the gun always hung. He returned a moment or two later, handling the gun as though it were no more than a stick of sugar-rock that he'd won at a fair.

'It's loaded,' said my grandfather.

'It's never anything else,' sneered the Spriv. 'You daren't let the damn thing off. Give us a mossel o' 'bacca.'

My grandfather meekly took out his pouch and the Spriv helped himself to a pinch of tobacco and rolled it into a chewing-quid.

'Hitch up, boy,' he said to me.

I moved along the box, and the Spriv, belching deeply and holding the gun carelessly across his knees, sat down beside me, reeking like a public-house on a market day, all stale beer and tobacco and horseflesh. We sat there for a moment or two watching the rain sweeping across the fields and washing away the droppings and footprints of the hens in the muddy yard, the Spriv chewing reflectively, as though trying to think of some boastful tale to tell us, until all at once we were disturbed by an unexpected voice, calling over the stackyard gate:

'Ye haven't a mite o' dry shelter for a fellow, have ye?'

It was a quick high-pitched voice, with a strange accent. The Spriv mocked it with contempt: 'A mite o' dry shelter,' he mouthed. 'Who the hell?' He stood upright and then took a step forward into the rain, the gun arrogantly under his arm, as though he owned it and were lord over the land and us too.

'It's a tramp,' he said, 'or a gypo. He's so big he can't see over the gate.'

We heard the click of the gate-hook and a moment later the stranger was coming towards us across the yard. He was not much more than a midget of a man and we could see by the way he came towards us, with quick perky steps, that he was as cheeky as a sparrow. He was wearing a turn-down faded green trilby and a blue seaman's jersey under his brass-buttoned jacket. His legs were slightly bowed and his face, sharp and pinched from the cold rain, had in it all the cocky mischief of a bird.

The Spriv, straddling, with the gun, eyed him with contempt as the wind half-blew him across the yard into the hovel.

'Ye'll be giving us a mite o' shelter, won't you?' cried the little man as he came and shook the rain from his jacket and hat under the hovel.

'You ain't big enough to git wet,' said the Spriv.

'Chrisht!' said the little man. 'And me walking from Grantham itself since breakfast.'

The Spriv looked at him with sudden suspicion, in silence, as though he were trying to reckon up whether it were forty miles to Grantham or fifty. Finally he said:

'That's a tidy way for a little 'un.'

'Ah! a little step, just a step.'

The Spriv spat. 'I walked there myself, and back,' he said, 'one Easter Monday. That was a wet day.'

'Ah now!' said the little man. 'Did ye? Ye didn't step on to Lincoln, did ye? I was walking from Lincoln to Grantham myself this morning before breakfast. It's a fine place.'

The Spriv said nothing. But he gazed at the little man with faint trouble in his eyes, as though trying to calculate how far it could be from Lincoln to Grantham.

'You can sit down,' said my grandfather to the little man. 'Boy, you come and sit along o' me.'

The little man took my place on the orange box as I went to sit on the mound of sacked potatoes by the chaff-cutter. He looked as though he had been rescued from drowning, his clothes shining black and shrunken with rain, his hat dripping water over his pale face like a leaking spout.

'Jesus,' he said with good-humour, 'it's a little damp.'

The Spriv, leaning against the hovel-post with the gun slanted under his arm and his mouth chewing with a sort of defiant self-importance, eyed the little man with contempt.

'Ah,' he said, 'you look as if —'

'Cripes,' the little man interrupted him, 'that's a fine gun ye have there.'

'Ah,' said the Spriv, deprecatory, yet fat with pride, 'I'd like as many pounds as hares I've knocked over wi' this gun.'

'I could see ye were a sportsman; I could see it,' said the little man enthusiastically.

The Spriv stood with his mouth open a little, as though feeding on these words of quick and oily flattery.

'Ah yes,' he began. 'I just —'

'I was shootin' meself once,' said the little man, unheeding, 'with a party, a fine party. It slips me memory whether there was twenty or twenty-wan of us, but that's nothing. I'm only after thinking now how many birds we shot. And Chrisht, will I ever forget?

That was a grand day, a grand day. We was all photographed for the papers that day, all standing there with the twenty-thousand birds laid out on the grass like a catch o' fish. Ah! that was a grand day.'

As the little man rattled off the story the Spriv stood eyeing him with a growing look of distrust, uneasily aggressive.

'And where the hell,' he said in a sort of half-menacing, half-derisive voice, 'was that?'

'Ah! that was in Ballaghadereen.'

'What?'

'Never mind it. You wouldn't know it.'

'Some foreign place,' said the Spriv, with airy contempt.

'It's a grand place. Ah! sure, a sportsman like yourself would be in his glory there. I can see ye can handle a gun. Ah, they'd have welcomed a sportsman like yourself there that day.'

The little man had put into his voice a tone of dark and sweet familiarity, as though he and the Spriv were the only men on earth who understood the ways of sportsmen. Flattered and mollified, the Spriv suddenly lost his expression of distrust and contempt, and over his face spread the old suave boastful look we knew so well.

'Come in out of the rain a bit,' urged the little man. 'Ye're such a grand man ye shut out the daylight.'

The Spriv swaggered in under the hovel and sat down on the orange box by the little Irishman.

'I hope you ain't got to go?' he said. He spoke with a sort of motherly kindness that was touching in its simplicity. 'Look's like raining all night to me.'

'Ah! sure, but I love the rain,' said the little man, 'there's music in it, music in it.'

'Music?' said the Spriv.

'I'm tellin' ye. As I was comin' along the road from Grantham this morning I could listen to it in the trees like it was meself playin' on me ould fiddle. It's a grand sound.'

'I'm a player myself,' said the Spriv.

'Ah! it was on the tip o' me tongue to say so. Didn't I know it? I could see by the fine look in ye handsome face ye were a musician. Sure now, that's a fine thing. And what insthrument? The fiddle, or what?'

'A trombone,' said the Spriv, with careless pride, 'a trombone.'

'And what in the name o' God,' said the Irishman, 'is a trombone?'

'You call yourself a musician,' began the Spriv, flushing, 'and not know —'

'Ah, it slipped me memory. I know the thing. It was me dad himself used to play the trombone at the opera house the time I was a little shrimp of a fellow fiddling at the old Duke's dances. Ah! the trombone. It's a fine insthrument.'

The Spriv had become suspicious again. And as though setting a trap for the Irishman he said suddenly:

'If you're a fiddler, where's your fiddle?'

The little man was ready for him with a sort of perky gaiety. 'Ah! I knew ye would be askin' that. I can see by ye face ye're a clever man,' he said. 'Ah! I wish ye was comin' wi' me where me fiddle is. I could do wi' the company of a grand musician like yourself. I wish ye was comin'.'

'Where?' said the Spriv.

'To London, that's where. Ye know London? But I can see ye do, I can see it.'

'I was there,' began the Spriv importantly, 'only last —'

'Ah! ye'd like to be there wi' me, a grand musician

like yourself. Listen, I'll tell ye something. D'ye know, did ye ever hear of a man named Pagliacci? The grand musician?'

'What name?' said the Spriv, very serious.

'Pagliacci. I. Pagliacci. The grand Italian musician? I. Pagliacci.'

'Ah yes, yes,' said the Spriv. 'I didn't catch it. I —.'

'Well, it's this fellow — No, no, after all I couldn't tell ye. It's the grand secret. I couldn't tell ye.'

'Ah, ye can trust me.'

'I know, I know. But it's not meself only.'

'Ah, go on.'

'Ye'll promise not to say half a word?' the Irishman whispered. 'Ah! but I can see ye're the grand fellow. Ye're a gentleman. Ye're a sportsman.'

'I know how it is,' said the Spriv. 'I was playing myself in London once in the — '

'I trust ye,' cried the Irishman. 'Well, it's this way I'm tellin' ye. This Pagliacci is my uncle . . . .'

And in his quick perky voice the Irishman began to pour into the Spriv's ears a strange long tale of how he used to go to London and play in all the grand orchestras with all the grand musicians under his uncle Pagliacci, who was the grand conductor. The tale went on as fast and persistent as the rain still pouring down over the desolate winter land lying beyond the stackyard, and the Spriv himself drank it in as the earth soaked up the rain. Whenever the Spriv grew uneasy or suspicious the little Irishman would repeat, 'Ah! but ye're the grand musician yourself. Ye'll understand,' like a soothing refrain. Sometimes the Spriv would try and break in upon the easy audacity of the tale with a boast of his own — 'I was playing before the Prince of . . .' — but the Irishman never paused, heaping lie upon lie inexhaustibly, with such compelling subtlety that at last the Spriv sat silent, too overwhelmed and overawed to speak, alternately fooled and flattered yet never suspecting. All the time my grandfather and I sat silent, without a sign, except that once he turned and winked at me.

Finally the little man took up his hat from where he had laid it on the dry bare earth and smoothed its sodden brim with a nonchalant flourish. Then he held the hat ready to put on his head with one hand, and with the other he made ready to shake hands with the Spriv.

'Ah! sure, I hate to be goin',' he said, 'and not be stoppin' to talk with a fine musician like yourself. It's been a grand pleasure.'

He held out his hand and the Spriv took it solemnly. 'And if ever,' began the Irishman, 'ye're in London — '

'I'm sure to be there,' said the Spriv. 'Sure to — '

'Sure, that's fine. It'll be the grand day when we meet again. Good day.'

'Good day,' said the Spriv.

'I hope ye'll have good sport — but I know ye will, I know ye will. Ye're too grand a sportsman ever to — '

A moment later his words were cut off and lost in the sound of the wind and rain and his little perky figure was driven across the half-flooded stackyard and through the gate to the road. The sky had the strange glassy look of early winter darkness and almost before we heard his feet scraping on the road the Irishman was lost to us in the rainy gloom.

For a moment or two the Spriv stood staring at the rain. When at last he came back into the hovel he turned upon us a look of aloof contempt, as though we were not to be numbered among the privileged. We said nothing.

But there must have been something in our silent eyes that he did not like, for suddenly he looked red and suspicious, then uneasy, and at last angry, as though he had an idea we were laughing at him.

A moment later he was swaggering off across the half-flooded yard, in great haste, not heeding the puddles or the rain, and my grandfather was calling after him:

'Don't you want the gun?'

But the Spriv did not turn or answer. He went across the stackyard and through the gate to the road as though he were in a great hurry to catch someone and the last we saw of him was as he disappeared down the road in the rain, looking like an angry and hopeless second in a walking race.

It was a long time before we saw him after that and longer still before he came to borrow the gun again.

SPRING SNOW

When the sun came out, suddenly, from behind racing white clouds, it was so hot in the cup of the precipice and the chalk face so fiercely white that for a minute it would be like summer. Then the cloud-shadows raced up the road again, and chalk and road and even grass seemed quite grey, only the yellow-gorse branches still bright on the cliff edge and against the chalk-dusty grass round the hut. All the time the wind was tearing in big gusts across the opening in the hillside so that the fire of gorse and dead wood raged wildly with flame.

Far off, the clouds looked heavy with spring snow. Going backwards and forwards from the gorse-clumps to the fire the girl would look at them, eyes still and motionless. She carried double armfuls of gorse to burn, carrying them in front of her, so that she seemed heavy with a pregnancy of flowers. She had a colourless face, almost Jewish. Doing the journeys, breaking flowers and burning them without any alteration of expression at all, she looked dreamy, far away. It took about five minutes for every journey. Every time she came to the fire the old woman started her prattle from the hut, her voice high in the wind.

'Last Good Friday was the day, dearie! Last Good Friday. Gawd, we took some dough. Run out o' bread and run out o' tea. Turned people away and then took eighteen pound. Dearie, you shoulda seen the money. You shoulda seen it!'

The girl, not answering, never stopped to listen. The old woman still prattled on long after she had left the fire. Big, dowdy-haired, shapeless, she would waddle down the hut steps with bits of furniture, white-painted tables and chairs and seats carpentered from beer-boxes, and set them out on the grass in the sun. Once she came out with a notice 'Café' and then another 'Motorists Pull Up'. She laid them on the trestle table outside. Then she came out with chairs and odd boxes and a smaller table. She set them all on the grass. For a big woman she moved very quickly, with an avaricious waddle, her fat body squabbing and jellying as she did the journeys up and down the steps. All over the face of the hut were notices, in blue paint, the big letters rain-washed: Pot of Tea 6d., Ham Roll 6d., Ham and one Egg 1s., Ham and two Eggs 1s. 6d., Café again. And over all, on a separate board: 'Charley's. Best and Cheapest.' Finally the old woman came down the steps empty-handed and called:

'Soon's you done that, dearie, come and help us have a sweep out here. Gawd, Charley'll be down with the stuff and on top of us 'fore we know what's what.'

The hut, from being shut up all winter, smelled of creosote. The girl caught the smell before ever she got to the steps, and it made her momentarily sick. She came almost before the old woman had finished speaking, as though not really in answer to her. Free of the gorse, she looked very heavy. She moved slowly. By the time she got to the hut her face was tight with pain.

She went straight up the steps and sat down in the sun.

'It's coming,' she said.

'What? Gawd, how can it?' Scared, the old woman came out of the hut quickly, thrusting out thick surprised lips. 'How can it? You ain't due. You ain't due till after Easter. Gawd, how can it come?'

'It's coming,' the girl said. 'I can feel it. I know.'

'You strained yourself,' the old woman said. 'You got a bit tired, carrying the wood.'

'No, it's coming,' the girl said. 'I feel it. I know. I feel it. Every now and then I have a pain.'

'Pain? What sorta pain? How often?'

'Every little while. Every five minutes.'

'It's when you quicken,' the old woman said. 'It's only when you quicken, that's all. That ain't nothing, dearie. It ain't nothing!'

'No, it's coming,' the girl said. 'I ought to know. I know. I know. I can feel it.'

She sat scared herself. The sun was blazing now, the smell of creosoted boards hot and strong. Across the grass the gorse-fire crackled fiercely, the spring trees beyond the road shimmering behind the rising cloud of heat.

Suddenly the sun went in and the pain came on the girl, and she sat quite cold and doubled up. It was almost all she could do to speak. She simply moaned the words, quietly:

'Oh! What can we do? What can we do? Oh! do something! Do something!'

The old woman stumped back across the bare boards of the hut with heavy impatience, in fear almost angry.

'Gawd, this would happen! This would happen! Good Friday to-morrow and all. Oh! Gawd!'

The girl, free suddenly of pain, came into the hut and sat on the bare boards opposite the door. No longer in anguish, she took off her coat and spread it over herself like a blanket. Her face, pinched up, looked more Jewish than ever. She lay propped up against the wall, her head back. Lying there, she watched the old woman light the oil stove and put the kettle on. Listening to her prattle, 'I'll get y' cup o' tea. That'll ease y'. I'll git y' cup o' tea', she was not really conscious of it. She was conscious of only one thing: the advent of pain. She waited for it with clenched hands.

But when it came, in a moment, it caught her so suddenly that she cried out.

'Oh! get somebody! Do something! Do something! Get the doctor! Oh! help me!'

'Doctor? Gawd, how can I git a doctor? You want me to leave you by yourself?'

'Oh! get somebody. Stop a car. Stop somebody going by. Oh! God!'

'Lay quiet. Lay easy,' the old woman said. 'Lay easy now.'

She spoke more softly and as she spoke the pain too softened and the girl lay relaxed, quieter, her eyes shut in relief, and something like shame at her outburst.

'What time is Charley coming?' she said.

'Not afore night.'

'I want him,' the girl said. 'Can't you telephone him?'

'How can I? What good? What could Charley do?'

'I want him,' the girl said. 'Telegraph for him. He'll come. Send him a telegram.'

'It's no good. Charley can't do no good. He's up in Camden Town. It wouldn't be no good. Gawd, what good could Charley do?'

'I just want him,' the girl said. 'That's all. I just want him.'

She stopped speaking, held herself tight, waited for the new pain. All of a sudden it came. Wracked, she lay pressed against the wall, in brief agony, her eyes shut again.

When it had passed she began to undress herself. 'It's coming, they're every three minutes now,' she said. She undressed slowly, taking off all her things, dress and shoes and stockings and knickers, with the exception of her skirt. Her bare legs and arms were covered with goose-skin and she pulled the coat over her again, cold and scared.

'How long will it be?' she said.

'The tea?'

'No. How long will *this* be? How long shall I be?'

'Gawd, I don' know. I was all night with Charley.'

'All night? Not all night?'

She lay silent, waiting again, afraid. Through the hut windows she could see four sections of sky, great snow-banks of cloud split with lakes of spring blue. She kept her eyes fixed on a single cloud, watching its course, thinking that if she watched the cloud she would forget the pain.

But it was an illusion. She suddenly cried out. She quivered and stretched out her legs and momentarily did not know what to do with herself for agony. She had no time or will even to shut her eyes. The old woman ran up, scared, and held her hands. 'Pull,' she said. 'Pull on me. Press y'self down and pull on me, dearie.' The girl groaned and pulled, the woman grunting for her, the two in time with each other until the spasm had gone. And finally when it had gone the girl lay bathed in a white sweat of anguish, weak and now quite terrified.

'It can't come,' she said. 'I can feel it. Something's stopping it. It can't come!'

'Gawd, you ain't started yet. You ain't started. I'll git you something to pull on, dearie. You ain't half started.'

'Get somebody,' the girl said. 'Stop a car. I don't want it to be born here. I don't want it!'

At the back of the hut the old woman found a length of clothes-line. She tied it on the inside of the doorknob and the girl held the other end so that, whenever the pain came, she could pull on the rope, her feet against a box of crockery. By that time also the tea was ready. After the girl had drunk hers it came out on her body at once, in sweat. All the time the old woman grunted and moaned a little: 'Gawd, why'd have to come jis now? Oh! Why'd have to come?' as though the anguish were her own.

Then, in a moment, the girl was staggered by un-precedented pain. She rolled on the bare floor in an agony that stupefied her. She clenched the rope madly. She whimpered a little in distress, without words, like a dumb person. Her bare feet were hard and bitterly pressed against the box of crockery, until she could feel the splinters in the soles of her feet and baby pressing downward inside her, the pain so fierce that it drove her momentarily beyond consciousness.

When she looked up again, through the windows it seemed as though it were raining. It looked like white thunder rain. Then she saw that it was snow. And far beyond the snow and the snow-clouds were blue lakes of sky, the same as ever, but now more brilliant and stormy and far distant. The girl watched the snow and pressed her feet against the box in a stupor of pain, trying hard to deliver herself and at the same time to obliterate what she felt and saw. The old woman moved about the hut in a waddle of distress, putting another kettle on the oil stove, holding the girl's hands, tearing up towels, ripping finally her own pinafore, crying a little. Shut up, the hut reeked of creosote and tea and the girl's sweat. It was full also of the wailing and moaning of the woman and the girl, sounds that went on unchecked and unbroken until the shout of triumph from the woman.

'It's coming! It's coming! Gawd, it's coming.

Hold me. Hold on t'me. Dearie, hold on to me. It's coming.'

The girl held on through the blind agony of deliverance. While it was happening, the snow ceased. The sun came out fierce and brilliant on the white chalk. Clouds and sky were so sunlit that to the girl they were momentarily dazzling. So that when she looked away again and down at herself and the floor she seemed to see lakes of blood instead of lakes of cloud and sky.

Then, suddenly, she saw that it was blood. She saw it spattered on her body and skirt, on the old woman, on the box, everywhere. It was strangely scarlet and sickening. Seeing it, she felt a rush of joy. She was through it! It was all over! Then she saw the old woman with knife upraised, to cut the cord, and it was more than she could bear. Sickness and fear and weakness annihilated her.

Long afterwards she lay flat and weary and without triumph. She had only one thought. She kept repeating it. 'Where's the baby? Where is it? What is it? Where's the baby?'

'Lay still, dearie, lay still,' the old woman would say. 'Lay still and get some rest.'

'Where's the baby? I want it. Where's the baby?'

Finally the old woman went out of the hut carrying the blood-spattered box. When she came back, empty-handed, the girl was crying. 'I know,' she said. 'I know. Don't tell me. I know.'

'Lay still, dearie, don't cry. It's all right. Lay still. It's better it's all over,' the old woman prattled. 'It's better. Better for you. Better for Charley. Better for all of us. Gawd, it's Good Friday to-morrow. If it's half the Good Friday it was last year — eighteen pound, ducky. Eighteen pound in one day!' She prattled on in a long rigmarole of comfort and memory. 'We only want it fine. Gawd love us, we only want it fine. Everything'll be all right if it's fine, dearie. Gawd, we'll take some dough if it's fine. We'll git the place cram jam full if it's fine.'

The girl lay still and said nothing. But a little later she raised herself on her elbows, so that she could look out of the windows. Cars going up and down the hill outside were the only moving things in the world except the snowy trees shaken in the wind.

'Gawd, see the cars going by a'ready? See 'em? There'll be some folks up here to-morrow. Gawd, we only want it fine. By Gawd, if only it don't snow again.'

Far off beyond the horizon and the farthest ridge of cloud, the sky was miraculously blue.

'It's going to be fine,' the girl said.

'See the cars? Hear 'em?' the old woman said.

The girl did not answer. She lay staring beyond the horizon. To her weak eyes it seemed farther than she had ever seen before.

Even so, it did not matter.

MILLENNIUM ALSO RAN

THE young reporter walked reluctantly out of the soft morning sunshine and up the half-dark iron-shod stairs which led to the office of his paper, *The Harlington Echo*. In strict truth the small bare draughty room behind the frosted-glass door at the head of the staircase was hardly an office; and he himself was scarcely a reporter. The room was in reality a disused lumber-room belonging to the wine-and-spirit merchant who occupied the premises below. It was not only bare and draughty but damp and mice-ridden, and except for two chairs placed against a small deal writing-table and a waste-paper basket overflowing with torn and screwed-up papers by the fireplace there was no furniture. Back numbers of the newspaper were strewn about the floor loosely or in dust-yellowed bundles tied up with packing string. A smell of mouldering paper and printing ink mingled with the vague odour of stale spirits or wine coming up from the warehouse below. Above all these was an odour of dust, old stale dust that showered mysteriously and everlastingly like yellowish pollen on the chairs and tables and papers. It had powdered the tea-cups standing on the iron mantelshelf above the fireplace, and at times the young reporter seemed to feel it penetrating to his mind also, poisoning and deadening it. He loved the place like a mortuary.

He arrived there a little after nine each morning. He was hardly a reporter because, except for odd cases of suicide and drunkenness, a weekly routine of weddings and funerals, births and birthday parties, there was nothing to report. The office was a branch only; he was there in readiness, an outpost who might any day be lucky enough to discover some scandalous or tragic human calamity. He came to the office every morning with the vague hope that during the night someone had shot his wife and burned the body. Without such tragedies he knew that his day, from nine o'clock in the morning to seven or eight at night, would be utterly filled with boredom, his mind soured by dust and silence and loneliness.

He threw up the window and put his hat on the mantelpiece. It was early June; he could hardly bear to look out of the window at the sunshine. He had bicycled in that morning from the country and he remembered almost with pain the odour of meadow-sweet, the singing of yellow-hammers, the hot strength of the sun.

Unfolding the morning paper, he sat down at the table. His first job each morning was to cut the lists of race-horses from the sporting pages of a London newspaper and then paste them on a sheet of cardboard which hung by the telephone on the wall. Two doors along the street stood the offices of a rival newspaper. In the afternoon, in order to defeat the rival, the young reporter would receive the race-winners and their starting-prices by telephone and then stamp them frenziedly in violet letters with a rubber-stamp on the stop-press columns of the early editions and deal out the papers to the newsboys who stood crowding on the dark stairs, deriding him impatiently. Sometimes he won; but often he checked the horses wrongly or printed them upside down and then lost. By four o'clock each day he was sick and tired with the frenzied haste and uncertainty of it all and the fear that at any moment, Mathers, the senior journalist, might burst in half-drunk and storm at him.

He tore the paper-scissors from the table-drawer

and then stopped. On the table lay a note for him, written on the back of an old ballot-paper in Mathers's tipsy-looking, half-illegible handwriting.

'Go round to No. 7 Salvation Street,' it said, 'and inquire why Parker hasn't been and if he will be coming again.' And as a kind of postscript: 'Nose round a bit.'

Parker was a paper-seller, a thin, sharp-nosed, colourless-eyed youth of eighteen or nineteen, who had failed to appear for three days. Mathers must have written the note late the previous night. He came to the office rarely, making unexpected and volcanic appearances, generally half-drunken haste and temper, a small, ferrety, bestial man, with shifty eyes that were raw pink from constant drinking and a short ginger moustache stained a dirty yellow nearest his thin lips. Both in winter and summer he wore a greasy mackintosh, a dirty yellow woollen scarf and a grey shapeless tweed hat from under which his fair hair struggled down unkempt and tawdry. He would rush into the office, bringing a smell of liquor against which the stale odours of wine and spirits from below seemed sweet, and sitting down at the table, still in his hat and scarf and mackintosh, he would proceed to write with frenzied excitement, as though he had come straight from the scene of some fresh murder. As he wrote he turned constantly to spit heavily into the fireplace, muttering and swearing in savage undertones between the spits. Then he would jump up as volcanically and suddenly as he had come in, hurl some savage command or criticism at the young reporter, and clatter downstairs, leaving behind him the stench of his breath and the loathsome hiss of his spittle dropping into the fire. Yet there were times when he came in with a sort of lugubrious sobriety. On these occasions he would solemnly sit down and lecture the young reporter. He would talk on the beauty of obedience and integrity, on duty, on moral cleanliness, on life itself, speaking in a soft oily voice with the repellent smugness of a preacher sermonizing, his beery pink eyes contradicting both his words and his voice. The youth's finest emotions would revolt as he listened, turning to a sickness which rose up in his throat and soured and remained there. He often could not speak for revulsion and unhappiness as he heard the suave criticisms of his conduct and work. He had come to the office in the belief that he might learn to write there. Mathers knew this and the youth's belief would serve as a sort of text for him.

'You want to learn to write, eh?' he would say. 'You want to cultivate style? Well, let me tell you, young man, that you won't cultivate a style by sitting on your backside waiting for something to happen. How do you suppose the great London journalists find the stories that fill their front pages? By sitting on their backsides, like you? Don't stare out of the window! Listen to me! Do you suppose I'm telling you this for the good of *my* soul? What the hell do you expect to learn by dreaming? You must get out! Go on, get out. Now. Find something to write about. Nose round a bit. And don't come back until you've found something.'

And so, this morning, he must go out and nose around a bit. He must forage among the blood and offal of human scandal and tragedy. The note seemed to mean that Mathers would not be in all day, and he finished cutting out and pasting the lists of race-horses at his leisure. While the paste was drying he read down the lists and then referred back to the paper for the tips given by the racing journalist.

There appeared to be a big race at three o'clock. He read the names of the horses half aloud: 'Irish Green, Sea Captain, White Rose, Moonraker, Volcano, Millennium, Double Quick, Black Tulip.' The tipsters seemed to fancy Millennium, and one wrote: 'We have always known, of course, that he was an animal of sterling abilities as well as achievements, and I have no doubt that in to-day's race he will add further lustre to his name. One might say, indeed, that to-day, for once, the Millennium will arrive.'

When he had finished reading he hung up the card by the telephone, put some sheets of ballot-paper in his pocket, locked up the office and went downstairs into the sunshine.

He walked down the street, towards the sun, past the sawdusted steps of the wine-and-spirit merchant and the offices of his rival newspaper. Before he could nose round a bit or inquire after Parker he must perform his morning ritual: he must see the police and the coroner. These were, so to speak, his incubators, from which he hoped every morning that exciting game like rape and murder and felony and suicide had hatched.

But on this morning, as on most others, nothing had happened. His 'Anything doing?' at the police-station was answered by the fat sergeant at the desk with a glance at the pile of charge-sheets, a shake of the head and a quick 'Have you 'eard this one?' He stopped to listen to the bawdy story and tried half-heartedly to join in with the sergeant's deep laughter, which went echoing in hollow waves of sound up and down the glazed-brick corridors leading to the cells.

From the police he went to the coroner. The town was small, provincial in its very odours of fish and cheap drapery. The awnings were already down over the shop-fronts. He felt with pleasure the hot sun on his neck.

He pushed open the swing-door of the dark, gauze-windowed coroner's office and repeated to the youth sitting inside on a high round stool at a desk his daily formula:

'Anything doing?'

'Nothing.'

'Which is the way to Salvation Street?' he asked.

The youth put his pen behind his ear and came to the door and gave the reporter directions.

'Go through the churchyard and then past the canal. It's the fourth street by the canal. Anybody will tell you.'

He walked through the churchyard. It was nearly eleven. A bed of white pinks growing over an old grave poured out a heavenly fragrance as he passed.

He passed through the shopping streets and the sloping alleys, like rabbit-runs, going down to the canal. He smelled the morning smells of fish and drapery and watered dust changing to the odours of the canal-streets.

He read the names of the streets by the canal, each a cul-de-sac: Lord Street, Jubilee Terrace, Charlotte's Row, Salvation Street. The houses, squat boxes of dirty yellow brick and grey slate, had an entry to each pair, like kennels, and the railway ran side by side with the canal, bridging the streets.

He walked up Salvation Street and knocked at the door of No. 7, and after an interval and a second knock he heard footsteps and a wriggling of the unused key in the dry lock.

The door opened a crack. An old woman showed her face, looking very white and startled at seeing him there.

'Can I have a word with Mr. Parker?' he said. 'I'm from the *Echo*.'

He saw tears begin to roll down her cheeks almost before he had formed the words, and as she cried she shook her head feebly, making her tears tumble and fall quickly down over her black blouse.

He tried to say something to her and excuse himself, but as suddenly as she had begun to cry she disappeared.

Waiting, he saw through the door-crack the room within: a broken couch heaped with rags and old shoes, the bare floor-boards foot-worn and broken, the holes nailed over here and there with the lids of sugar-boxes and odd scraps of colourless linoleum; the wall-paper ripped and damp-rotten, the largest gaps pasted over with sheets of his own paper, *The Harlington Echo*.

He was thinking of walking away when he heard the return of footsteps, and expecting to see the old woman again, he got ready to say that he had made a mistake, but the door was opened wider and he stood face to face with a young girl. She would be somewhere between seventeen or eighteen. She was in black.

'Can I speak to Mr. Parker?' he said.

The cruel and foolish futility of his words struck him before he had finished speaking, and he knew what her reply would be.

'He died yesterday,' she said, but he could hardly catch her words.

Confused and angry with himself, he looked straight at the girl's face in mute humility. She seemed to understand. Her face, narrow, bleak and very girlish, had a strange composure about it; she had gone beyond grief and even beyond resignation into a kind of stupidity, a sort of elevated, unemotional trance. Her eyes were dark and dry, without even the light of grief

123

or pain, her hands hanging loosely at her side, her fingers straight and outspread, her wedding-ring gleaming bright against their pale boniness. He felt that she had said all she wished or could say. And as he wondered what to say before he took leave of her he heard the cracked sobbing of the old woman and her voice speaking from the room between the sobs.

'Ask him if he'll put it in the paper.' Her tear-wet face appeared behind the girl's. 'Will you put it in the paper, eh? It was gallopin'. He was only bad three days. It'd make him that happy if you'd put it in the paper. God bless you if you'll put it in the paper.' And then:

'Would you like to have a look at him? He looks so lovely. You can come and look at him.'

All the time the old woman was speaking, the girl's face was changing and hardening into a consciousness of bitterness and pain. Her eyes awoke and became filled with an icy white light of hatred for the old woman and her garrulous sobbing. The old woman tried to open the door wide enough for him to enter, but the girl held it, clenching it with her white hand and jamming her foot against it.

'I must go if I'm to get it into the paper,' said the reporter.

'Come and look at him,' moaned the old woman. 'He looks lovely. You wouldn't think he was dead.'

But encouraged by the bitterness in the girl's eyes, he ignored the old woman.

'Is there anything I can do?' he said to the girl.

She shook her head.

'I'll put it in the paper, if you like.'

She shook her head again.

'Oh! have it put in,' moaned the old woman. 'It'd make me happy if you put it in.'

The girl was shaking her head and biting her lips vehemently.

'There may be some money to come from the paper,' said the reporter.

'I don't want the money!' the girl cried.

'Oh! you silly silly!' moaned the old woman. 'Oh! she don't know what she's saying. She's all upset. Don't take no notice of her. She ain't got a penny — not a penny, I tell yer. We ain't got enough to pay for a decent coffin for him. Don't listen to her.'

'If there's any money I'll send it,' he said, half-walking away.

'Oh! she'll be glad of every halfpenny!'

'Oh! be quiet! Be quiet!' shouted the girl.

As she shouted the words she pushed the old woman furiously behind her with one hand and slammed the door shut with the other. Before moving away he heard her cries echoing distractedly in the house, mingling with the weary complaint of the old woman trying to comfort her. A woman with a wet, patched sack-apron over her black skirt and a man's cap hat-pinned to her thin grey hair hurried past him as he walked down the street, wiping her soapy hands on her apron and her sharp nose on her hand. He heard her voice also mingled with the voices in the house where the dead youth lay:

'Anything I can do, my gal? Mrs. Parker, anything I can do?'

Finally he could hear no more. He walked under the railway bridge, along the canal and so back to the town. Should he put it in the paper? The scene hurt and depressed him, persisting vividly in his mind. Ought he to put it in? Wasn't this where he became a reporter? Half against himself he strung the phrases of a paragraph tentatively together. 'After an illness

of only three days, James Parker, 19, yesterday suc-
cumbed to . . . Deceased, who had for some time acted
in the capacity of newsman to this office, leaves a wife
and . . .' The trite easy phrases condemned themselves
and seemed to reproach him. He began to think that
instead he would write an article, an impassioned
account of the filthy house, the garrulous old woman,
the tragic young wife. He would describe it all with
vivid indignation and emotion, asking rhetorically if
this were civilization, if poverty were any less a crime
because it was also a tragedy? In imagination he saw
the article, with impassioned headlines, given a promi-
nent place in the paper, and he half-imagined an edi-
torial comment upon it: 'We draw the attention of our
readers to the report, given on another page, of what
we feel is not only a sad and distressing case but an
indictment of the social conditions under which we live
and for which, in a sense, we are also responsible.'
His mind hammered out the words angrily. He would
write a report that would stir the consciousness of all
who read it. His desire to write flamed up so power-
fully that he found himself walking along in an agita-
tion of rage and anxiety.

Back at the office he sat down and took up some
sheets of ballot-paper and began to write. He was
ashamed when the old easy phrases began to form
themselves and not the passionate words of righteous
accusation he had planned. 'After an illness of only
three days' duration . . .' He began to tear up the
sheets, trying fresh beginnings. 'Housed in a jerry-
built hovel on the banks of a canal which stinks in
summer and floods in winter, I to-day found Mrs.
Parker . . .' He knew that this was too strong and he
tore up the sheet, beginning again and again. At last
he desisted and went downstairs and across the road

to the eating-house opposite, bringing back the cup of tea which he allowed himself every day with his sandwiches.

He drank and ate a little and then, feeling calmer, began to write again. He succeeded in describing the street, the house and the conditions under which he had found the girl and the old woman living. Then, warming up to his subject, he covered several pages, eating and drinking as he wrote, his sense of time deadened.

But coming to the girl herself, he could not go on. He saw clearly enough her dumb negation, her look of unemotional immobility, and he could hear with painful clarity her voice crying reproachfully, 'I don't want the money! Be quiet! Be quiet!' but he could not put the words describing it on paper. He could not convey the sense of her grief, her youth, her unspoken bitterness. And he went on watching her face, as it were, in his mind, without being able to describe it, until he heard clumsy feet on the stairs below and the sound of the newsmen's voices talking about the afternoon's races.

He was surprised to find that it was nearly three o'clock. He put his written sheets aside and opened the table-drawer and took out the rubber-stamping apparatus in readiness for stop-pressing the results.

Heavy feet came up the stairs as he was doing so and the glass door opened. A bundle of newspapers was flung on the floor inside and a dirty-capped head appeared in the door crack and a hoarse news-voice whispered:

'Remember what I told yer?'

'No.'

'What? Didn't I tell yer it was a gift — Millennium? Ah! yer don't know a good thing when I give yer one.

127

It *can't* lose — unless it falls over. If that ain't a winner I don't know a mare from a cock-sparrow.'

Suddenly something occurred to the reporter:

'Is it too late now?' he said.

'Well, you don't hurt. What d'ye want on? Put your top-hat on?'

It had occurred to the reporter that he might back Millennium, using Parker's money and giving the winnings to his widow. If the horse lost he himself would stand the loss; and hastily he found the sales-book, checked the sales to Parker, and a moment later the newsman was clattering downstairs with five shillings for the bet.

The reporter sat back in his chair to wait for the telephone call. As he sat there he played idly with the rubber-stamp and its letters, setting up Millennium and printing it on the blotting-paper. In imagination he saw the girl's face as it would be if the horse won, contrasting it with the grief-stupid tragic mask he could recall so perfectly but could not describe. And suddenly he remembered also the vehement shaking of her head in reply to his 'I'll put it in the paper if you like', and he suddenly seized the sheets he had written with so much struggle and tore them up.

His heart leapt as the telephone rang. As he stood with the receiver to his ear, waiting, he could hear the hush of the newsboys as they listened on the stairs.

A voice on the telephone gave him the horses. He wrote them down before the consciousness of his failure struck him:

'Volcano, Double Quick, White Rose.'

He repeated them and put up the receiver. A moment later the newsboys were crowding at the door, he was setting up the type in the rubber-stamp and stamping the horses' names in violet letters in the stop-press columns. Voices clamoured and swore and urged him to hurry. He stamped frenziedly and dealt out the papers. Excited feet clattered noisily on the iron-rimmed stairs. 'What won? Volcano. Millennium also ran. Volcano won. Millennium also ran.' Little by little the voices faded away downstairs.

When the last of the papers had been stamped and dealt out he sat alone. The voices crying the papers came up from the streets outside, rising and falling, shrill and inarticulate. He had never been able to tell what they said. Now though he listened carefully their words still eluded him. And he sat there long after they had died away, the memory of their inarticulate sound persisting in his mind like the clamour of voices crying to be understood.

THE BLIND

ONCE a week, every market day, the man Osborn and his wife drove down to the town in the old Ford tourer piled up with chicken crates, to take their girl to the travelling optician. They called him the eye-doctor. 'Now then, look slippy,' the man would say. 'We don' wan' keep th' eye-doctor waiting.' Or the woman: 'You think th' eye-doctor's got all day to wait? Git y' things on quick. Look about you.' But they were never late. Punctually at half-past nine the car came down into the town, mud-spattered or chalk white from its journey across the field-track from the poultry farm, the man with rusty moustaches hanging down like loose tobacco from the pouch of his mouth; the woman like a hen herself with beak-nose and cherry-hung hat bobbing like a comb; and the girl sitting between them on the cart-cushion, staring with still stone-coloured eyes into the distance, as though she could see beyond the ends of the earth.

'Summat do wi' cat's eyes.' The man had become slightly addicted to boasting about it. He had a habit of blowing into his moustaches, with a sound of astonishment. 'Knock-out, ain't it? Think as the gal's got eyes like that? He reckons it gonna take about eight or nine months to cure it. Seven and six a time — that's money.'

The eye-doctor rented the front room of a house behind the market. He hung his card in the window, above the fern pots. 'J. I. Varipatana. Optician. Attendance Tuesdays 10 a.m. — 1 p.m. 2 p.m. — 4 p.m.' And punctually at ten o'clock he would come to open the door to them, with the shell-white smile dazzling on his dusky sand-coloured face, his dark hand extended, and his way of greeting them with impersonal courtesy.

'Mrs. Osborn. Mr. Osborn. Miss Osborn. Please enter.'

In the front room a number of cards with test numbers hung on the wall facing the light. The eye-doctor stood with his hands clasped behind his back, the white almost feminine smile constantly on his dark face. 'And how is business with Mister Osborn? Nice weather. And Mrs. Osborn? You look very well. And the little lady?'

The girl sat as though far away, dumb.

'Well, speak up. Th' eye-doctor's speaking to you. Lost your tongue?'

'The eyes are a little better?'

'Yes,' the girl would say.

'Good. Very good. Very good.' The voice slow, correct, rather beautiful. 'You persevered with the lotion?'

'Yes.'

'Come near the window.'

He would hold back one curtain a little, so that the light fell on the stone-coloured, almost dead eyes. 'Yes. Look up to me. Now shut the eyes. Now open. Look out of the window. Look just like that for one minute. Yes.' The voice soft, in rumination, suavely gentle. 'Now shut them again. Open now. Look sideways.'

And then, as she looked sideways, he would put his hands on her face, the fingers supporting her head, the thumbs touching the eyelids. Like that he would look down at her, still smiling, until the force of his own eyes drew her own back again. With his thumbs he peeled back the lids and then released them. The man and woman watched in silence, waiting for the verdict.

'The cataract is no worse.' The smile remained on the lips, even as they spoke and shut. 'Indeed perhaps a little better.'

By silence they demonstrated their complete faith in him. They saw him as someone who could perform a miracle. Still more, the girl took on importance because it was on her that the miracle was being performed. And they, in turn, took importance from her.

One week the woman grew impatient, impelled by fear. 'Ain't she never goin' to git no better?'

'My dear Mrs. Osborn.' The voice itself had something miraculous in it, some gentle hypnotic healing quality. 'I am not a magician. The eyes are very precious, very delicate. You see, think of it like this. If you cut your finger I can put something on it that will heal, that will destroy the germs. Some iodine, something to burn out the infection. But no — not on the eyes. No drastic measures can cure the eyes. Only time and faith can cure the eyes. You must be patient, and have faith.'

Continually, week by week, the girl herself had the impression that she could see less. At a distance of forty feet hung a curtain of mist that her eyes could not penetrate, and gradually, she felt, this mist began to close in on her. She began to see the hens at home only as vague lumps of colour, and on dull days, when the light was poor, the black hens were lost on her altogether. The hens, which she fed morning and evening, were the test for her, and gradually, with the range of vision lessening, she had to begin to rely less on sight than hearing. By hearing, by listening to the sound of hen noises, her mind conjured the vision that eyes could not see. She began to hear things with wonderful clarity.

In the eye-doctor's small front-room there were no

hens, no test for her. And she was always frightened. Partly through fear, partly through some notion that if she said a thing often enough it would eventually become a fact, she said, always, that she could see a little better.

At the end of the consultation the eye-doctor wrapped up a bottle of lotion in white paper and Osborn paid the seven and six. Osborn felt that by doing so he paid for something else besides a cure. He bought prestige, importance, some essence of slight mystery, a thing to boast about.

'Cost us pounds a'ready. Every week she's got 'ev this special tackle. You can't git it in England. He gits it from India — it's some rare herb or summat and it don't grow in England. Gits it from some head man over there. Ah! I tel y', costs us pounds, costs us a small fortune. You know what he told me? Reckons where he comes from they ain't got such things as bad eyes and like o' that. It's this herb as does it.'

Then one week the girl could read only the large capitals on the test-cards. At home the hens had begun to resemble balls of brown and white mist. With the mist closing down on her, she was more frightened than ever.

'Well, I think it may be only temporary. But just to be on the safe side, I am going to give you a new lotion.' The voice was easy, smooth, like a beautiful oil itself. 'Now Mr. Osborn, I should charge you one pound for this lotion. The herb from which it is distilled is very rare indeed and in my country it only grows on hills above ten thousand feet, and it can only be gathered after the snow has melted. My people have known about it centuries. You see? But wait, please — wait one for moment, please, one moment. I am not going to charge you one pound, not anything like one pound. Because

I know you, because I want your daughter to get better — half-price. To you only, half-price. Ten shillings.'

'Half a quid a week — that's what it costs us. Enough to break anybody — but there y'are. I don't care what it costs, I ain't goin' t'ave anybody say I was too mean to fork out the dough. Course, he ain't ordinary doctor — you don't expect to pay ordinary prices.'

One morning it was not the eye-doctor but a woman who opened the door, and the card was not in the window.

'No, he ain't come.'

'Very like had a break-down? — puncture or summat?'

'Well, it seems funny. He always drops me a card so as I get it first post Tuesdays. But to-day I ain't had one.'

'H'm, funny. Well, we'll go back to market and then come round again.'

At twelve and again in the afternoon Mr. Varipatana was not there. They drove home. 'Hope he ain't bad or nothing. You're sure he must be took bad or else he'd write?' They spoke with concern, making the illness of an important man a thing of importance for themselves.

To the girl it seemed as if they drove in semi-darkness. She could hear the wind, now, with the aggravated keenness of her hearing, as she had never heard it in her life. Her mind gathered the sounds and translated them into images. The sounds seemed to her to come through an immense expanse of space. She sat with her hands in her lap and when she touched one hand against another she was reminded of the sensation of Mr. Varipatana's hands pressing on her eyes. They seemed to be pressing her down into greater darkness.

'Well, I hope nothing's happened to the man. I hope he ain't been took bad or nothing. She's used every drop o' lotion up.'

They drove down to market as usual, a week later. Mr. Varipatana was not there.

'He ain't bad?'

'I dunno. He sent a letter saying he wasn't comin' no more. That's all I know.'

In the afternoon they drove back, the eyes of the man and woman depressed, short-focused, as though seeing nothing, the girl with her eyes still and fixed, as though on some illimitable distance. Osborn felt cheated, turning the lost money over and over in his mind.

The girl sat with her hands in her lap. She recalled the touch of Mr. Varipatana's hands on her eyelids, and it seemed suddenly as if the hands shut down the lids with suave finality, for ever.

The car stopped before she was aware of it. She was jerked back to reality. She felt the pressure of mist on her eyes and was frightened.

Instinctively she put out her hands.

ELEPHANT'S NEST IN A
RHUBARB TREE

THE summer I had the scarlet fever the only boy I could play with, during and after the scarlet fever, was Arty Whitehead. Arty had some buttons off and he lived with his uncle. His uncle had an elephant's nest in a rhubarb tree.

It was very hot that summer. As I leaned from the bedroom window and looked down on the street of new brick houses and waited for Arty to come and play with me the window-sill would scorch my elbows like hot sand-paper. On the wall of our house my father had planted a Virginia creeper. That summer, under the heat, it went mad. It pressed new shoots forward every day and they ran over the house and the house next door, and then the house on the corner, like bright green and wine-red lizards with tiny hands. One of the games I played was to watch how far the creeper grew in a week, sometimes how far it grew in a day. After three or four weeks it grew round the corner of the street and I could no longer see the new little lizards glueing their hands on the wall. So I would send Arty round the corner to look instead. 'How far's it grown now, Arty?' Arty would stand by the green railings of our house and look up. He had simple, tender eyes and his hair grew down in his neck and over his ears and he always talked with a smile, loosely. 'Growed right up to mother Kingsley's! Yeh, yeh! Growed up to the shop,' he'd say. Mother Kingsley's was a hundred yards up the next street. But I was only six, I couldn't see round the corner, and either I had to believe in Arty or believe in nobody. And gradually, as the summer went on, I got into the way of believing in Arty.

Arty came to play with me every day. Another game I played was blowing soap bubbles with a clay pipe. They floated down from the open window and Arty ran about the street, trying to catch them with his hands. One day I blew a bubble as big as a melon, the biggest bubble I'd ever seen, the biggest bubble that anyone would ever have seen if there'd been anyone in this street to see it. But there was no one but Arty. The great melon bubble floated slowly down in the hot sunshine and then along the scorched empty street. The funny thing about it was that it wouldn't burst. It floated beautifully away like a glass balloon polished by the sun, keeping about as high as the windows of the houses. When it got to the street-corner a puff of wind caught it and it turned the corner and disappeared. I called to Arty to run after it and he ran like mad after it with his cap in his hand. It was then about two o'clock in the afternoon but Arty didn't come back until six that evening.

When he came back again his lips were tired and looser than ever and I could see that he'd been a long way. 'Where you been?' I said.

'Arter the balloon.'

'All this time? Didn't it bust?' I said.

'No,' he said, 'it never busted. Just kept like that. Just went on. Never busted.'

'Where?' I said. 'How far?'

'Went right up past the school and over Collins's pond and over the fields. Right out to Newton. Past our farm.'

'Whose farm?'

'Our farm. Went right over. Never busted.'

'I never knew you had a farm,' I said.

'Yeh, yeh,' Arty said. 'My uncle gotta farm. Big farm.'

'Where?'

'Out there,' Arty said. 'Just out there. Great big farm. Catch foxes. Catch wild animals.'

'What wild animals?'

'Foxes. All sorts,' Arty said. 'All sorts. Elephants.'

'Not elephants,' I said.

'Yeh, yeh,' Arty said. 'Yeh! Catch elephants. My uncle found elephant's nest one day.' His eyes were pale and excited. 'Yeh! Elephant's nest in a rhubarb tree.'

That was the first I ever heard about it. In the beginning I had to believe Arty about the Virginia creeper, then I had to take his word for the bubble, which no one but Arty and I had ever seen. Then I did something else. Perhaps it was the after effects of the fever, the result of being shut up for nearly eight weeks in a bedroom which was almost like a boiler-house in the late afternoons; perhaps it was because I had temporarily forgotten what the world of reality, school and fields and sweetshops and trains, was like. Perhaps it was having Arty to talk to, and only Arty to play with. But gradually, from that day, I began to take his word too for the elephant's nest in a rhubarb tree.

After that, I began to ask him to tell me what it was like, but he never gave me the same description twice. 'Yeh,' he would say. 'It's big. Ever so big. Big rhubarb.' And then another day it was different. 'It's jus' a little squatty tree. Nest like a sparrow's. That's all. Little squatty tree.' Finally I was not sure what to believe in: whether the rhubarb tree was like a chestnut or an oak, with a nest of elephants like a haystack in the branches, or whether it was just rhubarb, just ordinary rhubarb, the rhubarb you eat, and it was a nest like a sparrow's, with little elephants, little shiny black elephants, like the ebony elephants that stood on my grandmother's piano. I was sure of only one thing: I wanted to go with Arty and see it for myself as soon as I got better.

It was early August when I came downstairs again and about the middle of August before I could walk any distance. When I went out into the street everything seemed strange. I had not walked on the earth for eight weeks. Now, when I walked on it, it seemed to bounce under my feet. The things I had thought were ordinary seemed suddenly odd. The streets I had not seen for eight weeks seemed far stranger than the thought of the elephant's nest in a rhubarb tree.

One of the first things I did when I got downstairs was to go and see how far the Virginia creeper had gone. When I got round the street-corner I saw that someone had cut that part of it down. The little wine and green lizards had been slashed with a knife; they were withered by sun and the tendril-fingers were dead and fixed to the wall. As I looked at it I was not only hurt but I also knew that there was no longer any means of believing whether Arty had been right about it or wrong. I had to take his word again.

Then about three weeks later Arty and I set off one morning to find the elephant's nest in a rhubarb tree on his uncle's farm. Arty was about twelve years old, with big sloppy legs and thick golden hair all over his face, so that he looked almost, to me, like a grown man. All the time I had a feeling of being sorry for him, of knowing that he was simple, and yet of trusting him. I wanted too to make a discovery that I felt my father and mother and sister and perhaps other people had never made. I wanted to go home with a story of something impossible made possible.

It was very hot as we walked through the bare wheat-fields out of the town. Heat danced like water on the distant edges of the white stubbles. We walked about a mile and then I asked Arty how much farther it was.

'Ain't much farther. Little way. Two, three more fields. Little way, that's all.'

I saw a farm in the near distance, against the woods. 'Is that your uncle's farm?'

'Yeh,' Arty said. 'That's it. That's it.'

'Where's the nest?' I said. 'This side the farm or the other?'

'Other side,' he said. 'Just other side. Just little way other side, that's all.'

We walked on for another half-hour and then when we reached the farm Arty said he'd made a mistake. His uncle's farm was the next farm. We walked on again and when we reached the next farm he said the same thing. Then the same thing again; then again. Finally I knew that it was time to turn back, that we were never going to see the thing we had come to see. As we walked back across the fields the heat of midday struck down on us as though it came through glass. Clear and direct and sickening on the sun-baked stubbles, it seemed to take away my strength and turn the tears of disappointment sour inside me.

When I got home I felt pale and weak and my feet were blistered and I felt like crying. Then when my mother asked me where I had been and I said, 'With Arty Whitehead, to find an elephant's nest in a rhubarb tree', they all burst out laughing. 'Why, Arty isn't all there! That's all it is,' they said, and I knew that they were right, and because I knew that they were right, and that what I had hoped to see never existed, I began crying at last.

Since that day, twenty-five years ago, a good deal has happened to me, but nothing at all has happened to

Arty Whitehead. I no longer live in the same town; I have been across the world and I have grown up. But Arty still lives in the same town; he has never been anywhere and he has never grown up. And now he never will grow up. He is now a man of nearly forty but he is still the boy who ran after the bubble as big as a melon.

For the last twenty years Arty has worked for a baker. All he does is sit in the cart and hold the reins and tell the horse to stop and go. He does something that a boy of six could do. At the end of the week the baker gives him a shilling or two and every night he gives him a loaf of bread. Arty understands that. He understands the most fundamental thing about living: a loaf of bread. He understands perhaps all that anyone needs to understand.

Sometimes when I go back home I go to have my hair cut. Occasionally, as I sit in the barber's shop, Arty comes in. 'Arty', the men say as they greet him, and I say 'Arty', too, but Arty does not recognize me. I have grown up, whereas Arty's face is still the face of a boy. His eyes are still simple and remote and tender and as the men in the barber's shop talk Arty does not listen. He does not need to listen. They talk about Hitler, war in China, Mussolini, the cup-ties, the newspapers, women. Arty does not know who Hitler is; he does not know where China is or what is happening to China; he does not know anything about women. He understands that he wants his hair cut. He understands a loaf of bread.

And there is also one other thing he understands. I sometimes see him walking out of the town. His glassy simple eyes are fixed on and perhaps beyond the distance. He does not walk very fast but he looks very happy. And because I know where he is going there is no doubt in my mind that he is very happy. He understands the most fundamental thing about living, a loaf of bread, and he also understands the most wonderful.

It seems to me that Arty understands what perhaps the rest of the world is trying to get at. He understands the elephant's nest in a rhubarb tree.

THE DOG AND MR. MORENCY

Mr. Alexander Morency, residing at Seaview Hotel, the Esplanade, had a little dog, Fritz, a Pomeranian. Mr. Morency came to a decision to shoot either the dog or Mrs. Morency. He could not make up his mind.

Curiously, Mr. Morency had first wanted the dog. This had been in the days when the Morencys lived at 'Morency', 3 Lilac Gardens, close to Regent's Park, and Mr. Morency was in business as a tea-broker, in the City. Mrs. Morency had not then wanted a dog. 'Me? A dog? What should I do with a dog?' she would say. 'All over the furniture, paddling in and out in wet weather. Besides, there's some other things I don't like about them.' Morency, a small, easy-going gentle fellow with a voice like smooth toffee, who wore rimless glasses, tried to persuade her otherwise. 'You see you're alone here all day, and that isn't good for you. One hears stories of fellows calling ostensibly to sell floor polish and well — You need company, and you can't have better company than a dog. Everybody knows that, and it will protect you as well.'

Mr. Morency had not at that time considered the question of breed, but he had in his mind the idea of a large dog, some kind of mastiff. He saw himself exercising this mastiff in the park on Sunday mornings, and felt the power of it on the leash, of the great neck straining magnificently forward, the muscles rippling silkily, hard as rubber. He wanted a dog that was a dog, a fighting dog, a dog that if necessary might have to be muzzled. He felt vaguely some latent power in himself expressed in the thought of such a dog.

'Well, if I must have a dog,' Mrs. Morency said at last, 'I'll have a Pomeranian.'

'Oh! no. Have a dog. Have a dog that you can call a dog.'

'Well, isn't a Pomeranian a dog? What's wrong with a Pomeranian?'

'In the first place,' Mr. Morency said, 'it's a dog of German origin. And we can do without German dogs, I think. Then the whole idea of your having a dog at all is for you to have protection.'

'You said companionship.'

'Well, if you like. Companionship as well if you like. But primarily protection. Because you're alone in the house. Now if you would make up your mind on some dog like an Alsatian — '

'Oh! no. Beastly things. I can't bear them.'

'Well, all right. A Labrador.'

'What's a Labrador?'

So Mr. Morency explained what a Labrador was, but Mrs. Morency was not impressed. Then he described a Collie, and then a Sheep Dog, subsequently other large dogs, including a Wolf-hound. He even went so far as to describe a St. Bernard. He became very enthusiastic about a St. Bernard, playing on Mrs. Morency's maternal instincts. Mr. and Mrs. Morency had had no children and Mr. Morency kept saying didn't Mrs. Morency know that it was the St. Bernard who, with brandy flask, rescued lost snow-bound little children from death in Alpine passes?

But Mrs. Morency merely pointed out that St. Bernards ate a lot.

'Well, yes,' Mr. Morency said, 'admitted. A lot for their size, yes. But — '

'I don't want a dog that eats a lot.'

'Well, have a Collie. They don't eat so much.'

'And I don't want a dog that needs a kennel. If I'm going to have a dog I'll have a dog that'll be easy to keep, and that can come into the house and eat with us.'

'Yes, but the whole idea — '

'I'll have a Pomeranian,' Mrs. Morency said.

'Oh! no. Please.'

'I'll have a Pomeranian,' Mrs. Morency said, 'and I'll call him Fritz.'

When the Pomeranian arrived Mr. Morency almost liked it. It was soft and odd and puppy-playful, and he would roll it into a little black woollen ball in his hands. It wetted the cushions, but Mrs. Morency said that was natural, wasn't it? and Mr. Morency forgave it when it rolled in the geraniums. Mrs. Morency called it Fritzie, and bought a dog basket and lined the basket with red silk. The dog slept in the box-room and for a night or two was frightened, whimpering, and Mrs. Morency woke up and put on her dressing-gown and went to comfort it. Another day Mrs. Morency was wildly excited when Mr. Morency came home. 'It drinks tea! I gave it tea in a saucer and it drank it! Tea! There's a knowing creature for you. You a tea-broker and it drinks tea! Couldn't you bring it home a little caddy with some nice special Darjeeling in it, all its own?'

Mr. Morency brought home a little half-pound caddy, filled with Darjeeling, and Mrs. Morency wrote a label on it — 'Fritz'. Then Sunday came and Mrs. Morency said, 'Dogs need exercise. Would you like to take Fritzie for an hour into the park?'

With great reluctance Mr. Morency took the dog into the park. There were a great many dogs in the park. It seemed to him that there were, that morning, unusually large numbers of large dogs. He saw Alsatians with wild cocked ears, big Collies, vast Labradors bounding after balls across the grass. Fritzie strained at the leash and Mr. Morency strained back, walking almost on his heels, trying to foster the illusion of power. But it was no good: he could not blind himself to the reality of the little Pomeranian, miserable and despicable, so absurd that it did not even know what a tree was for. And he felt that he was on the verge of hating it.

But it was not until some time afterwards that he felt his hatred become a reality. In the autumn of that year Mr. Morency retired from business, and the Morencys decided to go and live at the seaside.

'Of course,' Mr. Morency said, 'we shall have to get rid of Fritz.'

'Get what? What do you mean? Get rid of Fritz?'

'Why, yes. You can't take a dog to live in an hotel. No hotel will have it.'

'Oh! won't they? We'll see about that. We'll find an hotel that does.'

Mrs. Morency went to several hotels and even took Fritz down to them, to see the managers. Finally the Seaview Hotel said it did not mind little dogs, provided they were well-trained.

'He has his own bed and bath and even his own tea-caddy. Oh! yes, and he even has other necessary things too. He's an angel.'

So the Morencys moved into the Seaview Hotel, and every morning, before breakfast, and every evening, after supper, Mr. Morency exercised the Pomeranian along the Esplanade with the sea-wind in his face. Mr. Morency tried hard to foster the old illusion of grappling with a powerful animal. But it was no good: he saw only the wretched yelping and yapping little Fritz, who would never grow any bigger.

And in the hotel lounge, every day, the Pomeranian did his tricks. 'Fritzie sit up! up! Up! Steady, Fritzie, wait. Fritzie, wait. Naughty Fritzie. Fritzie,

wait, wait. Now — catch it!' And Fritzie would catch
the biscuit. 'Now,' Mrs. Morency would say, 'cow
jump over the moon.' And Mrs. Morency would hold
up a saucer and call to Fritzie: 'Cow jump over the
moon! Fritzie, now, Fritzie cow jump — Fritzie,
naughty Fritzie. Naughty Fritzie not looking. Now.
Cow jumps over — Fritzie, Fritzie. Naughty. No
jump, no cakey. Now cow — steady — cow jumps over
the moon!'

And the ladies in the lounge would say what a
wonderful little thing Fritzie was.

'Oh! yes. He's so knowing. He knows it's tea-time
when I rattle a spoon in a cup, and he knows it's walkie
time, don't you, Fritzie? if I just pick up his lead. And
he knows — well, he can *tell* me when he — '

And hearing the voice of Mrs. Morency praising
and explaining the dog and seeing the dog itself, paws
up, begging for biscuit day after day in the hotel
lounge, Mr. Morency felt the gradual growth and
hardening of a peculiar hatred towards them both. He
saw himself for the rest of his life exercising the dog
morning and evening, getting out of bed to give it its
saucer of early morning tea, hearing its silly yappings
of joy and misery, smelling the old dog-smell about the
room. He began to long for the day when the dog
would get run over by a bus, and in desperation, once
or twice, he called it suddenly across the road on the
off-chance that it would get run over by the bus. He
felt jealous of the dog because of his wife's affection for
it, jealous of his wife because of the dog's everlasting
yapping and stupid affection for her. He hated the
walk along the Esplanade, and he could not sleep at
night, the thought of the dog boring into his mind like
a gimblet. Until finally he felt he could bear it no
longer.

He decided to shoot the dog. He would take it down on the sea shore, one dark evening, and shoot it and let the tide wash it away. If there was any trouble afterwards, he would probably shoot Mrs. Morency too.

And one evening, after dinner, he took the dog far along the Esplanade. He had an old service revolver in his overcoat pocket and he would shoot the dog down under the cliffs, where the lamps ended. As he walked along he passed other men exercising other dogs, and suddenly, instead of being remorseful, he was struck by the whole outrageous idea of dogs on earth. He thought of all the dogs being exercised, for the same purpose, along that piece of sea-front, and then of all the dogs being exercised, still for the same purpose, along all the sea-fronts of England. He thought of the thousands of dogs all over England, and then of the millions of dogs all over Europe, and all the other millions of dogs from China to San Francisco, from Greenland to Honolulu. There were millions of dogs in the world and what were they worth? You couldn't milk them, you couldn't eat them, and sometimes, he felt bitterly, you couldn't trust them. They were pampered parasites, an outrage, and nobody saw it. They didn't even hunt their own food, like cats, and he saw all the vast unharnessed power of dog muscle all over the world as something which was worth nothing at all.

He tugged the Pomeranian down to the shore. In the half-darkness he could just see it: miserable, despicable, an absolute caricature of a dog. He thought of the dog he had wanted, the mastiff. He felt the tremendous pull of it on the sockets of his arms, the strength of a dog that was a dog.

He got the Pomeranian by the collar with his left hand and held it down against the still sea-wet shingle. Below him he could hear the tide going out, washing the pebbles. There was no other sound except the wind up on the cliffs. The dog was making no sound at all.

As Mr. Morency looked at it, there was just a faint light from the last lamp on the Esplanade, and unexpectedly Mr. Morency saw the dog's eyes. He looked at them and suddenly, for about a second, he saw in the reflecting eyes of the small dog a small reflection of himself. He saw the dim light of something abject, downtrodden, a little forlorn, deeply unhappy.

And in that moment he could have shot himself.

THE BANJO

Uncle and Clarkey were travelling with the baby's pram over hilly country, in the heat of July, making their way towards the coast. In the fields the standing wheat was rapidly turning a bright olive colour. The hot light beat down strongly on the oats, so that they shimmered opal on the crests of the distances. On either side of the tyre-worn track of the by-pass, smooth as alabaster, long swinging lines of scarlet poppies seemed to jump back off the ground, stabbing the eyes.

One wheel of the pram had lost its tyre and Clarkey's feet were hurting. The constant sawing of the iron wheel-rim on the concrete was like jagged glass on the fibres of his mind.

'Ain't no use, Uncle,' Clarkey kept saying. 'I gotta git some new shoes afore the day's gone. I gotta cadge a new pair somehow.'

'H'mph.'

'Either I git 'em too big or too little. Never git 'em right.' Clarkey's eyes lifted themselves from the hypnotic glare of the poppies and rested, almost dreamy, on the cooler spaces of corn. 'One day I'll git a pair o' shoes right, I know. I see I git a nice pair o' patent, I see I do. I'll go in a shop and put the money down and be measured.'

'H'mph,' Uncle said.

They had been together now for almost six months and got some sort of living travelling along the coast with the baby's pram, grinding knives and scissors. When there were no scissors to grind they collected rags from children and gave back gay coloured windmills of their own manufacture. When this was done Uncle played a little tune on the banjo.

THE BANJO

The banjo lay under the sacking cover of the pram with the hand-worked grindstone, a pile of odd rags and half a loaf of bread wrapped in newspaper. All except the banjo they shared on an equal basis. The banjo belonged to Uncle. He was a big slommacking fellow with heavy placid eyes and large shell-backed hands from which his crabbed fingers spread out with slow diffidence, like the shy feet of tortoises. When he had played one tune on the banjo he began to play what seemed to be another but which it became evident, after a time, was only the first, played a little differently. The tune had no beginning and no end, but seemed to swing like a spider's web out of nowhere. Uncle had picked it up somewhere on the African veldt, thirty years before, as a soldier in the Boer campaign. Perhaps it was Dutch. Uncle did not know. He did not know the name of his tune or if there were words to it, and he did not know any other.

Sometimes as they went along the pram hit a stone or a flaw in the concrete and the banjo, suddenly jolted, would give out a little melancholy twang of sound.

For a long time this sudden mournful little sound had been playing, like the glare of the poppies, the shoes and the scraping of the tyre-less pram-wheel, on Clarkey's mind. For a time it had been only a source of irritation. Now it began to mean something. It began to crystallize into a desire to possess the banjo.

With the banjo, Clarkey reasoned, he could buy new shoes. His eyes were small and dark and excitable and he had a way of walking springing on the toes of his feet, so that he looked almost like a lady. He seemed to take three steps to Uncle's one, like a dark-eyed ferret running behind a large dog, and as the concrete struck through the soles of his feet, paining them, there was a resultant pain in his mind, the pain of an awakening envy against Uncle, the pain of wanting the banjo for himself.

The more he thought about this, as they went on in the heat of the afternoon, the more it seemed to him that he had struck a great idea. With the banjo he could cancel out the things that were troubling him. He could get away from Uncle, start on his own, be free. Easy to pick up a pram somewhere, learn a jazz tune or two on the banjo. A banjo must be easy to play. Easy as pie. Easy was the word for all of it. With the banjo there would be no more pram-wheels scouring the edge off his brain, no more concrete bouncing white hot pain into the soles of his feet.

As he was thinking this, his mind becoming set in a track of fanatically simple ideas, they came up to a large roadside tea-house with a fleet of orange long-distance coaches parked across the concrete pull-in outside. It was the chance they had waited for all afternoon.

'Goin' to give 'em a tune, ain't we?' Clarkey said. 'Ain't we?'

'H'mph,' Uncle said.

Uncle pushed the pram on to the grass verge opposite the tea-house, and there got out the banjo from under the covering of sacks. He slung the banjo over his shoulder and with huge ponderous steps that suddenly maddened Clarkey by their slowness walked across the road and took up a stand. People were now coming out of the tea-house and were standing about among the coaches, talking, wiping the tea-sweat off their faces.

Presently Uncle's fingers uncurled themselves, like tortoise feet, and began to play the slow melancholy tune on the banjo. After Uncle had played the tune once and had begun to play it again Clarkey walked among the people with his cap, 'Something to help us on the road ma'am, thank you ma'am, thank you, much obliged I'm sure, yes ma'am hot's the word', his voice like the twanging of a wire spring in the hot air, his feet purposely dragged with pain across the concrete.

'Six and eightpence,' he said, ten minutes later, half a mile along the road. 'Ain't bad, eh? Ain't bad?'

'H'mph,' Uncle said. 'Ain't bad.'

Clarkey counted out half the money and gave it to Uncle, and Uncle put it in his pocket, not speaking. The poppies, which had ceased for a short distance each side the tea-house, had now begun again, huge trails of blood following the white-painted edge of the road. His eyes and feet hurting again, Clarkey lifted his gaze to the cool fields of olive-yellow corn, thinking of the money. He thought of the amount, the whole amount, six and eightpence. A lot of money. A hell of a lot. Made in five minutes. Made by a scrap of a tune on a banjo. Down on the coast there were second-hand clothes shops where he could get a pair of shoes for that money. A week with the banjo, and he could get shoes and a pram, meat for dinner, fags, live like a lord, with a proper kip at nights. Live easy, play the banjo on the esplanade of some sea-side town, live easy and make money. No more slugging on by-passes.

They had not sharpened a pair of scissors or a knife all that day, but an hour later they came to a house surrounded by heavy clumps of spruce and pine where, once or twice before, they had had a little cutlery to grind.

'Want me to go in and see if they got a thing or two to sharpen?' Clarkey said.

'H'mph.'

To Clarkey there was something suddenly maddening about this repeated grunt. As he went up the drive of the house under the cool black pines it seemed suddenly as if the man who could talk like that, and never say anything but that, hadn't much place in the world. Like the banjo all he had was one tune: one word, a grunt that did for everything. A man like that might just as well not be alive. Might just as well be dead.

Clarkey came down the drive, two or three minutes later, with a kitchen knife in his hand. It was a short knife, black handled, with a triangular blade coming to a point. 'Take your time over it,' the kitchen maid said. 'We use it for cutting the rind off the bacon in the mornings.'

'Yes, miss,' Clarkey said. 'Take our time and make a good job of it, betcha life. How soon you want it?'

'The cook's been swearing about it for a month,' the girl said. 'Don't bring it back till it cuts some sense.'

'About half an hour?' Clarkey said.

'Any time, so long as it cuts.'

'Right,' Clarkey said. 'About half an hour. May be a bit more.'

Outside on the roadside grass Uncle fitted up the little hand grindstone. Clarkey held the knife. 'Shall I sharpen it?'

'H'mph,' Uncle said.

He began to turn the grindstone, moistening it with a little water that they carried about with them in a screw-stoppered beer bottle. Clarkey held the knife lightly in his hands, horizontal, with the tips of his fingers. For a small man his hands were very long, quite white, and they seemed exceedingly flexible. They were never still. They seemed as if charged with a kind of ladylike electricity, recoiling with a little quiver of shock as the knife blade made its contact with the stone. In this way it seemed sometimes that the

knife leapt up from the stone, of its own volition, beyond his control. A moment later Clarkey would have
it back again, holding it in his light, ladylike fashion,
almost caressing stone with steel, generating a little
firework of sparks that was scarcely visible in the glare
of sunshine.

'Gotta take my time over it,' Clarkey said. 'Ain't
had a stone on it for a year.'

'H'mph.'

Uncle did not change or relax his movements, but
turned the little grindstone like a man turning the
handle of a musical instrument and producing the same
harsh melody. To Clarkey this sound brought back and
became identical with the sound of the tyreless pram-
wheel on the road that afternoon. It brought back in
turn the glare of heat and poppies, the sudden useless
twang of the banjo, the pointless maddening little tune
that was the only tune that Uncle could play. Under
the renewed contact of all this Clarkey was hit by a new
and insane impression. He felt as if his mind were the
soft revolving circle of stone, that the fine edge of all the
circumstances of the day was being held against it,
wearing it away. As he watched the knife silvered and
fined to a razor edge under his own hand he felt his
mind sharpened in the same way to a fine edge of frenzy.

When he finally got to his feet with the knife he felt
the hot afternoon spin swiftly about him, rocking his
brain. He walked away towards the drive of the house
slowly, not thinking. Up to that moment he had not
grasped that the knife might have its own significance.

Then suddenly he saw it. He was walking along
with the knife in his right hand. He was under the
dark trees, out of the sunshine, and the knife had in
his hand no more than the appearance of a blade of
light. When he turned the knife very slightly in his

ladylike fingers the light went out. In that moment he saw the significance of the knife. He stood still and looked back. The pine trees had cut him off from the road. In the same way, as he looked forward again, he saw that they separated him from the house. He took several paces off the gravel drive and stood behind a tree. He stood there for three or four minutes, waiting and listening. He did not move at all except once. It was to give the knife a little twist with his fingers before putting it in his pocket, like a light that is switched out.

When he walked back to the road again, out of the black shadows of the thick pine trees into the sunlight, he was no longer thinking. Thought had been transmuted into a repeated current of sensation. It was already driving through him like a charge of electrified madness.

This single sensation was so strong that it had the effect of nullifying all the others that had troubled him that afternoon: the pain of his feet, the filing away of the broken pram-wheel, the heat, the hard glare in his eyes of concrete and poppies, the maddening sound of the banjo making its mournful twang under the sacking in the pram.

It drove him along all the rest of the afternoon and into the evening, replacing the machinery of physical effort and thought, so that he became no longer tired. He had no sort of plan of action. He had ceased thinking. His plan was the sensation itself. At some culminative moment something would happen. His hand touched the knife in his pocket. The knife now lay dead, but at some point it would spring to life, like the filament of a lamp when the current is turned on.

His first return to reality was when he realized that Uncle had stopped with the pram. The poppies had ceased, and now woods were thick on both sides of the verge. Above the gap made by the road between the trees he became aware of a strangely elevated clarity in the sky. He realized a moment later that they had come almost to the sea.

For the first time it was Uncle who opened the conversation. His speech was soft, almost on one note, and tired.

'This is th' old place,' he said. 'Remember it, don't you? Brook down on the other side of the wood. Plenty o' water, remember?' He pushed the pram off the road and into a track going down into the woods. 'I reckon I'll wash my feet.'

Clarkey did not speak. But once in the wood, under the trees, he began to remember the place. It was very quiet. In the heart of the wood it was quite dark, but at the far end the evening sun was pouring down between the trees in long bright trumpets of horizontal light. He caught the strong odour of sunless earth, of rank elder.

The path widened out eventually to a forty-foot track. Uncle parked the pram under a large sloe bush, and began to go about at once looking for wood.

'Goin' wash your feet afore we eat?' Clarkey said.

'H'mph,' Uncle said. 'Afterwards.'

'Christ, I'll be glad to get my feet in water too.'

They ate a meal of bread and cheese, with tea stewed over the fire in a can. All through it Clarkey was very silent. The sensation, the insane pain generated by the idea of the knife, had now left him. He was thinking again, but the process of his thought was no longer in any way chaotic. It had become very simplified. He didn't want any trouble. Uncle was a big man, slow but enormous, and had been a soldier. No need to knock the house down to get the cash-box. No need for trouble. All he had to do was walk away with the

banjo. Uncle always played the little tune on it last
thing at night, before they dossed. Clarkey could walk
away with it in the night. They were now about four
miles from the sea. In an hour he could be down in the
town, get a night's doss, and lay low for a bit. In a
week he could be away somewhere down the coast
where Uncle would never think of going. After that,
no more slugging with a pram, no more torn, aching
feet. He'd live easy and get himself a pair of shoes to
measure.

The plan was so simple that he lay on his back,
thinking it out, trying to find a weakness in it, all the
time that Uncle had gone into the field beyond the
wood, to wash his feet. He went over it in his mind as
a man goes over a problem in arithmetic, working it
out in different ways, getting always the same answer.

It was already twilight when Uncle came back. He
seemed larger, more cumbrous and more simple than
ever in the falling darkness. To Clarkey's questions
he grunted always with the old soft monosyllable of
content.

Lying on his back, Clarkey watched Uncle get the
banjo out of the pram. He watched with motionless,
half-closed eyes. He saw Uncle tune up the banjo and
then saw the slow tortoise-feet hands uncurl themselves
and strike the strings.

Without being affected by it he heard the strange
little tune mournfully strike the quiet air. He heard it
again and saw the figure of Uncle sink into a still
lower attitude in the darkening grass. Already, over
the colourless fringe of trees, the stars were pricking
out, dim above the reddish afterglow of heat and light
still suspended in the direction of the sea. All the time
no part of Uncle moved except the slow crude hands,
heavily striking out the tune.

Clarkey heard the tune twice and then it began gradually to get on his nerves again. He turned restlessly in the grass. He began to feel the frayed ends of his patience sticking into his mind like raw ends of wire.

'Can't yer play some other tune?' Clarkey said.

Uncle did not speak; the little tune mournfully went on.

Then Clarkey remembered another question. It had troubled him for a long time.

'What do they call yer Uncle for? Are yer Uncle to somebody special or summat?'

Uncle gave a sort of negative grunt, barely audible above the sound of the banjo, in answer.

'Ain't yer Uncle to nobody?'

'No,' Uncle said. The tune had ended for the third time, his voice low but audible now.

'Ain't yer got no folks then?' Clarkey said.

'No,' Uncle said. 'I ain't got nobody.'

'Nobody, nowhere?'

'H'mph,' Uncle said, and now the tune, which seemed to have on Uncle an almost intoxicant effect, began again, fining the raw edges of Clarkey's impatience so that he turned swiftly in the grass.

'Can't yer give the music a rest now? I wanna get some sleep. It's bin a hell of a hot day.'

'H'mph, this ain't hot,' Uncle said. 'When we was out there, in Africa, it was a hundred and ten sometimes. And still with it. Quiet. Terrible still and quiet at nights. You got so's you slept easy and woke easy.'

'You git over it later?'

'No. I never got over it. I sleep as light as a kid now.'

Clarkey lay tense, thinking. Now he had an idea.

He began to unlace his boots. The sound of the banjo had ceased and it was silent and dark now, the figure of Uncle like a quiet and expressionless shadow as he moved across to put away the banjo in the pram.

'I think I'll change my mind,' Clarkey said, 'and go and wash my feet. They hurt like hell.'

He shuffled across the grass in his unlaced boots, then stopped and turned.

'You goin' get some sleep now?'

'H'mph,' Uncle said. 'Perhaps I will.'

Clarkey went down the track and into the field. He sat down on the edge of the small stream, low now after days of heat, and then took off his boots and socks and let his feet rest in the water. As he sat there, in the now almost full summer darkness, with the water stinging his feet, he could hear nothing at all but the occasional rush of a car passing on the road beyond the wood.

Then he heard something else. It was the little tune being played once again by Uncle. The sound of it maddened him, and the edges of his impatience were stripped raw again as he waited for it to end.

It ended after a moment or two and he waited tensely for it to begin again, his feet out of the water now, his sharp face turned upward, listening. He waited for three or four minutes, but there was no sound. He dried his feet on the handkerchief that he wore round his neck and then put on his socks and waited again. He knew how easily Uncle slept. He would be asleep in ten minutes, perhaps less. He put on his boots and laced them and then stood up. His feet felt light and cool and his hands were slightly stretched forward, ready to give him direction in the darkness.

He gave Uncle twenty minutes, as near as he could tell. Then he walked out of the field and back along the track, with his habitual ladylike springing steps exaggerated by the need for quietness. He reached the place under the sloe bushes where the solid shadows of the pram and Uncle were just distinguishable, side by side. He listened and it seemed to him that Uncle was asleep. He stood for a moment and then lifted the sacking of the pram. With the tips of his fingers he grasped the banjo and took it out. He knew that he had not made a single sound, that no single sound would now be necessary. Listening, he stood for a moment longer, and then moved away.

As he moved, the edge of his jacket very slightly struck the pram. Unbalanced on its three good wheels, the pram rocked a little, creaking the rusty springs.

A moment later he knew that Uncle was awake. He stirred and grunted and Clarkey, suddenly very frightened, began to run. He had not moved five yards before Uncle was lumbering after him.

In the instant that Uncle grabbed at him by the shoulders in the darkness it seemed to Clarkey that he reached the culminative point of all the day's impatience and anger, the extreme limit of pain. It was as if the long lines of poppies rose up again out of the darkness and struck him on the eyes. He felt his body flare up to a sort of frightened fury. Without knowing what he was doing he was swinging the knife.

He had not swung it more than once or twice before he felt the enormous cumbersome arms of Uncle close round him from behind. He had already dropped the banjo. Now he tried desperately to drop the knife. He could not do it because of the strength of Uncle's arms, which seemed to be crushing in his ribs, and suddenly he felt the knife force its way into his chest.

The huge powerful arms of Uncle went on squeezing him until he dropped, his breath choked so that he could make only a queer falling dribble of sound. As he fell and lay in the grass, Uncle stood away from him, bewildered, not fully knowing what had happened.

It occurred to him after a time to light a match. In its light he saw Clarkey lying at his feet. He did not know what to do. He stood with his heavy mournful eyes fixed on Clarkey and his slow tortoise hands suspended with dumb bewilderment and pain.

Finally he moved. He shuffled heavily forward. The match had gone out and in the darkness his feet struck against the banjo, lying in the grass.

As he did so he heard it give out a little mournful and ghastly twang of sound, like a dying complaint, that recalled for him the voice of his dead friend.

FUCHSIA

He wanted to put his feet up on his own fireplace, but he was well aware that twenty-eight weeks of idleness had lost him that privilege.

'And don't keep muttering at the girl!' his wife said. 'You mutter all day at me. Then when she comes home at night you start muttering at her. Can't you think of anything else to do? Go for a good walk.'

'I don't hold wi' this gadding out o' nights,' he said. 'I don't hold wi' it.'

'You never hold wi' anything,' she said. 'The girl wants some enjoyment, don't she?'

'I should think so!' the girl said. 'Who do you think you are?'

The words struck him into silence. He sat gazing heavily at the miserable little fire, backed up earlier in the day with a mass of wet potato-peelings, scraps of brussel-sprouts and a small quantity of wet slack. Damp clothes were drying about the overcrowded kitchen on lines and chair-backs. He was a heavy-boned man, with loose grey flesh and awkward hands rather like dead crabs. Twenty-eight weeks ago they had laid him off at the tannery. Now he looked indeterminately at the dead crust of fire and longed to poke it into flame. In the past his first act on coming home from work had been to seize the poker, exuberantly smash the fire into a blaze, and then put his feet on the hob. These acts had given him prestige. He could see even now where his feet had scarred the lid of the side-boiler. Yes: feet on the hob, then a kipper or a piece of haddock or eggs with his tea, then hot water from the boiler and a smoke and a look at the paper in his shirtsleeves before going out to the club.

Now things had changed. It was the girl who had the kipper, with the paper independently propped up by the teapot. It was she who brought the money home. It was she who had the prestige and kept things together.

The odour of fish made savagely delicious stabs at his senses. The girl, alternately intent on fish-bones and the paper, did not look at him. She was just twenty. One day she had been at school; the next day as it were he had looked up to see her fully grown, swinging her hips. She was pretty in a ripe, haughty sort of way. She earned good, easy money in a large machine laundry. She used lipstick and sometimes wore Woolworth ear-rings that made her look much older and, to him, almost a stranger. And now, for some time, he had been worried because she was having a gay time, staying out at all hours of the night.

As he sat there defeatedly contemplating the fire she got up from the table. He looked up, and a spark of the old authority sprang up in him.

'Jist you be in a good time,' he said.

'Ah! start that again!' the woman said. 'Start that again!'

'Well — '

'Well what? The girl earns good money, don't she? She's only young, ain't she? She's entitled to a few minutes' enjoyment, ain't she? The way you talk to her anybody'd think she couldn't look after herself.'

'You harbour her in it. That's what,' he said. 'I tell you.'

'Well, tell somebody else!' she said. 'I'm sick of it. All you do all day is maunder over the fire and jaw at folks. Take and get out and walk it off!'

'Yes!' the girl said again, 'who do you think you are?'

When he left the house, five minutes later, it was
as if these words drove him forward. After the bright
gas-light of the crowded little room, with damp clothes
drying on the ceiling-line and on the horse by the fire,
the streets seemed very dark and empty. The sky was
starless and quiet over the town. He heard the moan
of trams rising and falling above the murmur of other
traffic and saw above the darker horizon of buildings
the great reflection of lights flowering in apricot and
rose.

Well, who was he? The question, not answered,
settled at the back of his mind, dully pricking his consciousness. He walked with his hands in his pockets,
staring at the slightly wet pavements. At the bottom of the next street there was a corner pub, The
Flying Horse. He went past it. He would have liked
a glass of mild-and-bitter, an hour in the smoke of the
bar, but he knew it was not possible. Nothing was the
same now. He had lost the right to put his feet on his
own fireplace, the right to have a drink, the right to
expect a civil answer from his own daughter. Well,
who was he? Who did he think he was?

He walked on into the centre of the town. Fragmentary moments out of the past flashed across his
mind exactly as the sparks flashed along the elevated
tram-wires. He did not consciously think of things as
they had been. It was not possible to grasp the pictures
of himself, independent, in regular work, able to de-
mand a thing and pay for it or ask a question and get
an answer, before despondence absorbed and extin-
guished them again.

Five minutes later he was down among the shops.
It was Tuesday and now he saw that there was a street-
market. He walked slowly past stalls on which pyra-
mids of fruit glowed orange and green and scarlet

under white gas-flares. The odour of celery was clean and sweet in the damp, wintry air. The light broke up into diamond and multi-coloured sections the sloping counters of sweets and cakes iced with sugar and coconut.

He went slowly past them, as if not interested. He was not hungry. Hunger had nothing to do with it. Some part of himself had simply been taken away and in his wretchedness he was not able to place what it was. It had something to do with his daughter.

He felt that she no longer belonged to him. Why was it? For years he himself had been independent, with good money, proud, able to please himself. Now it was her turn. What did she do with herself at nights? How had he come to let her get like this? It seemed to him that she was growing into a common woman, a stranger, swinging her ear-rings and her hips along the street. How had it come about?

She was right. Who was he? How did she come to talk like that? His thoughts unconsciously beat him to a standstill.

A moment later he was no longer thinking. He found himself looking at many flowers blooming with shadowy brilliance under the light canvas of a stall. Behind cool wax pagodas of pink and mauve hyacinth and blue stars of cineraria and bowls of little lemon tulips a woman was sitting silently knitting by the light of an incandescent lamp. He stood looking at the flowers with immobile eyes. The damp wintry air had now become suddenly fragrant and light. He heard for a moment nothing but the softest click of the bone needles as the woman knitted, and gradually his interest concentrated itself on a single flower, a small pink and white fuchsia in a pot, which he picked up in his hands.

For two or three minutes he held the flower in his

large crab-like hands and looked at it. The slender upper petals, of clear cherry-red, were turned backwards. The lower petals were gathered thickly together like a skirt which swung lightly under the vibration of his unsteady hands.

At last he was aware of the woman looking up from her knitting, watching him. He made as if to hold the flower nearer the light, peering at it more closely. The woman remarked at last that it was a pretty pot, and he nodded.

'Ballet Girl,' she said.

'Eh?' He raised grey, unreceptive eyes.

'Ballet Girl,' she said. 'That's the name of it.'

'Ah,' he said.

He stood holding the flower for almost a minute longer, without a change of expression or another word.

'Ninepence,' the woman said. 'If you look at it closely you can see it's just like a girl. Like somebody dancing.'

He did not speak. He held the flower in his hands a little longer before moving again. When he did move, putting the pot down on the stall at last, the flowers swung briefly beneath the leaves in the quiet air.

And even then he still stood watching, his eyes lowered in the gaslight. It was only when he moved away from the stall and the flowers and the woman watching him over her poised needles that the expression in his eyes became quite clear.

He was looking straight before him into space, his eyes alight for a moment with happiness, with a momentary illusion it was clear they could not sustain.

THE MAN WHO LOVED CATS

THE Professor turned his toast and gently pushed the milk for the tortoiseshell farther along the hearth, away from the fire. The angora, asleep on his knees, curled up, was like a lady's fur. Her little snore was like a toy dynamo. The Professor stroked her silky ears with one hand, while he toasted with the other. Dear puss. Beautiful Angelica. It was a dream to touch her. As he stroked and toasted, the tortoiseshell lapped milk with pretty smacking noises, jingling the saucer against the fire-irons. Until at last he had to rebuke her, pushing the saucer still farther away. Greedy puss. Silly, silly Shell.

It was about five o'clock: November, a still, already dark afternoon. The house smelled faintly of cats and, more strongly, sourly, of fish. The Professor, used to it over a period of years, did not notice it. It was the natural smell of the house, the sweet soft cat atmosphere he loved. He ate and drank his tea with one hand, loving the angora with the other. He sat curled up in the chair, long and thin, with bony hands. Long love of cats had made him rather cat-like himself: lean and pawing and soft. Only his collar hardened him. It was a high butterfly collar, the wings of it cut deep, so that his scraggy Adam's apple was free. It was the collar that gave him the look of decayed depravity.

After about five minutes the street bell rang, and he got up, with the angora still asleep in his arms, to answer it. Before he could reach the door the tortoiseshell was through it: through her own little trap-door at the foot. It was an ingenious contrivance. With seventeen cats it saved much time. It was fitted to all doors except the front. And when he opened the front door the Professor kept his foot against the lintel.

'Ah, it's Miss Minot! Come in.'

The girl came in. She was about sixteen. She had gone just beyond gawkiness and was filling out, but she was shy, and the Professor did not help.

'I thought it sounded like your ring,' he said.

'My ring?' she said. 'But I don't ring differently?'

'Very much,' he said. 'You ring shortly — short and sweet. Very much. Very different from any other pupil.'

'But how do you tell?'

He smiled down at her: a curious and almost lop-sided smile, somehow feline and almost fascinating. 'How do you ever know anything? By memory,' he said. 'I remembered. I remembered you from last week.'

She stood in a little trance of embarrassment, not knowing what to say. 'What books have you brought?' he said.

'The Saintsbury and the *Introduction to Dramatic Art*.'

'Good. Take off your things and come in. Don't mind the cats. Shelley, Shelley. Silly Shell. Come away.' The tortoiseshell sleeked off across the hall and slid through the patent trap into the Professor's room.

In a moment the girl and the Professor followed. The Professor walked with a slight stoop: a little arched, like a cat offended. 'Sit down. Warm yourself,' he said.

She sat down, in the Professor's chair. Pointedly, he stood up. And all of a sudden, she saw her mistake. 'Oh! I'm in your chair!'

'Never mind, never mind.' He smiled: the slow feline smile that was almost, but not quite, fascinating.

'Never mind, my dear. It's big enough for two. I'll sit on the arm for a moment. I'll sit and hold Angelica.'

'Angelica? Is that the cat?'

'Yes, that's the cat. *The* cat. There are cats and cats, you know. Angelica's a queen. But what's your name? You didn't tell me last week.'

'Oh, it's a rotten name!' the girl said. 'I hate it.' She pouted.

'But tell me what it is. I'd like to know. I can't call you *Miss* Minot. Not for three months.'

'It's Viola. It's silly. It's so pi.'

'Viola.' He spoke it softly, purring, his voice a tone or two above the angora's snore, a sleepy purr of seduction. Speaking, he looked down at the girl. Her little bust, under the silky dress, was round and smooth, like a plum. He looked at her legs. She was opening the Saintsbury, the book drawing her dress tight across her knees. Her stockings were silvery in the lamplight. 'Viola,' he kept saying. 'Viola.' Nice legs. Lovely virginal legs. 'I suppose you think we ought to be doing some work?' he said.

'I was only thinking we hadn't much time, if I'm to cram for the exam.'

'My dear child, I'll teach you all you want to know in three months. I've never had a failure yet. Does Angelica upset you?'

'Not a bit. I like her.'

'No? I'll put her down anyway. She can sleep on the sofa. Anyway, I can't teach unless my hands are free.'

So he took the angora and laid her on the settee like a child, cushioning her with precious murmurs.

'How many cats have you,' the girl said, 'altogether?'

'Altogether seventeen.' He came back to her chair, bending, his body arched and slightly twisted, his smile false and sweet. 'But no kittens. There are no misdemeanours with my cats.' He sat on the chair-arm, pulling his fingers, cracking them softly. 'I can't have promiscuous Tommies in this house. It wouldn't do, would it? You know what cats are. She-cats too.'

The girl, not knowing quite how to take it, sat still somewhere between shyness and entrancement.

'After all, I ought to know,' he said. 'I've kept cats for so long. For thirty years now. I've written books about them.'

'Books? — just about cats?'

He leaned down and put one hand on her shoulder. It was a soft touch, light as silk, and just detached enough to be safe. 'My dear child, don't say just about cats. Cats are the most wonderful creatures in the world — with one exception.'

'And what's that?'

'Women. Cats and women go together. They were made for the same thing — for petting and loving and stroking. Oh, there are all sorts of points of similarity! However, this isn't English literature. We ought to get on.' He leaned over to shut the book on her knees. As he shut it, the book fell through her skirt, between her knees. 'There, forgive me. I've disarranged your dress,' he said. Her silky young knees fascinated him. 'Oh, don't pick up the Saintsbury! We shan't want him. Just sit still.'

She sat still: still as a cat, her body delightfully unobtrusive and soft in the Professor's big chair.

'Now where did we get to?'

'The Reformation,' she said. 'You were just running over things. Just to get a sort of skeleton idea.'

'The Restoration. Congreve and that crew. Wycherley and so on. It was a period of great licence.'

He had his hand on her shoulder still, and now, as

though from long habit, he was beginning to stroke it, with his long-boned fingers, in the same feline and almost fascinating fashion as he smiled. 'I mean that there was not only licence in art and drama, but in private and public life. It was a most licentious age. English literature would have been better without it.'

'We were supposed to do some of the plays last term,' the girl said, 'but Miss Brand passed them over. Of course she thought we were innocent.'

'And are you innocent?'

She did not speak. He let his hand run down her shoulder and down her arm. He squeezed her.

'You don't say anything. That means you are innocent.'

'It doesn't!'

'Oh, yes! How innocent?'

'It doesn't. I've read *The Way of the World*. Any of the sixth would be awfully piqued if you called them innocent.'

'All right,' he said. 'You're not innocent. So now we know.'

'Now you think I'm fast?' she said.

'Oh, no! Not fast. Very nice. As nice as Angelica. You don't mind if I stroke you? I feel you're just like a little cat and you must be stroked.'

'What came after the Reformation?' the girl said.

'You mean the Restoration?' He was stroking her absently, his fingers making tiny feline explorations across her dress. 'Pope. He was a lesson in himself. And then of course the novelists. They were a pretty outspoken lot too. Sterne and Smollett. I don't suppose you've read them?'

'We've had to do Sterne with Miss Brand. But she didn't take it all. We had private reading for it mostly.'

'You know your groundwork pretty well,' the Professor said. 'What you want is a fuller knowledge? You want to go deeper?'

'Yes, I want to know more detail. I think I'll be all right then.'

They sat for some minutes without speaking. For the Professor there was no need to speak. He expressed himself by silence and by the soft explorations of his hands, his fingers like feelers across the girl's dress. Once she quivered.

He had found the neck of her dress, and she pushed his hand away. But it came back again, sleepy and catlike and insistent. She could not resist or escape it. Until at last his hand was still on her small breast.

'Don't mind me at all,' he said. 'It doesn't mean anything at all. I must stroke something.'

He stroked her: it was restful and yet exciting. It gave her an extraordinary sensation, not where he stroked her, but in her legs and in the depth of her stomach.

'Is it because you've been stroking cats for so long?'

'Yes, it's because I've been stroking cats.'

She moved a little and gave a big sigh, so that the sensation in her legs and body fused and came up into her throat.

'Where are all the cats?' she said. 'There's only Angelica and the tortoiseshell.'

'They're all over the house. In their favourite places. Sleeping mostly. They do as they like. I let them.'

'Just as they like?'

'Yes, or just as I tell them. They know when I speak.'

'That's marvellous.'

'Just see,' he said. 'Shelley. Shelley. Silly Shell. Go out of the room, Shell. Shelley, go out, I say.'

The tortoiseshell uncurled from its place by the hearth, soodled across the floor, flapped open its little trap door and was gone.

'Send Angelica,' the girl said.

'You want me to? She's still asleep.'

'Yes, send her. See if she hears you while she's still asleep.'

Without turning the Professor called. 'Angelica, Angelica dear. Angel. Go out. Out of the room. Go out, Angelica dear.'

Listening, the girl heard in a moment the soft flapping of the cat's door, and then quietness.

'It's marvellous,' she said.

'Now we're alone,' the Professor said. He bent his head close to the girl's hair. It was soft and thick and silky, almost like the angora's. 'Now we can go on. Where exactly had we got to?'

MISTER LIVINGSTONE

'MISTER LIVINGSTONE!'

Livingstone knocked the nail into the fence, not quickly, as if in answer to the voice, but with a kind of sick drowsiness. Wasn't he sick? He gave a bit of a cough, weakly. Chronic. Then, the nail in at last, almost caressed into the rotten wood by his feeble hammer blows, he turned to look at the farmhouse. His face, in the hot sun, was ruddily purple, his neck sun-burnished. He could see Mrs. Kilham at the bedroom window.

She called again. 'Mister Livingstone!'

Livingstone opened his mouth. It was a sign that he heard, that he was listening. It was a big mouth, raw, red-lipped: a mouth proper to a man weighing, like Livingstone, nearly two hundred pounds. But by dropping it open Livingstone made it sick too.

'I'm going out,' Mrs. Kilham called. 'Don't let the calves get in, whatever you do. Get the fence mended.'

He made a sick sign of acquiescence, a nod, a half closing of eyes, the dumb response of a man too weak to speak.

'Whatever you do don't let the calves in again.' She was still straightening her white straw sun-hat. Livingstone blinked as though it dazzled him. 'I'll be back in half an hour. There's more nails in the kitchen if you want them. There'll be no peace until we get that fence mended.'

She disappeared and Livingstone dropped the hammer in the long rye-grass by the fence. Wearily, as if there were no peace anyway, he began to roll himself a cigarette. The fence divided the paddock from what had once been the garden and what was now a calf-stamped mass of dock and poor cabbages and cotton-headed thistle. No potatoes, no beans, nothing in cultivation. Livingstone kept it. First he had been too sick to dig it, and then automatically too late to plant it even if it had been dug. Then the calves would keep getting in. The pigs followed, snouted and tootled round the gooseberries, rubbed the fence into an even more rickety-decay. It was Livingstone's duty to mend the fence, to keep the calves out, to curb the pigs. But what could a sick man do? Kilhams expected him to do everything.

And when, two minutes later, Mrs. Kilham came out of the house and across the sun-baked, cow-stinking yard, he could tell by the way she shut the door that she was in one of her tempers. He dropped the rolled unlit cigarette into his waistcoat pocket.

'I'm only going to get a loaf,' she said. 'I'll be back in half an hour.'

'Boss about?' Livingstone said.

'He's down the bottom field,' she said, 'hoeing swedes.' As if to say: 'Hoeing swedes, where you ought to be.' Livingstone knew.

'We ought to get the fence mended as quick as we can now,' she said, as though, Livingstone thought, she were helping.

'I can't do two men's work,' he said. He looked at the fence, the long wind-smashed snaky line of rotten wood and wire. 'It wants one holding and one nailing.' He shook it, sharply, with too much strength, so that he had to shake it again, with proper feebleness. 'It's no naughty weight. It takes some holding. I can't do two — '

'I'll help you hold it when I get back,' she said. 'I can hold it.'

Before he had time to make a gesture she walked off. With his big cow-like eyes he watched her disappear beyond the pond and the damsons and then through the road-gate. She walked quickly, young bare legs very brown against her white skirt. Hold the fence. Her holding the fence. She wanted nailing together herself. He belched contempt: a strong, healthy belch of a man in full prime of strength and digestion. He knew she hated him, wanted to get him out, had her knife in him. But so long as he was sick . . .

Out in the road she herself walked along with no other emotion but that hatred. Livingstone this, Livingstone that, always Livingstone. Always Livingstone, Mister Livingstone. The afternoon heat and the heat of her own anger fused and burnt her up completely, so that she walked almost in a physical trance. Mister Livingstone, *Mister* Livingstone.

A year ago she had been a dentist's assistant: attending to patients, answering the telephone, a good job. And now look at her. Married to Fred Kilham, bound irrevocably to a derelict farm, to a life sucked dry by Livingstone before she could even taste it. She remembered the beginning: what big hopes she and Kilham had had, how they had searched for a farm, how they had found it, complete with Livingstone. She wondered, now, how they could have been deceived by Livingstone — Livingstone the caretaker, Livingstone the man left in charge, Livingstone who had been so sick, Livingstone who had his furniture stored in the best bedroom, Livingstone who would be out as soon as he was well enough to lift a finger.

She looked back on the struggle, to the gradual evolution of the conflict to make ends meet, of the conflict between herself and Livingstone. Eighteen months of it were focused down into a single needlepoint of clear hatred in her mind. She walked rapidly, downhill. First she had been compassionate, since Livingstone was sick, then suspicious, then depressed, then antagonistic, then in despair — always because Livingstone was sick.

Or rather because he was not sick. Had he ever been sick? She doubted it now. Why hadn't she seen it? Why hadn't Fred seen it? She remembered Livingstone's first wheedlings — to be allowed to stay a little longer, to be given a bit of a job, to be allowed to do the garden. And how gradually that had evolved into Livingstone will do it, ask Livingstone, leave it to Livingstone. Until at last Livingstone had become, to her at least, a kind of perpetual evil.

Livingstone this, Livingstone that. Always Livingstone. *Mister* Livingstone. When could they hope, now, ever to get him out? He would go next week — how often had he promised! He would go as soon as he was well. He was never well. They couldn't turn a sick man out, furniture and all, into the road, could they?

Coming back, later, with the loaf, she could see the farmhouse, with decayed roof patched with reddened corrugated iron, set among tarred shacks beyond the damson-fringed pond. Seeing it, she felt for some reason calmer, more reasonable. Why shouldn't they say to him 'Get out to-morrow. Pack your things and get out'. Why shouldn't they say that? She would say it herself. Why shouldn't she say it? She would say it simply, calmly, without fuss or fear or anger. They were all afraid of Livingstone. She would make him finish the fence, so that the calves never got in again. She would dig the garden herself. She would sow radishes in it, and next year peas and beans and potatoes. It would be like a beginning all over again.

She came in by the back of the house, across the cow-yard. Sunk down, the yard, between its barns, held the heat, the thick heat of sun and cow-water and cow-dung intermingled. The place almost made her angry again — always they were going to do so much with it, clean it, rebuild it, modernize it, put it into an altogether new order. And always they did nothing. She had seen herself, at one time, as a dairymaid, white smock, white hands, white milk. Oh! everything so white. It was a stupid illusion. The milk was not even clean. How could it be clean? In that muck. How could anything be clean? 'Oh, it'll do for now. We'll make shift. One day I'll get Livingstone t'ave a clean-out and we'll whitewash it.'

She heard Fred saying it, and the words were symbolic of all the ramshackle, hand-to-mouth, rotten methods by which the farm was run. And then, to be reminded again of that eternal fatuous reliance on Livingstone — it was too much. It sent her into a kind of furious despair. She walked through the yard and the cow-stinking hovels without any longer knowing what she meant to do.

And then, coming round to the house, she heard sounds — quiet sounds, muffled, the sound of calves' feet. She began to run. She knew, even before she came within sight of the fence and the garden and the young calves browsing among the few cabbages, what had happened. A dozen calves — no Livingstone. No Livingstone. She dashed into the garden, madly waving her hands and the loaf, shouting, stampeding the calves against and at last through and over the smashed-down fence.

And having done that, she heard another sound. It came from among the damson trees. It was Livingstone stirring in the orchard grass. She half ran

towards the trees with a fury that surprised even herself.

Livingstone sat up, sick-eyed. 'I didn't feel — '

'You pack your things and get out,' she said. 'To-
morrow. If you don't pack them I'll throw them
out!'

'I ain't well . . . I — '

'Don't tell me that! Don't . . . Why didn't you
mend that fence?'

'I didn't feel — '

'Whether you're well or not you get out to-morrow.
For good.'

'The boss — '

'Never mind about the boss. I'm boss! I'm boss!
You hear me? Get up and get that fence done. Get up!
Get up! Do as I tell you! Get up!'

Suddenly before Livingstone could make the
habitual sick sound of protest, she brought the loaf
down on his head. She brought it down with two
hands, like a thunderbolt. Livingstone went suddenly
drunk. Eyes upraised, he looked at her for one
moment with aggrieved astonishment. Before he
could move she brought the loaf down again, flatly,
two-handed, with full strength and hatred. Livingstone, this time, upraised his hands, put them de-
fensively on his head. She brought down a terrific
blow on them, crashed him into a momentary senseless-
ness. He fell slowly back on the grass. She got him
by the shirt and pulled him upright again and hit him
full in the face with the bread. His face changed from
its strong blood-richened purple to white, to the first
signs she had ever seen in it of sickness.

'Get up!' she shouted.

He made some kind of inarticulate sound of wrath
and despair.

'Get up!' She held the loaf like a bomb. 'Do you hear me? Get up!'

Meekly, sick in reality now, he got up out of the grass, over two hundred pounds of almost six feet of healthy flesh. On his feet, he staggered about for a moment like a man after a knock-out.

'Get on with that fence!'

'I . . . Boss'll . . . I —'

Get on with that fence!

'I lost the hammer —'

'Find it!' He moved. She raised the loaf, with a gesture that was meant to be terrible. He accepted it. Shuffling off under the trees, he found the hammer in ten seconds. He began on the fence.

'You get out to-morrow!' she shouted.

He did not speak.

'You hear me? You get out to-morrow.'

'Yes, Mrs. Kilham.'

He knocked in his fifth nail. Simultaneously she, for some reason, burst into tears and began to run into the house.

Livingstone did not look up. He felt that there was no need to look up. Hammering the nail with sick drowsiness into the wood that was too rotten to hold it, he felt suddenly that there was no need to worry any longer. The tears made it all right.

And she, crying in the house, hearing the feeble sound of hammer against rotten wood in the hot still air, felt that she was, after all, up against something besides Mister Livingstone. And it seemed worse because, in her misery, she did not know at all what it was.

SOMETHING SHORT AND SWEET

THE car was stationary, by the wood-side, under snow-wet beeches. The man and the young woman sat in the front seats. They were also quite still. Outside nothing moved except the snow, which fell wetly, a slither of watery whiteness on the wind-screen, a wet frosting on grass and branches. The car hood was ripped and some snow had feathered in on the piles of books on the back seat. They were all red books, all the same book. The man had one of them, open, in one hand, with the other hand palm downwards on the flattened page, so that momentarily he looked like a man expounding a sermon.

'What is it you don't understand?' he said.

The girl looked anaemically at the snow, without speaking. She was about twenty. Her face reflected the dull whiteness of the snow, making her eyes snow-glassy.

'Is it anything in the book?' the man said. 'In here? If it is I can explain it. Don't be afraid. Tell me. Is it the book?'

'Partly.'

'Which chapter?' He waited for her to speak. She said nothing. In the intervals of speech he twitched his weak eyes, as though his spectacles were troubling him. He was about forty, with very dark hair that was greasy, and his coat collar shone at the edges with a sort of lead-coloured wax, the result of years of rubbing. He had many raw pimples on his face. 'Tell me which part, which chapter?' he said. His hat sat low on his ears, giving him an almost fanatical look of correctness. 'The Displacement of Self by God?' he said. 'Is that it?

Is it that which is troubling you? I admit it's difficult to understand. Is it that?'

'I don't know what it is,' she said.

She sat huddled up, cold to the bone, simply looking at the snow.

'You're not losing faith?' he said.

She shook her head. Waiting for her to speak, he twitched his weak eyes rapidly.

'You need vision,' he said earnestly.

'I know, I know,' she said. 'But people are so rude!' she burst out. 'They're so rude. They treat you like dirt.'

'They don't know,' he said blandly. 'They don't understand. Vision hasn't been granted to them as it has been to us. Vision isn't granted to everybody. It's just what happened to Christ. When you've been in the mission as long as I have you'll understand. You're new to it. We must bear the burden. It's our task. It's our mission. Don't you believe it?'

'I believe it when you say it,' she said. 'But I'm not so sure when I say it myself.'

He wetted his thumb and began turning over the leaves of the book. Looking at him, she saw suddenly that he had a button off his overcoat.

'You've lost a button,' she said. 'I'll sew it on. Where did you lose that, I wonder?'

'Where? What button?' he said. 'Don't worry. Here, this is it. Here — '

But she was out of the car. Merely to get out was a blessed, almost hysterical relief to her. She went round to the back of the car quickly. It was snowing fat wet blots. She undid the suit-case strapped to the luggage-grid and foraged in it and found a needle and cotton. Above the grid, on the back of the car, was chalked 'Galilee Gospel. Prepare to Meet Thy God'. The snow was beginning to wash the words out a little.

Back in the car she tried to thread the needle, but her hands were numb. She tried and tried again, until she outdid the man in extreme earnestness of expression. And all the time, as she vainly wetted and screwed and pointed the thread, he was expounding from the book on his knees.

'So long as the self dominates there can be no God,' he read out. 'And until there is God we shall know no fulfilment of true happiness. The worship of self means the rejection of Our Lord. Vice versa the acceptance of our Lord means the burying of the graven image of self. God is with us for ever, but the self is not and must perish.'

He left off reading and blinked. 'Surely that's clear?' he said.

His voice startled her. By a great effort she had almost threaded the needle. When he spoke her fingers trembled and she felt suddenly upset. She looked for a second as if she would cry out. But she just did nothing. The man also did nothing, taking no notice of her. In a moment she took up the thread again and he went on expounding and saying: 'That's clear, isn't it? You understand, don't you? You must see. It's vision you need. That's all.'

As he was speaking she felt painfully hungry. It was long after midday. That morning they had come about thirty miles out of Oxford, from headquarters. In other districts other workers for Galilee would have covered the same distance, for the same purpose. It was part of the spring campaign. Clear of the town, the man would stop the car every mile or so and the girl would get out and with a large piece of chalk would print the symbols of the creed on field-gates and telegraph poles, while the man kept a look out and waited. 'In the Midst of Life we are in Death', she chalked, or 'The Kingdom of Heaven is at Hand'. At the top of hills she chalked, 'Prepare to Meet Thy God', in the biggest letters of all. It had been savagely cold from the very beginning. Then the snow came on, her hands got frozen, and she made the journeys in absolute misery, in slush up to her ankles. Once he had a brain-wave. 'The Canker of Self is Eating your Soul', he said. 'Put that.' She had to chalk the words on two gate bars. The snow blinded her. She felt the snow go right through her heart. Then whenever they came to houses or a village he stopped the car again and she took a bundle of books and went the round of doors and chanted what was really, for her, a meaningless rigmarole:

'I speak for the Galilee Mission. In this great book you will find the solution to the problem of our existence here on earth. God is at hand. At any moment he may strike you down. Have no fear. Find God in this book. We are offering it at our special price of half a crown. Normally it is ten shillings. You will never see such a chance again. Make your peace with God before it is too late.'

Sometimes, often, she never got as far as that. She stood on the doorstep and, after a moment found herself speaking to space. It was that which crushed not only her but the meaning of it all too. Malfry was always telling her to emulate him, to have vision, to be inspired. But what was the use of being inspired if nobody listened?

'Shall we have something to eat?' she said.

'Do you feel clear about it?' he said. 'Until you believe it yourself how can others believe it?'

His voice was impersonal, hard as bone. She stuck the unthreaded needle absently into the dashboard and looked all the time at the snow. Then she got out some food from among the books on the back seat: four beef sandwiches and an apple. She ate ravenously. The man ate without pleasure, ascetically. Afterwards there was a little tea, in a thermos flask. All the time, as they drank, the girl kept looking at the man, expectantly, waiting for some kind of softening and change in him. Nothing happened. He kept turning over the pages of the book, reading odd paragraphs, making pencil notes, his earnest eyes blinking.

Then, when the food was finished, she was still cold. The wind came through the slit canvas hood and made a continuous mournful draught. The snow slithered everlastingly down the windows and the girl shivered.

'I think I'll put another jumper on,' she said. 'Do you mind?'

'No, I don't mind.' He did not look up.

She got out of the car again and fetched in the suit-case. The snow was almost yellow on the road, the tyre-tracks a dirty orange. In the car, kneeling on the seat, she opened the suit-case and found a dark green jumper. Then she put the suit-case back among the books and took off her coat. Underneath it she had on a brown jumper.

Suddenly she gave one look at the man and took it off. Her heart was thumping. Her small breasts were just visible above the skirt top.

'Mr. Malfry, shall I look best in the green one or the brown one?' she said.

'Eh?' He looked up, blinking, with open mouth. 'Oh! which you like.'

She waited for him to do something. She turned the green jumper right side out and sat there almost stupidly expectant, her heart pounding.

'I never showed you my birth mark, did I,' she said.

'Look here at it, on my shoulder. It's like a walnut.'

She let down her right shoulder strap. The man just looked at the birth mark, blinking his eyes, as though he could not see it properly.

'Isn't it funny?' she said. 'I've always had it. It's just the shape of a walnut.'

'So it is.' He laid his hand on the book. 'I've marked all the passages in the Displacement of Self by God which I think are obscure. You can have a look at them to-night. It's only vision you need. It's only faith.'

She sat forward, so that the whole of her skirt fell loose, the shoulder strap down, her small apple breasts as nearly visible as she dare let them be.

'We'd better get on,' the man said.

'Yes. Don't you think it funny about my birth mark?' she said.

He did not speak. He started the car. Very slowly she pulled on first the green jumper and then the brown and then, just before the car started, her coat. Putting on her coat she half stood up and when she sat down again her skirt was pulled up over her knees and she did not put it back again.

In a minute the car moved off into the snow. She sat quiet, her anaemic face intent.

'Don't worry if people are rude,' he said. 'You've got to suffer that. That's our mission. You've got to suffer many things before people see as you do.'

Ten minutes later he pulled up. The gate was black. Far off a cyclist was coming, a dark spot in the snow.

'Quick,' he said. 'Something short. God is love. Something short and sweet.'

She got out of the car and staggered through the snow to the gate. Slowly, with bitterly cold hands, she chalked the words on it, though by that time she could hardly see.

I AM NOT MYSELF

IT was summer when the Arnoldsons first asked me to go and stay with them. I could not go. I did not go until the following winter, on January 5th. It was bitterly cold that day, with thin drifts of snow whipped up from the ground like fierce white sandstorms, and there was snow on the ground almost every day until I left, four days later.

The Arnoldsons lived about seven miles from the nearest town. The house is quite ordinary: plain red brick, double-fronted, with large bay-windows and a large brass-knockered front door and a spotless white doorstep. It is the colour of a new flower-pot and at the back in the garden there is a long pergola of bay trees which is like a tunnel leading to nowhere.

Before that day in January I did not know any of the Arnoldsons except Laurence. We were at school together but we had not seen each other for fifteen years. He was an architect and I had written a letter to a paper about country architecture and he had seen it and that was how the invitation to stay with them had come about. Laurence Arnoldson is a man of medium height, with straight dark hair brushed back. He wears plain ascetic-looking gold spectacles and is a man of meticulous habits; always paring his finger-nails, polishing his glasses, splitting life into millimetres. His craze for exactitude and his contempt for people who have no time for it have made him a prig. He holds his head very high and you can see him looking down his nose at the world. The best thing about him are his eyes:

they are weak but they are a deep, rather strange shade of brown. There is something remote about them.

Laurence met me at the station that day in a fairly old but carefully kept Morris-Oxford, a four-seater. His father was with him. He sat in the front seat, huddled in a black rug, with a large shaggy grey scarf muffled round his head. The scarf covered almost all of his face except his eyes. As Laurence introduced me I saw that his father's eyes had exactly the same deep remote brownness as the son's. It was snowing a little at the time and Laurence had left the windscreen wiper working and I could see the man's eyes mechanically following its pendulum motions. They slid to and fro like two brown ball-bearings moving in grey oil, fascinated by the clear glass arc made by the wiper in the furred snow.

Laurence's father did not speak to me and neither he nor Laurence exchanged a word as we drove slowly out into the frozen country. Their silence depressed me. I felt it had something to do with myself. Now and then I made a remark and once, about half a mile from the house, we passed a pond frozen over and I said something about skating, and Laurence said:

'Oh! Yes. That's the pond where my sister saw a fox walk across the ice yesterday.'

The Arnoldsons' house stands on what was formerly a private estate and there is a private gravel road half a mile long leading up to it through fenceless fields that are planted with groups of elm and lime.

There is no Mrs. Arnoldson. She has been dead for thirteen years, and the house has been run for all that time by her sister, aunt Wilcox. It was aunt Wilcox who met us at the front door that afternoon, a dumpy woman with white hair scraped back sharply from her soap-polished face. She came out of the house briskly, shook hands with me without waiting to be introduced and then helped Mr. Arnoldson out of the car. I thought at first he had been ill, but then as he stood upright I could see that there was nothing wrong with him and that he was really a big and rather powerful man. His hands were very large-boned and his head, hugely swathed in the great scarf, had a kind of ill-balanced power about it. It swayed slightly to and fro as he walked, as though it were loose on the spine. He did not speak to me.

Aunt Wilcox spoke with a strong Yorkshire accent. The Arnoldsons themselves are Yorkshire people and the house is furnished in Yorkshire fashion: a rocking-chair in every room, big dressers, patchwork cushions, heavy pink-and-gold tea services. In the large drawing-room the curtains are of some claret-coloured woollen material, with plush bobbles, and they hang from great mahogany rods by mahogany rings that are like the rings on a hoop-la. On the mantelpiece stand two large china dogs, spaniels, black and white. They face each other and they appear to be looking at the same thing. They are extraordinarily lifelike.

I had been upstairs to unpack my things and had come down again and was looking at these dogs when Laurence came in to say that tea was ready. We went across the hall into the opposite room. It was about four o'clock and the white reflected light of the fallen snow was prolonging by a few minutes the fall of darkness. We sat down to tea in this strange snow-twilight, aunt Wilcox and Mr. Arnoldson opposite each other at the ends of the table, Laurence and I opposite, I myself opposite the window. The room was the exact reflection of the other. At the windows were the same sort of heavy woollen-bobbled curtains and on the mantelpiece stood what might have been the same pair of china spaniels watching with extraordinary lifelike fixedness some invisible object between them.

We sat there eating and drinking, without saying much. Aunt Wilcox poured tea from a huge electro-plated pot that might have held a gallon. The cups were like pink and gold basins.

I drink my tea very hot, and suddenly, as aunt Wilcox was taking my empty cup, I saw someone coming up the road towards the house. I knew at once, somehow, that it was Laurence's sister. She was wearing a big brown coat, but no hat. Every now and then she stepped off the road on to the grass and wandered off, as though looking for something. She was like some-one playing follow-my-leader with herself. Once she wandered farther off than usual and in the half-darkness I lost her for a moment. Then I saw her again. She was running. She was running quite fast and all at once she fell down on her knees in the snow and then ran on again. She was still running when she came to the house.

Two minutes later she came in. Her knees and the fringe of her coat were covered with snow where she had fallen down and there was a small salt-sprinkling of snow on her hair. She was about twenty-three, but she looked much younger, and I shall never forget how she came in, out of breath, to look at us with the same remote brown eyes as Laurence's, intensely excited, with a stare that had nothing to do with earth at all.

'I saw him again,' she said.

For a moment no one spoke. Then Laurence said: 'Who? The fox?'

'Yes. I saw him run over the pond again and then I chased him up through the park and then just as I got near the house I lost him.'

No one spoke a word.

That evening, after supper, she told me more about the fox. She described him: how bright he was and how good-coloured and how it was only in snowy or frosty weather that she saw him, and as she described him I saw him, bright, quiet, his back feet slipping from under him a little as he sloped across the ice on the small pond. I saw him as she saw him, as she wanted me to see him.

She told me about the fox in two or three minutes. She talked rather quickly, but all her impressions were in reality created with her eyes; the images of fox and snow and frozen pond were thrown up in them with untarnishable clarity. Unlike a great many people she looked straight at me while talking. Her eyes were full of great candour. They looked straight forward, with natural ardour. You felt that they could never look sideways. They had in them an unblemished honesty that was very beautiful and also very convincing, but also, in some way, empty.

For those two or three minutes we were alone. We had all had supper and we were going to play cribbage. Laurence had gone into his room to finish a letter and aunt Wilcox was in the kitchen. Mr. Arnoldson had gone upstairs to find a new pack of cards.

'I'd like to come out in the morning,' I said, 'and see this fox.'

She did not say anything.

In a little while first Laurence, and then Mr. Arnoldson and then aunt Wilcox came back, and we made arrangements to play. Cribbage was the only card game all of us knew and we decided to play in two pairs, for a shilling a horse, man out scoring. We cut the cards, ace high, lowest out, and aunt Wilcox said:

'It's you, Christiana. Mind now, no edging.'

The girl had cut a two of hearts, and I realized suddenly that it was the first time I had heard her name.

Aunt Wilcox and I played together. We were both rather quick, downright players, quick to sense a hand. We always had the pips counted before we put them on the table. This was not the Arnoldson way. Deliberation, to me an increasingly irritating deliberation, marked everything Laurence and his father did. They weighed up their hands guardedly and put on poker expressions, giving nothing away. Just as the girl spoke with her eyes, they played with their eyes. Between the counting of the hands they did not speak a word.

The game was a near thing and it looked, for a moment, as if aunt Wilcox and I might die in the hole, but we got home and I noticed aunt Wilcox pocketing the shilling. The Arnoldsons were not at all satisfied, and Laurence went over the last hand again, architect fashion, checking up, before giving in.

Mr. Arnoldson looked at Christiana. I forgot to say that he had a large grey sheep-dog moustache. The expression of his mouth was thus hidden. The whole expression of his face was compressed into his eyes. They shone very brightly, with a rather queer glassy look of excitement.

For the second game aunt Wilcox dropped out and Christiana took her place, playing with me. She was the quickest player I had ever seen. Every player gets now and then a hand he cannot make up his mind about, but that never happened to her. She played by instinct, second sight. She hardly looked at the cards. She kept her eyes on me. Yet she made up her mind before we began. I felt that, in some miraculous way, she could see through the cards.

All through the game she sat with her eyes on me. This constant but completely passionless stare had me beaten. It was hypnotic, so that whenever I looked away from her I was conscious of being drawn back. At first I thought it was deliberate, that she was simply trying hard to attract me. Then I got into the way of accepting her stare, of returning it. But where there should have been some response, there was only an unchanged anonymity, a beautiful brown wateriness filled with a remote, quietly hypnotic strength. I saw her as one of those composite pictures of two people. Two personalities are fused and there remains no personality, only some discomforting anonymity that fascinates.

During the game the tension between Christiana and her father increased. She was constantly one leap ahead of us all. She knew; we guessed. She had good cards, twice a hand of twenty-four. All the time I could see Mr. Arnoldson fidgeting, his eyes generating new phases of resentment.

Aunt Wilcox seemed to understand this. The Christmas decorations were still hanging up in the house, sprays of holly, withering now, stuck up behind the pictures, and a wand or two of box and fir. Suddenly aunt Wilcox said:

'Twelfth day to-morrow. We mustn't forget the decorations.'

'Pancakes,' Christiana said.

'Fifteen two and a pair's four and three's seven,' I said. 'Pancakes?'

'A north-country custom,' aunt Wilcox said. 'You fry the pancakes with a fire of the evergreens.'

'I think,' Laurence said, 'I have a pair.' He slowly laid out his cards. 'Mind you don't set the chimney on fire.'

Suddenly Christiana's hand was on the table. She

counted it like a parrot saying something by heart. She
had three sixes and a nine and a three was up and she
rattled it off, running the words together, making
eighteen. Eighteen was quite right, but Mr. Arnoldson
sprang to his feet, as though he had not heard it.

'Nineteen, nineteen, you can't score nineteen!' he
shouted. 'It's not possible in crib!'

'I said eighteen!'

'Eighteen is right,' I began.

'She said nineteen. I heard her. I distinctly heard
her. You think I don't know her voice?'

'Eighteen!' she said.

You said nineteen and now you're lying on top of it!'

He was on his feet, shouting at her, grey with anger.
Suddenly he began to shake violently and I knew he
had lost control. He turned round and picked up the
heavy mahogany Yorkshire chair he had been sitting
in and swung it about, over his head. Aunt Wilcox got
hold of Christiana and half pushed, half dragged her
out of the room, and I automatically went after her,
shouting after her as she ran upstairs in the darkness.

When I went back into the room, a moment later,
Mr. Arnoldson was lying on the hearth-rug, on his
back, in a fit. The chair was lying smashed on the
table where he had brought it down. He was clenching
in his hands some bits of withered holly he had torn
down from one of the pictures. His hands were bleed-
ing and it was a long time before we could get them
open again.

III

The next morning Laurence, aunt Wilcox, Christiana and I sat down to a large and healthy breakfast,

plates of porridge, lumps of rather fat beefsteak with fried mashed potatoes and eggs, thick toast and very strong marmalade, with the usual basins of tea. It was all very solid, very real. Unlike the behaviour of Mr. Arnoldson on the previous night it was something you could get your hands on and understand. Mr. Arnoldson did not appear at breakfast and no one said anything about him.

During breakfast Laurence read his letters and said he had a couple of hours' work to do and would I mind amusing myself? In the afternoon we could go and look at some houses; there were one or two good stone mansions in the neighbourhood. It was still bitterly cold that morning, but there had been no more snow. The snow of yesterday had been driven, like white sand, into thin drifts, leaving exposed black islands of ice.

I decided to go for a walk, and after breakfast I asked Christiana to come with me. 'We could look for the fox,' I said.

Except for refusing, she did not say much. She was going to help aunt Wilcox. About the fox she was very evasive. It might not have existed. She might not have seen it.

'I'll have a look for it myself,' I said.

She looked at me emptily, not speaking. Her eyes had lost completely the natural ardour and candour, both very childlike, which had infused the picture of the fox with reality and which had made me believe in both it and her. At that moment she could not have made me believe in anything.

I got my overcoat and gloves and went out. It was an east wind, steady, bitter, the sky a dull iron colour, without sun. In the fields the grass had been driven flat by wind. The earth was like rock. In a scoop of the

land a small stream flowed down between squat clumps
of alder, catkins wind-frozen, cat-ice jagging out like
frosted-glass from the fringe of frost-burnt rushes on
both banks. Farther on a flock of pigeons clapped up
from a field of white kale, clattering wings on steel
leaves, spiralling up, gathering, separating again like
broken bits of the dead sky.

I went on until I found the pond. I knew it at once
because, a field away, I could see the road, and because
of what Christiana had said about it. She had described
the black sloe bushes barricading one side, the speared
army of dead rushes, and a broken-down, now half-
submerged cattle-trough on which the fox, she said, had
leapt and sat and stared at her. The pond was covered
with ice and the ice in turn with the fine salt snow swept
in a succession of smooth drifts across it.

I stood and looked at the pond. Then I walked
round it. At the opposite point, by the cattle-trough,
I stood and looked at it again. On the cattle-trough
the light snow crusts were unbroken, and on two sides
of it, away from the water, snow had drifted in long
arcs, rippled and firm as lard. On the trough and in
the snow drifted round it and all across the pond there
were no marks of any fox at all.

I V

When I got back to the house, about twelve, aunt
Wilcox and Christiana were taking down the decorations. Most of the evergreens had been hung up in the
hall, holly behind the pictures, sheaves of yew tied to
the newel-posts of the polished pine staircase, and a
very dry spray of mistletoe hung from the big brass

oil-lamp. Aunt Wilcox and Christiana were putting the evergreens into a zinc bath-tin.

'You're just in time,' Christiana said.

'Last come must last kiss,' aunt Wilcox said.

'And what does that mean?' I said.

'You've got to kiss us both.'

Laughing, aunt Wilcox stood under the mistletoe and I kissed her. Her lips were solid and sinewy, like beefsteak, and lukewarm wet. As she clasped me round the waist I felt her coopered, with stays, like a barrel. Then Christiana stood under the mistletoe and I kissed her. Just before I kissed her she looked at me for a moment. Her eyes had the same remote anonymity as on the previous day, the same tranquil but disturbing candour. As I kissed her she was quite still, without fuss. Kissing her was like kissing someone who was not there. It was a relationship of ghosts. For one moment I felt I was not there myself. The recollection of this unreal lightness of touch was something I carried about with me for the rest of the day.

That afternoon Laurence and I went for a walk. I asked after his father and he said he was better, but resting. We talked about him for a short time. He told me how he had begun as a pit-boy in a Yorkshire colliery, but had worked himself up, and had later become a schoolmaster. Then the war broke out and he felt suddenly that he was wasted in the class-room and had gone back to the pit, to become under-manager. After about six months there was a disaster in the pit, an explosion that had brought down a vast roof-fall, entombing thirty-five men. Arnoldson went down for rescue work. For two days he could hear the voices of the entombed men quite clearly, then for a whole day he could hear them intermittently, then they ceased. But though they ceased Arnoldson fancied all the time he could still hear them, the voices of the dead, of men he had known, screaming or whispering in his mind more sharply than in life. He went on hearing these voices for weeks, the voices of people who were not there, until they broke him down. Christiana had been born about a year later.

Laurence spoke of his father with a slight impatience. He spoke as though, occupied himself with concrete things, the small matter of voices disturbing the spirit of another man had no material importance for him. It was clear that he did not believe in voices. From the subject of his father we went on to the subject of himself. I walked with head slightly down, mouth set against the wind, saying yes and no, not really listening, my thoughts in reality a long way behind me, like a kite on a string.

When we got back to the house, about four o'clock, I noticed a curious thing as we went past the dining-room. The door of the room was open and I could see that one of the china spaniel dogs was missing from the mantelpiece. At the time I did not take much notice of this. I went upstairs to wash my hands and came down and went into the drawing-room. Christiana sat reading by the fire, but for about half a minute I did not look at her. One of the china dogs was missing from the mantelpiece.

It was only about ten seconds after this that I heard Laurence coming downstairs. His way of coming downstairs was unmistakable. I heard his feet clipping the edges of the stairs with the precision of an engine firing in all its cylinders: the assured descent of a man who knew he could never fall down.

As he came down into the hall Christiana suddenly went to the door and said in a loud voice:

'Tea's ready. You're just right.'

We went straight into the dining-room. Christiana was last. She shut the door of the drawing-room after her. On the mantelpiece of the dining-room the two china dogs sat facing each other.

All through tea I sat looking at Christiana. She sat looking at me, but without any relationship between the eyes and the mind. Her eyes rested on me with a stare of beautiful emptiness. It might have been a stare of wonder or distrust or adoration or appeal: I could not tell. There was no way of telling. For the first time I saw some connection between this expressive vacancy and the voices that Mr. Arnoldson had heard in his mind. Sitting still, eyes dead straight but not conscious, she looked as though she also were listening to some voices very far away.

Just as we were finishing tea, aunt Wilcox said to me: 'I hope you didn't get cold this afternoon. You look a bit peaked.'

'I'm all right,' I said. 'But I never really got my feet warm.'

'Why don't you go and put on your slippers?' Christiana said.

'I'd like to,' I said.

So I went upstairs to put on my slippers, while Laurence went to write his evening letters, and aunt Wilcox and Christiana cleared the table. It was Sunday and aunt Wilcox was going to chapel.

I came downstairs again in less than five minutes. Christiana was sitting by the fire in the drawing-room. The two china dogs sat on the mantelpiece. I looked at the dogs, then at Christiana, with double deliberation. She must have seen I was trying to reason it out, that perhaps I had reasoned it out, but she gave no sign.

I sat down and we began to talk. It was warm; the

small reading-lamp imprisoned us, as it were, in a small world of light, the rest of the room an outer darkness. I tried to get her to talk of the fox. There was no response. It was like pressing the buttons of a dead door-bell. Once I said something about her father. 'He's asleep,' she said. That was all. We went on to talk of various odd things. She lay back in the chair, facing the light, looking quietly at me. I fixed my eyes on hers. I had a feeling, very strong after a few minutes, that she wanted me to touch her. All at once she asked me had I ever been abroad? I said: 'Yes, to France once, and Holland once. That's all. Holland is lovely.' She did not say anything at once. She looked slowly away from me, down at the floor, as though she could see something in the darkness beyond the ring of light. Suddenly she said: 'I've been to Mexico, that's all.' I asked her for how long. She looked up at me. Without answering my question she began to tell me about Mexico. She told me about it as she had told me about the fox, speaking rather quickly, telling me where she had been, reciting the beautiful names of the places, talking about the food, the colour, the women's dresses. I had a feeling of travelling through a country in a train, in a hurry, getting the vivid transient panoramic effect of fields and villages, sun and trees, of faces and hands suddenly uplifted. She described everything quickly, her voice certain and regular, like a train passing over metals. She described an episode about Indians, how she had gone up into the mountains, to a small town where there was a market, where thin emaciated Indians came down to sell things, squatting close together on the ground in the cold, with phlegmatic and degenerate eyes downcast. There a woman had tried to sell her a few wizened tomatoes, holding them out with blue old veined hands, not speaking, simply holding the tomatoes out to her. Then suddenly, because the girl would not have them, the woman had squeezed one of them in a rage until seeds and juice ran out like reddish-yellow blood oozing out of the fissures between her frozen knuckles. As the girl told it, I felt rather than saw it. I felt the bitter coldness of the little town cut by mountain winds and the half-frozen juice of the tomato running down my own hands.

She went on talking, with intervals, for about an hour. After a time, some time after she had told me about the Indian woman, I had again the feeling that she wanted me to touch her. Her hands were spread out on her lap. I watched the light on them. I could see the slight upheaval of the white fingers, regular and intense, as she breathed, and this small but intense motion radiated a feeling of inordinate and almost fearful strength. The effect on me was as though I were looking down into very deep, not quite still water: an effect slightly hypnotic, slightly pleasurable, quietly governed by fear. I felt afraid to take my eyes away from her and I felt, after a time, that she did not want me to take them away.

After a time I did something else I knew she wanted me to do. I went and sat by her, in the same chair. I put my arms round her, not speaking a word. As I held her I could feel her listening. Perhaps she is listening, I thought, for someone to come. She did not speak. I could feel her fingers, outspread, clutching my back, as though she were falling into space. After a time she spoke.

'What did you say?' she said. I sat silent. 'What did you say?' she said. 'I thought I heard you say something.'

'No,' I said, 'I didn't speak.'

'Perhaps it was someone else?' she said.

I sat still. I did not say anything. Her breathing was slightly deeper. All the time I could feel her listening, as though waiting for the echo of some minute explosion on the other side of the earth.

'Don't you ever think you hear the voices of people who are not here?'

'Everybody does that,' I said.

'I mean you.'

'Sometimes.'

'Often?'

'Not often.'

The small reading-lamp stood on a table between the chair and the fireplace. I felt her stretch out her hand towards it. About us, for one moment the house seemed dead still. She put out the light. I heard the small click of the switch freeing us, as it were, from the restriction of light. She put her hands on my face, held it. I remember wondering suddenly what sort of night it was, if it were starlight, whether there was snow.

'Can you see me?' she said.

'No.'

'I can see you.'

I felt her withdraw herself very slightly from me. Then I knew why she could see me. I was sitting facing the window and through the slits of the dark curtains I could see blurred snow-white chinks of moonlight.

v

We did not have supper, that night, until nine o'clock. We had Yorkshire ham and pork pie, cold apple tart, with red cheese, mince pies and cheese-cakes, with large basins of strong tea. Aunt Wilcox had pickles and towards the end of the meal we pulled half a dozen crackers that had been left over from Christmas. Out of her cracker Christiana had a tall white paper hat in the twelfth-century style, pointed, like a cone. As she put it on I got an instant impression that the dark brown eyes, under the white cap, looked darker than ever, and that they were slightly strange, not quite real, and for the first time it hurt me to look at them.

This impression continued until the following day. The moonlight was very strong nearly all night and I did not sleep well. All through the next morning I wanted to be alone with Christiana, but the chance did not seem to come. Mr. Arnoldson came downstairs and sat all day in front of the drawing-room fire, wrapped in rugs, so that the drawing-room was never empty. The two china dogs sat on the mantelpiece there and were not, as on the previous day, changed at all. Once I heard the voices of aunt Wilcox and Christiana coming from the kitchen. They were talking about the dogs. 'It's in my room,' Christiana said. 'I've stuck it with seccotine.' I sat most of that morning in Laurence's study, reading. He went in mostly for technical books and towards the end of the morning I got bored and asked him if he had any books of travel. He said there were a few in his bedroom. I went up to his room and there, on his chest of drawers, I found a book on Mexico. I took it downstairs and in five minutes I was reading the episode about the tomato and the Indian woman in the little cold mountain town.

In the night there had been another fall of snow, but it was a little warmer. The sun was very brilliant on the snow and out of Laurence's study window I could see, high up, peewits flashing like semaphores, white and dark against the very blue winter sky. I felt I had to get out.

I went out and walked across the fields, in the snow, past the brook and over towards the pond. The white of the snow was dazzling and I felt a slightly dazed effect, the light too sharp for my eyes. Along by the brook the snow was beginning to melt a little on the branches of the alders, bringing down showers of bright ice rain. I could see everywhere where rabbits had loped about in the early morning snow and there were many prints of moorhens, but there was nothing that looked at all like the mark of a fox.

The snow had covered everything of the pond and the surface was smoother than water. I stood and looked at it for a moment and then went on. A little farther on I picked up the brook again and I did not come back for half an hour.

Coming back I saw Christiana. I could see where she had walked in the snow. She had walked round the pond and now she was about half a field away, going back towards the house. I called and she turned and waited for me, standing against the sun. She stood with her arms folded, her big coat lapped heavily over her. Her face was white with the strong upward reflection of snow.

We walked on together. She walked with her arms continually folded. 'Have you seen the fox?' I said.

She did not answer. I knew I did not expect her to answer. Farther on we had to cross the brook by a small wooden bridge. On the bridge I stopped her, holding her coat. I put my arms round her and held her for a moment. Holding her, I could feel, then, why she walked with her arms folded. She had something under her coat. She kissed me without speaking. All the time I could feel her holding some object under her coat, as hard as stone.

We stood there, above the sun-shining water, slightly dazzled by the world of snow, for about five minutes, and I kissed her again. She was acquiescent, but it was an acquiescence that was stronger, by a long way, than all the strange remote activity of her spirit had ever been. It was normal. I felt for the first time that she was there, very young, very sweet, very real, perhaps a little frightened. Up to that time we had said nothing at all about affection. I had not thought of it. Now I wanted her. It seemed very natural, an inevitable part of things.

'You like me, don't you?' I said. It was all I could think of saying.

'Yes,' she said.

'Very much?'

'Very much.'

She smiled very quietly. I did not know what to do except to smile back. We walked on. Out in the open snow I stopped and, before she could do or say anything, kissed her again.

'Someone will see us.'

'I don't care,' I said.

I was very happy. At that moment, out in the snow, walking away from the sun, watching our two blue shadows climbing before us up the slight slope to the house, I had no doubts about her. Half an hour before I had wanted to tell her that I knew there was no fox, that she had never been to Mexico, that all that she had told me was an imposture. Now it did not seem to matter. And the voices? They did not seem to matter either. Many people hear the voices of people who are not there, who have never been there. There is nothing strange in that.

I was worried only by one thing: what she was carrying under her coat. Then, when we went in for lunch

I knew, for certain, that it was the china dog. And that night I knew why it was.

Mr. Arnoldson went to bed very early that night, about half-past seven, and aunt Wilcox went upstairs with him, to see that he was all right. Laurence had gone down to the post office and I was sitting in the drawing-room, reading the morning paper. From the dining-room, suddenly, I could hear voices.

They went on for five minutes and I could not understand it. At last I got up and opened the drawing-room door. Across the hall the dining-room door was open a little and Christiana was sitting at the dining table, talking to a china dog.

'The fox,' she was saying, 'the fox!'

I stood looking. She was jabbering quite fast to the dog, strangely excited, her fingers tense.

'Christiana,' I said.

She did not hear me.

'Christiana.'

She got the dog by the neck and ran it across the mahogany table, towards a glass fruit dish, in crazy pursuit of something, jabbering, laughing a little, until I could see that the dog had the fox by the neck and that they were tearing each other to bits in the snow.

I saw it quite clearly for a moment, like a vision: the mahogany changed to snow, the fruit dish to fox, the china dog to a dog in reality, and in that moment, for the first time, I felt a little mad myself.

I went away on the following afternoon. Laurence drove me to the station. Nothing much happened. It was snowing fast and Christiana did not come outside to see us off. She stood at the window of the drawing-room, staring out. Except that her face was white with the reflection of the snow, she looked quite normal, quite herself. No one would have noticed anything.

But as we drove away I saw her, for one second, as someone imprisoned, cut off from the world, shut away.

We had not much time for the train and Laurence drove rather fast. 'You look a bit queer,' he said at the station. 'Are you all right?'

'Yes,' I said.

'Are you sure? Let me carry your bag. You don't look quite yourself.'

I could not speak. No, I thought, I am not myself.

THE WREATH

THE train was almost ready to start when the old man and the girl came into the carriage. The girl was very sweet with him, putting his travelling case and the wreath on the rack, reminding him of things, kissing him very tenderly good-bye.

'You know where you're going? Now don't forget. Ham Street. First stop and then you change and get the other train. You think you'll remember? Ham Street and change first stop?'

'Yes. I think I shall remember.'

'And carry the wreath this way up. Like this. You see, there's a little handle.'

He said yes, he would remember and carry it that way up, and then she kissed him good-bye through the open window and the train moved away.

'Oh! dear,' he said to me, 'we went to the wrong station and then had to run for it.'

He was dressed all in black. He had pure white hair and a very pink fresh face, and he looked rather like a picture of a French priest. He gave me a smile. 'When you get over eighty, running for trains isn't what it used to be.'

'You're not over eighty?' I said.

'Oh! yes. Eighty-three. You think I don't look it?'

He looked perhaps seventy. I said so.

'They all say that,' he said. 'No, eighty-three. At eighty I had an illness, a sort of stroke, and the doctors said, "You won't get better". Then I did get better and they said, "It's very remarkable. We'll give lectures on you", and so they've been giving lectures on me.' He looked up at the rack. 'Is the wreath all right?'

'Yes,' I said, 'it's all right.'

He was silent and I thought perhaps he was tired of talking and I handed him an evening paper.

'No,' he said, 'thank you. Thank you all the same. But since my illness I can't read. I can write, but I can't read.' He looked out of the window at the darkness. 'Yes,' he said, 'Yes.'

He looked at me. 'What were we talking about?'

'You were telling me,' I said, 'how you could write but not read.'

'Ah yes. Yes.' He began to forage in his pockets. 'Yes, I can write. I write quite well, quite straight.' He turned out first one pocket and then another. 'I am trying to find a specimen of my writing.' He found a piece of blue paper. 'No. That's who I am, where I'm travelling to. In case I get lost.'

He gave me the paper to read. It had written on it: 'Simpson. Travelling to Ham Street.'

'I am going to a funeral,' he said. 'Is the wreath all right?'

'Yes,' I said, 'it's all right.'

He took out his snuff-box, opened it and handed it to me. I thanked him and said no. The box was silver and on the lid were engraved figures of men cycling. He said, 'The arms of my cycling club. I do a great deal of cycling.'

'Still?'

'Oh, yes! In the summer. Oh, yes! I cycle all over the countryside.'

Again he looked out of the window, briefly, watching the darkness. Then he looked at me.

'What were we talking about?'

'About the cycling.'

'Ah, yes. Yes. About the cycling. Oh! yes, I'm energetic. I go into the bathroom every morning and wash in cold water and do my exercises. Take a bath once a week. Cycle in summer.'

He held out his hands to me.

'Are they the hands of a man of eighty-three?'

They were full, beautiful hands, wonderfully pink and fresh like his face.

'Oh, no!' he said. 'In summer I cycle from Ham Street to Rye, three times a week, to get a shave.'

'That's a long way.'

'Seven miles.'

For a time he told me about the cycling. Then he began to tell me about his youth.

'I was a grocer. An apprentice.' He stopped. 'But this is not fair to you. Talking about myself.'

'I like it,' I said.

'You have some way of making me do it,' he said. He paused, looked up. 'The wreath is all right?'

'Yes, it's all right. I'll watch it.'

'What were we talking about?'

I told him.

'Oh, yes. We sold everything. Provisions, furniture, blankets, stockings. A big connection. I used to drive about the country in a trap, taking orders. Ladies' stockings. Oh, yes! In those days you measured the length of the leg. Pleasant. Blankets was another thing. I remember selling a hundred pairs of blankets in one day, just by telling them that I'd dreamed it was going to be the coldest winter on record.'

'And now,' I said, 'it's all different?'

'Oh, yes!'

'You sit back and take it easy?'

'Oh, no! I'm the director of a company with a capital of five million.' He put his hand on his neck-tie. 'You see that pin?'

'The Prince of Wales's feathers?'

'Exactly. The late Edward VII gave it to me. Any time I like I can walk into Buckingham Palace.'

The train was rushing on. The wreath trembled as we swayed over points.

'What was I saying?'

I reminded him. He went on to talk about his daughter. 'She is a pianist. You may have heard of her?' He told me her name. I said yes, I had heard of her.

'You are musical yourself?' he said.

'Yes.'

'I knew it. You have a musical face.'

I told him how I heard his daughter, often, play the piano. He was touched. The train rushed on, lights were hurled past us in the darkness. Sitting silent, he suddenly looked frail and tender. I thought of him as a boy, measuring the ladies' legs for stockings, in the seventies. He took out his snuff-box.

'You really won't try any?'

I hesitated.

'Go on.'

'All right.'

'Snuff said!' he laughed.

We took snuff together, holding the pinches delicately in our hands, his own strong and pink, the sniff of his nostrils urgent and deep.

'I shan't forget you,' he said. 'I keep a diary. I shall put you in it.'

We sat silent. I felt suddenly very close to him, as though I had known him a long time. He looked out of the window, at the travelling blackness, then at me again.

'Where am I going?' he said, like a child.

'To Ham Street. Don't you remember?' I said.

'Oh, yes! I remember.'

We talked a little more, I blew the snuff down my nose, and then I saw lights flashing past, increasing, in the darkness, and the train began to slow down.

I got up. 'I'll get the wreath down for you,' I said.

I reached up and got down the wreath and the suit-case. I held the wreath by the little handle of string looped at one end. 'I'll carry it and find out about your train,' I said.

'It's very nice of you.'

When the train stopped at the junction we got out and I found out about his train and then took him to where it was waiting, in the opposite platform. He got into the carriage and I followed him and settled his things for him, putting the wreath on the rack above his head.

'You know where you're going?' I said.

'Yes. I haven't forgotten.'

We said good-bye and shook hands and slowly, in a little while, the train moved off. He waved his beautiful pink hands out of the window and the wreath trembled above his head.

THE MACHINE

EVERY evening, up at the farm, we saw the same men go past, out towards the villages, at the same time. They were coming home from the factories down in the valley: men escaping from the machine.

And though we got to know them well by sight, first the young chaps, racing hard, with flying mufflers, then the old stagers, the old tough shoe-finishers still wearing polish-blackened aprons, then the man with the black cork-leg and only one pedal to his bicycle, there was one we knew really well. His name was Simmons. We called him Waddo.

When Waddo went past we lifted hands from hoes or rakes, or even waved a cabbage that we might be cutting, and hailed him. 'Way up!' we called.

'Waddo!' he shouted, and sailed on.

But three times a year, at hay-time, harvest and threshing, when we needed extra hands, he stopped to help us. He rode his pink-tyred semi-racing bike into the stackyard, unstrapped his dinner-basket, rolled up his sleeves and looked round at us, as we stood stacking corn or unloading hay, with a look of tolerant contempt. As though to say, 'You poor miserable devils. Bin here since morning and all you done is stack up three ha'porth o' hay. Well, spit on me big toe, spit on it. If you ain't a bleedin' limit.' It was the look of a giant for a degenerate collection of pitch-fork pygmies. Waddo himself stood five feet three.

But when he came into that yard we were transformed. He flung himself to work with an almost daemonic fury of strength. The muscles of his small arms were tight as clockwork springs under the white factory-blanched flesh. His little head, with thin wire-brush hair worn bald at the temples, was like a bullet that might have gone off at any moment with an explosive bang of enthusiasm or disgust. He worked swiftly, with the slight puffed swagger of a man of mountainous physique, incessantly talking, always comic, spitting mouthsful of patient disgust for us who worked so hard all day and did nothing. There was some extra volcanic force in Waddo, who never tired, never gave up, and was never beaten. Coming from the machines, he was like a machine himself. 'Waddo,' we'd say to him, 'blowed if you don't go on wheels.'

'I bleedin' well have to,' he'd say, 'don't I?' And we knew, with his five-mile ride to work and his five miles back, his eight-hour day holding boots to the jaws of a stitcher in the factory, his seven children, his readiness to mow with his own hands, in his spare time, every blade of grass and every standing acre of corn in the parish, how true it was. 'I got a day's work to git through in half,' he'd say. 'Not like some folks.'

'What you need on this place,' he'd say at last, 'is machinery.'

In any discussion of the machine Waddo held us as it were at arm's length, in contempt. 'Call yourself bleedin' farmers, and ain't got a machine on the place. No binder, no hay-turner, no root-cutter. No tater-riddler, no nothing. Blimey, spit on me big toe, spit on it. Ain't you up to date? Here you are scrattin' about like old hens scrattin' for daylight, when a couple o' machines'd bring you right bang-slap up with the times. Machines — that's what you want. Save yourself time and money. See! They do away with the men.'

The machine was his god. It was exemplified in his racing bike, in the stitcher which he fed all day with boots like some omnivorous steel brute at the factory, in the threshing-drum we hired once every winter. Working so beautifully, swiftly and naturally with his own hands, he exalted the mechanism that could have cut out the element of man. It fed his devotion with the same daemonic energy as he worked, so that he preached at us with one hand on the futility of a machineless world and showed us, with the other, how incomparable and effective it could be. With the machinery of his two hands he swung a scythe with a masterly and precise beauty that no machine could ever have shown.

And at heart, I think, he knew it. He mowed very fast, as though carelessly, off-hand, apparently indifferent. He was often not so tall, by a foot, as the corn he cut. Head down, he had a certain air of detached dreaminess, as though the whole thing meant nothing to him at all.

Then, at the end of the swathe, he would turn and look back; and we would see, for a moment, the beauty of the work recaptured in his own eye, the small light of pleasure glinting out as though a bead of sweat had been caught in the pupil. He gazed, as we did, at the level alleys of stubble, short and straight as though the corn were sprouting up white again, the golden-white corn stalks shining as if sun-oiled, the sienna-gold sweep of ears and the straight wall of standing corn, and he must have known that he was a master hand.

But always in time, the obsession of the machine caught him up again. 'How many acres of wheat you got here? Ten? Gonna take us a week to move it. Now with a binder — '

We would say something about expense.

'Expense! Spit on me big toe. You can't see for looking. Expense! You can save the bleedin' cost of the thing in a couple o' years. Save money, save men. Don't you see?'

Sometimes he would work on into the still August moonlight, tireless as a machine himself, mowing, whetting the scythe, dropping the scythe to fall flat on some escaping leveret, mowing again, still arguing, still abusing us, then biking off, at last, across the moon-dewed land with the energy of a man just beginning a cycle race.

'Don't you want a light?' we'd say to him.

'Light? Spit on me big toe, I s'll be home and in bed with the missus afore you can strike a match.'

He abused and decried us all through harvest and hay-making. At threshing he got his reward. In the engine and drum he saw, at last, a sensible interpretation of life: a complicated system of power and steam, a miracle, a single unit doing the work of scores of men. 'Some sense,' he'd say, 'at last.'

He took a day off from the factory, then, to help us, arriving at six in the morning, and we saw then that we had never seen him except as a tired man. He skidded into the yard at full speed, bounced off his bicycle, seized his pitch-fork as though ready to lift a complete corn-stack with one finger. He argued vociferously, held us at the usual arm's length of contempt, laughed and joked and worked as always with the same casual and yet explosive and masterly rhythm. Working high up in the drum, on the edge of a maelstrom, he bawled down to us below with gigantic accents, though nobody could hear, feeding sheaves to the drum with the pleasure of a man feeding a favourite beast.

We threshed, one year, in November. The wind came down on us from the north-east, with intermittent bites of ice-rain, across bare land. The power of the wind roaring under the drum spouted up a terrific blast of chaff, all day long, that was like hail on the naked eyes. Above, chaff and chaff-dust were winnowed from the cracks of the drum in fierce little clouds, as though she were spitting ice vapour. Higher still, on the roof of the drum, the men caught by the full force of wind and up-blown chaff and wind-blasted straw worked all day half-blinded.

Waddo was on the drum. Exhilarant in that terrific wind, he worked as though the wind shot him new energy. He bawled down at us with a mouth that, against the roar of drum and engine and wind, was quite soundless. But we understood, we felt the words in his expression of contemptuous triumph. 'See? Didn't I tell you? Spit on me toe — didn't I tell you what a machine could save you?'

That day the rats began to run out of the first stack about eleven o'clock. We pursued and hemmed and cornered them, smashing them to lumps of grey-red jelly in the wind-littered straw. From above Waddo looked down on us like a director of operations, yelling and waving his fork.

As he stood there, jack-in-the-boxing, gesticulating, laughing, a rat leapt out of a sheaf he was lifting. We saw his own leap of energetic excitement and knew the words he yelled by long habit and the shaping of his lips:

'Spit on me big toe, spit on it! Waddo! Spit on me — '

We saw him slip. We knew how the iron-shod boots must have slid on the loose kernels of polished grain, on the straw-smoothed roof of the drum. He lifted a wild hand and he yelled and shouted. The engine-man threw on the brakes and we heard the shriek and moan of stopped machinery.

'Waddo!' we yelled, 'Waddo! For Christ's sake! Waddo!'

There was no answer; and in a world that stood still we knew that the machine had claimed him.

THE SHIP

My aunt Franklin, a long time ago, kept a small shop on the top of the high pavement. My uncle Franklin, who was dead, had been a taxidermist. But it is not about either of them that I want to tell you. They had a son, Ephraim Franklin, a sailor.

Whenever I went to see my aunt Franklin she was sitting in the room behind the shop. This room and the shop were filled with cases of stuffed animals and fish and butterflies and in this gloomy north facing little room, always so dull that even the colours of the butterflies seemed like dusty paint and the eyes of the animals as dull as shoe buttons, my aunt Franklin would sit talking or thinking about her son. His ship was called *The Mary Porter* and she was a sailing ship, a square rigger. Her port was Greenock and she made a fairly regular passage to Australia, taking a hundred days, even a hundred and fifty days; or she would be outward bound for Singapore, to await new orders there, going down afterwards to New Guinea, or Java, or Celebes, or Sumatra, or Borneo. And so because of this, because it took *The Mary Porter* a hundred and fifty days out and perhaps a hundred and fifty days back, the most my aunt Franklin could ever hope to see her son was once a year. And in the meantime, for two hundred and fifty or even three hundred days, all she thought of was Ephraim, anxiety for Ephraim, joy for Ephraim, Ephraim in the East Indies, Ephraim working hard to be second mate, Ephraim's photograph on the wall, until at last Ephraim himself came home, from the South Seas.

The first time I ever saw Ephraim I was about ten

or eleven. I went to see my aunt on a cold mizzling November afternoon and there, in the back room, home from a voyage of a hundred and thirty-five days from Sydney, sat Ephraim. He was then the second mate of *The Mary Porter*, a big man with a thick ginger beard and ice-blue eyes and stiff ginger hair on the backs of his hands. He talked to me all that afternoon; or rather he talked to my aunt, telling her stories. 'Mother, they was twice as long as this room, these codfish. They'll eat a man, I tell you,' or 'Mother, I'd tell you about the Mokoru tribe in New Guinea only it'd turn your stomach before tea,' or 'Yes, Mother, next voyage it'll be first mate. First mate. Mister Franklin.' And I listened to him all that afternoon as he sat picking bits of tobacco out of his teeth with a bodkin, his voice conjuring up for me the sight and smell of foreign parts, strange islands, *The Mary Porter* sailing beyond tropical horizons. He ate six soft-boiled eggs for tea that day, I shall always remember it, and then after tea he went upstairs and came down with a black tin box, carrying it by the handle. 'Mother,' he said, 'I'll give you six guesses.' So she sat there with her chin on her knuckles, an ivory-faced plain frail-looking little woman who looked the last person in the world to be the mother of a hairy second mate as big as he was, and guessed what it was he had brought her from the South Seas. She guessed a parrot, a pair of slippers, a comb, a shawl and then she gave it up. 'No,' he said, 'wrong every time.' It was an ivory box, carved with figures of fish and ships, and in it was a necklace of white coral. She loved them both and her face went as white as the coral and there were tears in her eyes. 'Ah! you wait,' he said, 'one day I'll bring you summat worth bringing. I'll bring you a necklace of black pearls. Black pearls. How's that, eh?' And suddenly he became aware of my standing there, listening and gaping at them both, and he said: 'Here, son, you nip off now and come in to-morrow. You come in to-morrow and I'll show you the model I'm making of *The Mary Porter.*'

The next day was Sunday and I could not go, but I went on Monday and he showed me the model of *The Mary Porter.* He had been making it for three voyages. When would it be finished? I said. 'When will it be finished?' he said. 'Oh! in about two more. I'll finish it before I get my master's ticket.' I stayed looking at the model of *The Mary Porter* all that afternoon. It fascinated me. Already it was a lovely thing, built as though in a shipyard, from the keel up, faithful in every detail, even below decks, to the ship in which Ephraim sailed. 'And next time I'm home,' he said, 'you'll see her rigging up, and then the next time she'll be carrying all her canvas.' As he told me about her I could already see her, in my mind, as a lovely and complete thing. For the next five weeks I got a glimpse of her whenever I could, and then, the day before Ephraim sailed again, I looked at her for the last time. He caught me looking at her very longingly, and suddenly, as though thinking perhaps that I were jealous of his having brought me nothing from that last voyage, he said:

'Well, son, you be a good boy now and keep your nose tidy and you know what I'll do? Eh? You know what I'll do if you're a good boy? I'll bring you a nigger gal.'

'Oh! Ephraim!' my aunt said, 'saying bits like that to the boy.'

'Ah, that's right, ain't it, son? You be a good boy and I'll bring you a black gal home. That's a promise, ain't it?'

He was so serious that I think, at the time, I half believed him and then, over the nine months' interval of that next voyage, I forgot about it. What I thought of was the ship. I would think of her assuming, in Ephraim's hands, her full shape, and of the beautiful light airy look that the rigging would give her. I would think of Ephraim knotting that rigging down in his cabin, under the hanging oil-lamp, on hot black tropical nights, moving the little ship gradually and patiently to its moment of completion.

Ephraim came home again in the October of the following year. I forget what he brought his mother that time, but I know that, as he had promised, the rigging of *The Mary Porter* was finished and true in every detail. It gave the ship that wonderful, lofty air, quite magical, that sailing ships have when they carry no canvas. I marvelled at that ship and for five weeks looked at it whenever he would let me, until he must have known how I coveted it. I marvelled too at Ephraim's patience. 'Yes,' he said, 'it takes a longish stretch. But then I'm working for my master's ticket and that takes up a lot o' time too. But I'll soon be finished with that now, I hope.'

He was finished with it that very time ashore. He got his master's ticket in London that November and in December the owners of *The Mary Porter* gave him his first command. The ship was another square-rigger, older than *The Mary Porter*, and I forget her name. 'And where will you be bound for?' I said.

'Singapore,' he said, 'and pick up fresh orders there.'

He sailed in January, and the day before he sailed he let me look at the model of *The Mary Porter* again.

'Shall you be able to finish it now?' I said.

'Finish it? Easy. All I got to do is get the sails

made and hoisted and I can do that with one hand tied behind my back.'

'When'll you be home?' I said.

'Home? Never tell,' he said. 'But you know what I told you, don't you? You be a good boy and I'll bring you a nigger gal. That's right, ain't it? You be a good boy and I'll bring you a nice fat blackie. She'll make your hair curl.'

'Ephraim,' my aunt said, 'give over, do.'

That time Ephraim was away nine months. My aunt did not know when he was coming home. She never knew. She would be sitting there in the back room, wondering if Ephraim were in the Bay of Biscay or the Indian Ocean or even at the bottom of the ocean, when suddenly the shop-bell would ring and a voice would shout, 'Shop, missus!' and it would be Ephraim home again.

But when he came home that following November, from that first command, he came into the shop without a word. It was Saturday afternoon and I was there in the back room with her. When she heard the shop-bell ring she got up and went to the glass-panelled, curtain-screened door that divided shop from living-room and she opened it. She opened it and then she just stood there. I heard her say 'Ephraim', and nothing else, in a not very loud voice. Then there was a silence, as though of completely stupefied astonishment. Then she went slowly forward into the shop. As she went forward I moved forward a few paces too. Through the still open door I could see Ephraim. There was someone with him. For a moment I could not see who it was, because aunt Franklin was standing there. Then she moved and I could see who it was. It was a woman. But for a moment I did not realize what woman or what sort of woman. Then suddenly, even in the bad light of the shop, I could see the colour of her face. It was black. For about ten seconds my heart stood still and I knew that Ephraim had brought home a black girl from the South Seas.

If I had any illusions about Ephraim having brought home that girl for me I know that they didn't last long. After about a minute Ephraim came slowly out of the shop into the back room. He was alone and he shut the door behind him. He did not seem to notice I was there. All he did was to put his hands on my aunt Franklin's shoulders and say: 'Mother, it's all right. She's all right. Honest, she's the only gal I ever wanted. It'll be all right.' But I knew, somehow, that it wasn't going to be all right. My aunt did not speak and she was crying.

Then, after a few moments, Ephraim noticed me. 'Hullo, son,' he said. 'You run along now and come in another day. And don't go chopsing all over the place either.'

I knew what that meant. I went away and I kept my mouth shut. But I remember, as I went out through the shop and passed the black girl still standing there looking at Ephraim and his mother through the lace curtains of the glass door, that I was suddenly frightened. Then it passed. She looked as completely scared as I was — scared and forlorn in the cheap high bandeau hat and blue serge costume that Ephraim must have bought her up in Glasgow.

That was my first picture of her, scared and forlorn and out of place. I did not see her again for more than a week. Then I saw her walking out with Ephraim in the High Street, and I saw then that she wasn't black, but brown, a soft, coffee-cream brown, with large, gentle eyes like ripe black grapes, and I thought she was lovely. Neither she nor Ephraim looked at me.

They did not seem to look at anyone. They walked down that crowded Saturday evening High Street as though they were walking along the empty sea-shore of some remote New Guinea island, completely oblivious of everyone, infinitely happy.

But if they were oblivious of everyone there was no one in the town, from my aunt Franklin downwards, who was oblivious of them. People were all talking about the scandal of Ephraim Franklin bringing home a black girl and they all called her a nigger. Somehow it was a terrible, outrageous, wicked thing, and one day when I went into my aunt Franklin's shop I heard my aunt and Ephraim quarrelling in the back room, she arguing from just that standpoint, how terrible it was, how wicked it was, and he trying to soothe her: 'Mother, she's only human, she's flesh and blood, she comes of very high class. It'll be better when she can speak English. You'll git along better then.' But this remark seemed to upset my aunt still more. 'That's it, that's the trouble. I shouldn't care if she could only speak to me!'

I went out of the shop, that day, without going into the back room, and I did not go back any more for a fortnight. When I went back Ephraim was not there. He had gone to Greenock, I think, to see the owners. I think there had been some trouble, perhaps about the black girl. At any rate, when I went into the back room neither Ephraim nor my aunt was there. The black girl sat there all alone, in a plain blue, ready-made frock that didn't fit her. It was a dark December day, with raw rain, near Christmas, and she was trying to keep herself warm by the fire. I don't think she could have been more than eighteen, perhaps even less than that, and now, instead of looking scared, she looked pleased to see me, showing the pleasure in a sudden pure white smile. 'Hullo,' I said, and to my astonishment she said 'Hullo' too.

Besides 'yes' and 'no' that was her only word of English. She kept repeating it. 'Hulloyes,' she would say, all in one word. Her voice was quite high, but smooth; it prolonged her three words of English to double their length, until they had a dreamy, mooning, regretful quality. I don't think she really knew what any of them meant, any more than she really understood anything much about that gloomy little shop, with its dead fish and animals, and the still gloomier little room behind. It must all have been sepulchrally strange and foreign to her, not quite real, with the lead-coloured December light shining on the dead glass that covered the dead animals, and the dead light itself gradually being watered away by the dark December rain beyond the windows. It must have sent her thoughts flying back to wherever it was she came from, and it must, I think, have made her unhappy, because now and then you would see her look far beyond windows and rain and dark sky with a look of unconscious pain.

But there were two things in that room that she did understand. One was a case of butterflies; they were tropical and I think perhaps, at one time, Ephraim had brought them home for his father. The other was Ephraim's ship, the model of *The Mary Porter*.

Ephraim had brought home the ship for the last time. It was finished and it stood on the mantelpiece above the fireplace. It stood raised up, on a wooden support, in front of a pier-glass. The glass was tilted so that, just now and then, you had the illusion of the ship, with all her canvas set, waiting for a breeze in the dead calm of some tropical latitude where sky and sea had fused to a sheet of glass.

And she understood that ship. She must have seen its original over and over again. It would provoke her into long moments of reflection, not painful, not really happy, but full of something inexpressible.

Nothing happened about the ship that afternoon. Soon after that first 'Hullo' my aunt came in with a bucket of small coal and kindling sticks that she had been chopping in the backyard and as she set down the bucket by the fireplace she looked old and yellow, like a woman who has just come through an illness. She muttered something about not being so young as she used to be and another remark about some people who were young enough to do things but never lifted a finger, and I knew she was bitter against the black girl. Then I had an idea. 'Let me come round every afternoon through the Christmas holidays,' I said, 'and get your sticks and coal in.'

So I began to go round every afternoon, and sometimes Ephraim's black girl would be sitting there, by the fire, doing nothing except staring at the ship or the sky or the butterflies. And sometimes Ephraim himself would be there and they would be talking together, in her language, softly, this barrier of language cutting them off from my aunt, who would sit silent and apart from them, her yellow face bone-hard with an extraordinary bitterness and jealousy.

Then on the last day but one of December I went there and Ephraim had gone. He had sailed that day for Singapore, master of a ship named *The Border Lass*, for different owners I think, and he had left the black girl behind. He had left her because, I think, neither the new owners nor the old nor any others would ever countenance the sailing of a white skipper with a coloured wife. How he had ever brought her in the first place I could never fathom. Why he had brought her was something which troubled my aunt still more.

And even I, a boy, could see what was going to happen. It would be nine months, perhaps longer, before Ephraim came back. And in the meantime? I could see nothing but tension: the tension of the long winter days in the gloomy room behind the shop, the girl with her three words of English able to express almost nothing of what she felt, my aunt expressing what she felt by jealousy and silence. I could see all this, but how it was going to end was beyond me.

Then something happened. Every Thursday afternoon my aunt shut the shop, and sometimes she took the train into the next town, to see some friends. One Thursday when I went round to the shop to get in the coal and sticks she had shut the shop and gone, leaving Ephraim's black girl alone in the back room.

'Hulloyes,' she said when I went into the back room, and smiled.

'Hullo,' I said.

I put the bucket of coal and sticks down by the fireplace, and then I didn't know what to say. Then suddenly she looked at the ship on the mantelpiece and said, 'Ephraim?'

'Ah!' I said, 'Ephraim on sea. Yes. Understand? On sea now. All right.'

She didn't understand. She just looked at me with a large bewildered smile.

'Ephraim on sea,' I said. 'Understand?'

No, she didn't understand. So at last I got the ship down and knelt on the hearthrug and began to rock the ship backwards and forwards and up and down. She would be just about like that now, I thought, in the Bay of Biscay. The girl understood. She knelt down on the hearthrug and began to push the ship backwards and forwards across it, steering it. The way she pushed it was different from the way I pushed it. She pushed it softly, sleepily. I could see she meant it to be in calm latitudes. 'Kimusa,' she said. 'Kimusa.' Now it was I who didn't understand and I shook my head. So she reached up and got down a book from my aunt's little bookshelf made of boards and cotton-reels that hung by the fireplace and put the book down on the hearthrug. Then she sailed Ephraim's ship close by the book and pointed to the book again and said, 'Kimusa.' Then suddenly I tumbled to it. Kimusa was an island, her island. I nodded and she smiled again. She was quite excited. She sailed the ship close to the island and suddenly I saw what she was trying to tell me: that this was Ephraim in *The Mary Porter*, off Kimusa, in the South Seas. She was talking rapidly now, smiling, very excited. And then she jumped up and pointed to the butterflies, fluttering her brown hands. And in that moment I could not only see it all but feel it all. I felt for a moment as if I were Ephraim Franklin, standing off that island in the New Guineas, with the tropical heat and motionless sea and white sand and palms and the almost savage blue butterflies like those Ephraim had once caught for his father. Looking down at the ship and hearing her excited, almost childishly excited voice, I felt it all as a boy would feel it and was momentarily lost in wonder.

When I looked up again she was crying. And that was the oddest thing of all. I could understand her crying, but what I couldn't understand was the colour of her tears. They were white. And I couldn't get over that. I had somehow expected that they couldn't be anything but black. And while these white, so ordinary-looking gentle tears were rolling down her brown face the outside shop-bell rang.

I went and unbolted the shop door and it was the

telegraph boy. I took in the telegram and came back into the room and put the envelope on the mantelpiece, not opening it. Then the girl and I went on playing with the ship, getting down more books, making more islands, sailing the ship dreamily among them, she laughing sometimes and then crying, overcome with joy at having found someone to make friends with at last.

Half an hour later my aunt came home. The mantelpiece was by that time empty of everything — all books and vases were islands — except the telegram. My aunt went straight to the telegram and opened it and read it. Then she stood utterly still.

And suddenly I knew it was about Ephraim. I did not know what to do or say. My aunt sank down into a chair and looked straight in front of her, saying 'Ephraim' and holding the telegram in her shaking hands.

When the girl heard my aunt say 'Ephraim', she got suddenly very excited. 'Ephraim yes?' she kep saying. 'Hulloyes Ephraim, yes?'

'Ephraim's dead,' my aunt said.

'Ephraim yes? Ephraim?' the girl said and she began laughing.

'Don't laugh!' my aunt said. 'He's dead. Stop it! He's been drowned. The ship went down. Everybody's drowned.'

The girl, not understanding, still so excited by the mention of Ephraim's name, kept on laughing.

My aunt began to cry, dryly, bitterly, without hope. She gave me the telegram. 'Tell her, make her understand,' she said. 'Tell her.'

For a moment I was so upset that I did not know what to do. Then after a moment or two I took hold of the ship. The girl watched me. I drove the ship across the hearthrug, tossing and pitching her terribly, giving her a great list to port, and then crashed her against the steel fender. I crashed her so hard, almost broadside on, that I cracked her planks on the starboard side and damaged her hull. When she heeled over I left her there and made great sea noises, washing the sea over her with my hands. Then suddenly I stopped and I just said 'Ephraim, Ephraim' and shook my head and let my hands fall by my side. Then the girl understood. She just stood still too and began to cry again with the white, gentle, ordinary-looking tears that were such a shock to me.

It is almost twenty-five years since all this happened. In six months the girl caught a chill and got pneumonia and died, and three months later my aunt died too. The shop is no longer there, and the ship, which my aunt gave me and which as I grew older I took less and less care of, has gone too.

But what I wanted to emphasize was this: that nothing can change the fact that for one afternoon I knew what it was like to be Ephraim Franklin, first mate and later master of *The Mary Porter*, and sail the seas in that ship, and anchor off the little island of Kimusa in the South Seas, and fall in love with a coloured girl.

THE BEAUTY OF THE DEAD

GRIMSHAW finished stopping up the cracks of the bedroom window with the putty knife and the scraps of dirty rag. Outside it was already snowing, in sharp wind-scurried bursts, with particles of ice that bounced like grains of rice on the black dry pavements. But it seemed warmer in the bedroom now, so Grimshaw thought, the east wind deadened by the rag in the cracks, and at last he turned with satisfaction to look at his wife, who lay dying on the bed.

'Feel any different?' he said.

'No. No different.'

'Warmer now, ain't it?'

'Yes, bit warmer,' she said.

'Doctor said I'd gotta git a fire,' Grimshaw said, 'but you don't want a fire, do you? Have one if you want one,' he added quickly.

'No. I'm warm enough.'

'Never had a fire in this room,' Grimshaw said. 'Don't see why we should start now, do you?'

'No,' she said.

Grimshaw's wife lay in a large and beautiful mahogany four-poster without hangings, its canopy looming over her like a dark attendant angel with carved scrolls for hands. As Grimshaw looked at her, a small meek-eyed woman with high blood pressure that showed in the sharp colour of her face and the rootlike veins of her hands, his eyes dwelt on the bed too. To Grimshaw's way of thinking the mahogany itself, deep as burgundy, gave out enough fire to keep the room warm. It was a very beautiful piece: one of the finest pieces he had. Yes, it was very beautiful. Over the small figure

233

in the bed was laid a brown horse-blanket with a yellow scorch-hole in it, and over that a tasselled white quilt that had been darned along the edges. Lower down the bed Grimshaw had laid an old Inverary cloak, and there was a bucket for slops under the bed.

'Feel like anythink t'eat?' Grimshaw said. 'It's goin' uphill for twelve.'

'I don't fancy much,' she said.

'I got that cold rice pudden,' Grimshaw said. 'I could hot that up.'

'All right. Hot that up for me.'

'I could go out and git a bit o' pig's fry. On'y it's snowing. I could go out though.'

'No,' she said, 'hot me the rice pudden.'

Scratching his thin grey hair, Grimshaw began to go towards the door, feeling his way between several Hepplewhite chairs and a William and Mary occasional table and a carved commode that were crowded together between the four-poster and the wall. At the door he stopped and peered back at her over string-tied glasses.

'How shall I hot it?' he said.

'Jist stand it over the kettle,' she said. 'It'll hot itself like that.'

'Ah. All right,' he said. 'A bit o' warm pudden'll do you good.'

Grimshaw went out of the bedroom and along the dark landing and downstairs between the rows of pictures and furniture and the many pieces of china suspended by wires from the frieze-rail. He went through the living-room, fireless too and crowded like the bedroom and the passages with many pieces of furniture, and so through to the kitchen. The kitchen was dirty, with a day's unwashed crockery in the sink, and in the range a small acrid fire of leather-bits that

Grimshaw cadged twice a week from the shoemaker round the corner. In the middle of the floor stood a pembroke-table, not a good specimen, that Grimshaw had once got for two shillings and had repaired in the workshop up the yard. On the table were spread sheets of newspaper, for a table-cloth, and on the newspaper stood a dirty cup and plate and a broken egg-shell, the remains of Grimshaw's breakfast. A brown teapot was stewing on the hob, the kettle simmering on the trivet beside it.

Grimshaw cleared the table of the dirty crocks. He put the crocks in the sink and the egg-shell in the fire and then, in the pantry cupboard, found the remains of the rice pudding, a chunk of solid brown-skinned substance in an enamel dish scorched at the rim. He put this on the kettle after taking off the kettle-lid, swinging the trivet across the fire.

While waiting for the rice pudding to warm Grimshaw fell into a kind of trance. The door from the kitchen to the living-room stood open, and from where he sat Grimshaw could see the little room crowded with furniture. His eyes, greyish-yellow, rheumily protuberant and almost lidless, were the focal point of his scraggy face. He was wearing several dirty waistcoats, and now that the weather had turned bitter again he had wrapped a dirty scarf round his chest, tucking the ends into his armpits. In this trancelike attitude, his scarf giving him the appearance of a man who is waiting to go out somewhere, he sat for some time and gazed at the furniture. The tops of the tables, the chair-seats, the face of a bureau seemed, like the bed upstairs, to give out an indefinable air of warmth. They seemed very beautiful. The sight of them touched Grimshaw's senses, colouring his acute and jealous sense of possession with a remotely poetic feeling. From his eyes, still protuberant but softer now, it was possible to see that the shape and tone of antique wood affected him like words or music. He seemed to be listening to its beauty in the semi-dark silence of the house round which the snow was now beating in thicker waves.

After some moments he remembered the rice pudding. He found the enamel dish warm to his touch. He took it off the kettle and poured a little hot water into the pudding, stirring and mashing it up with a spoon. Then he poured water into the teapot, stirring the stale stewed leaves with his finger. Finally he poured out a cup of tea, giving it a look of the milk and a half spoonful of sugar. The cup of tea, with half the pudding on a plate, he took upstairs.

His wife was lying just as he had left her. On this side of the house the snow was beating in thick white flakes at the windows. It was settling untouched on the roofs and the street trees, and the reflection of it in the mahogany was like a soft solution of silver.

Grimshaw, moving to set the pudding and the tea on a table, a Georgian pedestal, thought better of it, and set it on the floor. His wife began to struggle feebly up in bed, her lips pale and exhausted, and Grimshaw helped her into an upright position, giving her the tea and the pudding a moment later.

'You manage?' he said.

'Yes,' she said. 'I can manage. You go down now and have yours afore it gets cold.'

'Doctor'll be here soon, without the snow holds him up,' Grimshaw said.

He felt his way among the chairs and table again, and went downstairs. In the kitchen he sat and ate his dinner off the newspaper, eating the same as his wife, the now luke-warm pudding mashed with water, swilling it down with the rank stewed tea. What was good enough for her, he thought, was good enough for him. Yes, they shared and shared alike. They always had shared and shared alike. They always would.

He bolted the food quickly, staring outside at the now rapidly falling snow. The food did not mean anything to him. He had forgotten what good food was like. She never had been able to cook and now it didn't matter. You didn't eat so much when you got old anyway, didn't need so much. They had lived in the house now for forty years, after marrying fairly late, and gradually the furniture had accumulated round them like a silent family of children. All their money had gone into it, had been made out of it. At first Grimshaw had been a carpenter, repairing bits of furniture in the evenings for other people. Then gradually the furniture had bitten into him, had got hold of him like drink, until it had become a sort of single-minded passion. Now he went about the house touching the mahogany and walnut and oak and fruit-wood with trembling fingers; he stared at it for long periods with jealous, protuberant, poetic eyes. He was mad when a piece got chipped or scratched.

The jealousy and madness had got into her too — her upstairs, who was never anything to him but simply Her. She was passionately mad on the china and the glass. In the front-room and the hall and in some of the never-used bedrooms there were cupboards and cabinets of china to which no one had ever had the key. And now no one would ever have the key, because no one except the doctor came into the house. Grimshaw and Her were alone in the house. They wanted to be alone. They were quite happy like that, all alone, living on bread and tea and rice pudding, with the silent family of furniture about them and the countless pieces of china blooming in the dark and unopened cupboards like rows of everlasting flowers.

As he sat there finishing the pudding and the tea, Grimshaw heard the heavy front door open and swing to, and then quick feet mounting the stairs.

He knew that it was the doctor. He wiped his mouth on the back of his hand and went upstairs too, following the diminishing chips of snow on the newspapers that covered the turkey-red carpet on the stairs.

In the bedroom the doctor was sitting on the edge of the bed with a stethoscope in his ears. He took off the stethoscope and turned to look at Grimshaw as he came in.

'You ought to have a fire in here. I distinctly said that yesterday.'

'She says she's warm enough.'

'Never mind what she says. It's ten degrees colder to-day and it looks like being colder,' the doctor said. 'You must get a fire in here this afternoon.'

Grimshaw did not speak.

'There's another thing. It's more than time your wife had proper nursing.'

'She don't like strange people about,' Grimshaw said.

'Never mind that. What about relatives?'

'She ain't got none. Only a sister. And she never comes near.'

'Wouldn't she come if she knew about this?'

'She might.'

'Then get her to come. If she can't come you must tell me. I'll get a trained nurse instead. Of course I can't force you, but — '

The doctor got up from the bed and packed away the stethoscope into his bag. The woman on the bed did not stir and Grimshaw, looking at her for a sign of acquiescence or denial, did not speak.

As he went out of the door the doctor made a sign to Grimshaw, and Grimshaw followed him downstairs.

'Now listen,' the doctor said. 'The fire and the nurse are both very essential. If you don't give your consent to a nurse I am afraid I can't be responsible for what happens. Do you understand?'

'Yes.'

'How is she sleeping?'

'Says she sleeps all right, doctor.'

'Well, keep on with the medicine. I'll give another injection to-morrow.'

When the doctor had gone Grimshaw went upstairs again. He walked slowly, aggrieved and resentful at the idea of a stranger intruding in the house: a strange woman, with fresh bright hands scratching like pins at the virgin skin of the furniture, a woman breaking in with new and regular routine on the old sanctified system of the house. He did not want that. And what about her? If he knew anything about her she didn't want it either.

Still he was troubled, and was greatly relieved, on going into the bedroom, to hear her voice from the bed, gentle and small and scared, entreating him:

'You ain't goin' to get Emma in, are you?'

'She wouldn't come here,' Grimshaw said. 'You know that.'

'You ain't goin' to get a nurse or nobody in? I'm all right. I don't want nobody.'

'I'll do jist as you like,' he said. 'You want somebody, I'll get 'em in. You don't want nobody, you neent have nobody.'

'I don't want nobody.'

He was relieved, almost glad. He stood by the bed, over her. She was so small and frail and tired-looking, in spite of her high colour and the large veins on her hands, that he experienced a moment of tender anxiety for her, a spasmodic flutter of gentleness that had nothing to do with the starved cold remains of the rice pudding, the rags with which he had stopped up the window, the miserliness that in her eyes and after so many years did not seem like miserliness at all. The emotion fluttered his heart and he made a vague gesture or two of restlessness across his unshaven face with his yellow, dirt-clotted hands. 'You have somebody in if you want somebody,' he said.

'No. I don't want nobody here,' she said desperately. 'I don't want nobody traipsing all over the place.'

'All right,' he said. He picked up the dirty rice-pudding plate and the dirty cup. 'You goin' to git some sleep now?'

'I'll try,' she said. 'Where are you going to be?'

'I'm going to be up in the workshop.' He shuffled his way among the crowded snow-gleaming period pieces towards the door. 'Shall you be all right?'

'I shall be all right,' she said.

Grimshaw went downstairs again, put the dirty crocks into the sink and then went out across the asphalt yard behind the house and into the workshop at the end of it. Snow was falling faster and more softly now, settling everywhere in a crust of an inch or so, so that he made no noise as he walked. The big door of the workshop soundlessly pushed back an arc of snow as he opened it, and when he shut it again behind him the whole world seemed to dissolve into a great calmness. Falling softly into the dead air and catching itself now and then on the dead twigs of the plum tree growing on the wall of the workshop, by the window, the snow seemed to be the only living thing in the world.

On a set of three trestles, in the middle of the workshop, lay several planks of elm covered with sacking. Grimshaw took off the sacking and stood looking at the new, smooth wood. Presently he ran one flat crude hand along the surface of the uppermost plank. The wood had a beautiful living response which smoother things, like glass and steel, could never give. Under the slight pulsation of pleasure that the wood gave him he put his other hand on the plank and ran that too backwards and forwards. The wood was smooth, but he knew that he could get it smoother than that yet. He had spent all yesterday afternoon planing it. Now he could spend all afternoon rubbing it down. In time he would get it as smooth as ebony. It had been several years since Grimshaw had made a coffin. In his day as a carpenter there was always a hurry for a coffin, but now he did not want to hurry. Even though he knew she was dying, he wanted to make this coffin with care, with his own hands; he wanted to make it lovingly. He wanted to put a little decent scroll-work on it and silver handles, and make it as smooth as ebony. He had had the handles for a long time, put away in a box on the top shelf at the end of the shop. They didn't eat anything. The elm was the best he could get. It would be a beautiful coffin and there was another thing: because he was making it himself it would come out cheaper.

There was the grave too. He thought about it at intervals as he worked on at the job of rubbing down the elm throughout the afternoon, with the snow falling more thickly than ever outside and the snowlight falling more and more brightly on the wood-shavings, the tools and the elm, the snow at last standing like flowers of coral on the black branches of the plum tree. In the silence he could think of the grave without interruption, and gradually it took shape in his mind as a beautiful thing.

He had long since decided that the grave was going to be something more than a hole in the ground. Every inch of it was going to be lined with painted tiles. There were three or four hundred of these tiles packed away in a chest upstairs: painted with flowers, birds, bits of scenery. He had watched her collect them over a period of years. He had watched her gradually collect her own grave together, and now no one in the world was going to be buried more beautifully.

He worked at the elm until, even with the snow-light, it was impossible to see any longer. He packed up at last and went back into the house, not realizing until he crossed the yard in the three or four inches of snow how bitterly cold it still was. When he realized it he went back into the workshop and scraped up a handful of shavings and wood-chips and took them into the kitchen. The fire was dead, and he put a match to the shavings and the wood, piling a handful of leather-bits on top. He swung the kettle over the trivet, and then went upstairs again.

It was very dark on the stairs and almost dark in the bedroom. He went into the room very quietly, greeting her with a whisper, 'You all right? You bin to sleep?' which she did not answer.

He stood by the bed and looked down at her. She lay exactly as he had left her, but he knew that there was something different about her. At last he put down his hand and touched her face. Her eyes were cold and closed and he realized that she had gone to sleep and had died without waking up again.

For some moments he stood looking at her, perfectly motionless. Then his thoughts went back to the work-shop. Then gradually he came to himself and began to move with the gentle deliberation of a man who has for a long time had something deeply planned in his mind. He pulled back the horse-blanket and the quilt and began to lay out her body.

It was quite dark when he had finished, and downstairs in the kitchen he lit the tin lamp that stood on the mantelpiece. The kettle was boiling and he poured water on to the stale tea-leaves for the third time that day, adding half a spoonful of fresh leaf to the pot. He poured out a cup of tea and spread himself a slice of bread and shop-lard, salting the lard, eating it standing up.

When he had finished the tea he took the lamp and walked across the yard into the workshop. It was still snowing and again an enormous calmness closed in behind him as he shut the door, the calmness of snow and darkness and the thought of death.

He turned up the lamp and set it on the bench and began to work straightaway at the coffin. From that moment, and on through the night, he did not know whether it snowed or not. He did not know anything except that the conception of the coffin took shape under his hands. He did not feel the crystallization of any emotion. He kept back his emotions as a policeman keeps back the crowd from the scene of a disaster.

It was about eight o'clock next morning when he really looked up and saw that the snow had ceased, that it lay thick and frozen like years of coral-flower on the bowed branches of the plum tree. When he blew out the lamp, the strong snow-light came in at the windows, turning the almost completed coffin quite white. He worked on for just over another hour, not hungry, still not feeling any emotion, fixing the silver handles at last; and then soon after nine o'clock he slid the coffin on to his shoulders and took it into the house.

When he moved across the yard in the foot-deep snow he heard the sound of shovels scraping on pavements as people moved the snow up and down the street. The sound whipped up in him a realization of the outside world. It died almost immediately as he went into the house. He had stopped thinking what the outside world felt or did or thought. He was alone in the house, with her, the coffin and the tiles with their flowers and birds, but he did not feel alone. They had lived alone together for a long time. The furniture and the glass had taken the place, gradually, of people and fields, friends and outside things. No one could understand how they felt, how he himself felt, about the beauty of the things for which they had starved and cheated themselves. There are different ideas of how to live, and he did not expect anybody to understand. That was why she had not wanted a strange person in the house. That was why he wanted to be alone now.

And as he went upstairs, very slowly, bending himself almost horizontal so as to take the coffin, he felt the presence of the things about him acutely, more real than anything of the outside world had ever been. He felt the beauty of the polished wood as he steadied himself between the tables and chairs with a sudden outstretched hand.

In the bedroom the blinds were still undrawn and the room was filled with the strong light of the snow. It melted in the shining surfaces of walnut and mahogany and hung on the ceiling like a cotton sheet. It struck brightly in his eyes after the gloom of the stairs, filling him with momentary tiredness. But he did not stop. He laid the coffin on the bed and after a time succeeded in laying her in it.

When it was all finished he stood away from the bed, with his back to the snow, and looked at her as she lay in the new bright coffin. As he stood there the emotions he had kept back during the night gradually flooded over him. The light of the snow was very white on her face and he stood looking at her with his ugly stained hands loose at his sides and his ugly tired face sunk on his shoulders.

With tears in his eyes he stood like that for a long time, taking in the beauty of the snow-light that was growing stronger every moment, and the beauty of the dead.

MR. PENFOLD

MR. PENFOLD, a travelling draper and haberdasher, easy terms arranged, a painfully shy, retreating man with almost invisible eyelashes, who looked as if he would have been much happier walking backwards, struggled out into the countryside every other Thursday on a massive basket-work tricycle, and called on Mrs. Armitage, a war-widow, and her daughter Katie. Mr. Penfold, who was in his early forties, was a single man.

Mr. Penfold had been calling on Mrs. Armitage and her daughter ever since the war: so long that he had become like one of the family. To the Armitages, who lived at the bottom of a hill, in a red-brick house surrounded by large clumps of lilac under which there was a great trembling spread of snowdrops in early spring, Mr. Penfold had become an institution. 'Well, it's Mr. Penfold's day,' they said, every other Thursday; then, as the clock drew on to five in the afternoon, 'It's nearly Mr. Penfold's time'; and then, at last, as they heard the huge wicker-work carrier of the tricycle squeak and clump over the grass verge outside the house, 'That'll be Mr. Penfold'. Then they waited for Mr. Penfold's knock: a gentle retreating kind of knock, as if Mr. Penfold had made it and run away. Finally, when with great timidity and decency Mr. Penfold stepped over the threshold they would say, 'Well, it's Mr. Penfold!' as if he were a stranger turned up from a far country.

On this same afternoon once a fortnight there was always a cup of tea for Mr. Penfold in the Armitages' comfortable living-room, and with it whatever the

Armitages had: a boiled egg, tinned salmon, cake, fresh lettuce in summer. In return, after tea was over and the table cleared, Mr. Penfold would carefully and almost religiously lay out his lines, stockings, knickers, handkerchiefs, ribbons, elastic, buttons, woollen combinations. And there would suddenly hang in the air a smell which, after so many years, had become to symbolize Mr. Penfold: the dry, discreet odour of new drapery, a smell that had become to stand for the grave and timid discretion of a man who appeared to be for ever on the verge of folding himself up and putting himself away. It seemed sometimes as if this discretion might flower into something else. It seemed to Mrs. Armitage, who was lonely and who had nothing to look forward to except the careful saving of her meagre pension and the growing up and perhaps finally the loss of Katie, that it might flower into something beyond friendship. For many years it seemed as if this might happen, but every Thursday she watched Mr. Penfold go through the same painful, too-discreet process of folding himself up and putting himself away for another fortnight. She watched him manœuvre the tricycle away from the house, and felt a strange conflict of anger and despair, and became resigned at last to the fact that Mr. Penfold would never change, was perhaps incapable of change, except under the impetus of a revolution.

Though she did not notice it, this revolution was going on under her eyes, and once every fortnight under the eyes of Mr. Penfold, though for many years he did not notice it either. There was a revolution going on in the young girl, Katie. When Mr. Penfold first began to call on Mrs. Armitage there was a baby in the house, and sometimes he would take the child on his knee. He had a small gold watch which struck the hours like a little bell, and the child would listen to it for a long time, with dark eyes that had alternate moods of sulkiness and vivacity. As she sat on Mr. Penfold's knee he would stroke his hand backwards and forwards with grave pleasure across her hair, which was the colour of sun-bleached straw and which, Mrs. Armitage said, would grow darker as she grew older. But for some reason, and to Mr. Penfold's secret happiness, the hair never grew darker, but remained the one constant and beautiful element in the changing and growing girl.

For some years there were no changes in the girl that could startle Mr. Penfold. He would see sometimes that the child had grown from one fortnight to another; there periodically came a time when she needed the next size in underclothes. When he expressed any feeling about the way the girl was growing and changing it was always one of surprise: surprise that time could go so quickly. 'She'll be telling us what to do before we know where we are,' he would say.

Then one summer, during the whole month of August, Katie went away to stay with an aunt, and it was six weeks before Mr. Penfold saw her again. During this time there were changes, but to Mr. Penfold unnoticed changes, in the behaviour of Mrs. Armitage. One afternoon she said that the plums were ripe in the garden. Would he like to see them? He said yes, and in his simple way, that had no connection with and did not understand subtleties, he went into the garden with her. The plums were dark and thick on the high tree, the skins warm in the rich August sunshine. He took off his coat and climbed the long high ladder and found himself in a deep sun-trembling world of fruit and leaves, his basket hooked on a

branch, his two hands free for the great bunches of
plums that hung everywhere like blue grapes on the
brittle branches. After a time he heard Mrs. Armitage's voice and looked down and saw her coming up
the ladder. It was very warm and she had loosened the
neck of her dress. She was a neat, firm little woman
with dark brown crinkled hair and a still young figure,
and he had only to glance down in order to see the
hollow of her breasts opening darkly in her loosened
dress. She came up the ladder smiling, with slightly
parted lips, but he did not seem to see either her
breasts or her smile, and it did not occur to him that he
had only to reach down and she would fall into his life
more easily than the plums were falling into his hands.

He remained in the plum tree with her for more
than two hours that afternoon, and at no time did he
come near to understanding what had brought and
kept him there. When he breathed the sweet, almost
autumnal fragrance of ripe plums and saw the sunlight
breaking through and quivering between the leaf-
shadows on his hands and he said how lovely it was in
the country, he did not grasp the meaning of her
answer, that it was lovely but that you only understood
how lovely it was until you lived there always. And
when finally they left the tree and he carried the plums
indoors for her and she gave him two glasses of her
cool home-made wine to drink and begged him to stay
and have a little supper, he was still as remote from the
meaning of it all as ever. It was still as if he could
never reverse the fixed process of habit and nature, and
for once unfold and give himself, instead of folding
himself up and putting himself away.

She was more angry than despairing when he went
away that evening, but he did not know that either.
He could not begin to know it, incapable as he was of

understanding an inner meaning, kept as he had been by great shyness from any entry into a single great experience. He understood simple, visible things like a yard of velvet, a tree of plums, snowdrops in bloom, a pair of combinations. He understood that Mrs. Armitage had been buying things from him every fortnight more or less for fifteen years and that she paid him by a system of rather parsimonious instalments which in his shyness he called 'this week's', but he did not understand that she was lonely and unsatisfied.

A fortnight later he called again as usual, knocking in his timid way and waiting for an answer. But when the door opened he got for a moment the impression that it had been answered by a stranger.

This impression, which went stabbing through his mind like a needle, was gone almost at once, and he saw that the stranger was Katie. He saw with astonishment a clear, unmistakable thing before his eyes. In her absence Katie had grown up. She was some inches taller, but he saw more than that. She stood very erect, her young, newly-formed breasts pushing against her frock, and it seemed to him that she looked at him with eyes that had in them a kind of sulky hostility. The one thing about her that had not changed was her hair: it had the same shining blondeness, but now against the dark self-conscious eyes it seemed doubly beautiful and striking.

He was so affected by this transition in the girl that as he came into the house he felt as if something were waiting to explode behind his shyness. He wanted to talk about it, to remark to Mrs. Armitage how suddenly and unmistakably Katie had grown up. But he could not say anything and gradually his great sense of astonishment was repressed and folded away, to become in turn part of his shyness, to become as time went on something that he could not speak about or reveal.

But that afternoon he found himself forced to face the change in the girl in other ways. It was time, Mrs. Armitage said, that Katie wore some sort of support. She believed in support early; there was nothing like it, she always held, for starting a good figure.

'Besides, she's going to leave school, and start to work.'

'Work?' Mr. Penfold said. 'Why, what work, where?'

'She's going to work down in Denton,' she said, 'in Chapman's office. She starts next week. Yes, she's starting to work.'

'Well,' Mr. Penfold said. 'It doesn't seem five minutes since she was a baby.'

As he said this, Mr. Penfold looked up at the girl, who was standing in the room, her back against a high dresser, her arms folded behind her. He smiled, half expecting her to smile back, but he saw on her face only the new-born, adolescent resentment, not yet hostility, to what he suddenly felt was a foolish remark. Her direct, sulky stare brought all his own self-consciousness rushing to the surface, and he felt strangely, miserably foolish.

He turned hurriedly to the things on the table, and was immediately faced with a new problem. It was very rare that he carried such lines as belts or brassières and in fact corsetry was rather out of his line, and he knew that he had nothing suitable for the girl. 'But I could run the tape round her and bring some over special to-morrow.'

'Well, that would do as well,' Mrs. Armitage said. 'Katie, let Mr. Penfold run the tape over you.'

Mr. Penfold produced the tape-measure from his

pocket and unrolled it in his hands, but before he could do anything the girl sprung away from the dresser and went swiftly out of the room.

'Well!' Mrs. Armitage said. 'Well! And that's how she's been ever since she got back. Too big to be spoken to, too big to do anything. And now throwing her weight about. Well!'

'It's all right,' Mr. Penfold said. 'Leave her alone. Shall I bring some sizes over to-morrow and she can try them on?'

'I don't know,' Mrs. Armitage said. 'I'm sure I don't know. Perhaps we'd better go down to Lee and Porters and go up into the ladies' department and get it there.'

'All right,' Mr. Penfold said.

'Seems they grow up to be ladies while your back's turned.'

The girl did not come into the room again, and later Mr. Penfold took away with him the startling impression of her sudden transition and the still more startling impression of her exit from the room. Whenever he thought of the two things he was filled with a sense of her beauty and rebellion. He was aware of the presence in her of moods and attributes which he had never foreseen in the child who had once sat on his knee, listening to his watch as it chimed the hours like a little bell.

When he called at the house again, a fortnight later, Katie was not there. Mrs. Armitage looked at the clock on the mantelpiece and said, 'She'll be here very shortly She gets home about half-past five. Sometimes six.'

'Does she like it?'

'You better ask her!' Mrs. Armitage said. 'I can't get a word out of her whether she likes it or not. She's got that proud she won't tell you anything.'

Mr. Penfold did not know what to say. Proud? It was a strange thing to be angry about. He sat down at the table as usual and Mrs. Armitage gave him a cup of tea. And then, about half an hour later, he heard the door open and shut and the footsteps of the girl going upstairs.

'That's her,' Mrs. Armitage said. 'One time o' day you couldn't horsewhip her into washing her hands before she sat down to table. Now she finicks about with them for hours.'

Once again Mr. Penfold did not say anything. He lingered over his tea with even more diffidence than usual, partly because the egg that Mrs. Armitage had set before him seemed suddenly distasteful, partly because he wanted to remain in the room until the girl herself came down. In this mood of uncertainty, in which there was also a strange feeling of suspense, he let his tea grow cold, drinking it without quite knowing what he was doing.

The cup was actually at his lips when the girl came in, proud and silent and very soft-moving, so that she slipped into her chair, opposite him, as soundlessly as a soft blonde cat. He bade her good-evening, the tea still cold on his lips, and she answered him in a low voice. He saw at once that she had grown still more and that the transition from childhood to adolescence, just begun when he had seen her last, was now complete. Every movement and lack of movement now was mutinous with the self-conscious sense of her own beauty, so that he felt his own sense of surprise grow and change into a kind of absent-minded wonder, the cold tea-cup still in his hands and still foolishly suspended midway between his lips and the table, until he abruptly realized it and set it down with a clatter against the spoon.

A moment later he got up from the table and made some excuse about going. He knew that he could not sit there at the table with the girl any longer without something happening: something momentous or foolish or even, to his way of thinking, something terrible. He went out into the warm early September evening with a feeling very like fear uppermost in his heart. He did not know what he had to be afraid about; he was not even sure that what he felt was fear. But like fear the emotion propelled him forward, deeply disquieted, uncertain. That evening it still seemed like summer, with delicate fingers of honeysuckle outspread in the hedges, and the sun flat and warm and golden on the bright renewed September grass. The papers were saying that it was the finest September for many years, but now all at once he realized that he felt its beauty keenly not just because it was splendid weather but because it was emotionally linked with the beauty of the girl. He saw in the straw-gold colour of the honeysuckle the exact shade of her hair reproduced with fearful and lovely fidelity. The honeysuckle floated dreamily by him as he cycled past and in the same way he felt his dreamy thoughts about her run past him and gather in the distance, too numerous and diffident and troubled to catch.

From this moment he went on thinking of her, as it were, from a distance. He called at the house every other Thursday, not as if nothing had happened but in the hope that as time went on something would happen. Sometimes he saw the girl, but always with her mother; sometimes she was late from the office. More often than not he never spoke to her. She continued to remain mutinous and cool, her lips richly defiant, her young breasts rapidly growing ripe, to be carried soon with a new and conscious air of voluptuousness. In her presence he felt shyer than ever: shy, painfully inexperienced and sometimes foolish, the girl old and mature and fixed in beautiful contempt above him.

It was not until three years later that he suddenly found himself alone with her one evening. He had been held up by a puncture three miles away late in the afternoon and had mended it himself on the roadside. It was almost seven o'clock when he got to the house. He knocked shyly on the door as usual, and waited, and it was the girl herself who came in answer.

'Oh! it's Mr. Penfold,' she said. 'Come in.'

He went into the house. It was November and the milk-globed lamp was alight on the table. The light shone upward into the girl's blonde face and on her bright blue jumper and on her bare smooth arms and hands. But it was not only the beauty of her body, in the milky lamplight, that struck him. There was something else. There was a change in her voice and manner.

A moment later he knew the reason. 'Is your mother in?' he said.

'No,' the girl said. 'She thought you couldn't be coming. She waited till six and now she's gone down to the village.'

Her voice was amazingly friendly and free of all the old mutinous reserve. He had not time to understand it before in a warm, eager way she asked him if he would like some tea. He excused himself by saying it was too late but she said no, a place had been left for him and all she had to do was boil the kettle.

His astonishment at this change in her manner was tremendous. He felt as if he were speaking to her for the first time. He sat and warmed himself by the fire while waiting for the tea and then, as she began to pour it out, the curve of her bare arm clean as marble in the lamplight, he saw that she had brought two cups.

Yes, she said, she would have a cup with him, and if he didn't mind she was a bit cold and she would have it sitting on the rug. Before he knew what to say she curled herself up between a chair and the fender, her legs shining with the silvery-pink of ripe oat-straw in the firelight, her breasts drawn up under the close blue wool whenever she turned to look up at him. Then the reason for her prolonged strained attitude began gradually to be clear to him. He did not know what began it, but they began to talk about money. He was saying that the business was there if only the money was behind it. But he was finding money very tight. It had been tight all that year. 'Not that I'm grumbling. I've saved and taken care of what I have had,' he said, 'only it's difficult to go on putting it by if you don't have it coming in.'

When she spoke there was a flash of the old rebellion in her voice. 'Yes, and it would puzzle you still more to save if you never had any to save,' she said.

For a moment he did not grasp her meaning. Then it all began to come out, as if she had waited for a long time for a moment like this. She began to talk in a rapid, emotional voice, telling him her troubles. She had been at work for three years now and she was still being carried about by her mother. She worked with other girls who had freedom, took some part of their wages as a right, and had fun in the evenings. She had no money and no fun. All of her money went back to her mother, to be doled back in sixpences when she asked for it, to be sparingly saved in a penny-bank and, once saved, never touched again. All that the girl asked was a little freedom, some fun, a dance or two, an evening out once in a while. 'That's all I want,' she said passionately. 'That's all I want. I want fun. That's all. And all the time she wants to keep me locked in a glass case.'

Mr. Penfold listened without knowing what to say, the tea once again growing cold in his hands. The girl would be about nineteen now and it grieved him deeply to see her reaching out for something, for happiness and fun, and not getting it.

He looked down at her a moment later and saw that she was crying. He found himself almost glad of her tears, which now saved him from the painful necessity of talking. He let her cry for a few moments and then put his hands lightly on her shoulders. It was the first time he had touched her. She did not move but, as though unaware of him, cried quietly and immovably into her hands. He wanted to move his own hands and grasp her tightly and in that way express the sympathy and affection he felt for her, but for what seemed a long time he could not overcome his shyness. At last he did overcome it and very gently moved his hands across her shoulders and partially embraced her.

They were sitting like this when Mrs. Armitage suddenly burst into the room, almost as if she had been standing outside in the kitchen, listening. Mr. Penfold hastily sat back in his chair and said that Katie was getting him some tea.

'Funny way of getting tea,' Mrs. Armitage said.

He went away shortly afterwards, without speaking again to the girl and without another word being said about her or about what Mrs. Armitage had seen.

But when he called, a fortnight later, he knew that something had happened. That day he purposely changed his route, not arriving till six o'clock, but the girl was not there and it seemed to him that the atmosphere of the house was strange. He felt that the hostility that had so long been the girl's had for some reason suddenly been transferred to her mother. The table was not laid for tea and Mrs. Armitage's hat and gloves and Mr. Penfold's weekly payment book were on the table. No, she didn't want anything. No, there was nothing at all, and she was sorry but she had to go out in a hurry now.

'Where's Katie?' he said.

She looked at him with frank hostility and he knew that she was blaming him for something.

'Katie?' she said. 'Katie's started to live in lodgings in Denton. She's been worrying about it long enough and now she's got her way.'

'Oh,' he said. He did not know what to say. It came to him that it was a very strange, sudden decision. There must be a reason for such an abrupt change of attitude. Suddenly he looked at Mrs. Armitage. Her dark eyes were fixed on him with clear rebellious resentment and he knew then that the reason was himself. He knew that, prompted by some bitter, narrow sense of jealousy, she had taken the girl away from him.

'Will there be anything next time?' he said. It was all he could think to say. He had never said it in fifteen years.

'No!' she said. 'I don't think there will.'

'I'll call, just in case.'

'Just as you like!' she said. She stood with her hat and gloves, waiting for him to go.

Two weeks later, for the first time in fifteen years, he did not call. He pushed the heavy tricycle about the lanes with a deep and pointless sense of frustration. He found himself taking the complication of events like a skein of tangled wool and trying to roll them into a simple ball. For what he wanted now was very simple. He wanted the love and beauty of the girl for himself.

He wanted to open a little shop in the town and give up the tricycle. At the back of the shop there would be, he imagined, a room where they could eat, and over the shop a room where they could sit and look down at people passing in the street below. As he lived now he did not eat very well: hasty cold meals in the country, bits of bread and cheese washed down by cocoa in the evenings. But in the shop there would be contentment and comfort and the smell of steak and onions.

Finally he could bear it no longer. He decided to go back and call once again on Mrs. Armitage. Conquering his shyness, he would somehow tell her what it was all about. For once he would unfold himself, and say how he wanted the girl, how he could go on no longer without her.

The following week, almost six weeks after his last call, he again knocked with his habitual timidity on the door, and then waited. It was a grey January afternoon, not quite dark, the land settled deep in winter, and he saw that the snowdrops were not yet out in the grass. It was Mrs. Armitage who answered his knock, and she said:

'Oh! it's Mr. Penfold.'

She held open the door and he went into the house. As he entered the room he almost stopped. It seemed to him, just as it had once before, that a strange girl was sitting by the fire. It was Katie. She was wearing the same bright blue jumper as before and her hair, still as pale as honeysuckle, was brushed in the same way, yet she looked like an inexpressibly strange person, farther away from him than ever. As he came in she stood up, smiling a little. In a moment he knew that the smile, sudden and a little forced and without a trace of hostility, was the signal that something was the matter, and before he could speak to her she went out of the room.

He was surprised by that action but not really troubled. Perhaps it would be easier without her. 'Has Katie come back?' he said. 'I mean for good.'

'I don't know what you mean, good,' Mrs. Armitage said. 'She's come back.'

'Is anything the matter?' he said.

'Matter?' she said. She walked away from him and stood looking bitterly into the fire. 'She's going to be married.'

He stood immovable; he felt deeply and inexpressibly sick at heart.

'She's got to be married,' she said, 'that's all. You might as well know first as last.'

He stood there for some moments before realizing fully what she had said. Then he knew that there was nothing he could do or say, and he went out of the house. It was dark outside, and he lit the lamp of his tricycle. As he rode away he recalled that in the papers that morning there had been a forecast of rain, and now he could feel it spitting on his face and hands out of the strong heavy western wind.

He rode on for some distance before the gradient of the road made him dismount. He could not think clearly, but was conscious only of the strange, once rebellious and now resigned beauty of the girl filling and troubling his heart. He did not feel any bitterness, but only that behind his lifelong shyness something terrible was at last preparing to explode and shatter him. It was as if he had no longer anything to which he could look forward. He walked heavily, oblivious of the rain. The winter was dead all about him and back in the Armitages' house the snowdrops had not yet come in the grass. 'Oh! my God,' he said to himself, 'Oh! my God, my God.'

THE BRIDGE

I

THE summer my father died my sister and I decided to start a guest-house together. Of course we were fools, but I think we both thought it time to make something of the too large red-brick family house where for so long there had been no family. Mother had been dead six years: and now, for the first time, we were feeling our independence.

All through that summer the weather was lovely. My father had died in March, and we spent the whole of May, June and July replanning and redecorating the house, putting in new baths, central heating, even a second staircase. We hoped to be ready by August, and all through these weeks of clear dry weather we had every window open and there was that fine exhilarating smell of new paint and new wood in every corner of the house. My father had been a country solicitor of a solid and careful type who felt tradition to be of supreme importance in life. For that reason the disappointment of having two daughters had shaken him greatly, and although he had borne with my sister, who is older than I by seven years, he had never really been able to bear with me. I have always done my best to understand this and not bear him any ill-will because of it. He wanted sons to follow him in a profession where sons had followed for five generations, and to have had tradition broken by a girl who grew up to be a little irresponsible, rather self-centred and highly impracticable, was a shock from which he never properly recovered. He took a sort of revenge on me, whether by conscious or unconscious means I could never tell, by showing a certain partiality towards my sister. I was hurt by this partiality, but I have since tried to understand it too. What I can't understand is why my father did not make the most revolutionary possible break with tradition and take my sister into the solicitor's profession with him. Dora would have made an admirable solicitor. She is utterly practical, resourceful, conscientious and in a way very ingenious. Her straight brown hair is and always has been parted directly in the middle: so straight and accurate and unchanging that it gives the feeling of being the result of a positive and ingenious mathematical calculation. In the same way her clear, rather white-skinned face has something of the same surely defined, uninspired beauty as a careful copperplate hand in a ledger.

I do not know quite what gave us this idea of a guest-house. Parkinford is just a small pleasant country town, with a thirteenth-century church and a row of almshouses and a tiny square surrounded by sycamore trees; the river flows past one end of the town, under a stone hump-backed bridge, past irregular clumps of weeping willows that hang down like disentangled water-weed, brushing the water with their pale green branches in spring and summer. There was a time when I thought it a very dull town. Then I went away from it and — well, I shall come to all that in a moment. All I wish to say now is that apart from the public-houses and a temperance commercial hotel down by the station we suddenly realized that our guest-house would be the only place where a certain class of tourist could get a room for the night. The fact that there were very few tourists who wanted to stop a night in Parkinford didn't discourage us; my sister quite rightly reasoned that it was our business to attract tourists. In time we should build up a reputation.

Among other things my sister is a beautiful cook. She turns out tarts and pies and a great variety of dishes with the same ease and precise, mathematical beauty as she manipulates figures. I couldn't cook at all, I hadn't the slightest interest in mathematics, but I was young and, that first summer of the new boarding-house, I had no doubts about my own beauty. I had very thick deeply-waved blonde hair and clear blue eyes. I was full, too, of that deep emotional energy that springs naturally with youthful beauty — my heart full of it and hurting and not knowing where to direct itself. There is a snapshot taken of me just about this time: it shows me in a short white dress standing in front of a large lime tree at the back of the house. You can see in this picture a young, eager-looking girl with a smile on her face; but what you cannot see or hear or feel are the millions of delicate blossoms on the lime, the surge of bees in them and the scented honey-dew falling on my hair and on my hands and on the brown summer grass. What this photograph does not show is the dreaming, urgent creature behind the gaiety and the beauty. It does not show how that young girl of twenty-two felt, dreaming and in love with herself and rather foolishly conscious of having a soul.

We opened the guest-house at last in the middle of August, and we started off immediately with two guests. One was a Mr. Bernard Parker, who had been my father's clerk for twenty years and had lived in disgraceful back-room lodgings most of the time and had never married; the other was a Miss Millay, librarian at the public library, a studious sort of girl who had been friendly with my sister for many years. These would form the permanent background for casual tourists, for which of course it was really too late that year.

Then, no sooner had we opened, than we had a considerable shock. It was announced in the papers, and soon everyone was talking about it, that a new by-pass was to be constructed immediately on the south side, the river side, of Parkinford. This would not only cut out the old hump-backed bridge, but by means of a great new concrete bridge would span the river, the railway line, and the meadows that were almost always flooded in winter. It was a project that had been talked of for years and the realization of which had been almost abandoned. Everyone was now very jubilant about it. It was only we who had reason to hate the thought of it. We felt that nothing could have smashed so completely our hopes of tourists and our hope for the future. My sister, less emotional than I, more balanced and more resourceful, took it with a sort of logical stoicism, but from the first I made up my mind I hated that bridge.

The project of the new bridge had been announced about a month and preliminary work had already begun across the meadows by the river and the railway line when something else happened. I had been down into the town shopping one evening and I came back about seven o'clock to find my sister talking to a young man in what we called the reception room. He had two large leather suit-cases with him and I knew, even before my sister spoke, that we had another guest.

'Oh! there you are, Linda,' my sister said. 'May I introduce Mr. Lawrence? Mr. Lawrence is coming to stay with us.'

'Oh!' I said. 'For long?'

'Well, for quite a time, I think,' he said. 'I've a job in the town that'll keep me busy for about eighteen months.'

'Oh! Yes,' I said.

He looked at me and smiled. It was a curious smile. It gave me the strangest sort of feeling: the feeling that I had been singled out to receive it. There are some people who smile with the eyes, hardly moving the lips; others who show their teeth and keep the eyes immovable. This smile came from the slightest quiver of a mouth that did not open. I did not see it then, but it was a weak mouth. It was handsome and impertinent and it seemed to me to have all sorts of subtle and compelling qualities that were not analysable at a first glance, but you could see without thinking that it was vain and passionate and in a way sensitive too. I knew that I was right about the vanity. You could see that by the way he dressed: the smart grey suit, the brown suede shoes, the silk wine-coloured tie, the soft green Homburg hat. Oh! yes, you could see that he felt himself to be somebody that was somebody.

Instantly I didn't like him. I said something about I hoped he would be comfortable and he said 'I hope so', almost mocking; and then my sister said she would show him to his room. He insisted on carrying his bags upstairs and in walking behind my sister. I must say that the back view of him was even more impressive than the front. It was curious how you got a feeling of jauntiness and class and vanity from the smooth cut of that grey suit and the even smoother sweep of his very black, oiled hair. It was curious how repellent and attractive it was.

My sister came down again in two or three minutes, and she said at once, 'Well, what do you think?'

'Well, he certainly doesn't undervalue himself,' I said.

'Linda,' she said, 'I think it ought to be our first rule not to criticize guests. We've set out to make a business proposition of this place, and personalities have got to be kept out.' That was just like Dora: sound and practical and admirably logical. 'The main point is whether he pays his bill. In any case it's a very good let — eighteen months. It will do something to compensate us for that wretched bridge.'

'I only hope we're good enough for him,' I said.

'Well, if you want my opinion,' she said, 'I think he's perfectly all right.'

'You didn't ask him what his job was?' I said.

'No, I didn't. That's something else we ought to avoid. Inquisitiveness. We'll find out soon enough what his job is.'

My sister was quite right. We did find out. Every morning, before breakfast, we had our separate jobs to do. Dora cooked breakfast and took up early morning tea to the guests; I prepared the tables and tidied the dining-room. We had only one servant, Elsie, and she would be busy stoking the boiler-fire and sweeping the hall and stairs. One of my jobs was to take in the morning papers and the post. The second morning I was astonished to see the size of Mr. Lawrence's correspondence: a dozen or more letters, one registered, and several large flat packages. One of these packages was marked *Ministry of Transport: Urgent*, and then I knew who and what he was.

Soon, of course, everyone knew what I knew. Everyone knew Mr. Lawrence, the government engineer in charge of the new bridge. And everyone, including even my sister, seemed quite honoured by the presence in Parkinford of a government engineer. In fact the instant reaction in Parkinford was a sort of emotional dog-fight — half the women became at once raving jealous over him. Even Elsie and Miss Millay were jealous.

My own instant reaction was quite simple. I disliked him intensely. At twenty-two it is possible to hate some person or object or creed with a peculiarly pure, straightforward hatred, and to gain some kind of inverse pleasure from that hatred. This is how it was with J. Eric Lawrence and I. You will notice this J. Eric Lawrence — that's how he always styled himself: just that extra initial that put him a little above other men. I hated him more out of deliberation than out of any genuine feeling of revulsion. I cheated myself into thinking I hated him more than anything because he stood for the conception of the new bridge. He stood for something new and aloof and outside us and I took great pleasure in hating that something, whatever it was, tremendously. I also got a special feeling of pleasure out of behaving perversely. If J. Eric Lawrence was nice to me, as he could be so easily and often was, I took great pleasure in being despicably rude and aggravating towards him. I took great pains to be contemptuous of his precious bridge, although it did not begin to take shape until the following spring. Above all I was disappointed whenever he was not there, as I had hoped, to offer himself for one of my attacks. The strange thing was that he did not mind my hatred. He accepted it with a kind of amused amiability. He accepted it with that smile of his: that very handsome, vain, and important smile, with its flicker of impertinence.

There isn't much doubt, I think, that all this would have worn off gradually; this childish, mechanized hatred certainly couldn't have gone on for ever. But after J. Eric Lawrence had been with us about two months something else happened.

I began to notice a remarkable change in my sister.

From the first my sister had accepted J. Eric Lawrence with a sort of frank, businesslike cordiality. It was very natural that they had a great deal in common. My sister, with her mathematical, resourceful mind, could understand and be interested in and even become enthusiastic about an engineering project like a bridge. To some people arithmetic is, I suppose, a form of music, and the calculation and planning and creation of that bridge must have had the quality of music to J. Eric Lawrence. And gradually and quite naturally my sister began to take an interest in that music. It began to have the deepest and most disturbing and most beautiful effect on her mind.

It was very strange how I first noticed this. My sister has never been given to very easy self-expression. Any other girl would have begun to express reactions of love and happiness as soon as the cause of them became clear to her. But my sister is abnormally passive. She is capable of feeling but not of demonstrating any great emotion: so that it is easy for anyone who does not know her to conclude that she is almost incapable of feeling emotion at all. Also she takes after my father, who was a negative, unattractive man with colourless, bony features. She has the trim, practical appearance of a cloth-bound book. In consequence she has no means of expressing by physical beauty any great depth of emotion, however beautiful it is in itself. It is beyond her to fall in love actively. Her way would be to fall in love with dismal passivity, quietly, tragically, out of sight.

There are women who would have found another quite simple way of expressing their feelings, but my sister could not even do that. She could not even cook

her way to J. Eric Lawrence's heart. She was too practical for that. All our guests, unless they asked specially,
ate the same food. It was against all my sister's prin-
ciples to make an exception even of J. Eric Lawrence —
yet one of her special smoked salmon omelettes, which
were delicious and which she only turned out on rare
occasions, must have shown him that she had some
positive, individual feeling for him. But she couldn't
even do that.

No: my sister's way of showing that she was in love
with J. Eric Lawrence was to go for a walk every
evening. That was an old habit of hers: a walk into
the town to post some letters, or as far as the common,
or down to the public library to meet Miss Millay.
She had always varied her route. But now it became
obvious that her walk every evening was in the same
direction and to the same place. She went down to
J. Eric Lawrence's bridge.

It did not strike me until later how odd it was that
for me the bridge was a means of hatred, whereas for
my sister it was exactly the opposite. It was odd how
that inanimate and at that time almost non-existent
object — there was very little to be seen except huge
piles of timber, iron and concrete lying about the
meadows — should have affected our lives so much.
Of course we were fools. There was I cheating myself
into hating the man because I hated the bridge; and
there was my sister, too inhibited and passive to express
her love, going out every night, wet or fine, to gaze on
a pile of raw materials lying in a field and a line of red
signal lamps where the road had begun. Can you
imagine anything sillier than that?

Perhaps that is what made me so angry. It all seemed
so silly and irrational and pointless. It was Miss Millay
who first told us about it. 'Dora always used to meet me

out of the library two nights a week,' she said. 'Now she never does. I can't understand it.' I couldn't understand it either. Then gradually we found out where she was going, and I began to understand.

Without waiting to think it over, I felt terribly angry. Although I had never been directly angry with J. Eric Lawrence I felt my antagonism suddenly shift from him towards my sister. I found all sorts of reasons for my feelings. There is nothing a woman dislikes more than to see another woman running after a man, and it seemed to me that this was what my sister was doing. Another thing, it seemed cheap; it also seemed very clumsy and, in such a calm, rational person as my sister, very absurd and very childish. No: it did not once occur to me that perhaps she was deeply, terribly, mortally unhappy.

Then I began to notice something else. My sister began to display the strangest and most comprehensive knowledge of bridge construction. It was winter now, and sometimes J. Eric Lawrence spent the evening playing chess with Mr. Parker in the drawing-room. One evening I went into the room just in time to hear my sister say:

'Isn't the chief object of steel in reinforced concrete to resist tensile stresses?'

'Yes, that's right,' he said.

'And the concrete, I suppose, offers resistance to compression?'

'That's it,' he said, and smiled a little: the old, handsome smile with its captivating impertinence.

I was staggered to hear my sister talk like this. To me a bridge was a bridge; it had never occurred to me that there was a science of bridge-making, and when my sister began to use terms like the theory of the resolution of forces, elastic deformation, the neutral axis and the relationship of stress to strain I saw I was listening to a new form of love-attraction. She was trying to express her love for J. Eric Lawrence by her knowledge of something dear to him, by her brains and her ingenuity. There was something pathetic and absurd about it, and again I was strangely angry.

For a time J. Eric Lawrence was very interested in this talk of my sister's. He was very clever, naturally, very clever; he had once said that even as a boy he ate and slept and dreamed mathematics. I could well believe it. But a passion for mathematics is not inexhaustible, and a woman who elects to talk of tensile stresses has only herself to blame if after a time she becomes very boring. And gradually, that night, I saw J. Eric Lawrence becoming more and more bored by the dry, desperate, mathematical mind of my sister.

All this time I had been sitting by the fire, not saying anything. I could see his face. It was the sort of restless, sensuous, self-indulgent face that needs and is always looking for an emotionally responsive face of its own kind. A large part of the mind behind it had no interest in tensile stresses; it was bored by all thought of such things as weight of steel in superstructure. It depended for its existence on emotion, warmth, excitable beauty. I saw him look at the clock, down at his hands, at the chess-board. Yes, he was bored, bored by the talk, the game, insufferably bored above all by my sister, and I felt glad about it. Then suddenly he looked up at me. It was just a repetition of an habitual look, quick, attractive, rather impertinent. But now there was something else about it too. It had a kind of confidential softness in it — but I had not time to analyse it or do anything before he hurriedly got up from the chess-board.

'I knew there was something I'd forgotten,' he said.

'I knew there was something. I'd meant to see Garbo in that film at the Ritz, and to-night is the only possible night I can go. I knew there was something.'

He looked at my sister. Of course it was a weak excuse. He must have known that she never went to the cinema. She had always kept away on principle: thought it rather silly. He must have known that. Yet he said, 'How about coming too?'

'Me?' she said. 'Oh! no.' Her face began to colour deeply. 'Oh! no, no thanks, I never go. I'd rather not.'

He looked at me.

'What about you, Linda? You'll come, won't you?'

I got up. 'Yes,' I said. I spoke without thinking. 'Yes. I love Garbo.'

'Good,' he said. 'How many hours will it take you to get ready?'

'Two minutes,' I said. 'I just have to run upstairs.'

'All right, I'll get my coat,' he said.

I went upstairs and he went into the cloakroom to get his coat. After two or three minutes I came down again, and at the same moment he came out of the cloakroom.

'Ready?' he said.

'I'll just say good night to Dora,' I said. 'In case we're late.'

Opening the drawing-room door, I began to say, 'I'll just say good night, Dora, just in case — ' when I saw that Mr. Parker was sitting there alone. 'Oh! where's Dora?' I said.

'I think she went out for her walk,' he said.

I did not say anything. But as I went out into the darkness with J. Eric Lawrence I felt a rush of jealousy, hatred and triumph combine in an intolerable feeling of excitement in my heart.

At precisely that moment there began a new antagonism against my sister.

THE BRIDGE

All that winter the building of the bridge, of course, went on; and all that winter the feeling of antagonism against my sister deepened and got stronger. The two structures were gradually built up together.

The construction of a bridge is a slow process: similarly the building up of a certain state of emotion, like deep affection or revenge, needs time. My early feeling of hatred towards J. Eric Lawrence was superficial; I did not know him then. Yes, it was superficial, and it might have gone on being superficial if it had not been for my sister. If my sister had not fallen in love with him I might not have acted as I did. For the plain fact is that all that winter, and on into the next spring, I set myself to fall in love with J. Eric Lawrence purposely, simply in order to spite my sister.

I have already said that my father had always shown great partiality towards my sister, and had seemed to take an unconscious or conscious revenge on me. It may be that this lay behind what I felt or did. I don't know. I only know that I took a despicable delight in doing what I did — in taking J. Eric Lawrence away from her, in appealing to the side of his nature that was foreign to her, in throwing at him all my youthful, excitable beauty and greatly rejoicing in it.

All this did not happen suddenly. It was accomplished slowly, by little things — things like visits to the movies together, glances, a dance or two, by our coming into the dark, quiet house very late at night, I in a flimsy dress with bare arms, and both of us warm and excited, and once by the snow lying in light soft flakes on my fur coat and on my gloves and my hair and he standing in the lighted hall and telling me how much I looked like something off a Christmas tree, in just the flattering, sentimental way that a young girl would love, whether she admitted it or not.

Yet all that winter there was no feeling of permanence about what was happening. I had the feeling first of not giving the best part of myself, then of not trusting him. At the first opportunity I felt he would drop me and run. All the time I felt I wanted something much more secure and beautiful.

It wasn't until the next summer that anything important happened. Then one evening J. Eric Lawrence and I were walking round the garden. For some reason or other we stopped under the lime tree. I have already spoken about this lime tree. It was quite large and must have been fairly old, and it overshadowed completely the west side of the house. Already that summer the grass had stopped growing underneath it and already in the warm early June evening it was possible to breathe the almost intolerably sweet scent of the first lime flowers.

We stood underneath the tree and then J. Eric Lawrence suddenly began to say something about the roots of such a large tree must be having a damaging effect on the foundations of the house. 'You ought to do something about it,' he said.

'What could we do?' I said.

'Well, if it were mine,' he said, 'I should have it down.'

At that moment I turned and saw my sister coming along the path from the house. That was rather her way: coming upon us suddenly, as if she couldn't leave us alone together. The evening was beautifully clear and calm, and she must have heard what J. Eric Lawrence had said.

'So you want to cut down the lime tree, Mr. Lawrence?' she said.

'Well, I'm only speaking from a practical point of view,' he said.

'But why?'

'It probably keeps the house damper than it should be,' he said, 'and it certainly shuts out light and air. And I should think it adversely affects the foundations.'

Well, that was practical enough — just the sort of practical, sober reasoning that ought normally to have appealed to my sister. But she wouldn't have it. She suddenly showed that she had an enormous sentimental attachment to that tree. She flushed hotly and said:

'You may want it down, but I don't. I don't, and I never shall!'

'I think Mr. Lawrence is right,' I said.

I spoke quickly. The reaction was instinctive. If I had thought a moment I should have realized how much I myself loved that tree, which with its first lovely olive-green leaves, the honey-fragrant blossom and the masses of claret-coloured branches in winter was the most beautiful thing in our overgrown neglected garden. Yes, it was a beautiful thing, but suddenly I wanted it down. I wanted to be against my sister; I wanted to show her that J. Eric Lawrence and I were on one side and she on another. I wanted to be able to revel in an aggravated sense of triumphant superiority.

'After all,' I said, 'the tree is no good to us.'

'All the same, I love it and I'd rather die,' she said, 'than have it down.'

'Well, there's no need to come over all sentimental about it.'

'Perhaps I am sentimental,' she said.

'Perhaps!' I said. 'Just hark at her,' I said to J. Eric Lawrence. 'She must think we're a pretty hard-bitten pair.'

'I don't think anything,' she said. 'I'm only saying what I feel.'

'All right,' I said, 'you're not obliged to cry over it.'

That was a bitter thing to say and she did not answer it. Instead she turned and walked back into the house. In that moment, as I now see it, a break was made between us: she on one side, J. Eric Lawrence and I on the other. When she had gone it seemed suddenly very silent. It was growing dark and the leaves of the lime tree were wonderfully still. By the trunk of the tree there was an old iron seat and we sat down on it. For some time we sat without saying anything. There are evenings in summer when it never grows cool and the nectar keeps rising in all the flowers in the warm darkness, until the darkness itself is inexpressibly deep with scent. You feel it would be good to sit there all night long and it was like that as we sat there under the lime tree. My mind, young and excitable and at its best deeply sensitive, suddenly took a new direction. I felt very moved by the evening, the silence, the strange atmosphere of protectiveness given out by the lime tree spreading itself above me.

We sat there for a long time. The lights in the house began to go out, and when the last one had completed the darkness J. Eric Lawrence turned to me and asked whose it was and I said it was my sister's.

'Is your room on the other side?' he said.

'Yes,' I said. I had made up my mind what I wanted now. 'You know it's just at the top of the new staircase,' I said, 'where it comes up from the kitchen.'

I V

He used to come to my room very often that summer and autumn, using the second staircase, until the bridge was finished. I don't know if my sister knew about it. She may have done; she may not. She knew that he was in the habit of working very late at night, at correspondence and plans and such things, and it is possible that she never suspected.

The odd thing is that I was not afraid of her knowing. On the contrary I was afraid of her not knowing. I wanted her to know. I wanted to confront her with the whole thing, to show her that what I felt for J. Eric Lawrence was something more real and more exciting and splendid than anything she could feel on that solitary nightly walk of hers down to the bridge. How often she walked down to that bridge I don't know. I cannot begin to think what she felt for it, unless it was that in her level-headed, practical way she could never let herself fall in love with a person directly, but only with something symbolic of that person, like J. Eric Lawrence's bridge. I only know that she was in love with him, very deeply, very passively, at a distance, a sort of love by remote control, and I only knew that later.

Then in October that year, my sister had a great shock. She could not have been more greatly shocked if she had walked into my room one night and found J. Eric Lawrence there.

One morning, when she took J. Eric Lawrence's coffee and eggs into the dining-room, she found Mr. Parker and Miss Millay shaking him enthusiastically by the hand.

'Why,' she said, 'is it a birthday or something?'

'No,' Miss Millay said, very excited, 'it's better than that. Better than that. It's the bridge. The bridge.'

'The bridge?' my sister said.

'Yes!' Miss Millay said, 'it's to be opened on November the fifteenth.'

'The fifteenth?' my sister said. 'But that's only three weeks away.'

'Nevertheless,' Mr. Parker said, 'that's the date.'

My sister looked at J. Eric Lawrence. 'But it was to take eighteen months,' she said. 'It's hardly been fifteen.'

'We had special orders from the Ministry some weeks ago to get a move on,' he said. 'We're anxious to get the new road open before there's any chance of flooding on the old one. I'm told it floods very easily down there.'

'Then it means you'll soon be going?' my sister said.

'Yes, soon now,' he said.

It was Miss Millay who told me how my sister reacted to that simple and, as it seemed, purposely abrupt statement. She went deathly white. There are women who would have rushed out of the room, made a demonstration. But there was only one demonstration my sister could make. It was the simple, silent demonstration that she was terribly sick at heart. I do not suppose J. Eric Lawrence noticed anything. That would be like him. Nor was I upset by the news that the bridge would soon be finished and that by the beginning of December J. Eric Lawrence would have gone away. My reason for not being upset was quite simple. I was determined that if he went away I should go with him.

That night I made him promise that. For him, as I see it now, it must have been a very simple thing to promise. I was very young, very excitable and in a dangerously credulous state of mind. In the darkness of the bedroom I could not of course see his face. All I wanted was a simple answer. All he had to say was 'Yes, you can come with me', and that, of course, is exactly what he did say.

It was the next day when I realized that there was just one thing more that I wanted.

'If we're going away we ought to tell Dora,' I said.

'Must we? It'll be several weeks yet.'

'We ought to tell her,' I said. 'I want to tell her.'

'Now?'

'As soon as possible.'

'Look,' he said. He smiled at me in the old, completely captivating way. 'Let's wait until the bridge is finished. Won't that do?'

'All right,' I said.

So we waited until the bridge was finished, and until the day the bridge was opened I went about with what must have been an impossibly conceited air of only partially disguised triumph. But it was nothing to the triumph that I saw on my sister's face when she stood with the privileged spectators on the bridge that soft clear November afternoon, with the dead leaves of the neighbouring willow trees blowing idly along the new white concrete, over the new stone parapets and falling lightly on to the grass, on the railway track and on the clear water of the river below. There were many people there and they cheered loudly as the Minister of Transport, accompanied by a large group of important townsmen, cut the tape and made the usual joke about paying for the scissors and then shook hands with J. Eric Lawrence. The triumph on my sister's face was at that moment complete. It was wonderfully characteristic: passive, but deep, quite strong, but beautifully unselfish and secure. The most wonderful thing about it was that it lacked all direction; it was not a triumph against anyone. Only my sister can tell what she felt, of course, high up on that shining white bridge in the clear golden

November air, but it seemed to me as if she might have regarded the bridge as her own spiritual triumph.

As soon as the bridge was opened the traffic began to drive over it, and shortly afterwards the Minister of Transport and the officials drove back to London, and then my sister, J. Eric Lawrence and I walked slowly home through the town. It had been a tense day for all of us and we did not speak much. My sister was too shy and too passive even to congratulate J. Eric Lawrence on his achievement, but all the time I knew she was still nursing that deep, private sense of triumph.

I too was nursing something, and I knew that I could not keep it much longer. My sister had had her triumph. Now it was my turn. And that evening, just before Miss Millay and Mr. Parker came down to supper, and when there were only the three of us in the sitting-room, my sister smiled at J. Eric Lawrence and said she supposed it was only a question of time now before he packed his bags?

'You mean our bags,' I said.

My sister did not speak. Her mouth was open a little, and I remember thinking how foolish, unreliant and vacantly frightened she looked.

'You must have known,' I said, looking straight at her. I had waited so long for that particular moment that now there seemed nothing in it. The tragic surprised vacancy in my sister's face made everything else seem sterile.

'You must have known,' I said. 'Now the bridge is finished we're going away together.'

My sister did not speak. I had no more to say either. Somehow the whole thing seemed extraordinarily empty. A fortnight later J. Eric Lawrence left for London. I was to follow him four days later and meet him at the Park Hotel.

It is now summer again and I am back in Parkinford. The summer has been a good one and, contrary to all our early fears, the bridge and the by-pass have made no difference to business with us. We have been very busy all summer and by evening, by eight or nine o'clock, after supper is over, we are both tired out. My sister does not go for her walk now, and I do not go out either. I have got into the habit of sitting in what used to be my father's study. It used to be a very dark, gloomy little room, but it is very light now. The reason for this is that my sister has had all the branches of the lime tree cut off, leaving the trunk stark and bare, so that now there is nothing to shut out the light.

But this is not what I am trying to say, and perhaps it would be better if I came to the point. I have never been a very practical person and the truth is that there are things about J. Eric Lawrence that I should have found out but which, because I was young and romantic and excitable, I did not trouble about. But then my sister, who is so extremely practical and far-sighted and realistic, did not trouble about them either. Of course we were fools, and it did not occur to either of us that J. Eric Lawrence was a married man who had for some years not lived with his wife. Even now my sister does not know that. She does not know that I went to the Park Hotel and found a letter telling me, in the most charming and persuasive terms of course, that simple and final fact, without giving an address to which I could send an answer. No, she does not know that, and if there is any question of triumph now it lies with her. She knows that my love-affair with J. Eric Lawrence is over. She knows that he will never come back of course, but there must always be for her the secret and perhaps exciting hope that one day he might drop in for tea, stay on to supper, and talk once again of bridges and tensile stresses and smile at us in the old charming, self-indulgent, impertinent way and proceed to captivate us all completely again.

Of course he won't come. I know that. We were both fools. The strange thing is that I do not hold him responsible. I am responsible. If it had not been for that recurrent and inexplicable feeling of antagonism towards my sister it would never have happened. My sister would have fallen in love with him in her own way, with unspoken passivity, and when he went away she would have locked it all away very nicely in her heart. For a time she would have brooded over it, squeezed from it a few drops of miserable, solitary pleasure, and then probably after a time have got over it.

The point is that it is not all over. J. Eric Lawrence has gone, the bridge has long since become an unnoticed part of our everyday life, the beauty and excitement and trouble of last summer are things of the past; but the antagonism remains.

It is, however, not only that. There is still something else. It might be possible to do something about the antagonism itself, but now something else has happened in this house where for so many years nothing ever happened at all.

We have another permanent guest. He is a youngish man named Barnes, and he has just been transferred to one of the banks here. He is a very pleasant, courteous, fair-haired man who could not cherish a moment's antagonism against a soul. He is gentle without being at all docile. He rushes to open doors for us, and moves with discretion when he comes in late at night from the bank. He plays the piano rather well, and you get the impression when he plays that the hammers are muffled with wool. There is nothing impertinent or passionate or vain about him, he could never build a bridge over a river, but it seems to me that he is the sort of person in whom you could confide an enormous amount of trouble. He listens with the gravest attention to all you say, and it is obvious he would not hurt a soul. He is like a well-made cushion on which you could rest your head.

And that is exactly how I feel. After the bitterness and shock and tumultuous emotion of the affair with J. Eric Lawrence I feel that I should like to rest. I should like to rest for a long time. I should like to find someone in whom I can confide and who will never think of hurting me — someone who will be decent to me for the rest of my life.

It is the simplest, most natural desire in the world, and yet I am immensely frightened of it. And I am frightened of it because my sister has begun to think exactly as I do. She is also thinking of Mr. Barnes. There is something in her quiet, passive nature which would appeal enormously to a man like him, and it is easy to see that in a very prosaic, very inglorious sort of way he could fall in love with her.

I am at the moment sitting in my father's former study, looking out of the window. In my absence last winter, as I said, my sister lopped the branches of the lime tree. A few fresh twigs, now a deep claret colour, have shot out from the trunk, but there are no flowers this year, and what was once a large, dark, graceful tree now looks hateful. You would not believe what a difference it makes. You see things you could never see before, and there is light everywhere.

Downstairs in the drawing-room Mr. Barnes is very softly playing the piano. I have been listening to him, but I cannot tell exactly what it is he is playing. It is something very soothing and subdued, in a minor key, and I have no doubt that somewhere in the house my sister is listening too.

It is almost dark and I have been looking and listening for a long time. The bridge has been built. I have been away and have come back again. My sister has lopped the branches of the lime tree and now in the house there is the sound of this gentle Mr. Barnes playing the piano. Things have changed, and yet in a way they have remained the same. For God's sake, what is going to happen now?

THE FERRY

RICHARDSON drove his car down to the river, and there a woman of sixty or more ferried him and the car across. The water, chopped by the motion of the crossing, flapped against the low mud banks, the piles of the disused wharf and mournfully against the clumps of dying reed. The sky was dirty over the interminably flat land, very low, with breaks of wintry evening sunlight that were here and there reflected in the dark water of the dykes. When the ferry hit the opposite bank the big woman lumbered off, caught the rope and pulled on it, digging her great gum-booted feet into the turf.

'You can drive off now!'

At that moment something made him turn and look back. He saw on the bank, standing back, the low mud-plastered pub that had perhaps been the ferry-house for more than a hundred years. Three boats were drawn up in the yard. It was November, but they were still not covered for the winter, and on one side the wind had piled up against them like a golden shoal a great drift of fallen willow-leaves.

'Any fishing here?' he said.

'About as much here as anywhere,' she said. 'Pike-fishing mostly. Some tidy roach though.'

'I've been trying all day farther up,' he said. 'Nothing doing at all.'

'Over-fished,' she said. 'When it ain't that it's poison from the tanneries. Nothing left but water-rats and gudgeon.'

She still stood braced on the rope, her heavy feet dug into the earth, while he took one more look at the pub, the boats and the shoals of leaves on the wooden jetty.

'Ain't you coming off?' she said.

'I just wondered if you let rooms,' he said. 'I might stay the night and try a day here to-morrow.'

'We got a room or two,' she said. 'We get a fisherman or two here most week-ends.'

Without surprise, as if it were something that had happened very often before, she began to ferry him back again. On that return journey he noticed the great strength of her thick legs and arms, straining on the rope. Her jaw had the square set of a boat broad and clumsy in the bows. Most of the lines of her face ran vertical, like dry seams opened by weather. Her mouth was thin and fine but not bitter, fixed with a kind of dry smile that she did not know was there.

It began to rain as they went together across the yard. The wind sprang up across the dykes in a sudden dirty burst, and the ferry rocked on the slopping water, banging the chain.

'I'll give you the back room,' she said. 'If there's a mite o' wind you'll hear things slapping about all night.'

'You think it'll set in?' he said, 'the rain?'

'The wind's about right,' she said. 'It's bin raining off and on for two days now.'

She took him straight through the small front passage and up the narrow varnished stairs. It was growing darker every moment. Suddenly, as he followed her, he got for an instant the impression of a movement behind him. He turned round and saw at the foot of the stairs a thin pale woman of sixty or so watching him. As he saw her she began to move away, slowly but dead silent. She had in her hands a candle that was not lighted, and for a moment he thought she had the air of someone who resented something but had forgotten what it was.

He went up into his room. The brass bedstead shone cold in the wintry light. The big woman ran her great brown hands across the white quilt, smoothing it, saying she hoped it was all right for him. 'And what about your tea? You'd like something to eat now?' He said he would, and she said she would cook whatever she could, eggs and ham or fish if she had it. 'Sometimes we get a boat coming up from Lynn and they drop in with a little sea-fish. But gen'lly we don't see nobody much, only week-ends.'

She went out of the room, but from the passage outside she called back: 'You can go down and sit in the parlour. There's a fire there. The bar ain't properly open till six.'

Rain beat desolately on the windows while he unpacked his things. Looking out, he saw it raking the air far across the endlessly flat landscape of already blackened earth. The bones of willow trees alone broke the skyline, and stacks of brown reed the empty desolation of fields bound everywhere by dark lines of water.

Going downstairs, he found the parlour by the glow of the fire coming through the open door. He went in, and was startled to see the thin pale woman sitting by the fire, her hands in her lap, her head turned away from him.

'Good evening,' he said.

She did not answer; as far as he could tell she did not move at all.

'Wretched weather,' he said.

She coughed slightly into her hands, once or twice, dryly, almost without a sound. Then she drew in her breath, as if to cough again, but nothing happened.

Her body retracted slowly and her hands fell into her lap. He saw then that they were long, bony, inanimate hands, beside which the hands of the other woman now seemed exceeding powerful. For some time he stood there waiting for her to do or say something, but nothing happened and at last he went out of the room.

He stood for a time in the darkening bar, looking seawards through the heavy rain. By the time the voice of the other woman called that his tea was ready he could no longer see even the nearer fields; he could see the ferry rocking and slapping against the bank and the water of the river wildly broken by the bullet hail of rain, but the pub seemed now to be standing on the edge of a vast dark plain that had no end.

He thought as he went in for his tea that no one would come in there that night, and for a long time he was right. He ate his meal of eggs and ham and sausages slowly, by lamplight, alone except at the beginning of it, when for a few moments the big woman stood by, telling him how there was no fish, that the boats had not been by all day. 'I don't know whether you see the papers,' she said, 'but the water's pretty high on the Level. It'll be a high tide to-night with the wind where it is too. We had a big break across here two year back.'

'How far away?' he said. 'How big?'

'Three or four mile down. Big enough to flood a farm or two out. We had everybody working at it as could work. Had seven feet of water here in the cellars.'

'I remember reading about it,' he said. 'It was bad.'

'It was bad, but you get used to it. You're born with your feet in water here. You live on water and you die on water.'

She left him to eat alone and when he saw her

again, in the bar, it was as he had expected. She too was alone; no one at all had come in. The continuous crash of rain from far across the immense flat space of land on all sides struck the house with a force that shattered them both, at intervals, into silence. Small tin oil-lamps lighted with a deep yellow glow the varnished walls of the little bar, and the scales of a twenty-pound pike shone with savage beauty in a glass case above the low back-room door. As he looked at this pike, meaning to ask her who had caught it and when, he noticed something else. The spirit bottles on the bar shelves were marked with many small horizontal white lines: the chalk marks of successive drinks. He asked her then if it was a tied house or a free house, and she said, rather proudly but a little wearily too he thought, 'A free house. We own it. We've kept the ferry for thirty years.'

'We?'

'Me and my sister.'

'Was it your sister,' he said, 'that was sitting in the parlour?'

'That was her.'

'I spoke to her,' he said, 'but she didn't seem to hear me.'

'No.'

'You're not much alike,' he said.

'No,' she said. 'No.'

Directly afterwards the door opened and the wind battered into the bar a man in a heavy reefer jacket and high gum-boots. Behind the bar the woman reached for the whisky. 'Evenin', Dave,' she said.

'Evenin', evenin',' he said. He looked at Richardson. 'Evenin'.'

'Evening,' Richardson said. 'Have it on me. And you,' he said to the woman. 'Let's all have one.'

'No,' she said. 'No. No thanks.' She poured two whiskies and set them on the bar. 'What's it like, Dave?'

'Water's riz a foot,' he said. 'And still rising. Busted the bank a bit on th' old river. I just bin up there. Fast as they bung it up one place it starts in another. They'll want all the help they can get.'

'You'll be getting water in the cellar again,' Richardson said.

The woman did not answer. The man set the empty whisky glass on the bar, looking at Richardson. 'Another? I got to go.'

Richardson said thanks, and they had another whisky. 'You're going back to help?' Richardson said.

'Yeh.'

'Any good if I came?'

'You don't want to go, sir,' the woman said. 'Slopping about in that Fen clay up to your eyes. You be ruled by me, don't you go, sir. Don't you go.'

She seemed almost frightened: not for him, but for herself, as if not wanting to be alone.

'I'd like to go,' he said. 'I won't get any fishing anyway.'

'But it's a dirty night. You'd be better here. There's nothing like a dirty Fenland night.'

'I'll just go up and look,' he said. 'I'll go up for an hour and come back. What time do you close up?'

'Ten, sir,' she said. 'But I'll be up until you come.'

It was strange, he thought, that she had suddenly begun calling him sir. He went upstairs to his room and put on his mackintosh and his fishing boots and sou'-wester. As he came back through the passage behind the bar he saw a light shining upward from the open door of the cellar. He passed quickly, and did not see if anyone was there. In the bar the big woman

watched him go without another word except a low
'Good night'.

Outside, the rain struck with a succession of heavy
blasts across the yard above the jetty, smashing the
ferry with eternal melancholy janglings of the chain
against the wooden piles. He groped his way to the
car, blinded by darkness, calling the other man. The
reply was snatched up and hammered away by the lash
of wind, but finally he reached the car and got in,
switching on the headlights. In the interior calmness
he heard the voice of the other man now shouting
beyond the black glass of the windows and saw a pair
of yellow gesticulating hands, the voice and hands both
like those of a person trapped and trying to escape.
He opened the side-window of the car and shouted
'Get in!'

'You won't get far with a car,' the man shouted.
'There'll be water on the road.'

'Never mind, we'll try. Go as far as we can. How
far is it?'

'Two mile or more.'

'All right. Get in.' He started the car and switched
on the wind-screen wipers, peering ahead through the
arc of smoothed black glass. 'Keep a look out for
water.'

Driving away from the ferry, travelling for a time
in low gear, not nervous but simply tense, not yet
used to the light, he felt on both sides of the narrow
dyked road a great solidity of darkness out of which
wind and rain hammered with heavy violence on the
car, beating it like a drum. In this atmosphere there
was not much he could say. He slowed down once or
twice, imagining he saw water lying ahead, but the
man beside him would say, 'It's all right, it's all right.
You won't git no water here. I'll tell you when you'll

git water.' He saw a light: a moment later a house floated past like a whitewashed boat, swiftly drifting away. And then something about the solitary house reminded him of the pub, solitary too by the river edge, and the big woman back there leaning her muscular and yet uneasy body on the bar, suddenly calling him sir and not wanting him to go. It reminded him too of the other woman sitting alone in the parlour, not speaking, thin, strange, inanimate and yet in a way alert. It reminded him of the light in the cellar.

'They'll be flooded out at the pub,' Richardson said, 'won't they, if this keeps on?'

'Ah! they'll cop out. They always cop out. Did y'ever see the flood marks in the cellar? Y' ought to look at 'em. Plenty o' times six or seven feet o' water down there.'

Richardson did not speak again. Ahead, now, he could see lights and as they sprang increasingly out of the darkness the man at his side shouted.

'Water!'

Richardson stopped the car. Flowing like a stream, clay-coloured water came up to the front wheels. The man got out, and in the beam of the headlights Richardson saw him wading ahead, calf-deep in water. Presently he came back. 'All right. Go on now. But steady.'

'How far?'

'Twenty or thirty yards. It's the water from the break. You can see the lights on the Level.'

They came slowly through the water, drove on a short distance and then stopped. They got out of the car and began to walk towards the lights. Sounds of human voices, disembodied, remote, irregularly driven across the short intervening space of darkness, became louder and more living as Richardson saw the shape of the Level, vaguely marked out by lights, a wall of earth rising thirty or forty feet above the black flat land.

It was some time later, when his eyes became used to the darkness, that he saw what was happening. Figures of men, working in the light of oil-lamps and here and there by an inspection-lamp plugged by a lead to a standing car, swarmed darkly on and about the bank like stooping ants, sucked down into heavy postures of determination by the clay they cut and shovelled and carried. He saw sometimes the steel gleam of a spade as it carved the clay that in turn caught the yellow glow of lamplight; he saw it piled on barrows and wheeled away on the plank-lines and at last effaced by the dark torrent of ceaseless rain. He watched for a time the men coming and going out of the darkness. Then he walked up the road to the point where it bridged the Level. The wind was strong and cold. On the far side he could see for a few yards the ripple of flood-water beaten up by wind and rain, but beyond that nothing. Solid, like a wall of black clay, the darkness shut out whatever lay beyond the ripple of water.

Up there, and again when he came down to the lower point of the road, he began to be aware of the smell of water. It was cold and powerful, and with it rose the sour dead odour of clay. It seemed to rise out of the earth; it rose straight into his nostrils, biting them. He gulped it into his mouth in icy gasps of rain.

After a time he got hold of a spade and began working. At the first stroke or two of the spade the great force of suction pulled at his heart. He realized he was not used to it and made a great effort, stooping and gripping the spade with all his power. And still, even then, the clay and the water under the clay sucked at the muscles of his arms and chest and heart and even the muscles of his neck. It caught at his boots; his feet were held in a trap. For a moment he suffered a spasm of childlike terror, feeling as if something unknown and limitless and powerful were sucking him down. He felt the sudden lifting of the clay, at last, like the tearing away of a piece of his own flesh. He was struck by shock and pain, and then by a shudder of relief, followed by a blank of stupidity.

He worked on for a long time like this, bravely and clumsily carving the grey sour clay out of the darkness, stupid, sucked down, not thinking. The clay he cut and loaded was carried away into the rain along the plank-lines to some point of danger he never saw. Farther beyond still the tide was rising. The land and the water and the darkness and himself were part of a great conflict. The rain stood like a cold sweat on his face. When he wiped it away with his hands his fingers left on his flesh the colder smeared impression of the clay.

Some hours later he struggled to his car and drove back to the ferry. As he went into the lighted bar his weariness took the form of a temporary blindness. He did not know what time it was and he stood by the bar, leaning heavily on his elbows, not seeing. The clay had partially dried on his hands, contracting the skin, so that his fingers too felt dead.

'I'll have a whisky,' he said.

After almost half a minute he looked up to find that no one had answered him. To his surprise the bar was empty. By the clock above the bar-shelves it was seven or eight minutes to ten.

Some moments later he heard voices. They seemed to come from somewhere in the passage behind the bar. After listening a moment he walked into the passage. He could see the light, now, coming up from the cellar; the voices were coming from there too, the voices of the two women, low, hollow, in argument, unconscious of him.

What he saw down there at the foot of the cellar steps, in the lamplight, puzzled and startled him. Water had begun to rise already in the cellar, so that the beer-barrels seemed almost to be floating. The lamplight fell with a cloudy glow on the dark barrels, the whitewashed walls and on the still water itself. It cast upward the heavy shadows of the two women, who were watching. One, the big woman, was standing on the lowest of the cellar steps, which the water had not yet reached. Her body seemed more than ever huge, anxious and in some way helpless. But it was clear that what she was really watching was not the water. He knew that she must have seen that many times before: many times, and worse, much worse. He remembered the story of the marks on the wall. What she was really watching was the other woman, and it was she, dreadfully thin, thin and worn-out and obsessed by some kind of parsimonious terror, who in turn was really watching the water. And as he stood there looking down, watching the small figure sitting on one of the pub chairs in the middle of the rising water, her feet on the rung, her body thin and frail but tight with a fanatical stubbornness, he knew that this too must have happened before, and he knew the reason for the big woman's fear and anxiety. He knew why she had not wanted him to go.

He moved at last, and the big woman, hearing him suddenly, turned her startled eyes upwards. Seeing him, she scrambled heavily up the steps. Behind her, as if nothing had happened, the little woman did not move.

In the bar he saw the big brown hands trembling as they drew the whisky. 'Won't you have one too?' he asked her.

'No. No sir, no thanks, no thanks.'

She tried to keep her hands still by pressing them together, and he knew she was alarmed by what he had seen.

'Is there anything I can do?' he said.

She shook her head.

'Nothing?' he said.

'No sir, no sir.' She stood silent again, defensive, trembling. He took a drink of whisky, and saw that it was a minute or so past ten o'clock. She realized it too and went across the bar and proceeded to draw the heavy bolts of the door, locking it afterwards.

'You've been working on the Level,' she said as she came back. 'I can see you're tired. You'll want some supper, won't you?'

'I don't think I'll have anything,' he said.

'What time would you like breakfast?' she said. She wanted him to go. He drank his whisky, hesitating. He wanted to say to her, 'Why does she sit down there? What makes her do that?' but somehow he couldn't. It was after all no concern of his: what they did or felt, why even they were there, why one of them should behave in that strange silent way, watching the water.

Then all at once she began to speak. She began to tell him why it was, in a voice unamazed, low, rather mechanical. While she spoke she kept her eyes lowered, and he felt sorry for her: the big hands flat on the bar, the heavy embarrassed face that could not lift itself, the difficult statement of painful words.

'She's got some idea that there'll be a second Flood.'

He did not speak. He let her go quietly on, telling

him how the other woman would sit there in the cellar, not only when rain came and the water was rising, but when there was no rain, even in summer: how she would sit there waiting, watching the flood-marks on the wall, and then how she would come up into the bar, obsessed by hours of watching these marks, and begin to make the marks he had seen on the spirit-bottles behind the bar. She was afraid and had been afraid now for many years that the waters would rise and cover them in the night and sometimes, as on nights like this, nothing could make her go to bed. There was nothing so very strange in that, he thought. There were people who lived their lives under the oppression of just such fears, the fear of being drowned or burned or suffocated while they slept. What was so strange, he thought, was that they had not acted about it in the most simple, obvious way.

'Why don't you move and go somewhere else?' he said.

'Us?' she said. 'Move?' She looked up at him at last, explaining. If the water was bad in one way it was good in another. It was their living: the ferry, the boats in summer, the fishing, the pub. 'We couldn't move,' she said. 'We couldn't move. What'd we do, at our age? Start again?'

'You could sell up,' he said.

'No,' she said. 'We can't sell up. It's entailed. We couldn't sell up if we wanted to.'

'But sitting down there, like that,' he said. 'She'll be ill.'

'She is ill,' she said.

He finished his whisky and then stood looking into the empty glass, not knowing what to say.

'Was the water rising much up on the Level?' she said.

'A bit. It'll be worse with the tide.'

'Yes,' she said. 'It'll be worse. And sometimes I wish it would get worse. I wish there'd be a flood. A big, second flood, like the one in the Bible. Like she wants. That'd be the end of it all.'

She had nothing to say after that, and after a moment or two he said good night and went upstairs to bed.

Long afterwards he lay listening to the sound of water. It was falling and rising everywhere about him with tremendous force. He heard it beating on the roof-tiles and the bare branches of the trees and on the raging surface of the river. He heard the constant melancholy beating of the ferry-chain as it struck against the piles of the jetty. He heard the rain roaring across the great level miles of darkness across which the tide too was coming in from the sea. And hearing it and thinking of the woman down below, he felt his heart grow cold.

THE LOVED ONE

ALICE WOODMAN had a soft loving face and brown
almond eyes that seemed to be always on the verge of
smiling at something. At twenty-two she married a
man who manufactured mustard.

A few weeks after they were married she began to
go about the district with her husband, in a small
10 h.p. van marked Pypper's Prepared Mustard, trying
to establish this commodity on the market. Her husband, a man of inexhaustible and changeable enthusiasm, was convinced that one-half of the world was
dying to eat a really decent mustard and that the other
half was dying because it did not eat mustard at all.
It was quite true that former manufacturers of mustard
had made fortunes out of what was left on the plate.
But here was a mustard you did not leave on the plate.
It was a prepared mustard, in the French manner, and
it was wonderful. It kept indefinitely in the little
brown stone jars of which the 10 h.p. van was always
full. At forty James Pypper had been a vacuum cleaner
salesman, an agent for fire-extinguishers, a traveller in
boiled sweets, a door-to-door salesman of cures and
preventives for rheumatism, a partner in a firm of
patent corset manufacturers. He spoke of the vacuum
cleaners and the fire-extinguishers, the boiled sweets,
the rheumatism and the corsets, much as he spoke of
the French mustard. Every household in the kingdom
was in danger of fire. Everyone ate sweets. There were
more deaths every year from rheumatism than from
any other disease. Every woman wore corsets. Alice,

who was slim and delicate, did not wear corsets; she had given up eating sweets and did not suffer from rheumatism. She had a warm, contemplative, loving face but she did not eat mustard.

As time went on, however, she began to be affected by the tireless enthusiasm of James Pypper for the mustard he was trying to sell to country grocers, village stores and even to public houses and wayside tea-shacks. For the first few weeks, whenever they came to a shop or some other place where the mustard might possibly be sold, Alice would sit in the car outside and wait for James Pypper to come out again. As she sat there she would look at the shop and sometimes she would see James Pypper talking with earnest rapidity to the shopman, waving his arms and striking the little brown sample pot of mustard on the counter: a man preaching a mustard sermon. This went on for several weeks; and then Alice, who at first had been shy of doing such a thing, began to go into shops herself and try to induce people to take sample orders. To her surprise and to James Pypper's surprise she was very successful. She did not preach about the mustard, she did not wave her hands and she did not strike the pot on the counter. She would look straight at the shopkeeper with her lovable, candid eyes and say in a simple way that the mustard was beautiful. Almost immediately it was as though the shopkeeper became confused between the beauty of the mustard and the quiet, lovable beauty of the girl who was speaking. He would give an order, 'Well, can't be no harm in trying a dozen. See if they've moved next time you come,' and he would watch her out of the shop, hoping that next time would not be long.

In this way Alice got many orders for James Pypper's brand of prepared mustard. James Pypper, however, did not notice it. When Alice returned from shops which had taken an order he would say 'Knew he would. Couldn't help it. You see, I told you.' Her going and coming and her success were simple proof of his enthusiastic creed that people needed mustard. It could never occur to him that they were proof that Alice was a lovable creature; he was concerned with saleable products only.

As they drove about the countryside Alice had a way of looking, in spring time, over the heads of the flowering chestnut trees, the cream clouds of may, the olive mountains of oak; or in summer over the long swinging distances of corn and the uniform green of distant trees. As she looked she appeared to be smiling. This supposed smile, completely unconscious, had first attracted James Pypper. He had seen Alice smiling like this at a dance, had taken it automatically to mean that she was enchanted by James Pypper, about to embark on a great enterprise. Now he was often irritated by it. 'What on earth are you smiling at?'

'I don't think I was smiling at anything.'

'Think? Don't you know? Don't you know whether you smile or not?'

'Yes. But perhaps I wasn't thinking.'

At times Alice would wonder whether James Pypper really did or really ever had loved her; then it became obvious that there were more important things on his mind than Alice's love, her almond eyes and her smile. It became obvious that the mustard was failing. It became obvious, by September, that the world did not eat mustard at all.

Up to this time Alice and James Pypper had lived in the middle of the town; theirs was a big, ill-proportioned house of ugly white brick with grey iron railings round it. The mustard was made in a little two-storied factory, formerly a warehouse, farther down the street. James Pypper had begun by employing three men and a boy, then one man and two boys, and then, as the mustard began to fail, a boy and an old man. He was just about to ask Alice if she too would leave the house and come to help retrieve the fortunes of the factory when something happened. James Pypper was in a grocer's shop one day when a man walked in with two huge baskets of white and brown eggs. James Pypper looked at them casually, then with a sudden jump of interest, and then realized all at once that he was seeing eggs for the first time in his life. He asked the man how many eggs there could be in a basket. 'About ten score each basket,' the man said. James Pypper wanted to know how many days' laying that represented and the man said: 'That's two days' lay. Eggs are falling off a bit.' James Pypper went out of the shop impelled by a terrific idea: the stunning cataclysmic, revolutionary idea of the egg.

As he rushed home to tell Alice of this, his mind worked out like an arithmetical machine the whole scheme of egg production, egg distribution, egg profit. He realized that he had got hold of something truly stupendous. He couldn't think why he, and indeed anyone else, had never thought of it before. He was seized with a primitive fever of simple wonder for one of the basic forces of the universe: the egg.

As he told it to Alice it was like a daydream worked out by figures. The mustard was forgotten now, but the story of the egg was literally the story of the mustard over again.

'Don't you see? Every man, woman and child in the country must eat an average of one egg per day. You wouldn't call that an extravagant estimate, would you? Eggs for breakfast, eggs in puddings, eggs for tea, omelettes, custards, cakes, thousands of things. One egg per day per person,' James Pypper said, striking one hand into another. 'That's forty million eggs a day. In round figures that's fifteen thousand million eggs a year. Just think of it. The average price of an egg is twopence. That means that roughly £125,000,000 are spent on eggs annually in this country. Think of it. It's colossal! It's almost pitiful.'

Alice sat staring into the distance, seeming to smile.

'You're not listening?' James Pypper said.

'Yes, I am listening. I am.'

'You're not only not listening. You're laughing about it too.'

'Oh, no!'

'It's not a laughing matter!' James Pypper said. 'It's colossal! There's a fortune in it. All big fortunes have been made out of something very simple, like this. We must get started on it. The thing's so infernally simple. We must.'

Nearly a week later James Pypper had closed down the mustard business. He rushed home to Alice one day to say that he had rented a house and four acres of land out in the country. That afternoon he and Alice drove out in the 10-h.p van to see the house and land.

When she saw the house Alice was too appalled to say anything. It stood on high exposed ground like a slice cut out of a working-class street. It seemed as if it had been cut out of a strange impoverished town, dumped down and that the occupants had hastily fled because of the raw hideousness of the place, because they were miles from anybody or anywhere, because of some bleak, sour quality of loneliness in the surrounding land. Then Alice saw another reason why they had fled. Out of the distance came the sound of a train. It came shrieking and piping up a deep cutting fifty yards from the house, its long line of white smoke rising, hanging for a few moments and then vanishing in the clear sunny autumn air.

A few minutes later, while James Pypper was enthusiastically pacing up and down on the neglected patch of grass adjoining the house, Alice walked the short distance along the road to the railway cutting. She was surprised to find it very deep. At the track the road made a dead end. There was no bridge, but steps went down the cutting, and over the single set of metals there was a wooden foot-crossing.

Alice climbed the stile in the hedge and went down the wooden steps towards the permanent way. Along the railway banks yellow flags of ragwort, torn about by early autumn winds, waved between bright pink patches of late willow herb. Now that the train had passed the air was at rest, with settled echoes. Alice walked down the steps, stood still at the bottom of them, and gazed up and down the line with her habitual expression of unconsciously smiling repose. The lines, chromium bright in the sun, stretched away dead straight on either side. The train that had passed had come down a long steep gradient and farther up the slope deep woods closed in on both sides of the track. Beyond this wooded gully, at the crest of the gradient, stood a white signal-box. As Alice stood looking at it the track became so quiet that small companies of rabbits began to come and feed on the grass and wood pigeons began to moan softly in the woods, the low sounds coming down the lines like softly telegraphed messages.

Alice stood looking up the line for almost five minutes, before James Pypper's voice, calling her name from the vicinity of the house, aroused her. All

this time her brown almond eyes had been fixed on
the signal box, with remote and disquieted thoughtful-
ness, as though she were thinking deeply about something or even not thinking at all.

I I

For some time, on into the beginning of the next
year, things went fairly well with James Pypper's
simple scheme for making a fortune out of the egg.
Neat rows of expensive mobile chicken-houses covered
the field by the house, and sometimes the broken
ruminative talk of two or three hundred brown and
white hens was the only sound Alice heard, except the
sound of the trains, on the dark quiet winter afternoons. Sometimes, when James Pypper left early to
go to one market or another with the crates of eggs
that now replaced the pots of mustard in the 10-h.p.
van, it was the only sound she heard all day. After a
time it seemed that she did not hear the trains. At first
they had shaken and disturbed her, shaking crockery
in the house, shaking the windows so that she did not
sleep at nights. They had shaken and broken the days
by their shrieking and clamour into harsh sections that
made her so nervous that she felt sometimes that the
north-bound trains, expressing down the gradient,
were coming straight into the house. Then gradually
she grew used to them, gradually forgot them.

On some days the only living soul she saw was the
boy who cleaned the chicken-houses and collected the
eggs and made himself generally useful. Working out
in the raw open air of the bare hillside she became
strong and healthy, her breasts and arms filling out,
her face warmly fresh. But her brown almond eyes

still retained their disquieting habit of smiling at in-
conceivably remote distances or simply at nothing at
all, and soon, twice or three times a week, they were
smiling or seeming to smile at the men who drove up
the road and turned into the gateway with lorry loads
of chicken feed or peat-litter or simply with the vans
delivering meat and groceries. By the simple and unconscious habit of appearing to smile she seemed to
confer on each of them a special sort of affection. She
had another habit by which she curled her left arm
completely over her head, so that she could play softly
with the lobe of her right ear. Standing like this,
against the door-post, the shape of one breast and one
arm beautifully exposed, she had an air of serene and
disturbing invitation. In a gentle sort of way she was
very fascinating and soon the men were driving up
the dead-end road on the pretext of having forgotten
an order or on no pretext whatsoever. Sometimes on
cold mornings, as she gave them cups of hot tea and
lumps of bread and cheese, treating them all equally
at various times, they would remind her of things she
might have forgotten — 'Any corn, Mrs. Pypper, any
sausages, any coke this time?' — and she would say,
perhaps, 'No, not this time, perhaps next time', and
like the men behind the grocers' counters they would
hope that next time would not be long. And as signs
of spring began to show themselves in the longer days
and the stronger light over the claret-coloured buds of
the birch trees that fringed the woods on the railway
line, there would be greetings like 'Beautiful morning,
Mrs. Pypper, lovely day', and again it would seem as
if the beauty of the day became confused in the men's
minds with the charming lovable beauty of the girl
leaning on the door-post, playing with her ear and
smiling at the fresh spring sky.

But occasionally, in the afternoons, she was not there to answer the door. As spring came on she began to find more and more pleasure in walking along the banks of the railway. Beyond the hedge a path ran along the crest of the bank and she gradually got into the habit of walking there for an hour or so on fine spring afternoons.

By this time, on the sheltered part of the bank, under the woods, primroses were making soft yellow rosettes in the wintry grass, and wands of silvery wine pussy-willow were pushing out from the mass of darker leafless trees. Except for the trains and an occasional plate-layer walking below her by the line and the dainty patter of pheasants' feet on the dry leaves under the birch trees in the woods there would be scarcely a sound or movement during the whole of her walk up the track and back again. It was not only out of this secluded sort of quietness and the primroses and the sight of the young birch trees that she got a happiness that she did not ever experience with James Pypper, but out of the mere sight and nearness of the endless lines of steel running below her. In the shining metals, running away into the distances, her vague smile into space seemed to find its foundation. It seemed to be able to follow the lines to some point of permanence and reality.

One afternoon she walked as far as the signal-box. She had primroses in her hand and as she sat down opposite the box she kept touching her face with the flowers, disturbing velvety breaths of scent.

She sat and looked at the signal-box. She could see the signalman working inside it, pulling levers. She heard the ringing of the telegraphs, strange urgent sounds in the silence of the track, and she could see a tall red geranium flowering in one of the windows.

For a long time she sat there fascinated. She could see for miles up and down the empty metals, and presently she realized that the signal-box was on the highest point of the gradient and that, by watching, she could see the signals give their responses to the levers.

In about five minutes she heard the sound of a train coming uphill from the north. Though it was an express it came fairly slowly, forcing its way up the gradient laboriously. As it came nearer she felt a curious rising emotion, an advance of a moment of dramatic power. With the approach of the great double-engined train she began to tremble, and she realized that the moment would come when the train passed the signal-box. The intensity of her feeling was sharpened because the train came slowly. It had the effect of drawing out her emotion like a thread of bright hot glass.

In the middle of feeling all this she saw that the signalman had opened the window of his box and was leaning out, watching the approaching train. She had just time to note that he was a lean dark young man in his shirt sleeves before the train rose to the high point of the gradient and passed the box. At this moment the hot glass thread of her emotions seemed to solidify, become brittle and splinter violently. She was aware of being suddenly relieved and happy: the sort of feeling that might have followed the aversion of a catastrophe. She discovered that she was smiling, really smiling this time, and was waving her hand. To add to her delight the signalman was waving his hand too.

When the train had finally gone by there was an interval of about half a minute before the signalman went back into his box. In this moment he looked up at her. She was still smiling and it seemed for a second as if he smiled too.

She remained there for another hour, watching the trains and between the trains watching the shadowy figure of the signalman at work in the box below. Each train produced in her the same effect of drawn-out emotion, as of hot glass drawing out, hardening and smashing explosively into relief and happiness. She knew that the signalman must have been aware of her sitting there, yet he did not appear at the window again.

The next day she walked up the track at the same time and sat down in the same place and remained for about the same length of time. She saw the same train come laboriously up the gradient again, and experienced the same deep emotion, terrifying in its peculiar and too-fine ecstasy. Once again she had primroses in her hand, and once again she waved her hand and smiled at the man in the signal-box and it seemed again as if he smiled too.

The next day she was there again. And that day she had no doubt that the signalman was very aware of her presence. He came several times to the window, and once to the door of the signal-box. He looked up at her and she smiled. It was now a real smile, its true perspective fixed, its direction and object fully conscious. She felt that nothing could have been more soothing and beautiful than this fully realized moment of her smile and its return from a man she did not know and perhaps could never speak to.

After this she began to go up to the signal-box almost every afternoon. She complained to James Pypper, when he asked why she left the chickens, that the oil from the incubators gave her a headache and that the walk would do her good. James Pypper did not protest. Spring was coming on and there were a million eggs too many in the world and he was preoccupied by all the problems that an egg can raise.

Spring also began to strengthen and become very beautiful along the railway track. There were violets now, white snowdroplike buds in the grass and patches of dark purple and pale mauve lace all along the slanting yellow banks of primroses. The birches were showing a little leaf and the sallows had bright golden beards that trembled with bees in the sun.

There was something else, besides the trains, the excitement and the beauty of spring breaking on the woodsides, that appeared to Alice very wonderful. It was the awakening and stilling and reawakening of many voices in the woods by the passing of the trains. If she could not speak to the man in the signal-box — and she did not see how it could ever be possible — this clamour of voices and echoes could be a kind of common speech between them: the speech of the trains which now controlled so much of both their lives, though their lives had no other contact.

Then one day something new happened. Alice sat on in the sunshine above the bright glistening metals until six o'clock. Just before six o'clock she saw another man coming down the opposite bank. She saw him enter the signal-box and realized that it was time for the change of shift.

She waited to see what would happen. In about a minute she saw the first man, the dark lean young man, come out of the box. She saw that he was carrying the red geranium: perhaps to take home for a window, perhaps to re-pot it, perhaps, she thought, to give it to her. And suddenly she wanted him to give it to her. She wanted him to come across the track and say something and give her the geranium.

She wanted him to take the first step that would lead to friendship, perhaps affection, perhaps intimacy.

And having come down the steps of the signal-box the signalman paused on the edge of the track as if the same thought were in his mind. He must have been puzzled by her. He must have reasoned out for himself that it was not because of the spring or the thrill of trains or the voices in the woods that she came there smiling, but solely because of himself. He stood there for about half a minute, holding the bright red geranium, trying, it seemed, to make up his mind to come across the lines to her. Then, perhaps because he was self-consciously aware of being watched by the other man in the box, he decided against it. He turned and walked up the diagonal path of the bank.

By the time he had reached the top of the bank Alice had got to her feet and was walking along too. They walked a little way in the same direction, as it were side by side, although separated by the tracks. This short walk produced in her a deep sense of intimacy, so deep that a train roared down the gradient and passed them before she had time to realize it had come and gone.

A moment later the signalman stopped and climbed a fence on the edge of the wood. For a moment Alice stopped too. Then he waved his hand. She waved her hand back to him and kept waving it as she slowly walked away.

This same thing began to happen every evening. Gradually she knew that she was more intimate with the signalman, to whom she never spoke and from whom she was continually separated by the tracks of a railway, than she had been or could ever be with James Pypper, now struggling with increasing desperation with all the maddening problems of the egg.

She had become not only intimate, but she had an increasingly deep conviction that she was in love. But it was not so much that she was in love as that she herself was the loved one. The structure of both the love she was giving and the love she was being given was built on things that had nothing to do with love: on the passing of trains, the strange ringing of telegraphs in the silence of the spring afternoons, the fall and rise of signals. The emotion of the passing trains was now identified with her feelings for the signalman, waving his hand each night before going home through the wood. She began to feel that her life was stretched out to the limitless extent of the metals; that it was so tenuous and delicate that it might suddenly snap, like bright hair-thin glass.

Finally she could bear it no longer. One evening the sky was duller than usual and there was a heavy unkind wind blowing loudly down the empty track. She was cold and she felt that she could not go home without speaking to the signalman at last.

She waved her hand as usual as he reached the woodside, and then she called him.

'Come over a minute!'

The wind took her words and broke them up, so that they could not travel. He raised his hand, as though to say that he could not hear.

'Come over a minute!'

She was smiling. There was something in the smile that was like a concentration of all the remote, tenderly captivating smiles she had ever given. It went across the track with an intimate and secret swiftness that held the man momentarily spellbound.

Then he started to run down the bank. The way he ran, not heeding anything, made it seem as if this was the moment he too had been waiting for. He ran with arms out, to steady himself, as if ready to embrace her. He was running without thinking and suddenly she knew that he could not stop himself.

She did not exactly hear the approaching train. She felt all of a sudden the intense dramatic emotion that the approach of a train always gave her. The train was coming very fast down the gradient. She looked with great horror across the track and she saw that in a moment the man and the train would meet.

A moment later her life lay all along the metals, an illimitable thread of glass smashed by the train that had passed. The echoes were smashing the dark woods to pieces and she could not see anything except on the lines below a splash of scarlet that might have been a red geranium.

Some weeks later James Pypper found that he could not master the problem of making a fortune out of the egg. He sold the chickens and the chicken-houses as suddenly as he had bought them, and he and Alice moved away from the house that was like a harsh slice cut from a street in a town.

Summer was coming on and James Pypper now had a wonderful idea. It was the idea of making a pile of quick money out of a dance-hall, in which he had bought part interest at a seaside resort. During the summer months it was bound to be a good thing, James Pypper said, a very good thing, a wonderful thing, because at some time or other everybody felt like dancing.

Alice, who had not liked mustard and had become indifferent towards the many problems of the egg, went with him. But she had lost her way of smiling, and she did not feel like dancing now.

TIME TO KILL

HE inquired at the station if they knew anyone named Edwards, but at first they did not know. Then a second porter came and stood thoughtfully looking up the empty single track, where the bright spring evening sun flashed on the metals and on the slanting sallow trees that broke with grey and silver the bare monotony of the cutting beyond the coal-yards.

'Y'see there's so many folks named Edwards.'

'Yes, I know that.'

'Same all round. At Hardwick it's nothing but Baxters. Over at Stanford they're all Drages or Bowens. Here it's all Edwardses.'

Hanson began to wish he hadn't come.

'But wait a minute,' he said. 'You might know them if I tell you who the woman was before she was married. Her name was Claridge.'

'Ah well,' the porter said. 'Well. Now I know who you mean. Now I know. You mean Clem Edwards. Got a milk-round. Comes round in a three-wheeler. That's who you mean.'

'Where do they live?' Hanson said. 'I haven't got much time.'

'Well, without you go across fields it's a dinkin' long way round. Place called Ash Trees. It's no naughty walk if you go round by road.'

'Which way do I go by field?'

The porter began to tell him the field way, pointing an arm over the tracks. Hanson turned to look and felt the north-east wind slice his face from across the low flat land, cutting away the thin warmth of the sun. When the porter had finished Hanson said, 'Does that give me time to get back for the 7.47?'

'Just about,' the porter said. 'Only it's 7.53 now. Been altered.'

'Thanks,' Hanson said. 'Thank you very much.'

He walked away up the platform and over the iron footbridge and took the gravel path that went beyond the coal-yards and the last few houses of the town. The March sunlight was sharp and low on the level fields, making the young wind-pressed shoots of corn gleam like wire. In the naked ash trees that broke the lines of the hedges thrushes were singing high up against the sun, wild and clear in the bright wind. When he looked ahead Hanson could see the path quite clearly marked out, clay-brown in the young wheat, brighter green in the pasture.

He walked about a mile and a half before coming within sight of the house. A little distance off he stopped and looked at it. It was a small farm, a square flat-windowed house of light-red brick with a roof of blue slate that somebody had once left like a forgotten box on the flat land. He could see no ash trees, but above and beyond the outhouses and the wire fences a group of high black poplars were swinging heavily to and fro in the wind.

Coming into the farmyard he saw a man standing under a cart-shed, watching him. He held a spanner in his hand. He was small, with the high sharp cheek-bones of the district, rounded shoulders, and steady hostile eyes.

'Want somebody?'

'Yes,' Hanson said. 'Can I see Mrs. Edwards?'

'You can go and try.'

He stood weighing the spanner in his hand, hostile, intent, slightly puzzled.

'If it's got anything to do wi' insurance we don't want none.'

'That's all right,' Hanson said. 'It's not that.'

He walked on across the yard towards the house, uneasy, aware of the man still watching him. About the dry earth hens' feathers were being bounced by the wind among the many dark claret poplar catkins that had fallen from the trees.

Round the corner of the house, out of sight of the figure watching him, he knocked at the back door and waited. The voices of children crying in a room upstairs broke for a moment and then began again and in the short interval of silence he heard the beat of footsteps.

The face of the young woman who opened the door was not quite what he had expected. She stood shocked too, her dark bleak eyes beaten dead by the moment of astonishment. She stood looking at him with brief, inert silence, and then suddenly she came to herself and began to pull her stained torn pinafore over her head, ruffling her black short hair and then smoothing it, almost beating it down with her small narrow hands.

'Arthur,' she said. 'Arthur, whatever made you come up here?'

'I had some time to kill at the junction,' he said. 'I thought I'd just have time to come up on the branch. Just to see you.'

She did not speak.

'You didn't answer my Christmas card,' he said. 'You didn't send one.'

'No.'

'I wondered if you were all right.'

'I'm all right,' she said. Unconsciously, in perplexity, she had screwed up the pinafore like a bundle of rag. 'You'd better come in, hadn't you?'

She stood back from the door, which had dropped

on its hinges and would not open any further. He went into the kitchen. A cold sour odour of milk, a stale breath of boiled onions, met him. Milk pans, waiting to be scoured, stood about the brick floor of the kitchen and the small dairy place leading off from it. Beyond, in the living-room, tea was partly laid on a deal table. Thick slices of white bread were waiting to be toasted on the hearth, where socks and napkins were drying on a line below the mantelshelf. More clothes were hanging diagonally across the lamp-darkened ceiling, by the staircase door. The wind rattled the window on the east side.

She asked him to sit down. She had dropped her pinafore in the kitchen and now stood with empty hands. If there was some slight hostility in the way she kept standing it was unconscious and he did not notice it. He looked hastily round the room, taking in the details, and saw through the windows the edges of the great poplars beating against the sky. A moment later he looked back at her and suddenly saw her, uneasy, untidy, taken unawares, as the remnant of the girl he had decided not to marry, for some trivial reason, six years before.

A child began crying upstairs before either of them could speak.

'Is it two children you've got?' he said, knowing it quite well.

'Two,' she said.

The child cried loudly. Outside, the cries seemed to be reproduced in the short hollow sounds of a spanner beating on metal.

'There's nothing wrong, is there?' he said. The crying of the child had on him an effect of nervous distraction.

'It's earache,' she said. 'I'd better go up. Take

your coat off.' She looked at him with unhappy, disturbed eyes. 'You'll have a cup of tea when I come down again?'

'Only if it's ready,' he said. 'Don't make it specially.'

'It's our tea-time, now,' she said, in a dead voice.

When she had gone upstairs he sat staring at the tea-table without having taken off his coat. He tried to remember what things had been like six or seven years before, but the details were at first dead and would not revive in the oppressive ugly little room. Only the girl herself at once came back, involuntarily recalled in sudden, time-sharpened images. In those days they had both lived in the town. She was a school-teacher and belonged to one of those large, boisterous, clannish families who always stick and die together. There were five sisters and two brothers, all dark and rather self-willed, the girls very pretty, with small, proud faces. Several times a year the Claridges managed to find an excuse for a party, a coming-of-age, a wedding, New Year, in the big draughty local drill-hall. It was at one of these parties that Hanson, attending as the local reporter, had met Kitty Claridge. He remembered what a bright, impulsive, argumentative creature she had been: how she had argued with him all that evening, with militant smiles of triumph, on the merits of some writer whose name he had long ago forgotten, how every dance had been an exhausting, fascinating affair of beauty and conflict. After that they could never see enough of each other. On summer evenings, when there was little doing on the local paper, they would hire a boat and go on the river and float downstream between the willow trees to villages beyond the town, and in time the peace of the evening would be broken by the question of his going away and working on a larger paper. It gradually became apparent that she had no ambition to live anywhere but in the small, branch-line town, with the one tired newspaper, the flat countryside parched to concrete by the spring sea-winds, and the little river with the waving willow trees; it seemed that all she wanted was to remain, even after marriage, part of the large, proud, boisterous family, as if there were no other life and she would get all the emotion and excitement and beauty she needed in their way and not his.

The end of it was that they had broken up on some such point as this, quite trivial in itself, but really part of the larger question of his also marrying the family, which at heart he disliked intensely. He remembered that the Claridges were very affronted at the affair, and never spoke to his own family again. Shortly afterwards he got another job and gladly moved out of the circle of small-town family hatred. But with Kitty it was different. They had kept up a correspondence which after a time had dwindled down to a Christmas card: but he knew all the same that the correspondence of the mind, with its half-captured passages of warm, regretful thought, had gone on.

She had been married four or five years now. He did not know how it had come about. At the back of his mind lay the uneasy thought, dropped there by something he had heard, that the family no longer had anything to do with her. For some reason the boisterous, proud loyalty had been broken.

He was once more beginning to wonder about the oppressive little room, the isolated farm with the sea-winds striking at the poplars, and the man with the spanner outside, when she herself came downstairs again.

He was unaware of it until that moment, but the crying of the child had already ceased. For one moment the window ceased rattling, and he stood up, looking at her in the sudden silence. He wanted to say something to her: about the child, the weather, to tell her that she was not to make tea for him specially. But for some time he did not say anything, and she came over to the fireplace and began mechanically to remove the drying clothes, folding them and pressing them into a small heap with her hands.

'Don't move them for me,' he said.

'No?'

In this one word it seemed to him that he heard the indirect echo of antagonism, but when he looked up at her, quite sharply, there was nothing on her face but the same look of bleak surprise. She was rather thin and he saw that she found it difficult to keep her eyes quite still. They were weak and dark with nervous pain.

After the clothes were folded she went away for a moment, into the kitchen, coming back with empty hands. She came to the fire for the kettle, to make tea, her dark head bent down. Abruptly the window rattled like a machine-gun.

'I had an idea your husband was a mechanic,' he said. 'How did you come up here?'

'His chest was weak.'

She set the metal tea-pot in the hearth, afterwards turning away to the table. He looked after her and suddenly saw her come momentarily to life, setting the things on the table straight, moving cups, smoothing the cloth, her pride rising.

'The doctor ordered it. There was this little milk-round, so we took it — until something better turns up. We're not stopping here.' She turned round and spoke for a moment with defensive pride, holding up her head. 'It's only something temporary. We shan't stop another winter.'

Behind the pride he could detect the fear of it all in her voice; she seemed to know this and all of a sudden said something in a hurried whisper and then went out. He heard the outer door grating against the bricks as she tugged it open and afterwards, above the wind, he thought he heard her calling.

After two or three minutes she came back. Her hair was ragged from the wind, and in her hands she was clasping a bunch of coloured primroses, washed-blue and pink and red, tangled with scraps of leaf and grass, that she had hastily snatched up from somewhere. She put them into a cup of water which she set in the centre of the table, her face turned away from him as she did so.

And for a minute it was painful for him to look at her. He saw in the bland, soft glowing flowers the inexpressible recollection of other things. He again wanted to say something to her, but it was no use. He hated suddenly the flat drabness of the little room thrown into relief by the small glowing centrepiece of flowers. He was driven to hatred of the drying clothes under the ceiling, the rattling window, the sour smell of milk, the slight whimpering of the child which had again begun overhead.

He was saved from expressing or hiding what he felt by the noise of someone entering the kitchen, and a minute later the man with the spanner came into the living-room. He changed the spanner from one oil-greased hand to another as the woman spoke. 'This is my husband — Mr. Hanson,' she said.

'You're the paper bloke,' the man said.

'That's me.'

'You want tell 'em to write some sense in some o' the papers.'

'Yes?'

'Yeh, you do an' all!'

He wiped his oily palms on the flanks of his trousers and sat down at the table.

'Will you sit here?' she said to Hanson, and he sat down too. He heard the husband give a short laugh as he cut himself a lump of cheese, leaving on the wedge the greenish imprint of a finger.

'Flower show early, ain't it?' He pointed the cheese at the cup of primroses, ironically. 'Well, well. Very nice. Very nice.'

As she poured out tea the woman gave no sign. Upstairs the short whimpered cries of the child became fused into a single unbroken cry, and the father lifted his head.

'What's up wi' Jean?'

'Earache again.'

'Then why the bleedin' hell don't you fetch her down?' He ceased gnawing at the cheese with small chimbling bites like those of a rat. 'Sittin' here jawin' and lettin' the kid bawl.'

'I'll fetch her,' she said.

'You neen't bother!' he said. 'I'll fetch her meself. I'll fetch her.'

He went with a show of temper out of the room, and she stood for a moment in silence, looking painfully down at her hands, not able to speak.

'I think I'll go,' Hanson said.

'I —'

Her words would not come, and she made instead a brief, stupefied gesture towards the cups and the food. Before he could reply he could hear footsteps on the stairs, and then for a second her voice came to life. 'Don't take too much notice. He's not strong. It's because he's not really well. He can't hold his temper. It's just when strangers come.'

322

Hanson could not speak.

'It's nothing. I get used to it, I get used to it,' she said.

A second later the man came in with the child, a girl of three, in his arms. At the sight of a stranger the child turned away her puffed tear-damp face. The man brought her to the table, holding her on his knee, talking to her in a new, wheedling, tender voice, pouring out tea for her in a saucer and then sopping into it lumps of broken cake. 'Make old ear better, won't it? Dad make old ear better?'

In the few minutes before Hanson got up to go the father continued to hold the child apart, in a kind of alliance with himself against the mother and even, Hanson thought, against him. During all this time the child did not speak. In the silences the window broke into the renewed chattering of a machine-gun, and sometimes the echo of the sea itself could be heard in the mournful beating of the poplars.

'If I'm to get that train,' Hanson said, 'I ought to go.'

He got up from the table, saying good-bye to the child, who did not answer. Without holding out his hand, he said good afternoon to the father, who grunted in answer something about getting the newspapers to write the truth about things. They were at the root, he said, of everything, damn near everything. One way or another you could trace it all to the newspapers.

Hanson said a final good afternoon and went into the kitchen and so outside, the woman going with him. In the strong March wind her hair was flung tortuously about her cold face. For a moment she stood gazing at the earth and then said, 'I'll walk as far as the gate with you', and they walked together across the wind-dried yard with its storm-driven litter of feathers and straw and golden-claret catkins. All the time it appeared to him as if she were about to stop and say something. She wanted perhaps to express regret for things: or she wanted to get off her mind some oppressive, tortured explanation.

Whatever she wanted to say was never spoken. She halted by the gate in the wire fence and said good-bye, holding out her hand. The wind had beaten her hair unmercifully, giving her face a wild, bloodless look. He searched it in vain for a sign of pride or vivacity, but the eyes that were lifted up to him were quite dark and cold, and strangely repressed, as if they had got into the habit of not looking far.

After walking away at last he turned and looked back. She was walking back to the house, pressing her body against the wind and at the same time gazing down at the earth. He halted a moment in the hope that she would turn round, but nothing happened and he went on.

When he turned again she had disappeared altogether and nothing moved against the dead little house except the high sunless poplars beaten by the sea-wind.

THE LITTLE JEWELLER

I

MR. ELISHA PEACOCK woke suddenly at four o'clock in the morning, in the dead of darkness, feeling very ill. For some moments immediately before waking he was aware of a strange sound of tinkling glass, of his whole body fighting a violent constricton in his chest. When he woke at last it was some time before he realized that the sound was that of the night wind shaking the coloured glass chandelier above his head, that the conflict in his body was in reality a wire of pain boring down into his heart.

It was then that he realized he was very ill. In the moment of realization he suddenly heard too the striking of ten or a dozen clocks downstairs in the small jeweller's shop he had kept for thirty-five years. The sounds, not quite simultaneous, at first clear and then discordantly confused, rolled over and over his half-wakened mind in waves of metallic tumult. He managed at last to struggle up on one elbow. The pain, as if a hot gimlet were being turned slowly down into his chest, had now slightly lessened. The clocks had ceased. In the night silence he could hear no sound except the small renewed clash of the glass hangings above his head, and there was only one thought in his mind. It was the strange, painful thought that he, Elisha Peacock, after sixty-eight years of tranquil living, had reached the point where he must die in the night, alone, frightened like a child by the silence and the darkness, before anyone could reach him or he could get downstairs to the telephone.

With this thought in his mind he managed to get

slowly out of bed and put his feet into his slippers. The pain in his heart had now ceased to have direction or motion, and lay there only like a dull embedded bullet. He felt that he wanted to press it away and so held both hands locked across his chest, staggering a little as he walked. He felt very weak as he walked downstairs, slowly, not troubling to put on the lights, feeling his way by the cold walls of the staircase, and he was troubled by a remote but fierce idea that he did not want to die. By the time he reached the passage which led from the stairs to the glass door of the shop this thought had replaced all others: had become not merely a wish but a determination. He at last put on the lights of the shop, where the telephone was, and then stood still: a small, grey, perplexed little figure, his pain-washed eyes blinking in the white reflected light that sprang at him from the cabinets and shelves of glass and silver with which the shop was full.

For one moment he looked at the telephone, thought better of it, and then went into the room behind the shop, switching on the light. By the fireplace, in which the fire was quite dead, there was a cupboard. He stood with his hand on the brass knob of it, intending to get himself a glass of brandy. But for a long time he could not move. The upward motion of his arm had brought on the pain in his heart again. Suddenly he shut his eyes and felt that he was falling.

It was some moments later that he came to himself, knowing that he must have fainted. He pulled himself up to the cupboard and found the bottle of brandy and a glass. He poured out a little brandy and drank it. It smoothed away the harsh edges of his weakness and pain and for a second or two he looked vaguely about him, slowly coming back to his senses before going back upstairs, still carrying the bottle and the glass, still half-stupefied, so that he forgot to switch off the lights.

From that moment until eight o'clock he lay in bed, thinking. The pain in his heart had ceased, there remained in its place a huge, accumulative fear. He felt that he had been down to the edge of life, had looked over into a vast space of unknown darkness, and had only just managed to come back. This fear was sometimes so strong that he held himself immobile, not daring to move. He lay looking at the grey winter morning light distribute itself reluctantly on the tiny pieces of rose and emerald glass of the chandelier, which still shook and tinkled in the moving air. After sixty-eight years something almost catastrophic had happened to him, and now fear of its recurrence drove his thoughts back into the past. He recalled his life in the shop. He was not married. Outside, in permanent gilt lettering, he had had put up a quarter of a century ago a large notice: 'Peacock for Presents. Pence to Pounds,' and on this simple motto he had built up a secure, comfortable business. He had tried during all that time not to harm anyone; he felt he could recall honestly that he had never cheated a single person out of a single penny. He was not afraid of the opinion of any man. He had tried to be decent, upright, considerate, and he felt that perhaps he had succeeded. No, he was not afraid of that.

It was only the conscious realization of his fear of death that disturbed him. He knew suddenly, as he lay looking at the pieces of glass quivering above his head in the increasing light, that he had been afraid of it for years. The desire never to give pain to others had made him sensitive to the thought of any pain to himself. In one sense it had made him an ultra-careful man — he remembered how in the days of gas-lighting he would never go to bed without turning off the main for fear of being blown up or asphyxiated in the night — in another, quite careless. What had happened that morning had brought to his mind another result of his fear. Somehow he had shrunk from making a will.

But now he would rectify that. Yes, now he must see to it. When Edward came at eight o'clock he would explain what had happened; they would call in a solicitor. Edward would understand; you could talk to Edward. Edward was his assistant: a thoughtful, conscientious young man remarkable for resource and promptitude. He was not only a shop-assistant, but he came in every morning an hour earlier than opening time in order to cook breakfast. When he thought of Edward the little jeweller felt his mind instantly strengthened and tranquillized.

At eight o'clock the clocks downstairs began striking the hour and they had no sooner finished than he heard the sound of Edward unlocking and opening the back door. He lay still for a few moments, listening, and then called.

'Edward!' he called. 'Edward!'

He was surprised at the weakness of his own voice. It dissolved against the walls of the room, unheard. He tried to raise himself slightly on his elbow, but it seemed as if his body were made of wax that dissolved too under its own slight motion. He could only lie back on the pillows, weakly repeating Edward's name.

A few moments later he heard the young man mounting the stairs; then his voice:

'Mr. Peacock! Are you there, Mr. Peacock? Was that you calling? Mr. Peacock!'

'In here, Edward,' was all he could say. 'In here.'

Edward came hurriedly into the bedroom, a bespectacled young man with brown, alarmed eyes.

'Oh! there you are, Mr. Peacock. All the lights were

on downstairs, Mr. Peacock, and I couldn't make it out. Whatever's the matter?'

'Nasty turn, Edward,' he said. 'In the night. About four o'clock.' He tried to smile. 'An awful pain in my heart, Edward. Nasty.' He tried again to struggle up in bed.

'I wouldn't try to get up if I were you, Mr. Peacock,' Edward said.

'No good lying here, Edward.'

'That's all very well, Mr. Peacock,' Edward said, 'but if you're not well, I ought to ring up the doctor. Shall I?'

'I don't know, Edward. I don't know what to say. I've never been like this before, Edward. I don't know — '

He tried again to get up. For the second time his body melted like wax on the pillows. He shut his eyes for a moment, weak and tired, and when he opened them again Edward had gone out of the room, and he called after him:

'Edward! Edward!'

It was only after he had called six or seven times that he realized once more how weak his voice was, that it had no more strength than the gentle, insistent sound of the chandelier trembling above his head, that it was now very like the voice of a child, crying in trouble and getting no answer.

II

He lay in the bedroom all that day, irritated and tired, yet restless. Frequently he found himself troubled by the motions and the sound of the chandelier. It was a very strange thing that he had never noticed it before. Yet now it troubled him. Once or twice he settled back on the pillows, trying to sleep, but the tinkling of the little pieces of glass, stirring in the wind blowing in at the open window, made a tiny maddening curtain between himself and oblivion. At other times he lay thinking: about the shop, then Edward, about the chrysanthemums in his little green-house behind the shop, about the doctor. When the doctor had been and departed he turned over in his mind what he had said. He tried to read into his reticent words at first more and then less than they seemed to mean. 'The heart has had a nasty bump, Mr. Peacock, that's the trouble. A nasty little bump. It needs rest and quiet, that's all, Mr. Peacock. If I were you I should get someone in to look after you.' In time these words began to have on him the same effect of irritation as the sound of the chandelier. They told him nothing. Very clever to say the heart had had a nasty bump; wonderful to advise getting someone in. The trouble was that he had nobody: except a sister who lived at the far end of the town, married to a third-rate insurance-agent who rolled his own miserable ragged cigarettes for the sake of economy. He did not like either his sister or her husband; he did not think they liked him. It annoyed him that he should be forced even to think of them now.

He was glad when, about twelve o'clock, Edward came upstairs to say that his solicitor had arrived. Yet once again his feelings instantly took the form of fresh irritation.

'All right, all right, all right!' he said. 'Show him up! What's the sense in tramping upstairs twenty times when once will do?'

'Yes, Mr. Peacock, yes.' Edward hurriedly left the room.

'Wasting shoe leather!'

He lay back on the pillows, ashamed. His heart was beating very rapidly. He had not intended to speak like that. Far from it. No. He did not know at all what was coming over him. A few minutes later his solicitor came in, a tall narrow-jawed man who enjoyed a little shooting two or three days a week and who now entered the room with great heartiness, smiling. Suddenly the little jeweller, who had lived for so many years without contention or malice, felt that he hated him. He felt illogically that the solicitor and the idea of the will were the causes and not the result of his pain. His mouth set itself coldly against the bed-sheet, his eyes levelly transfixed.

'Sorry to see you like this, Mr. Peacock. Awfully sorry. Understand you wanted to see me?'

'No!' the little jeweller said. 'No!'

'Well, Mr. Peacock — '

'I don't want to see you! I don't want to see anybody!'

'All right, Mr. Peacock, all right, all right. As you like, Mr. Peacock. As you like. Perhaps I might come in again to-morrow?'

'No!' the little jeweller shouted. 'No!'

For some moments after the solicitor had gone he was still speaking, repeating that angry monosyllable in a voice that was foreign to him. When he had finished he was again ashamed. He lay silent, his hands pressing his nightshirt against his heart. Closing his eyes, he tried to search for the causes of his strange behaviour. He then discovered that he was lonely. He felt suddenly a great need for companionship, for some objective event or circumstance that would make him forget his fear.

Lying there, he recalled the chrysanthemums in his

little greenhouse behind the shop, and it seemed to him that he had found a solution. He felt a great hunger for the sight of the flowers. He called Edward, and then when Edward came upstairs he began to explain what he wanted: how Edward was to go downstairs to the greenhouse and cut the chrysanthemums. The young man stood listening reticently, with an expression of grave concern, asking at last how many chrysanthemums he was to bring? Something about the young man's earnest gravity suddenly seemed very funny to the little jeweller and he began laughing.

'Cut them all,' he said. 'Cut them all, Edward. Bring them up here so that I can look at them. All of them, Edward, all of them! Go on! Go on!'

'You don't mean it, Mr. Peacock?'

'Bless me, mean it? Of course I mean it. Why should I say it if I didn't mean it?'

'What shall I do for vases, Mr. Peacock?'

The little jeweller suddenly began laughing again, telling the young man that he was to get the vases out of the shop. The assistant looked very troubled but said, 'Yes, Mr. Peacock', and left the room. Ten minutes later he began to bring up the first of the flowers, great stalks of bronze and yellow and amber and pink, which he held at arm's length, like torches. He laid them first on the bed, where the little jeweller could reach out and touch them with the tips of his fingers, and then began to arrange them in bowls and vases brought up from the living-room and the shop. The little jeweller watched him with bright, alert eyes, the chandelier and the solicitor and the pain in his heart momentarily forgotten. It seemed to him now that the room was alight. For the first time that day he lay untroubled by fear. He let the lids of his eyes relax and from his prostrate position on the bed he watched the great curled chrysanthemums swim about the room like constellations that brightened and soothed his mind. He asked at last how many flowers there were. The young assistant said he did not know, and the little jeweller said, 'Count them, Edward, there must be fifty or sixty'.

'Yes, Mr. Peacock,' the young man said and began to move his hands, counting the flowers, turning his head at last to say, 'Sixty, Mr. Peacock. Exactly sixty. Funny how you guessed.'

'Guessed?' The little jeweller began laughing in a strange way again. 'No, Edward, no. I counted them! Counted them.' He laughed at the young man's grave disturbed face. 'Caught you that time, Edward, eh? Caught you?'

'Yes, Mr. Peacock,' Edward said.

'Caught you nicely, eh, Edward?' He continued for some moments to laugh with bright eyes. He ceased only to turn again to the young man and speak.

'Like having sixty moons shining in the room together,' he said. 'Eh, Edward, eh?'

I I I

Later that afternoon he fell asleep, awaking with fear in his heart about half-past three, momentarily disturbed by the November twilight and the sound of the chandelier. Earlier, before sleeping, he had been along to the bathroom. The catch of the bedroom door had not fastened properly, and the door now stood partially open. In this way he could hear voices. He lay listening intently for some moments, and then it came to him that they were the voices of his sister and her husband, talking to Edward at the foot of the stairs.

For some time he could not hear what they were saying. He caught only the tone of their voices. They seemed almost to be arguing. He heard Edward make a sudden exclamation, as if in protest. He heard the aggressively pitched note of his sister's voice, surprised, resentful, dominating Edward. He did not know why he concluded that his brother-in-law was there: except perhaps because he was completely silent.

Soon the voices came nearer. He heard the sound of feet on the stairs, and caught a sentence of his sister's: 'Well, then I think we'll go up and see what just *is* the matter.'

He lay gripping his hands under the sheet. He did not know why he should feel suddenly so antagonistic towards his sister, towards everyone. He had never liked his sister, but his attitude had been one of remote indifference. But now pain had ripped away the neat edge of his nerves, and he was angry because his sister had somehow been able to discover that he was ill.

He had withdrawn himself almost entirely under the sheets by the time his sister, preceding Edward and her husband, came into the room: a small, juiceless, volatile woman, with crinkled skin, her hands grasping a large patent leather handbag.

'Well?' she said. 'Well! What have you been doing to yourself?'

He muttered sounds of denial and protest that had on her the effect of a challenge.

'Well, of course, if you're going to be like that after we've traipsed all the way up from North End!'

'Like what?' he murmured. 'Like what?'

'Jumping down folks' throats! Muttering!' she said. 'Muttering!'

He did not say anything. The slight exertion of protest had made him feel once again old and tired. In a moment the tranquillizing effect of sleep and flowers had been lost. He turned with slight weariness in the bed.

At that moment he saw that his sister had seen the flowers. Her eyes were behaving like lights of warning in their wrinkled sockets. Her mouth, falling open, revealed a colourless dark gap between the plate of her false teeth and the roof of her mouth; but a single word of speech was enough to bring the plate into place again with a click of acid astonishment.

'Well!' she said. 'I wonder what next, I wonder what next!'

The little jeweller clenched his hands even harder under the sheets. As he did so his brother-in-law spoke for the first time.

'Been bringing the greenhouse indoors, eh?' He spoke with false robustness, as if trying to be funny. His words became as it were knotted in his moustache, which his habit of smoking loose cheap cigarettes had turned a gingery yellow.

'And what if I have?' the little jeweller said. 'What if I have? What exactly is it to do with you?'

'Mr. Peacock,' Edward said. 'Mr. Peacock. The doctor said you were on no account to get excited.'

'Excited?' the woman said. 'Excited. It looks as if that's the trouble. Over-excitement about something. Bringing a greenhouseful of flowers into the house.'

'Can't I do what I like with them?' he said, trying to raise his voice. 'They're my flowers! Without you interfering?'

'Mr. Peacock,' Edward began.

'Be quiet, Edward!' he said. 'Get downstairs! Get down to the shop. What do you suppose customers will be doing? Get down to the shop!'

As the young assistant went reluctantly out of the room the little jeweller's sister began speaking again, in protest, but he suddenly cut her off with an attack of angry words, at the same time throwing up his hands and bringing them down on the sheets.

'And you get out too! Both of you. Before I lose my temper. How can I get rest if you come up here arguing? How can I? How can I?'

'All right!' his sister said. 'All right! But it looks to me as if you want someone to look after you!'

'I don't want anything except a little peace and quiet!' he shouted. 'Get out!'

Rather hurriedly his brother-in-law went out of the room, his sister following, her lips strangely set. Suddenly he shouted after them that they could leave the door open. He wanted a little fresh air in there, a little fresh air!

The door was left slightly open. Exhausted, astonished at himself, feeling slightly ashamed, he lay back on the pillows. It took him some moments to get his breath. Then in the silence he lay listening, hearing again the voices from downstairs.

It was only after three or four minutes, after his anger was really passed and had become in recollection something foreign and meaningless to him, that he got out of bed, put on his slippers, and went to his bedroom door. As he opened it, he took his grey woollen dressing-gown off the door-peg and slipped it over his shoulders. Then he went slowly along the landing. The voices had already become clearer, yet not distinct. It was already late in the afternoon and as he went cautiously down the first few steps of the stairs he could see the chinks of electric light splintering sharply the darkness between stairs and shop. Half-way down the stairs he sat down, looking very small, slightly perplexed with his head to one side, and very solitary. He could hear the voices quite clearly now.

They came from the living-room: mainly the voices of his sister, catechizing, and of Edward, answering. His sister seemed to be immensely concerned about the flowers.

'Didn't it strike you as very funny,' she said to Edward, 'that he should ask you to cut *all* the flowers?'

'Well, it did rather. Yes.'

'Fifty of them if there's one,' she said.

'There's just sixty,' Edward said. 'Mr. Peacock counted them. He said it was like having sixty moons shining together in the bedroom.'

'What?' she said. '*What?*'

The little jeweller heard Edward repeat what he had said.

'Well!' she said. 'Well! Well, that settles it, that settles it. I'm stopping here until things are straightened out a bit. First he acts funny with the solicitor, then with us. Then he talks about seeing moons shining in the room. I think it's a good job we found out about it when we did.'

The little jeweller made his way slowly back upstairs while she was still speaking, catching now and then some more strident passage in what she was saying. In the bedroom the colour of the many flowers had died, but the room was full of a strong odour of chrysanthemums that hung pleasantly on the damp November air. Tired now, he lay down in bed. As he began to try to think, turning over in his mind what he had just heard, the chandelier stirred and began to drop down on him its small tinkling irritant bits of sound. It was this repetitive maddening sound, he thought suddenly, that throughout the day had goaded him into brief fits of anger. Why was it? He did not want to be angry. He felt recurrently ashamed of himself, miserable. Yet underneath the shame he was aware of a strange, dormant anxiety. It seemed to him that unless he took a terribly firm hold on himself he must sooner or later leap up in bed and seize the chandelier and smash it to pieces.

He was struggling with the perplexity brought about by this desire when his sister came upstairs and into the darkening room. Though he did not see it, she had taken off her hat and coat. It was in explanation of this that she addressed him in a challenging voice:

'Well, I've decided to stay for a night or two and look after you, Elisha, whether you like it or not. I've sent Fred home for the things. I hope you hear what I say?'

He did not answer. In a momentary flash of cunning he decided to lie still and silent, in a pretence of sleep.

I V

When he woke again it was late in the evening; the room was dark and still, and he was no longer tired. He did not know what time it was, but soon he caught from the street outside the broken echoes of passing voices and traffic and then, raising himself on his elbow, he looked out of the uncurtained window and saw lights in the street below. He felt briefly reassured, and then turned to look at the bedroom. He could see better now, and suddenly he realized that something strange had happened.

The flowers had gone. He sat up in bed and switched on the light. An accidental breath of wind stirred the hanging glasses of the chandelier, and in this moment he felt all the violence of the day's anger renew itself with tremendous strength. It was beyond mere irritation now. It no longer sprang from within him. It was an external force which seemed to take hold of him bodily and jerk him out of bed.

For a few moments he stood in the centre of the room, in his nightshirt, staring before him. Yes: the flowers had gone. They had gone and he knew that only one person could have taken them away. His anger at these simple facts beat him into violent movement. He put out the light and began to dress. Anger directed his hands to things he did not consciously know were there: trousers, coat, a loose black beret which he often wore in the shop, his boots, which he did not lace up. It seemed to take hold of him and lead him downstairs: the same immense external anger aroused simply by the fact that his flowers had gone. Outside on the landing he almost stumbled over the vases of flowers lined up against the railings of the stairs, but his anger did not cease. It drove him from the stairs into the passage that ran between stairs and living-room, shining through the glass door of which he could see a light.

This light made him stop. Through the lighted glass door he could see his sister and her husband. They had taken possession. They were having supper at a table directly under the electric light. Beating straight down, the light threw their faces into shadow, depressing them. Bottles of stout stood on the table. He saw his sister, mouth full, reach out her hand and grasp the glass of stout and drink rapidly, her face excited by food and drink and some expounded intention he could not hear.

He turned away and went back along the passage. He unlocked the side door at the foot of the stairs and went out into the street. It seemed again as if anger had driven him there. The night air was not cold, and he was still not tired. He began to walk rapidly, knowing in a strange way that he was not fully responsible for his movements.

But soon, as he walked along the street, his anger underwent a change. It became an idea. It was the idea that his sister and her husband had installed themselves at the house for the sole purpose of taking away his money. He moved under the street lights with an oblivious swaying movement, looking at the ground. From the nucleus of his single idea sprang others. He began to walk more quickly, impelled by the idea of escape. He became aware of the idea that he was being persecuted. They had taken away his flowers, they had come to take away his money. In time, if he did not escape, they would take away him.

He struggled along to the next corner, and then he had another idea. Out of the darkness there came a taxi, driven slowly, going home perhaps after meeting the last important train at the station. He put up his hand and shouted. The taxi pulled up and he told the driver to go straight to Mr. Archibald Foster's house, forty-five Edward Street.

'What street?' the driver said.

'Edward Street.'

'Edward Street?' the driver said. 'Never heard of it. Edward Street?'

The little jeweller stood slightly swaying by the side of the taxi, trying to think. Edward Street? No, that was not right. It couldn't be right. He was thinking of Edward. It occurred to him suddenly that he needed Edward. What street did Edward live in? Foster Street? Archibald Street? He ran his hand vaguely across his face. No, he thought, no, what was he thinking about? Archibald was the name of his solicitor, who lived in Foster Street. It was his solicitor he needed, Mr. Archibald. He needed to make his will. Then he remembered that Mr. Archibald was dead, that the firm was carried on by somebody of another name. Mr. Foster? No: he recalled abruptly that Foster was his sister's married name. He stood swaying on his feet, his mind for the space of several seconds quite blank. Where did he want to go? What was he trying to remember?

The voice of the taxi-driver aroused him at last. 'Thought of it yet?'

'No,' the little jeweller said, 'I haven't thought of it.' He now suddenly felt weak and cold from standing. 'Let me get in. You can drive on and I'll tell you when I remember. I shall remember it in a minute.'

What was it? he thought. What was it? As he lay back on the cushions of the taxi he tried desperately to beat his mind into a coherent effort of memory. What in God's name was it? He shut his eyes, pressing his hands against his forehead. The taxi swung from side to side, turning a corner, swinging him as if he were suspended by a rope. He knew again that he was very ill. His mind had ceased in its reactions. The knowledge of his illness was part of the darkness, the street lights swinging giddily past, the strange droning noise of the taxi boring with infinite melancholy down into his brain. Once the driver turned and spoke to him, but he did not reply. He was seized by the idea that he was being forcibly carried away into the darkness of a strange place. He had long since ceased his effort of memory. He felt now that he was fighting to escape. He felt very frightened by the dark confinement of the taxi and suddenly began to shout like a child.

'Let me get out!' he shouted. 'Let me get out!' He wiped his hand across his face and found his forehead cold with the sweat of great anguish. 'Let me out! Stop it! Stop it! Stop it! Stop it!' he shouted. 'Please stop it now!'

When he came to himself again he did not recognize his own skinny white hands lying on the dark grey blanket of the bed. In the same way, when he lifted one of his hands and drew it unsteadily across his face, he could not recall who he was. The strange details of the face, a growth of beard, the fleshless cheek-bones, the deep-sunken eyes, might have been those of some other person. He knew that the bed, too, was strange. He fixed in his mind the reality of its black iron shape, the grey blanket, the grey light falling on it from a distant window. Then he realized that it was one of many others.

Where was he? His eyes cast themselves with slow weariness from side to side. They alighted and dwelt upon a double row of grey beds. In these beds, all exactly resembling his own, other men were lying, one or two asleep. He tried to understand his relationship to them. He looked at the walls of the room, the ceiling. The whitewash had begun in places to peel away. He considered again the grey winter light falling through the high narrow windows, trying to determine what time of day it was.

Gradually his mind began to clear. Wakefulness itself had broken a tiny hole of light in his troubled consciousness. It now began to widen, and as the distribution of light quickened he gripped his hands tightly on the blanket, remembering. Fixing his eyes on the ceiling he remembered the chandelier, his bedroom, the flowers, his sister. But between these things and the present moment he was aware of a great blank. Then slowly he realized that this blankness was the key to where he was.

He looked again at the faces of the men about him.

Some were staring at the ceiling, some straight before them, out of the windows; a few were asleep. With an abrupt calmness of pity he saw them as the faces of men not responsible for themselves: the faces of the partially insane. For a moment or two this realization did not trouble him. He saw calmly, with detachment, that it did not affect him. He himself was not one of those silent staring creatures; he had no part in their strange immobility. He understood and was sorry for them, his heart no longer calm but crying unspeakably with pity.

Suddenly it was as if he had stepped on a revolving trap. He seemed to take a step forward and was flung violently out of calmness into a pit of terror. He had a sensation of being hit on the head. He struggled to save himself, and all at once was completely calm again. This new calmness remained for a moment unbroken. Then it was shattered by his own voice, shouting at him in his own brain. 'You are one of them!' it shouted at him. 'You are one of them! You are! *You are!*'

As the voice died, he lay very still. A voice calling in his mind? In answer he felt fear slowly begin to creep back to him: not merely his former, shadowy fear of death, but the very cold, terrible fear of truth.

He lay for a long time trying to reason things out. He found memory very difficult, but finally he had an idea. As it came to him he looked slowly round the room. The figures of the men, staring and wooden, had not moved. Cautiously he moved his legs under the blanket, bending his knees. At either end of the room were double glass doors, beyond which he could see a corridor. He watched this corridor during some moments for a sign of life, but nothing happened. He was thinking with peculiar clearness now.

Suddenly he leapt out of bed, flung himself bodily

at the swing doors at the nearer end of the room, and rushed down the corridor. He heard behind him an abrupt murmur of voices, which the closing of the swing doors cut off again. For a short space he was alone in the corridor, running along the grey stone floors in his bare feet. Then he heard other feet running behind him. They were feet with heavy boots on them. They ran fast, catching up with him. He turned to look, involuntarily holding up his hands. The feet with boots belonged to a man in a brown uniform. The man rushed at him and locked his arms behind his back. The little jeweller began to struggle. He felt himself possessed suddenly by a colossal strength. He began shouting. The attendant put one of his hands over his mouth, bruising his lips. The little jeweller swung one arm free and then the attendant began to hit him, striking him again on the face and the body. He continued to fight violently and the attendant continued to hit him, until at last he gave up the struggle.

'Come on,' the attendant said. 'Back you go. They all try this trick once, but you'll learn better. Come on. Back again.'

It was almost two hours later when he opened his eyes to see two figures, a doctor and a nurse, standing over him.

'Where am I?' he said. 'Where is this?'

The doctor did not answer the question. 'You're all right now?' he said. 'Better?'

'I want to go home, please.'

'In time.'

'I want to know who brought me here? Please who brought me here? A lady?'

'Your sister.'

'I want to see my doctor,' he said. 'My own doctor.

344

You know him — Doctor — Doctor — ' he tried to make a great effort of memory, 'Doctor — '

'It's all right. I'm your doctor.'

'I want Edward,' he said. He suddenly felt an intense revulsion of feeling against his sister. 'Why did she do this?' he said, raising his voice. 'Why did she do it? She'd no right! I never did anyone any harm! I never did anything.' He clenched his hands. 'Damn her! Damn her!'

'Please,' the doctor said.

'She wants my money!' he shouted. 'Damn her!'

'Listen,' the doctor said. 'Quietly. Your sister is paying to keep you here. She is struggling to pay as best she can. Don't misjudge her. How can she have your money if it's safe in the bank?' The doctor spoke with heavy kindness, as if in reality the little jeweller had no money and was under an immense delusion. 'Now how can she?'

'She gets it if I die!' he said. 'There's no one else. She gets it if I die!'

'I know,' the doctor said. 'But you're not going to die.' He held clean light fingers on the little jeweller's pulse. 'You've been getting excited. You mustn't do that. If you want us to help you, you must help us. Couldn't you manage some sleep again?'

'I want to go home,' the little jeweller said. 'Please, I want to go home.'

The doctor walked away, passing like a white ghost out of the swing doors. Seeing him go, the little jeweller lay back on his pillows, determined for one moment to be quite calm. The nurse remained about his bed, tucking in his blankets. He looked at her face, quite young, alive and soft, and it seemed to him suddenly the most human thing he had seen since waking in the grey, impersonal room.

'Nurse,' he said. He held himself rigid under the blankets, more than ever determined to be quite calm.

'Yes,' she said, 'yes?'

'Nurse,' he said, 'Nurse.' He was speaking with great earnestness, in a whisper, unaware that his eyes were glancing rapidly to and fro about the room, for fear of listeners. 'Nurse, I've got money,' he said. 'Plenty of money. Two or three thousand. See? Plenty.' He spoke in a whisper of desperation. 'If you'll help me get away I'll see that you get something. A cheque for fifty pounds. More than that.' He stared at her with terrible earnestness, almost wildly. 'You can come to my shop and pick yourself a little jewellery. Anything. You see? You see?'

For a moment there was no response in her face except a remote smile. Then she spoke. 'Jewellery. Well, that's nice,' she said. 'Jewellery?'

He wanted to speak again, but he could not. He looked instead at her eyes, which contained no hint of understanding. They were regarding him instead with a kind of impersonal pity.

He knew then what she was thinking. He lay back and closed his eyes in order to shut her out, and when he opened them again she was gone. On the walls and the blanket and on the scarred ceiling the grey light was growing greyer now with the dying of the afternoon.

When the nurse came back past the bed again she saw the little jeweller lying with closed eyes and the palms of his small, shrunken hands upturned across the bed. His lips were moving very slightly, but with her casual glance she did not notice them.

Nor could she hear what he was saying now. 'Take me away. Take me away, please. O Lord! take me away.'

LOVE IS NOT LOVE

I

ACCIDENTALLY, almost against her will, Lilian Jordan fell in love one springtime with a man named Harry Travers. Sometimes she could not imagine how it had come about, unless perhaps it was because Travers had a wooden leg.

At that time she was working from nine to five in the offices of a wholesale garment factory: a girl with a sensitive oval face, creamy brown skin and extremely kind, trustful brown eyes, a girl of brave and gentle temperament, who kept much to herself. In another room, on a lower floor, there worked a young man named Arthur Austin, who suffered from pimples on his face, and who from time to time, when she was out of the room, brought her notes which he laid on her desk with casual and painful secrecy. Like all the girls she laughed at Austin, and for some time it did not occur to her that he too might be in love.

One day, before she met Travers, she was persuaded by Austin to go out to lunch with him. At the small café round the corner they had a course of meat and vegetables, followed by tapioca pudding. At first she hardly noticed that Austin did not eat much; then she saw his pale-grey eyes begin to turn a watery yellow and his lips become gradually dry and nervous, and suddenly she sensed that he was about to declare his love for her over the tapioca. For some moments she went on eating as if she had not noticed anything, unable in reality to look at the nervous pimpled face, the eyes sick with an emotion they could not otherwise express and the red bony hands hovering with painful inertia above the already cold white pudding.

Suddenly, with great abruptness, Austin began to say what he felt about her. She heard a rush of earnest, entangled words that left her cold. 'Can't you come out with me sometimes, please, just for a walk, come to the pictures, I know I'm not much, I know I'm not much, but you can come sometimes, can't you please, can't you?'

'No,' she said at last. 'I can't. I'm sorry. I can't.'

'Why not? Please, why can't you?' He kept smoothing his dark straight hair fiercely with the palm of his hand; in the hope, evidently, of looking stronger and more determined. 'Please, why not?'

She did not answer.

'Please,' he said again, wiping his hair, 'why not? Tell me straight out what it is. Don't you like me? Don't you want to?'

'No,' she said. 'At least, not enough.'

'Why not?' he said. 'Why don't you like me? Tell me straight out. Go on, tell me straight out. Is it because I'm not good enough?'

'I don't know.' She sought desperately to find an excuse that would finish it all. 'I don't know.' She suddenly looked straight at his weak, unhealthy face. 'You don't take enough exercise.'

'Is that the honest truth?' he said. 'Is that what you feel? Is that all?'

'Yes,' she said, 'that's what I feel. You don't take enough exercise. You go to the pictures too much.' She tried to speak with conviction, not really believing all she said. 'You eat too many sweet things. You smoke too much. You don't take care of yourself physically. That's what's the matter.'

Then suddenly, before she could finish speaking, Austin got up and went out of the café.

After this incident she sometimes went to have

lunch at the café alone. Austin gave up speaking to her, and then a week later she heard that he had given in his notice and had left the factory. No one knew why it was. It was now early springtime, and as she looked out of the windows of the café she saw tender green mists, deep olive and sometimes almost yellow, skeined across the sunlit branches of the street trees. Lilacs were now budded with dark red knots in the surrounding gardens and daffodils were shaking brightly against the sun in the window-boxes of the café. Looking at them and thinking of Austin, she felt that perhaps it had been foolish to speak to him as she had done. Foolish and perhaps pointless too. Because it could make no difference, as she well knew, whether a man were physically fine or not. Looking at the daffodils and thinking of Austin, she knew that she wanted something more.

It was soon after this that she began to notice Travers; or rather she began to notice how Travers noticed her. She saw that he was in the café every Tuesday and Friday. He was a man of thirty-five or six, with bushy brown hair and rather heavy, kindly features. He seemed to her to be a man of certain fixed ideas because of his habit of coming to the café on certain days, of always sitting at the same corner table, and of remaining for a long time with his face tenderly supported by one hand, not moving, heavy blue eyes transfixed, watching her.

One Friday she noticed that he was not there. It was as if she had looked out of the window to find, suddenly, that the branches of the trees were bare again. As she went out of the café she began to feel oppressed by an overpowering sense of emptiness.

It vanished suddenly as she came out into the sunlight. She saw then that Travers was sitting in an old blue saloon car drawn up with a trailer at the edge of the kerb; and she knew for some reason that he was waiting for her. She stopped involuntarily on the pavement, and then he spoke. He said simply, 'We're always looking at each other. I thought we might meet for a change,' and she said, 'Yes', and felt in a moment very friendly and liberated and glad.

For another five minutes she stood on the pavement, in the warm spring sunlight, talking to him. She saw his hands resting on the wheel of the car. She noticed that they were fleshy, muscular, expansive hands, the hands of a working man. Watching them, she drew the conclusion that they were part of someone of calm, conclusive temperament. It did not occur to her until afterwards that they seemed too large for the rest of his body.

Just before she went Travers asked if she would meet him on the following day. 'We could drive out into the country,' he said. 'You could come and see where I live.'

'Where do you live?'

'I've got a cottage at Felmersford,' he said, 'up the river. Do you know the river there?'

'No,' she said. 'I don't know the country. It's one of the things I want to know more about.'

The next day Travers met her outside the office at one o'clock. He sat in the car, now without the trailer, and opened the door for her without getting out. 'What about your lunch?' he said. She saw his large hand resting on the quivering gear-lever. 'I've had something,' she said. 'I'm not hungry.' The car presently moved forward through streets of sunlight.

'I thought we'd go straight out into the country,' he said. 'We'll get early tea.'

She did not answer. She saw that, in the calm conclusive way of which she had already seen signs, he had planned things out. Above everything she was aware of the car going forward, as it were, to meet the spring. It was a day of light cloudless wind, and sleepy sun. Through the light frail leaves of the birch copses she saw the sunlight flickering down on the dark unflowered spears of bluebells; and everywhere, in the grass by the hedgerows or under clumps of golden hazel or in the woods that began to close in on the roadsides, she saw the falling light transform itself into fragmentary shining patches of primroses, unshaken by the light wind swinging the uppermost branches of the saplings. Looking at them, watching the blue bonnet of the car sliding forward, she was unaware of not thinking much of Travers.

Four or five miles out of the town, Travers stopped the car. He lowered the off-side window but did not get out. She felt the light fragrant spring wind blow gently into her face. She saw, a short way ahead, a white double farm-gate and a house of pale cold yellow brick standing back from the road behind an avenue of young willow-trees.

'Listen a minute,' Travers said. 'Listen.'

She turned up to him her kind, serious brown eyes, puzzled.

'Can't you hear?' he said. He smiled a little at her bewildered face until she focused the sound. Then she lifted her eyes completely and looked up and through the open roof of the car saw countless bees working with a heavy moan of sound in the olive-golden flowers of a willow-tree just in front of the gate. Travers seemed delighted at her motionless and enraptured air of quiet astonishment. 'My bees,' he said, and she saw him smiling as he drove the car slowly forward and through the white gates. Bees were working thickly too in the young willow-trees on either side of the track. Beyond the trees, on one side, a few sheep with young white lambs were grazing under a new orchard of slender interplanted cherries and plums, and at the foot of each plum tree a light sprinkle of white petals had fallen on the sheep-shortened grass.

A moment or two later the car pulled up at the house. She opened the door and got out simultaneously with Travers. She stood for a moment with uplifted face, the sound of bees still audible from the long double line of willow-blossom in the quiet air. Travers too stood still, and then said, 'Are you glad you came?' and she said, 'Yes. Very glad. Very very glad.'

'Let's go in then,' he said. 'I'd like you to meet my mother.'

He then began to move towards her from the other side of the car, limping. She instantly became aware, for the first time, of what was wrong with him. She saw the meaning of the too-large expansive hands, the heavy, benign features. She looked at the leg quickly and then away again, as if she had not noticed it.

Following Travers into the house, she was no longer aware of moving. She heard the sound of the wooden leg striking the ground, but it evoked no response in her. Under the stupefying effect of her shocked astonishment her face, suddenly averted, remained arrested as if she were experiencing a remembrance of sharp displeasure.

When she began to feel and be aware of moving again she found herself in the house, shaking hands with Travers's mother. She saw a small woman whose eyes, out of necessity, were constantly uplifted, sorrowful with a heavy compression of pity. The bony hands were hastily wiped on a pinafore before they could shake her own. The grey, anxious mouth repeated everything twice, half-smiling.

'You're welcome I'm sure, you're welcome I'm sure. Any friend of Harry's is welcome, any friend of Harry's is welcome, I'm sure.'

From these words and from things that were said once or twice during the afternoon, she gained the impression that the Traverses had few friends.

I I

During the afternoon she learned too what they were doing there. They had had the small-holding, with the house of cold bone-yellow brick, for nearly three years. In the effort to make it pay they were keeping and raising, buying and selling, practically everything they could lay hands on. Everywhere on the surrounding five acres of land she saw, or was taken to see, the marks of their enterprise. The Traverses explained how they had planted the young fruit trees; how they had bought and bred the few lambs and sheep that were grazing under the first plum-blossom; how they had bought young store pigs, chickens, tame rabbits, a flock of geese, a mare which they used for ploughing and a dung-cart. Since they had planted the young avenue of willow-trees with branches cut from an old tree that overshadowed completely the brick courtyard at the back of the house, they had begun to keep the bees which were working the willow-flowers. She discovered the reason why she had regularly seen Travers on Tuesdays and Fridays: not because he was a man of fixed habit so much as because Tuesdays and Fridays were market days and because he then drove down into the town with the car, bringing the things he had to sell. She saw how, on a south-facing strip of land under a hawthorn hedge, they had planted twenty lines of raspberry canes. Next to them sun-dried ridges of early potatoes were edged by rows of strawed rhubarb blanched in oil-drums, and they in turn by a solitary line of daffodils, which Travers cut for market. They had no cow, but that would come, the woman said with heavy, sorrowful conviction, that would come.

She noticed that Travers walked very quickly. He moved with intense agility, a fierce will to overcome the disability of the leg. When he moved like this, hopping about the yard to show her the tame Flemish hares and the bee-hives, or along the dry earth by the daffodils, she could not look at him. The desire to be with him at once broke up and splintered into fragments of shocked bewilderment. Yet she remained all the time aware of the gentle friendliness of his face and voice. She understood how he felt and what he was doing. She saw how he wanted to make the little farm pay its way; she knew how determined he was not to be left behind, how he wanted the things that other people had. She knew that he wanted to live and get on and make friends and ultimately make love as if the physical handicap did not exist.

She knew that sooner or later she must hear about the leg; but it did not happen that day. She stayed on until the early evening, having tea with Travers and his mother in the sitting-room that Travers himself had painted and decorated with a remnant of old-fashioned paper of blue rose design. The room, with its harmonium and chenille tablecloth, had about it a warm, overcrowded air of friendliness; the sunlight lay on the new shiny wallpaper like segments of yellow glass. A jar of daffodils from the farm had softened and drooped in the sleepy sun in the front window. When she looked at Travers across the table she forgot the existence of the leg and saw only the same tender reflective face that had first attracted her.

Even so she had already made up her mind, some time before this, that she was not coming again. She felt the predetermined relief of final departure as she drove away in the car with Travers that evening, holding his gift of a pot of honey and a bunch of daffodils. She felt the relief of escape from pain.

But a week later she was back again. She had not the heart to refuse Travers's invitation. The daffodils, in the hot April sun, were by now fully blown, and Travers had conceived the idea of selling them in bunches by the roadside. When she arrived at the white gate with Travers it was to see his mother sitting with useless immobile patience at a deal table covered with bunches and stone jam-jars of newly gathered daffodils and a piece of sheet iron ingeniously bent into a triangle, with 'Daffs. 3d.' daubed white on two sides.

In the sight of Travers's mother sitting there, lifting irresolutely the same bunch of daffodils to every passing car, she saw some of the reason for her own return. She was too kind not to be touched by their struggle for existence. She saw that they wanted friendship; she was touched because they were lonely people.

'I'm so glad you come, I'm so glad you come. I said to Harry I hoped you'd come, that I did, I said to Harry.'

'It's such a lovely day,' the girl said.

'Any luck?' Travers said to his mother.

'Well, it's early yit, it's early. Nobody's had their dinners much yit, nobody's had their dinners.'

The girl looked at the uplifted eyes, the stone-jars filled with daffodils.

'Perhaps I could help?' she said.

'No,' the woman said. 'No. Go on with you, go on with you. I'm all right. You go with Harry, I can content meself, you go with Harry.'

'I want to help,' the girl said. 'I'd like to.'

Travers laughed. 'Let her help, Mother,' he said, 'if she wants to.'

'Well, all right,' Travers's mother said, 'sit along o' me, if you want to, sit along o' me.'

The girl sat at the table all the afternoon, until four o'clock. At intervals she too lifted the daffodils towards the passing cars and the sun. Cars rarely stopped; sometimes they slowed down, the occupants stared indecisively at the two women and the daffodils and the yellow house behind the rows of fading plum-blossom and then went on.

'I'm glad you come, I'm glad you come because Harry's never bin one to make friends easy,' Travers's mother said. 'When we come here we never knowed a soul. Sometimes never seed a soul one week's end to another. Never seed a soul.'

Not speaking much, the girl waited for what she knew was coming.

'I expect you wonder about Harry's leg?' Travers's mother said. 'I expect you wonder.'

'The war?'

'No, he wadn't old enough for that, no it wadn't that.' A car approached and she held up the daffodils with a mechanical motion and remained holding them after the car had passed. 'No, he used to work on a road job — ganger on a road job. You seen 'em riding home o' nights on them lorries, ain't you, you seen 'em how they ride home? All sitting in the back of the lorry? Well, that's how it were, that's how it were. He got pitched off somehow, and two or three others

356

with him. They was blood all over the road they said. I never seed it, but folks as seed it said they was blood all over the road.'

The voice, briefly excited and then saddened by memory, quickened and ceased. Another car approached rather fast, but the woman did not see it.

'Go too fast by half,' the woman said. 'Too fast by half.' She laid one hand on the table-top and remained for some time looking at it in a steadfast dream.

'Well, they kep him in hospital for I dunno emmany weeks, I dunno emmany weeks now. Then they took his leg off. Then it were weeks and months afore he could git about. Then they was ever such a to-do about the money part on it, you never heard such a to-do in your life as they made. And in th' end he never got a penny.'

'No compensation?' the girl said. 'But that's wrong! That's not right. Not to get anything.'

'Well, I won't have it said as I told a lie. He got his club-money, he did git his club-money. But that's all he did git.'

'But what about insurance? He could claim. Surely he could claim?'

'Yes, yes,' Travers's mother said. 'Yes, claim all right. But claiming and paying ain't the same thing. You can claim, you can go on claiming. On'y he got no business riding on that lorry like that, he got no business.' She looked up at last from the steadfast contemplation of her hands. 'He knows that now. But that don't git his leg back for him, does it, that don't git his leg back?'

The woman ceased for a moment, tired from talking but angerless, and then began to talk again, saying how at last they had come to rent the farm.

'He couldn't go back on no road job, and he'd got to

do summat, he'd got to do summat. So in th' end I lent him what mite I'd got saved and we took this 'ere place on. We got most o' the stuff on th' instalment. I don't hold with it, I never did, but Harry says it's all right, it's a way o' saving money, he says.'

She paused, trying to smile. 'And we're gittin' on a bit now, be degrees, we're gittin' on a bit now. But it's bin a struggle, no mistake it has.'

The smile on her face, after a short interval of silence, became a reality. 'We git things paid for a bit Harry'll git a proper leg. That old thing gives him gee-up some days, but he won't hear about a new 'un until we git things paid for, I know that. That's jis like him. Puts 'isself last.'

Before the voice had ceased again the girl was on her feet. A car was coming slowly out of the flat, sunlit distance, chromium glistening in the sun. Her lips were tightly and bravely set. She felt that if the car did not stop she might commit some desperate act of folly. She would seize one of the stone-jars of daffodils and hurl it at the car windows and smash them and make it stop. Then suddenly the car slowed down.

As she went forward with the daffodils, holding them at arm's length, proud and relieved, she began to smile. She did not realize until afterwards how happy she felt, or that she had now become part of the struggle in what the Traverses were trying to do.

III

She became more and more part of this struggle as the summer went on. By July the fronds of the rhubarb leaves had spread over the oil-drums like dark metallic canopies. Beyond the rows of potatoes, now in purple flower, the raspberries were fruiting for the first time, pink and ruby on the sugar-brown canes among the green and silver leaves. The land was dusty in the sun. After the office had closed on Saturday the girl, sometimes in Travers's car, sometimes by bus, went out to the little farm to spend first the afternoon only, then the night, then the whole week-end. She began to do things naturally about the house and the yard: drawing water, making tea, digging and peeling potatoes, pulling weeds. When the raspberry season began she stayed over Sunday and helped with the picking of the berries that Travers would take into town on Monday. Travers and his mother and she would begin at the picking when the sun first began to go down. Across the flat bright land she would hear for a time the sound of bells ringing in the country churches for evening service, but silence would come down as flat and level as the land itself when the bells had ceased, leaving the summer air so quiet that she could hear the tap of thrushes breaking snails on the bricks of the courtyard of the house. They would go on picking the ripe, velvet berries until very late. Across the land the long valleys of evening shade and sunlight would stretch for great distances and sometimes vanish completely before half the canes were stripped. Once they worked on by the light of full moon, the ripe berries and the stains on their hands black in the cheese-yellow light, the stack of chip-baskets rising like a white paper pagoda on the earth before Travers at last draped it with a hay-tarpaulin for the night.

Travers's mother, very tired, went on into the house half an hour before Travers and the girl. 'Git you both a mite o' summat t'eat. You'll be hungry when you come in.' When the time came Travers and the girl walked across the silent field to the house. The moonlight lay like bright cream on the dark potato-flowers, on the raspberry-leaves, on the slate roof of the yellow house. The tired, sore hands of the girl dropped at her side.

All of a sudden Travers stopped and placed his hands on her shoulders, then against her cheeks. He stood for some time looking down at her face, upturned in the moonlight. She could smell the fragrance of the crushed raspberries on his hands and she could feel the trembling of the heavy fingers.

'I know you're tired,' he began to say. 'I know — '

'No,' she said, 'I'm all right.'

'I wanted to say something,' he said. 'It's important, but I don't want to if you're tired.'

'I'm all right. I'm not tired. I'm not tired really.'

She felt his hands fall and grasp her shoulders with abrupt tenderness before he spoke again.

'I want to know when you're going to marry me,' he said. 'No,' he corrected himself, 'not when. I don't mean it like that. I mean if — if you will. That's all. I only mean if you will.'

She stood looking beyond him, not knowing what to do or say.

'I don't want you to say now,' he said. 'Not necessarily now.'

She still could not move or speak, and stood only looking at the moonlight, vacantly.

'You know I like you,' he said. 'You know that. And I know you like me, or you wouldn't have kept on coming. You wouldn't have kept on coming and staying if you hadn't felt something.'

'Yes,' she said, 'I like you.'

She could not now keep the tiredness and indecision out of her voice, and hearing it, he said again, 'I don't want you to say now. You want to make up your mind.' He began to speak with a great effort, more quickly. 'I know what it is. I know all right what it is. That's the reason I haven't said anything. That's the reason why I want you to make up your mind.'

'Would it be all right if I told you next week?' she said.

'Yes,' he said mechanically, 'yes.' His hands fell away from her shoulders. 'Yes, that'll do. Only will you promise? Will you make a promise to me?'

'Yes,' she said, almost against her will. 'I'll promise.' She looked away from him over the empty moonlit fields. 'Only you go in now, by yourself. I'll come in in a minute. I want to be by myself a moment, and then I'll come in.'

He walked away down the potato-rows towards the house, but she did not watch him. Only, when she turned eventually and went too, eyes downcast, looking at the brightly outlined earth in the moonlight, she could see where he had walked: where the stump of the leg had made dark holes in the dry earth by the edge of the potatoes.

One day during the next week a surprising thing happened. From the windows of the office, late one afternoon, she saw a young man in a light-grey flannel suit continually walking up and down the pavement on the opposite side of the street. When she left the office this young man came up and raised his hat to her. She saw with surprise that it was Austin.

'I didn't know you. I really didn't,' she said.

Austin was very much changed. His face had lost its narrow, pimpled look; he had no longer an air of pained nervousness when he tried to look at her.

She wanted to know where he had been.

'I'm an insurance man now,' he said. 'I've got a

small book. Takes me out into the country. I bike mostly. And you were right about the exercise. It's done me a world of good.'

As he talked they walked up the street in the sunshine. Without knowing it at first, she kept looking at his feet. Then she realized why she was doing it and why they attracted her.

'Anything wrong with my shoes?' Austin said.

'No,' she said. 'No. I was just looking at them, that's all — thinking how nice they were.' But she knew that in reality it was because it was strange to be walking with a man who had two feet. And she remembered too how she once told herself that it could make no difference whether a man were physically fine or not.

'I wanted to ask you if you'd come out with me again,' Austin said.

'I don't know about that,' she said.

'Just sometimes. Week-ends.'

'I'll see.'

'Just sometimes. I'm still mad about you. Say you'll come sometimes. Just now and then.'

'You'll be better with some other girl,' she said, 'not me.'

'No, I won't.'

'All right, but I've got to go now,' she said. 'I really must go now.'

The impression made on her by Austin remained painfully deep for some days. It was strange to be impressed and pained not by a man's voice or his looks or by what he said, but by the simple fact that he had feet like other men. In this mood she went about for some days looking at the feet of people walking. She knew that she did not love Austin, but she felt immensely grateful towards him for showing her what the feet of people could mean. She saw feet that were huge, flat, heavy and tired; feet that were assertive and militant and possessive; feet that were slender and jaunty and delicate; and she became aware of something very beautiful in all of them. Only when she thought of Travers she was aware also of something like terror.

When she came to the farm on the following Saturday afternoon Travers did not fetch her, because she had written to say that she would come by bus. As she walked along the road the heat of mid-afternoon seemed to strike her a series of flat sickening blows on the head. In the orchard the sheep were huddled against the hedgerows for shade and the leaves of young willows had begun to drop, curled and yellowed by heat, along the track leading to the house.

The doors of the house stood wide open, but the yard and the field were deserted. She went into the house by the front door, taking off her moist town-gloves. Her brown eyes, ordinarily kind and spirited, now seemed dull and defensive. She had made up her mind already what she was going to say, and even what she was going to do. Except for her gloves her hands were empty. For the first time for several weeks she had not brought her things for the night.

As she went into the living-room she saw that it was empty too. She sat down for a moment on the piano stool by the harmonium, twisting her gloves in her hands. On the table stood an empty tea-cup and on the old-fashioned horsehair sofa lay the opened sheets of the day's newspaper. She sat for some moments looking at this, dully reading the headlines sideways, and then finally she picked it up. As she did so she stopped quite dead. Underneath the newspaper — as if the heat had tried him very much and he had taken it off to rest — lay Travers's wooden leg.

She walked straight out into the sunlight again with a feeling of faint sickness and terror. She was not really aware of moving until she heard Travers's voice suddenly calling her quietly from a bedroom window.

'Hullo, there you are. Wait a minute, Mother's having a sleep. I'll be down in a minute.' His voice was excited by the pleasure of seeing her. 'Don't stand in the sun. I'm coming down.'

She walked vacantly round the back of the house, into the raspberry field. Standing looking at the canes, oppressed by an increasing sense of unhappiness, she saw that the hot weather had almost finished the crop, that the few berries looked dark and bruised, and that the leaves were very brittle in the sun.

As she stood there Travers came out of the house. She stood dully watching him hop over the ground, happy at her arrival.

'I've been having a bit of a sleep too,' he said, 'on the sofa.' For some reason he noticed her empty hands. 'Where've you put your case? I didn't see it in the living-room.'

She stood quite still.

'I didn't bring my case.'

'You didn't bring it?'

'No.'

He hopped sideways on one leg, as if about to lose his balance.

'You're not going to stay?' he said, 'is that it?' His eyes began to tremble with pain.

'No,' she said. 'I'm not going to stay. I'm not coming any more.'

'What we talked about last week — you mean you can't?' he said.

'Yes.'

'I know how you feel,' he began to say, 'but if you —'

'I just can't!' she said. 'That's all. I just can't.'

Afraid of crying, and suddenly wanting to end it all completely, she began to walk away across the field. She had walked about a dozen yards in the hot sun when she heard him call something after her.

'I know how you feel,' he said, 'I know. But why did you keep on coming? Why did you keep on coming if you didn't feel anything? Why did you? Why did you keep on coming?'

Hearing what he said, she could not go on. She stopped and slowly turned and saw him standing against the rows of shrivelled canes in the beating sunlight. She saw him standing like someone struck into inertia by heat and pain, his huge hands apathetically held at his side.

She stood for a moment longer watching him before she ran back to him. The tears were rising bitterly in her eyes and she made a slight cry of pity and terror as she beat her hands on his arms and shoulders.

'Oh! I will. I will. I do love you. I do love you. I do really love you. Please believe me. I do really love you. Please believe that I do. Please, please believe me now.'

THE EARTH

ALL that the Johnsons had was the earth. Very often it seemed as if it were all they had ever had.

It was true that they also had possessions — a plough, a two-wheeled cart, tools, a bony brown mare which slowly dragged the plough and the cart about their rough four-acre plot — but without the earth these things were useless. It was true that they also had a son.

The Johnsons' son was named Benjy, and it was more than thirty years since they had surrendered to the idea that he was not right in his head. It was not that he was insane or imbecile or even that he could not read and write and count figures, but only that he was simple, not quite like other people. And because he was their only son, the Johnsons had spent many years being a little too kind, too anxious and too sacrificial towards him, so that he had grown up to seem worse, in their eyes, than he really was. Benjy had the large loose limbs that often belong to the simple-minded, and thick soft fair hair on his face. He had the look of being a simple-hearted man as well as a simple-minded man. His eyes were blue and all day long he had a simple smile on his face. But somewhere behind the blue eyes, the simple smile and the soft childish hair, simplicity seemed gradually to have become a kind of cunning.

It was more than thirty years since the Johnsons, realizing that he was not quite like others, had taken Benjy to a doctor. This doctor had persuaded them that he needed interests that would strengthen his mind. It would be good if they gave him something to do, some occupation, which would help his development. It would help a great deal if they gave him a special interest, to feed his sense of responsibility. 'You are people on the land,' the doctor said, 'let him keep hens.'

So for many years Benjy had kept hens, and what the earth was to his mother and father the hens were to Benjy: they were almost all he had. When he came from school, cut off by his simplicity from other children, Benjy went straight home to his hens, which he kept in a wire coop that his father had made at the back of the house. At first he kept ten or a dozen hens, all colours and breeds, brown and speckled and black and white, and the coop was small. He fed the hens simply, on scraps from the table, seeded cabbages strung from the wire, a little maize, on corn-ears which he gleaned in the late summer from his father's acre of stubble. It is possible that a hen, being a simple creature, thrives best on simple treatment. Benjy understood the first and last thing about a hen: that it exists for the purpose of laying eggs. In those days this simple process had not become scientific; nor had it become highly complicated and commercialized. Eggs were cheap; hens mysteriously pecked nourishment off the bare earth. They sat in a home-made nesting-box, on straw, and laid the eggs expected of them.

Benjy understood another thing about the business of hens, and that was that eggs could be sold for money. At the very beginning Benjy's eggs were sold to callers at the back door of the house, in scores and half-scores and fives, and the money from these eggs was put carefully, almost religiously, into a large white basin that stood on the top shelf of the kitchen cupboard. The basin was beyond Benjy's reach. 'But one day,' his mother would tell him, 'the money will be yours.

You understand? Your father and me are going to save the money. When there's enough we shall put it in the bank. The bank will give interest on it and then one day, when you're twenty-one, it will be yours by rights. It'll be all yours and you can do what you like with it. Do you understand?' And Benjy would smile simply at his mother and say yes, he understood.

As time went on Benjy began to keep many more hens. Soon there were more eggs than could be sold at the back door, and by the time Benjy left school at fourteen he had forty or fifty hens and about as many laying pullets, and these were producing an average of two hundred eggs a week. Soon he would set off three times a week with a large basket of eggs on a wheel-truck, and hawk them in Castor, the nearest town. By this time the money no longer went into the basin, but straight into the bank. Benjy could read, and a year or two afterwards he read in a paper that it was better to segregate breeds of hens, keeping White Leghorns separate from Rhode Islands, and young from old. This meant new coops, and at the same time Benjy read that hens needed air and exercise and dry hygienic places to sleep. Benjy was very strong and understood a simple thing like nailing wire-netting to wood and began himself to build new houses and coops for the new, segregated breeds of hens. For all this he needed space, and so his father and mother gave him a strip of land running from the back of the house half-way across the field. In this way they gave him something more precious than they had ever given before. For the first time, without fully realizing it, they gave him a piece of the earth.

All this time they themselves had struggled hard and almost vainly with the earth. At the back of their minds lay a precious belief that Benjy would one day grow out of his simplicity. In the same way they cherished a silent belief that the earth would one day outgrow its poverty. The earth had yielded stubbornly for them, and the reason, like Benjy, was simple. The reason was not in the earth, but in themselves. For most of their lives they had put rather more value on faith than sweat.

For many years Benjy's father had been a local preacher, a man with quite a gift of talking. He liked not only to talk on Sundays, to village congregations in small still chapels far out in the countryside, but he liked to talk at the back-door, over the field gate, on the road outside the house. He talked so much that he must have had an idea that the earth, designed, created, and nourished by God, would take care of itself. While he talked thistles seeded and choked his wheat, rabbits broke in and gnawed his cabbages, storms smashed his standing corn. He struggled on like a man chained by bad luck, and while he knew that his land was poor and that Benjy was a simple man, no one had ever had the need or courage to tell him that he himself was a lazy man with too large a trust in Providence.

And while his father talked Benjy went on steadfastly with the simple business of making hens lay eggs. Part of the field at the back of his father's house began to resemble a quivering chequer-board of black and brown and white feathers. For a long time now the eggs had been too many for the wheel-truck, and Benjy at regular intervals borrowed his father's horse and cart, taking the eggs not only down into the town but also into market. All the time Benjy wore the simple smile of a simple-hearted man on his face, and all the time the money went religiously into the bank in his name.

When Benjy was twenty-one his mother and father

planned and carried out a little ceremony. They got his pass-book from the bank and at supper his father made a sort of speech, almost in the tone of a public address, in which he talked as if he had been a diligent man all his life, setting an example of thrift and industry, and that this, the pass-book, was Benjy's natural reward for following it. He talked as if he were talking to a child who still does not know one from two, and at last he gave Benjy the pass-book. 'This is your money, Benjy,' he said. 'Now you're twenty-one this is your money. Do you understand?'

'Yes,' Benjy said and he took the pass-book. He opened it and looked at it, and saw in it an amount of more than two hundred and thirty pounds. Then he shut up the pass-book and put it into his pocket.

Benjy's mother and father did not speak. A strange tremor of a peculiar emotion went through them both: a mixture of disappointment, fear, pride and pain. The amount in Benjy's pass-book was more than they themselves had ever amassed from the earth in their lives. They did not hope and did not mean that Benjy should give it back to them, but there was something about the silent, simple finality of his putting the pass-book into his pocket that struck them like a blow in the face. They had expected something else: a word of thanks, perhaps a concession, a willingness that they should share the money they had helped to save. It hurt them momentarily that Benjy should appear so completely indifferent to them and to all they felt. Then they remembered why it was. It was because Benjy was still simple. There were shades of feeling and conduct that were beyond his understanding. They were touched with pity for him, and understood.

'What are you going to do with the money?' they said.

'I'm going to buy a piece of land,' Benjy said.

'Land?' they said. 'What land? Where?'

'Mr. Whitmore wants to sell the four acres next to us,' Benjy said.

'But, Benjy,' they said, 'how did you know? How did you find out?'

Benjy had a very simple answer.

'I asked Mr. Whitmore,' he said.

'Well,' they said, 'that is a very good idea. A wonderful good idea. You couldn't do anything better.'

As time went on, and Benjy acquired the land, his father and mother not only felt that it was a good idea but they felt very proud of him. They had the kind of pride in him that parents have in a child that says its first word or takes its first step. Benjy, a simple-minded man, had taken his first step in normal, adult things. It was wonderful, too, that he had taken this step without help, without force or prompting. All his life they had treated him as a child that will not grow up and now, suddenly, he had grown up. Though they could scarcely realize it, Benjy was a man of property.

For the next four or five years Benjy went on creating more houses for more hens, and then selling more eggs and making more money. He was still a simple man. He could not have made a pair of boots; he knew nothing about the stock-markets. But he knew everything about a hen. His hens were still to him what the earth was to his parents: all he had, and all he understood.

There was only one difference between Benjy's hens and his parents' land. The hens belonged to Benjy. The land had never belonged to his parents, who had rented it now for forty years, on a yearly tenancy, from a man named Sanders. They had often spoken of buying the land, but somehow the scheme never came to anything. It was easier for Benjy's father to stand at the door and talk, or to talk in the pulpit and trust in God, than to make a business proposition. And now, at sixty-five, they were too old to think of buying land, even if there had been any money for buying land.

And suddenly the land was for sale: their land, their earth, which was all they had. The town was spreading, the man named Sanders said, and everywhere people wanted land for building. Either he must sell the land for building, or he must sell the land to them.

They felt lost and distracted. They had lived a vague, trusting life without system, with a simple-minded son to rear, with an infinite faith in God but with little or no faith in fertilizers. As a result they had nothing. Even the earth, which they had regarded as inviolate, was not theirs and was about to be taken away from them.

Deeply and painfully upset, they went to the man named Sanders, and told him how it was.

'I don't see no way of gitting the money,' Benjy's father said. 'So we must git out at Michaelmas. That's all.'

'Don't you worry,' Sanders said. 'Don't surprise me you can't see your way to do it. But I can tell you this, if you can't buy it, somebody not far away will.'

'Who'll buy it?' they said.

'Benjy,' he said.

They went home feeling that this was the supremely important moment in their lives. It seemed like the moment of reward. If their faith had been shaken, it was now completely whole again. They saw that there could be joy and satisfaction and ultimate good even in the raising of a simple-minded son.

'We never knew, Benjy. We never even suspected,'

they said. 'What made you do it? What are you going to do?'

'I'm going to put up more incubator houses,' Benjy said.

Again, as when they had given Benjy the pass-book, they did not speak. They had expected something else, without quite knowing what: a word, a small concession perhaps, an assurance that things would go on as before. But there was nothing, only the same simple finality as when Benjy had taken possession of the pass-book. They were momentarily pained. Then they knew, again, why it was. There are some things which are forgivable to a simple-minded man. The simple-minded, as they knew quite well, do not always understand.

By this time Benjy was almost forty, and it was only to them that he remained a simple-minded man. As his new hygienic chicken houses began to cover first one strip of his father's former land and then another, with the grey patches of hen-dung eating their way into the brown tilled earth, he began to be the largest poultry farmer on that side of the town. In appearance he had changed too. Always big-limbed, he had now become rather fat. His eyes were still a simple blue, and soft fair hair still grew thickly on his face, but now, set in fat flesh, the eyes seemed much smaller. They were no longer the eyes of a simple-minded man. They were the eyes of a man who, in a simple way, is quite cunning.

No one but Benjy, at this time, knew how many hens and chickens he possessed. No one knew how many eggs the collective-system lorries fetched from him every week; no one knew the amount in his pass-book. It was possible to gauge his progress only by the new chicken houses covering his father's former land,

and by the fact that he now employed people to help him.

One of these people was a girl named Florence. She had thick heavy legs and loose lips and unreflective grey eyes that matched Benjy's in their apparent simplicity. When Florence bent down to clean the chicken houses, which were raised up off the ground, Benjy could see a gap of bare flesh above her grey lisle stockings or the shadows of deep breasts beneath her smock. In a little while Benjy was catching Florence about the waist in the warm dark incubator houses, and for the first time in his life he had some other interest besides hens.

It became clear to him that his father and mother did not like Florence, this simple, undistinguished girl with ugly legs and a mouth that would not keep shut. But Benjy did not need a distinguished, intelligent girl, even if one would have looked at him. He needed a woman to help with the hens, and soon he was saying that he and Florence would be married.

As with the pass-book and the land, his father and mother were not prepared for that.

'Married? Aren't you all right as you are? Don't you want time to consider it? Where are you going to live?'

'Here,' Benjy said.

And that autumn, at the end of his fortieth year, Benjy moved into the house with Florence as his wife.

'We'll want the front bedroom,' Benjy said.

All their lives his father and mother had slept in the front bedroom. Now they vacated it and moved into the back. This removal hurt them deeply. But because it was now Benjy's house, because Benjy asked it, they moved without protest, adding a little more to the long chronicle of sacrifice, forgiving Benjy because the simple-minded cannot be expected to understand.

But the problem of the girl was different. It seemed to them that the girl was about to take Benjy away from them. The air in the house became charged deeply with antagonism, the house itself invisibly but clearly divided. And then presently it became divided in actuality. Up to that time the four people had eaten together. Suddenly Benjy's mother did not like the way Florence scoured the saucepans. 'I always scour 'em with soda. Soda's always been good enough for me and always will.'

When Benjy heard of the quarrel he had a very simple solution. 'That settles it,' he said. 'Now you eat in the kitchen, and we'll eat in the other room.'

And throughout that winter Benjy and his wife lived in one part of the house, and his father and mother in the other. To the old people the days began now to seem very long, and as they looked out on the land they could see the reason. Where there had once been brown bare earth, rows of winter beans, patches of wheat, there were now only Benjy's chicken houses. The earth was still there, but the purpose of it no longer concerned them. The plough, the mare, the cart and their few tools stood about in the yard, but now it was truer than ever that without the earth they were useless.

As the winter went on, and the four people were more and more confined indoors, the division in the house became an enormous gap. The two women passed each other on the stairs with glances of antagonism, not speaking. When Benjy's father walked out to preach on Sundays he walked slowly and brokenly, with the steps of an old man. Only Benjy appeared not to be upset. Preoccupied with his hens, it was as if the emotions of normal people never penetrated beyond his plump hairy face and the eyes that looked so harmless and simple still.

But in the end it was Benjy who made the decision.

'Mum and Dad,' he said, 'it would be a lot better if you went somewheres else to live.'

'Benjy,' they said.

'A lot better,' he said. 'This is our house now. We want it. I bought the house and I want it now.'

'Benjy.'

'I bought it and I want it,' Benjy said again. 'I want you to go.'

'Benjy, we can't go,' his mother said. 'We got nowhere to go. We got nowhere.'

'You got to get out!' Benjy shouted.

As he shouted they realized, more fully than at any time in their lives, that Benjy was really not right in his head. His simple blue eyes were shot suddenly with a wild expression of insane anger. They not only knew that Benjy was a simple-minded man who was not fully responsible for his actions, but for the first time, struck by this wild-eyed burst of anger, they were frightened of Benjy too.

'All right,' they said, 'we'll find some way to go.'

It was little more than a week later when Benjy drove his mother and father down into the town. He now had a small Ford van and as he drove the van, with his mother and father on the driving seat, he showed no sign of normal emotion. It was clear that he did not understand the meaning of affection, or of bewilderment, or despair. He felt and spoke and thought only in the simplest terms, with the cruel simplicity of a child.

'You'll be better by yourselves in lodgings,' he said. 'You'll be better by yourselves.'

They did not answer. They sat with faces made

completely immobile by a kind of stupefied resignation very near to grief. They listened silently and, because for forty years they had believed Benjy to be not right in his head, they made allowances for the last time.

Down in the town the car stopped in a street filled entirely with houses. Benjy did not get out of the van. His father's and mother's belongings had already gone on and now they alighted empty-handed. As they stood on the pavement Benjy spoke a few words to them, looked at them with unmoved simple eyes and then drove away.

When the van had gone they stood alone on the pavement, looking at the ground. They stood as if they had alighted in a strange place, were not sure of themselves, and did not know what to do.

Once they had had the earth. Now it was not possible to tell, from their downcast and silent faces, whether they altogether realized that it, too, had gone.

THE WHITE PONY

ALEXANDER went down the farm-yard past the hay stacks and the bramble cart-shed and out into the field beyond the sycamore trees, looking for the white pony. The mist of the summer morning lay cottoned far across the valley, so that he moved in a world above clouds that seemed to float upward and envelop him as he went down the slope. Here and there he came across places in the grass where the pony had lain during the night, buttercups and moon-daisies pressed flat as in a prayer-book by the fat flanks, and he could see where hoofs had broken the ground by stamping and had exploded the ginger ant-hills. But there was no white pony. The mist was creeping rapidly up the field and soon he could see nothing except grass and the floating foam of white and golden flowers flowing as on a smooth tide out of the mist, and could hear nothing except the blunted voices of birds in the deep mist-silence of the fields.

The pony was a week old. Somewhere, for someone else, he had had another life, but for Alexander it had no meaning. All of his life that mattered had begun from the minute, a week past, when Uncle Bishop had bought him to replace the rough chestnut, and a new life had begun for Alexander. To the boy the white pony was now a miracle. 'See how straight he stands,' he had heard a man say. 'Breedin' there. Mighta bin a race-horse.' They called him Snowy, and he began to call the name as he went down the field, singing it, low and high, inverting the sound of the cuckoos coming from the spinneys. But there was still no pony and he went down to the farthest fences without seeing him. The pony had been there, kicking white scars into the ashpales sometime not long before, leaving fresh mushrooms of steaming dung in the grass. The boy stood swinging the halter like a lasso, wishing it could be a lasso and he himself a wild boy alone in a wild world.

After a minute he moved away, calling again, wondering a little, and at that instant the mist swung upwards. It seemed to lift with the suddenness of a released balloon, leaving the field suffused with warm apricot light, the daisies china-white in the sun, and in the centre of it the white pony standing dead still, feet together, head splendidly aloof and erect, a statue of chalk.

Seeing him, Alexander ran across the field, taking two haunches of bread out of his pocket as he went. The pony waited, not moving. 'Snowy', the boy said, 'Snowy'. He held the bread out in one hand, flat, touching the pony's nose with the other, and the pony lowered his head and took the bread, the teeth warm and slimy on the palm of the boy's hand. After the bread had gone, Alexander fixed the halter. 'Snowy', he kept saying, 'Good boy, Snowy', deeply glad of the moment of being alone there with the horse, smelling the strong warm horse smell, feeling the sun already warm on his own neck and on the body of the horse as he led him away.

Back at the fence he drew the horse closely parallel to the rails and then climbed up and got on. He sat well up, knees bent. The flanks of the pony under his bare knees seemed smoother and more friendly than anything on earth and as he moved forward the boy felt that he and the pony were part of each other, indivisible in a new affection. He moved gently and as the boy called him again 'Snowy, giddup, Snowy', the ears flickered and were still in a second of response and knowledge. And suddenly, from the new height of the pony's back, the boy felt extraordinarily excited and solitary, completely alone in the side of the valley, with the sun breaking the mist and the fields lining up into distant battalions of colour and the farms waking beyond the river.

As he began to ride back to the farm the mood of pride and delight continued: his pony, his world, his time to use as he liked. He smoothed his hand down the pony's neck. The long muscles rippled like a strong current of water under his hand and he felt a sudden impulse to gallop. He took a quick look behind him and then let the pony go across the broad field that was shut away from the farm-house by the spinneys. He dug his knees hard into the flanks and held the halter grimly with both hands and it seemed as if the response of the horse were electric. He's got racing blood all right, he thought. He's got it. He's a masterpiece, a wonder. The morning air was warm already as it rushed past his face and he saw the ground skidding dangerously away from him as the pony rose to the slope, his heart panting deeply as they reached the hurdle by the spinney, the beauty and exhilaration of speed exciting him down to the extreme tips of his limbs.

He dismounted at the hurdle and walked the rest of the way up to the house, past cart-sheds and stacks and into the little rectangular farm-yard flanked by pig-sties and hen-houses. He led the horse with a kind of indifferent sedateness: the idea being innocence. 'Don't you let that boy gallop that horse — you want to break his neck?' he remembered his Aunt Bishop's words, and then his Uncle Bishop's — 'She says if you gallop him again she'll warm you and pack you back home.' But as he led the pony over to the stables there was no warning shout from anybody or anywhere. The yard was dead quiet, dung-steeped and drowsy already with sun, the pigs silent.

Suddenly, this deep silence seemed ominous.

He stopped by the stable door. Now, from the far side of the yard, from behind the hen-houses, he could hear voices. They seemed to be strange voices. They seemed to be arguing about something. Not understanding it, he listened for a moment and then tied the pony to the stable door and went across the yard.

'Th'aint bin a fox yit as could unscrew the side of a hen-place and walk out wi' the hens under his arm. So don't try and tell me they is.'

'Oh! What's this then? Ain't they fox-marks? Just by your feet there? Plain as daylight.'

'No, they ain't. Them are dug prints. I know dug prints when I see 'em.'

'Yis, an' I know fox prints. I seen 'em afore.'

'When?'

'Over at Jim Harris's place. When they lost that lot o' hens last Michaelmas. That was a fox all right, and so was this, I tell y'.'

'Yis? I tell y' if this was a fox it was a two-legged 'un. Thass what it was.'

Alexander stood by the corner of the hen-roost, listening, his mouth open. Three men were arguing: his Uncle Bishop, limbs as fat as bladders of lard in his shining trousers, a policeman in plain clothes, braces showing from under his open sports jacket, police boots gleaming from under police trousers, and Maxie, the cow-man, a cunning little man with small rivet eyes and a striped celluloid collar fixed with a brass stud and no tie.

It was Maxie who said: 'Fox? If that was a fox I'm a bloody cart-horse. Ain't a fox as ever took twenty hens in one night.'

'Only a two-legged fox,' Uncle Bishop said.

'Oh, ain't they?' the policeman said.

No, they ain't,' Uncle Bishop said, 'and I want summat done.'

'Well,' the policeman said, 'jist as you like, jist as you like. Have it your own way. I'll git back to breakfast now and be back in hour and do me measurin' up. But if you be ruled by me you'll sit up with a gun to-night.'

I I

An hour later that morning Alexander sat on a wooden bin in the little hovel next to the stable where corn was kept for the hens and pollard for the pigs, and Maxie sat on another bin, thumb on cold bacon and bread, jack-knife upraised, having his breakfast.

'Yis, boy,' Maxie said, 'it's a two-legged fox or else my old woman's a Dutchman, and she ain't. It's a two-legged fox and we're goin' to git it. To-night.'

'How?'

'We're jis goin' wait,' Maxie said, 'jis goin' wait wi' a coupla guns. Thass all. And whoever it is 'll git oles blown in 'is trousis.'

'Supposing he don't come to-night?'

'Then we're goin' wait till he does come. We'll wait till bull's noon.'

Maxie took a large piece of cold grey-red bacon on the end of his knife and with it a large piece of bread and put them both into his mouth. His little eyes bulged and stared like a hare's and something in his throat waggled up and down like an imprisoned frog.

Alexander stared, fascinated, and said 'You think you know who it is, Maxie?'

Maxie did not answer. He took up his beer-bottle, slowly unscrewed the stopper and wiped the top with his sleeve. He had the bland, secretive air of a man who has a miracle up his sleeve. His eyes, smaller now, were cocked at the distant dark cobwebs in the corners of the little hut. 'I ain't sayin' I know. An' I ain't sayin' I don't know.'

'But you've got an idea?'

Maxie tilted the bottle, closed his little weasel mouth over the top and the frog took a series of prolonged jumps in his throat. It was silent in the little hut while he drank, but outside the day was fully awake, the mist cleared away, the cuckoos in the spinney and down through the fields warmed into stuttering excitement of sun, the blackbirds rich and mad in the long hedge of pink-fading hawthorn dividing the road from the house. The boy felt a deep sense of excitement and secrecy in both sound and silence, and leaned forward to Maxie.

'I won't tell, Maxie. I'll keep it. I won't tell.'

'Skin y'alive if you do.'

'I won't tell.'

'Well,' Maxie said. He speared bread and bacon with his knife, held it aloft, and the boy waited in fascination and wonder. 'No doubt about it,' Maxie said. 'Gippos.'

'Does Uncle Bishop think it's gippos?'

'Yis,' Maxie said. 'Thinks like me. We know dug prints when we see 'em and we know fox-prints. And we know gippo prints.'

'You think it's Shako?'

'Th' ain't no more gippos about here,' Maxie said, 'only Shako and his lot.' He suddenly began to wave the knife at the boy, losing patience. 'Y' Uncle Bishop's too easy, boy. Too easy. Lets 'em do what they like, don't he? Lets 'em have that field down by the brook, don't he, and don't charge nothing? Lets 'em leave a cart here when they move round and don't wanta to be bothered wi' too much clutter. Lets 'em come here cadgin'. Don't he? Mite o' straw, a few turnips, sack o' taters, anything. Don't he?'

'Yes.'

'Well, you see where it gits 'im! Twenty hens gone in one night.' Maxie got up, sharp snappy little voice like a terrier's, the back of his hand screwing crumbs and drink from his mouth. 'But if I have my way it's gone far enough. I'll blow enough holes in Shako's behind to turn him into a bloody colander.'

Maxie went out of the hut into the sunshine, the boy following him.

'You never see nothin' funny down in the field when you went to fetch Snowy, did you? No gates left open? No hen feathers about nowhere?'

'No. It was too misty to see.'

'Well, you keep your eyes open. Very like you'll see summat yit.'

Maxie moved over towards the stables. Alexander, fretted suddenly by wild ideas, inspired by Maxie's words, went with him. 'You going to need Snowy this afternoon, Maxie?' he said.

'Well, I'm goin' to use him this morning to git a load or two o' faggots for a stack-bottom. Oughta be finished be dinner.'

Maxie opened the lower half of the stable door. 'Look a' that,' he said. The stable-pin had worked loose from its socket, the door was scarred by yellow slashes of hoofs. 'Done that yesterday,' Maxie said. 'One day he'll kick the damn door down.'

'He kicks that bottom fence like that. Kicks it to bits nearly every night.'

'Yis, I know. Allus looks to me as if he's got too much energy. Wants to be kickin' and runnin' all the time.'

'Do you think he was ever a race-horse?' Alexander said.

'Doubt it,' Maxie said. 'But he's good. He's got breedin'. Look at how he stan's. Look at it.'

The boy looked lovingly at the horse. It was a joy to see him there, white and almost translucent in the darkness of the stable, the head motionless and well up, the black beautiful eyes alone moving under the tickling of a solitary fly. He put one hand on the staunch smooth flank with a manly and important gesture of love and possession, and in that instant all the wild ideas in his mind crystallized into a proper purpose. He was so excited by that purpose that he hardly listened to Maxie saying something about 'Well, it's no use, I gotta get harnessed up and doing something', his own words of departure so vague and sudden that he scarcely knew he had spoken them, 'I'm going now, Maxie. Going to look for a pudden'-bag's nest down the brook', Maxie's answer only reaching him after he was out in the sunshine again, 'Bit late for a pudden-bag's, ain't it?' and even then not meaning anything.

He left the farm by the way he had come into it an hour or two before with the horse, going down by the stone track into the long field that sloped away to the brook and farther on to the river. It was hot now, the sky blue and silky, and he could see the heat dancing on the distances. As he went lower and lower down the slope, under the shelter of the big hawthorns and ashes and wind-beaten willows, the buttercups powdering his boots with a deep lemon dust of pollen, he felt himself sucked down by the luxuriance of summer into a world that seemed to belong to no one but himself. It gave a great sense of secrecy to what he was about to do. Farther down the slope the grasses were breast high and the path went through a narrow spinney of ash and poplar and flower-tousled elders on the fringe of it and a floor of dead bluebells, bringing him out at the other side on the crest of a short stone cliff, once a quarry face, with a grass road and the brook itself flowing along in the hollow underneath.

He went cautiously out of the spinney and, behind a large hawthorn that had already shed its flowers like drifts of washed pink and orange confetti, lay down on his belly. He could see, on the old grass road directly below, the gipsy camp: the round yellow varnished caravan, a couple of disused prams, washing spread on the grass, a black mare hobbled and grazing on the brook edge, a fire slowly eating a grey white hole in the bright grass. He took it in without any great excitement, as something he had seen before. What excited him were the things he couldn't see.

The trap wasn't there, and the strong brown little cob that went with it. The women weren't there. More important still, there was no sign of Shako and the men. There was no sign of life except the mare and the washing on the grass. Although he lay with his heart pumping madly into the grass, it was all as he had expected it, as he hoped it would be. He took the signs of suspicion and fused them by the heat of momentary excitement into a conviction of Shako's guilt.

He waited for a long time, the sun hot on his back and the back of his neck, for something to happen. But almost nothing moved in the hollow below him except the mare taking limping steps along the brook-

side, working her way into a shade, and a solitary
kingfisher swooping up the brook and then some time
afterwards down again, a blue electric message sparking
in and out of the overhanging leaves.

It was almost half an hour later when he slipped
quietly down the short grass of the slope between the
stunted bushes of seedling hawthorn and the ledges of
overhanging rock, warm as new eggs on the palm of
his hand as he rested his weight on them. He went
cautiously and, though his whole body was beating
excitement, with that air of indifferent innocence he
had used back in the farmyard. Down in the camp he
saw that the fire, almost out now, must have been
lighted hours before. He put his hand on an iron-grey
shirt of Shakos lying on the ground in the sun. It was
so dry that it seemed to lie stiffly perched on the tops
of the buttercup stems. Then he saw something else.
It startled him so much that he felt his head rock faintly
in the sun.

On the grass, among many new prints of horses'
hoofs, lay odd lumps of grey-green hen dung. He
turned one over with his dust-yellow boots. It was
fresh and soft. Then suddenly he thought of something
else: feathers. He began to walk about, his eyes searching the grass, his excitement and the heat in the
sheltered hollow making him almost sick. He had
hardly moved a dozen yards when he heard a shout.
'Hi! Hi'yup!' It came from the far bank of the brook
and it came with a shrill unexpectedness that made his
heart go off like a trap.

He stood very still, scared, waiting. He saw the
elder branches on the bank of the brook stir and shake
apart. He felt a second of intense fear, then another of
intense relief.

Coming up from the brook was young Shako: the

boy of his own age, in man's cap and long trousers braced up with binder string, eyes deep and bright as blackberries in the sun, coal-coloured hair hanging in bobtail curls in his neck.

'Hi! What you doin'?' He had a flat osier basket of watercresses in his hand.

'Looking for you,' Alexander said. 'Thought there was nobody here.'

'Lookin' for me?'

Alexander's fear seemed to evaporate through his mouth, leaving his tongue queer and dry. He and young Shako knew each other. Young Shako had often been up at the farm; once they had tried fishing for young silver trout no bigger than teaspoons in the upper reaches of the stream. Shako had seen Snowy too.

'Yes,' Alexander said. 'When're you coming for a ride with the cob and me and Snowy? You reckoned you'd come this week.'

'Won't be to-day,' young Shako said. 'The cob ain' here.'

'Where's he gone?' Alexander said. 'Where's everybody?'

'Old Gal's hawkin' down in Ferrers. Dad and Charley and Plum gone over to Huntingdon.'

'Long way.'

'Ain't nothing,' young Shako said. 'Jis skipped over about some ducks.'

'Ducks?'

'Selling some ducks or summat.'

Young Shako sat down on the grass, Alexander with him, careless, as though he knew nothing and nothing had happened. Ducks? Ducks was funny. He lay on the grass, some inner part of himself alert and listening. Ducks was very funny.

'You said we'd have a race,' he said. 'You on the cob and me on Snowy.'

'Cob'd eat 'im.'

'Who would? What would?' Alexander said. 'Snowy's been a race-horse.'

'Well, so's the cob. We bought 'im from a jockey-fella. Out at Newmarket. Jockey-fella named Adams. Best jockey in England. You heard on 'im, ain' y'?'

'Yes, but what's that? Snowy's a real race-horse. You can see it. Some hunters came by the other day and he nearly went mad. He can smell the difference in horses. Besides, we know he's been a race-horse. Ask Maxie. He's got his pedigree.'

'Pedigree? What the blarming oojah?' Young Shako said. 'That's nothing. You know what a pedigree is?'

'Yes.'

'What is it?'

'Well, it's what he is. What he's been.'

'What the blarming oojah?' Shako said. 'It's summat wrong with 'is legs. Any fool knows that. Pedigree — any fool knows it's summat wrong wi' his legs.'

Alexander sat silent, almost defeated, then coming back again.

'You're frightened to race, that's all. Make out the cob's gone to Huntingdon because you daren't race.'

'Frit?' Shako said. 'Who's frit? I'll race y' any day. Any time.'

'All right. To-morrow,' Alexander said.

'No.'

'See. I told you. Daren't.'

'What the blarming oojah! They ain't goin' be back from Huntingdon till Friday.'

Alexander stared at the sky, indifferent.

'What time did they go?' he said.

'Middle o' the night sometime,' young Shako said. 'They were gone when I got up.'

They lay for a little while longer on the grass, talking, young Shako trying to talk of big two-pound trout seen farther downstream, in the still golden hollows of the backwater where the mill had been, but the mind of Alexander could not concentrate and he had eyes for nothing except the tiniest of sand-coloured hen feathers clinging like extra petals to the edges of flowers and grass, suddenly visible because he could see them horizontally, a hen's-eye view — the same pale creamy-brown feathers that he sometimes found stuck by blood to the eggs that he collected morning and evening from the orange-boxes in the hen-roost at the farm. When he saw them, realizing fully what they meant, he lost track of what Shako was saying altogether. He got to his feet and made some excuse about going back to the farm. Shako got to his feet too, saying, 'Yis, I gotta meet the old woman and hawk this cress', his deep black eyes careless and tired and Spaniard-like in the full sun, his voice calling Alexander back from the dozen paces he had taken across the field.

'You wanna race Friday I'll race you if they're back. If they ain't back I'll race you Saturday.'

'All right.' In that second Alexander came to his senses. 'I'll come down and see when they are back,' he said.

He made the climb back up the slope, over the warm projecting rocks and up through the spinney and into the warm security of the breast-high grasses beyond it in a state of such excitement that he could not think or speak to himself. He could only beat his hands like drumsticks on his brown bare knees in a tattoo of triumph and delight.

That night he knew that his uncle Bishop and
Maxie sat up in the farm-yard with loaded guns,
Maxie in the little corn-hovel, his Uncle under the
cart-shed, from somewhere about midnight to the first
colour of daylight about three o'clock, waiting for
Shako. In the small back bedroom where in autumn
and winter the long brown-papered trays of apples and
pears would be laid out under his bed and over every
inch of the cold linoleum of the floor, so that there was
a good excuse for never kneeling to say his prayers, he
kept awake for a long time, listening for something to
happen, yet hoping and really knowing it wouldn't
happen, suddenly falling asleep in a moment when as
it were he wasn't looking, and waking an hour too late
to fetch Snowy from the field.

Of what had happened down at the brook with
young Shako he did not say a word all that day,
Thursday, and all the next. He heard more talk of
two-legged foxes, talked to Maxie himself of the way
the men had sat up listening and waiting and hearing
nothing but the sound of Snowy kicking the fences
over the dead quiet fields. He saw the constable come
into the yard again, making a pretence of taking
measurements, arguing, really whiling away, as Maxie
said, the bleedin' government's time and doing nothing. He knew that his Uncle and Maxie sat up that
night again, waiting for a Shako that he alone knew
would not come, and he let it happen partly out of a
queer impulse of secrecy and partly because of a fear
that no one would ever believe his simple and exciting
piece of detective fantasy.

It was Friday afternoon when he rode Snowy down
the track by the spinney and out across the buttercup

field and down to the edge of the quarry. He sat bare-back, the only way he knew how to ride, and the warm sweat of a canter in the hot sun across the shadeless field broke out on his legs and seemed to glue him to the pony. The delight of being alone, in the heat and silence of a midsummer afternoon that seemed to grow more and more intense as the ripe grasses deepened about the pony's legs like dusty wheat, was something he loved and could hardly bear. The may-blossom was over now, like cream soured and gone in the sun, and elderberry had taken its place, sweet-sour itself, the summery vanilla odour putting the whole sheltered hollow to sleep. So that as he halted Snowy and called down to the camp to young Shako, who was lying alone in the grass by the side of the hobbled little brown cob, his voice was like the sudden cracking of a cup in the stillness.

'Ready to race?'

'Eh?'

Young Shako turned sharply and rolled to his feet like a black untidy puppy, blinking in the sun.

'Now?' he called back.

'It's Friday!' Alexander said. 'You said Friday.'

'Right-o!' Wait'll I git the cob.'

Young Shako began to untie the rope hobbling the cob's fore-legs, but Alexander was no longer looking at him. The camp was deserted again except for the cob and the boy, but down under the caravan Alexander could see suddenly a white-washed crate, an empty hen-crate. It startled and excited him so much that he hardly realized that Young Shako was ready and already calling his name.

'Hiyup! You go along the top and I'll go along the bottom and meet you!'

'Right-o!'

Alexander turned the white pony and almost simultaneously young Shako scrambled belly-wise on the cob's back and turned him in the same direction along the brookside. They rode along together, hoofs making no noise in the thick grass, the excitement of silence beating deeply in the boy's breast and throat. It seemed to him too that Snowy was excited, sensing something. His head seemed exceptionally high up, splendid in the sun, with a sort of alert nobility, his beauty and strength flowing out to the boy, so that he felt outlandishly proud and strong himself.

Gradually the quarry-face shallowed down until the land was entirely on one level. Alexander halted Snowy and waited for young Shako to come up to him. The land had begun to be broken up by sedge and to Alexander it looked as though the cob, struggling between the stiff rushes on ground bubbled by ant-hills, was ugly and ordinary and short-winded. Until that moment the boys had not spoken again, but now Shako said where were they going to race? Up on the top field above the marsh? And Alexander said 'Yes, up in the top field', and they rode the horses away from the brook together, skirting the marsh where even the high spears of reed were dead still in the windless afternoon, blades of dark green steel sharp in the sun above the torches of lemon iris and islands of emerald grass among the fly-freckled pools.

'So they got back from Huntingdon?' Alexander said.

'Yeh! Got back. Got back late last night.'

'Gone somewhere to-day?'

'Only down to the market. Be back any time now.'

'How far are we going to race?'

'Far as you like.'

'Make it from the fence over to the first sycamore, shall we?' Alexander said.

'Ain't very far.'

'All right. Make it from the fence over to the feed-trough. That's a good way.'

'All right,' Shako said. 'Anybody who falls off loses.'

The sun beat down on them strongly as they turned up the field to meet it. Snowy lifted his head and Alexander could feel in him a sudden excited vibration of strength. His own heart was beating with such deep sickness that as they reached the fences and turned the horses he could not speak. He sat tense and silent, his senses cancelled out by the suspense of excitement. In this moment the world too was cancelled out except for the dazzling blaze of buttercups and the poised chalk statue of Snowy's head and the murmur of grasshoppers breaking and carrying away the silence on tremulous and infinite waves of sound.

Another second and young Shako counted three and lifted his hand and dropped it and Alexander did not know anything except that something amazing and un-earthly happened to Snowy. He became something tearing its way off the golden rim of the earth. He felt him to be like a great white hare bouncing madly into space. He leaned forward and clung to his neck, frightened of falling or being thrown. The sycamore trees sailed past like balloons broken adrift and five seconds later he saw the two stone feed-troughs flash past him like boats torn from their moorings too.

Snowy did not come to a standstill until they reached the hedge and the end of the field. He stood for a moment fretting and panting deeply. It had been like a burst of majestic fury. It filled Alexander with a pride and astonishment that momentarily took his speech away, so that as he turned and saw young Shako and the cob clumsily pulling up at the troughs he could not speak.

He walked Snowy slowly back. His pride was one with the pony's, deep, quiet, almost dignified. It sprang out of the pony's heart. It stirred him to a few seconds of such love for the horse that he suddenly dismounted and seized his warm dribbling head in his hands.

'You see, I told you,' he said to Shako at last. 'He's been a race-horse.'

'Wadn't much,' Shako said. The deep Spaniard eyes were prouder in defeat than Alexander's were in triumph. 'Cob was just tired after that long journey from Huntingdon. Bet y' I'd race you to-morrow and win y' easy. What y' goin' be up to now? Going home?'

Alexander remembered how Old Shako and his brothers Plum and Charley must be back from market soon, perhaps now, already.

'No,' he said, 'I'll come back a bit with you. Cool Snowy off and perhaps give him a drink.'

'Don't wanna give him no drink while he's so ragin' hot.'

'No, I know that. I'll just walk steady back with you. I want a drink myself.'

They walked back down the field towards the stream, not saying much. Snowy was oily with sweat and the heat caught Alexander in the nape of the neck like a blow as they came into the sheltered ground beyond the quarry.

It was at that moment he saw that old Shako and Plum and Charley were back, one of the women with them. He saw the flare of the woman's yellow blouse and the dark beet-red skirt. The men were gaunt, hungry as hawks, shifty, with untranslatable darkness behind the friendliness of their eyes.

'Young Bish!' Old Shako said. He grinned with

white eager teeth. 'Thass nice pony you got. Fus' time I see him.'

'Nice pony,' Shako's brothers said.

The three men came round the horse, laying long dark hands on the white flanks.

'Nice pony.' Old Shako looked at Snowy's mouth, and Alexander felt proud that Snowy stood so still and lovably dignified.

'Nice pony. On'y thing is he's gettin' old,' Shako said. 'Been about awhile.'

'Nice pony though,' Charley said.

'Yis. Nice pony,' Shako said. 'You wanna look after him. Be gettin' 'im pinched else. Nice pony like that.'

The dark hands were smoothed on the white flanks again, and it seemed suddenly to Alexander that they might be hands of possession. His fears were suddenly heightened by something Shako said. 'Knew a man once, Cakey Smith, he had a white horse and got it pinched. Somebody painted it black. Right, ain't it, Charley?'

'Right,' Charley said.

Alexander did not speak. He knew that they were kidding him. He saw sparks of lying winks flash out of Shako's eyes, but he was suddenly frightened. He got hold of Snowy's bridle and prepared to lead him away and all at once the woman's voice came sing-songing from the caravan:

'Oh! the boy's lucky. Got a lucky face all right. Got a lucky face. Nobody'll pinch nothing from him. A lucky nice face he's got. Lucky. He'll be all right.'

'Well, so long,' Alexander said.

'So long,' young Shako said. 'Race y' to-morrow if y' want.'

Suddenly Alexander's wits came back. He remembered why he was here, what it was all about. He remembered what his wild plan had been.

'I can't come to-morrow,' he said. 'Not Saturday.' He felt new sweat break and flush his face as he told the lie. 'We're going out. All of us. Over to Aunt Tilda's for the night. Going to-morrow afternoon and not coming back till Sunday.'

'Lucky boy,' the woman said. 'Oh! You're a lucky boy.'

He walked away with her voice following him calling him lucky, and feeling the sombre eyes of the men swivelling after him. Once up the slope and beyond the spinney he could not walk fast enough. He stopped Snowy by a fence and got on his back. He rode up the track under a deep impulse of excitement and an imagination flared by the behaviour of Snowy and the gipsies and all he had heard.

He rode into the farmyard to put up the basking hens in a scared squawking clutter of brown and white wings. He leapt off the horse and felt the terrific excitement of a kind of heroism as he ran into the house, knowing that the time had come when he could keep things to himself no longer, knowing that he had to tell somebody now.

I V

The following night, Saturday, Alexander lay in the little iron bedstead in the apple bedroom with his trousers on and his boots in readiness under the bed. 'No!' Aunt Bishop had said, 'they ain't goin' to sit up for no fox and no nothing else, so there! And even if they was you'd get to bed and get your sleep just the same. So don't whittle your belly about that!'

Very excited, he lay listening for a long time in the warm darkness of the little room. Twice he got up and stood at the window and looked out, smelling the summer night, seeing nothing to break the colour of darkness except the rosy-orange flowering of distant iron-ore furnaces on the hills beyond the river, hearing nothing to break the sound except a momentary lift of breeze stirring the pear-leaves on the house-wall under the window. For long periods he sat up in bed, eyes wide open so that they should not close altogether, and once he got up and, for the first time in his life, voluntarily washed his face. The cold water woke him afresh and after what seemed to him hours he heard the twang-clanging of the American clock, with the view of Philadelphia in 1867, being wound by his Aunt Bishop in the living-room below, and then her feet on the stairs and finally the latch of her bedroom door breaking one silence and beginning another.

He waited for what he felt was five minutes and then got up and put on his jacket and tied his boots round his neck. He opened the door of his room and waited, listening. His heart seemed to pound at the darkness. He knew that the stairs creaked at every step and finally he lay on the banisters and slid down with no sound but a faint snake-like slither. The kitchen door was unlocked and he went out that way, sitting on the door-mat to put on his boots.

In the darkness his senses were so sharpened by excitement that he could feel the presence of his Uncle Bishop and Maxie before he heard the whispers of their voices. They were sitting together under the cart-shed. For a minute he did not know what to do. Then he remembered the warm kindly face of his Uncle Bishop and the favourite phrase of his aunt, 'Can't see nothing wrong in that boy, can you? I don'

know! You'd give him your head if he asked for it,'
and he ran suddenly across the stack-yard, calling in a
whisper who he was. 'It's all right, it's me, it's Alexander', his heart bumping with guilt and excitement.

'Be God, you'll git me hung,' his Uncle Bishop said.

'Lucky for you y'aint in Kingdom Come,' Maxie
said. 'I was half a mind to shoot.'

'Young gallus!' his uncle said. 'Frightning folks to
death.'

'Can I stop?' Alexander said.

'Looks as y're stopping,' Maxie said. 'Jis be quiet.
Y' oughta ding 'is ear,' he said to Uncle Bishop. 'Too
soft with 'im be 'arf.'

'I told you they were coming,' Alexander said.

'We don' know as they are coming,' Maxie said,
'yit.'

For a long time nobody spoke again. The fields
were dead silent all round the house and when Alexander looked out from the hovel he was so excited that
he felt that the stars swung in their courses over the
straw-stacks and the trees. His hands trembled and
he pressed them between his knees to quieten them.
And then he heard something. It startled him by its
closeness and familiarity: the clopping of Snowy's hoofs
on the ground.

'Where's Snowy?' he said.

'In the stable,' Maxie said. 'We shut him up so's
they should think we'd really gone. See?'

'Diddling 'em?'

'Diddlin' 'em,' Maxie said. 'Gotta be artful wi'
gippos. Else they diddle you.'

They sat silent for a long time again, the night
broken by no sound except the occasional clop of
Snowy's hoofs and a brief whisking of wind stirring
into the stacks and sometimes an odd sleepy murmur

from the hens. A sort of drugged suspense took hold of Alexander, so that once he lost count of time and place and himself, as though he were asleep on his feet.

It was Maxie's voice that sprung him back to full consciousness and excitement. 'Ain't that somebody moochin' about behind the pig-sties?'

'Somebody or summat round there. Them 'ugs ain't rootlin' up for nothing.'

'Listen! Somebody's comin' up round the back.'

Alexander and the two men sat tense, waiting. The boy could hear the sound of someone moving in the deep nettles and grass behind the pig-sties. The sound came nearer, was in the yard itself, was translated suddenly into moving figures. Maxie moved out of the hovel. The boy knelt on his hands and knees, clawing with his finger-nails at a flint embedded in the dry earth, loosening it at last and weighing it in his hand. He felt astonishingly brave and angry and excited. Down across the yard there was a sound of wood being gently splintered: of the plank, as before, being prised out of the side of the locked hen-house. As he heard it he felt the pressure of his Uncle Bishop's hand against his chest, forcing him back a pace or two into the cart-shed. As he moved back he caught his heel against the lowered shaft of the pony cart and slipped. He groped wildly and fell against the side of the shed, the impact clattering the loose corrugated iron roof like a tin skeleton.

When he picked himself up again Maxie and his uncle were already running across the yard, shouting. He began running too. Somebody was slashing a way out through the nettles behind the pig-sties, out towards the orchard. The sows had woken up and were thundering against the sty-doors and the hens had set up a wild cluttering of terror. Alexander flung the flint wildly in the darkness. It hit the iron roof of the pig-sties like a huge explosive cap going off and the next moment, at the gate of the orchard, Maxie fired a shot. For a moment Alexander felt that he had been knocked off his feet. The shot seemed to reverberate across half the world, the boomerang of echoes came smashing back and stirred cattle and hens and pigs to hysteria in which he too was yelling madly.

He was half-way across the orchard, Maxie in front, his Uncle Bishop waddling behind, the gippos already lost somewhere beyond the farthest trees, when he realized that there was a new sound of hysteria in the yard behind him. He stopped, and knew suddenly that it was Snowy, kicking the stable down.

He ran straight back, seeing better now in the darkness but still blundering against low branches of fruit trees, barking his shins on pig-troughs in the stack-yard, brushing past the fat outspread arms of his Uncle Bishop, yelling at him to come. As he reached the stack-yard, mounting straight over the muck-hill, he heard the crack of the stable-door as it split the staple and the final frenzied hammering of Snowy's hoofs as they beat back the swinging door again and again until Snowy himself was free. The horse swung out of the dark hole of the stable like the ghost of a flying horse on a roundabout, circling wildly out of sight behind the far stacks, making drivelling noises of terror. The boy ran to and fro in the dark yard like someone demented himself, calling his uncle, then Maxie.

'Be God, what the nation is it? Boy, what is it? Boy, wheer the devil are y'?'

'It's Snowy!' he yelled. 'Maxie! It's Snowy. It's Snowy. Maxie! Uncle!'

He was almost crying now. The men were rushing about the yard. His Aunt Bishop, from an upstairs window, was shouting incomprehensible threats or questions or advice, no one listening to her.

They were listening only to Alexander, to what he had to say. 'Which way did he go, boy? Did you see him go? Which way?' And when he had nothing to say except, 'I saw him go by the stacks, that's all', they stood listening to a sound coming from far down the road, and he stood listening with them, his heart very scared, fear and excitement beating his brain dizzy.

It was a sound like the noise of a tune played on handbones: the sound of Snowy galloping on the road, far away already towards the river.

v

By nine o'clock on Sunday morning the three of them, Uncle Bishop and Maxie with Alexander riding on the carrier of Maxie's bicycle, had reached a point where the brook ran over the road, under a white handrail bridge between an arch of alders, four miles up-stream. Zigzagging across the countryside, they had been riding and walking since six o'clock, asking every-one they met, a shepherd with his dog, a parson out walking before breakfast, labourers, a tramp or two: 'Y' ain't seen a white horse nowhere? Got out last night. Ain't got no bridle on nor nothing', but no one had seen him and Alexander's heart had begun to curl up like a small tired animal on the verge of sickness.

A small hill, not much more than a green breast-work, curved up from one side of the brook, and Maxie clambered up it on thick squat legs to take a squint over the surrounding land. He came down shaking his head, pressing tired heels in the slope. Sun hit the bubbling surface of the water as it lippled over the road, the dazzling quicksilver light flashing back in Alexander's eyes, making him tired too.

'No sign on 'im,' Maxie said. 'No tellin' wheer he is got to. Rate he was runnin' he'll very like be half-way round England.'

'More likely busted issself up on something. On a fence or something, barbed wire or something,' Uncle Bishop said.

'Well,' Maxie said, 'ain't no use stannin' about. Let's get on as far as Shelton. We can ask Fat Sturman if he's seed 'im.'

'Fat Sturman?' Uncle Bishop said. 'It's Sunday morning. He won't be able to tell a white horse from a black for another twenty-four hours. Allus sozzled Saddays and Sundays, you know that.'

'I forgot,' Maxie said. 'Well, we can ask somebody. Ask the fust man we meet.'

They walked despondently up the hill, pushing the bicycles. It was hot and silent everywhere, bees thick in the grass, the flat empty Sunday morning stillness seeming to Alexander to stretch far over the quivering horizon. Climbing, he looked at his boots. The lace-holes looked back at him from the pollen-yellow leather with the sad stoical eyes of Chinamen.

When he looked up again he was surprised to see an oldish woman coming down the hill, walking in a prim lardidardy way as though she had springs in the heels of her flat cloth-sided boots. On the top of an ant-hill of grey hair she had a huge fruit basket of a hat that reminded him of the glass-case of artificial grapes and pears and cherries that stood on the bible in his Aunt Bishop's parlour. The woman was carrying a prayer-book in her hand and Alexander could see her turning to smile at the trees as she went past, as though she had hidden friends in them.

'Shall we ask her?' Uncle Bishop whispered.

'Won't know a horse from a dead donkey,' Maxie said.

'Never know,' Uncle Bishop said. 'Way she's bouncing down the hill she might a bin a jockey.'

'Well, you ask her. Not me.'

Half a minute later Uncle Bishop had taken off his hat and was making a little speech in a strange aristocratic voice to the old lady, who stood with hands clasped over the prayer-book, smiling with a kind of saintly beatitude. 'Hexcuse me, madam, but hi suppose you hain't seen a white pony nowheer? He 'scaped last night. Much hobliged lady, if you seen hany sign on 'im.'

The old lady took one smiling, saintly look at the two men and Alexander.

'Yes,' she said, 'I have.'

'My God,' Maxie said, 'wheer?'

The old lady looked at Maxie. 'Did you use the name of God?'

'Yis, but — '

'In front of the little boy?'

'Yis, but — '

'My man, you ought to burn in hell!'

Sheepish and exasperated and at a loss, Uncle Bishop and Maxie stood looking at the ground, not knowing what to say, and the old lady suddenly began to make a strange rambling speech of reproval, preaching decency and godliness and respect for the Sabbath, her voice by turns like vinegar and honey, one hand sometimes upraised in a little gesture to the sky, until finally Alexander could stand it no longer.

'Please,' he said, 'please tell us where the horse is. Something might have happened to him. He might be bad. He might be dying.'

404

'Everybody is dying,' she said.

His heart sank; tears of anger and frustration hit his eyes and sprang back. 'Tell us where he is,' he said. 'Please. Tell us where he is.'

She was still smiling, saintly, slightly but rather nicely mad, and for one second the boy did not believe a word of all she had said. Then all at once she turned and pointed up the hill.

'He's at the top of the hill. Lying on the grass. Lying under a tree.'

Maxie and Alexander and Uncle Bishop ran up the hill. 'God bless you,' the old lady called, but they scarcely heard it.

The white pony was lying as the old lady had said in the shade of an ash tree at the top of the hill. As he heard footsteps and voices he lifted his head, and a small black explosion of flies rose from one eye. The boy called his name and with a great eager effort, making odd noises in his throat, the pony tried to struggle to his feet. He made the effort and sank back and Maxie knelt down by his head. 'All right, Snowy. All right Goo' boy. Goo' boy then. All right.'

'We got to git 'im up,' Uncle Bishop said.

'Yis,' Maxie said, 'we got to git 'im up. Stan' back, boy. Very like he'll make a bit of a to-do. Stan' back.'

Alexander stood back but the white pony could not rise. 'Come on, Snowy,' the men said, 'come on now. Come on,' but nothing happened. It was cool under the ash tree but it seemed to the boy that the pony was held down by the heat of a great exhaustion. Each time he lifted his head the flies broke away in a small black explosion and then settled again.

They tried for almost half an hour to get the pony to his feet, but Maxie said at last: 'It's no good. We gotta git somebody else to look at him. You wait here and

I'll bike into Shelton and git Jeff Emery. He's a knacker.'

'Knacker?' Uncle Bishop said.

'Well, he's a bit of a vet too. Does both. He'll know what to do if anybody does.'

Maxie got on his bicycle and rode away up the hill. Alexander and Uncle Bishop stood and looked at the white pony. The depth of silence seemed to increase when Maxie had gone, bees moaning in the honeysuckle and the blackberry flowers, yellow hammers chipping mournful notes on the hedge-rows, a bell for morning service donging a thin hole in the distance over the hill.

'Think he'll get up?' the boy said.

'He'll get up, he's just tired. You would be if you'd galloped about all night.'

'Shako says he's old. He's not, is he?'

'He ain't young.'

'You think he's been a race-horse and the shot made him think he was in a race again?'

'I count that's what it was.' Uncle Bishop took another look at the pony. 'Well, it's no good. I gotta see a man about a dog. You comin'?' and he and Alexander went and stood over by the far hedge. 'Hedge-roses out nice,' Uncle Bishop said. 'Grow all the better for a little water.'

When they turned again something had happened. Very quiet and looking in some way very fragile, the white pony was on his feet. The boy's heart seemed to turn somersaults of happiness. He ran and put his hands on the pony's head, smoothing his nose, talking softly. 'Snowy. Good Snowy. Good boy, Snowy.'

'You think he's all right?' he said.

'You think he could walk as far as the brook? Perhaps he wants a drink?'

'Yeh. Let him walk if he will. Don't force him. Let him go how he likes.'

'Come on, Snowy,' the boy said. 'Come on, Snowy. Good Snowy. Good boy. Come on.'

The pony walked slowly down the hill in hot sunshine. At the bottom of the hill, where the brook ran over the road, he put his lips to the water. He let the water run into and past his mouth, not really drinking. He stood like that for a long time, not moving at all.

Suddenly he went down on his fore-legs and sank into the water. Alexander and Uncle Bishop had not time to do anything before they heard a shout and saw Maxie, with a man in breeches and leggings, coming down the hill.

'Summat we can do, Jeff, ain't there?' Maxie said. 'Summat we can do?'

The man did not answer. He knelt down by the pony, pressing his hands gently on the flanks.

'Well, there's jis' one thing we can do, that's all.'

The boy stood scared and dumb, watching the water break against the body of the horse, not seeing the men's faces.

'All right,' Maxie said. He took Alexander by the arm. 'Boy, you git hold o' my bike and take it across the bridge and put it underneath that furdest ash tree, outa the sun. I don't want the tyres bustin'.'

'Is Snowy going to be all right?' the boy said.

'Yis. He's going to be all right.'

Alexander took the bicycle and wheeled it across the bridge and along the road. The ash tree was fifty yards away. He reached it and laid the bicycle against the trunk in the shade. The bell tinkled as it touched the tree and at the same time as if the bell were a signal, he heard a sharp, dull report from the brook, and he turned in time to see the man in breeches and leggings holding a strange-looking pistol in his hand.

Running wildly back to the brook, trying to shout and not shouting, he saw the white pony's head lying flat and limp in the water. The water was lapping over the eyes, and out of the head and mouth a long scarf of blood was slowly unwinding itself downstream. The men had their backs turned away from him as though they did not want to look at him, and he knew that the white pony had gone for ever.

What he did not know until long afterwards was that there, at that moment, in the dead silence of the summer morning, with the sun blazing down on the white pony and the crimson water and the buttercups rich as paint in the grass, some part of his life had gone for ever too.

NO COUNTRY

OSCAR'S wife was Jewish. She was crying hard when I
got to the court. Her mother, a dusky, heavy Jewess
with sausage hands and a mouth wracked by the
immemorial pain of the race, was crying with her. It
was not like ordinary crying; it was far removed from
the crying of mere relief or apprehension. It was the
traditional subdued wailing of intuition and pain: as if
they knew that Oscar was doomed.

I did not see Oscar himself for two or three minutes.
It was raining outside, sour January rain, and I came
into the lobby quickly. Groups of policemen with
greased hair were standing talking, waiting to give
evidence, ready to answer questions. Two courts were
in sitting. The lobby was crowded, mothers sitting
on the benches, with meek bad boys, old women half
dozing, solicitors talking with lowered heads, touts,
fancy ladies, men waiting all alone. Then suddenly,
among them, I saw Oscar. His face was strange, very
yellow. It was as though he knew he were doomed
himself.

'They'll deport me,' he said, when I went to him.
He was tied up in knots of fear, almost beside himself.
'They'll turn me over to the Nazis. I know. They'll
deport me.'

'Have you said anything?' I said. 'Have you signed
anything?'

'I made a statement.'

He was done. I knew it. 'Did they *make* you do
that?' I said.

No. He went down, voluntarily. He dictated it.
He had to. He knew if he didn't they'd send him back
to Germany. To the Nazis. That's why he did it.

Now he'd put the statement in they'd give him a month and it would all be over.

'But you didn't do it,' I said. 'You haven't done anything. Just because somebody steals books and then brings them to you to sell doesn't mean you're a criminal. You didn't do anything.'

But it was a plant! They put it up. Didn't I see? They knew he was a communist. It was a political case. The books were just a blind. They had to get him somehow. It was political. It was political.

Then Oscar's solicitor came up and asked me to step on one side with him. He was piteously nervous, more nervous than Oscar himself, as though he didn't like being mixed up with the case of an alien who was also a communist, a man caught between the twin fires of the English police and Hitlerism.

'Oscar has made a statement,' he said.

'I know,' I said. 'Can I do anything? Give evidence?'

'That's what I wanted to say. Will you just give some evidence — just formal evidence — as to character?'

I said I would. When I looked round again Oscar had gone. Over against the wall Oscar's wife and her mother were still lost in a Jewish luxury of anguish. I went over to them and said:

'It'll be all right. They can't convict a man for something he didn't do. They can't do it.'

'It isn't that!' Oscar's wife said. 'It's intrigue, I tell you! It's political. The communists hate him and the Nazis think he's a communist. He's got nobody. He's got nobody. They're all against him! It's put up! It's put up!'

'Ach!' the old woman wailed, softly. 'Don', don'. Iss all ri'. Iss all ri'. Iss will be all ri'.'

'It'll be all right,' I said.

Then, quite suddenly, the court door was flung open and the usher bawled my name. I went into the court where Oscar was. It was a small court. It was like a schoolroom, bare-walled, hard. I looked at once for Oscar. There, in the dock, he seemed not only doomed but already dead. His face had gone beyond yellow to dead whiteness, beyond fear of not knowing into the terror of knowledge. Standing very erect, he looked very German.

Taking the oath, I looked from Oscar to the magistrate. He was small and fat, like a polished bladder of pink lard.

'Well? What're you — what're you — what's this man here to tell us?'

'He is here to give evidence, sir, as to the character of the defendant.'

'Is he? H'm. Well, come on — let's hear it. Who is he? What is he, eh?'

'He is a literary man, sir.'

'Eh? What? A what?'

'A literary man, sir. Books, sir.'

'Oh! books. Books, eh?'

As though to say mumps, or as though books were some childish complaint of the human mind. And suddenly he turned about savagely on me:

'You know something about books? What about these books? On this table. You ever seen these books before?'

Many books were stacked and strewn on the table before him, the stolen books of the case. I had not seen them before. 'No,' I said.

'Oh! Not seen them? Anywhere? At all?'

'No.'

'Oh! H'm.'

As though to say lucky for you.

Then, after a moment, the solicitor began to ask me questions. How long had I known Oscar? What was he like? What sort of man? Did I buy books from him? Did I sell books to him?

But suddenly the magistrate was bored or sickened or tired of it all. 'That'll do for you. Stand down. Write books, eh? Well, you must write a book about this some day. Eh?'

Laughter in court. I was annihilated, suddenly, by the smashing of questions at Oscar.

'Well, Obermann? What about you? What have you got to say? You have told us you are a German. You're not naturalized?'

'No, sir.'

'Still a German?'

'No, sir.'

'What? No nationality? Is that it? No country?'

'No, sir. No country.'

Sitting at the back of the court, I could see the round pink bladder of the magistrate's face in full, but only the back of Oscar's head.

'When did you first come to London?'

'In 1907, sir.'

'What did you do then for a living?'

'I peddled scissors, sir.'

'Eh? What? Speak up. What did you do?'

'I peddled scissors, sir.'

'You what? I can't hear. What's he say?'

They all explained, clerk, court missionary, solicitor: 'He peddled scissors, sir.'

'Oh! Scissors.' As though to say bombs, or balloons. The contempt made his face gross and sulky. 'Yes. And then what? After that? When did you begin the bookselling?'

'After the war, sir. I —'

'War? What happened to you in the war? What did you do?'

'I was interned.'

'Interned? Oh!' He made a note, as though that also were a bad mark against Oscar. 'Well, and after that? How did you get this shop? Save up?'

'I got married.'

'Eh?' Then it dawned on him. 'Oh! I see. Got married. Married the girl and the shop too. Is that it?'

Laughter in court again. And again silence.

'Well, and about these books? Eh? You say, here, in the statement, that it was very silly of you, that you must have known they were stolen. Is that right?'

'Yes, sir.'

'You were in difficulties? Trade was not good?'

'It was the slump, sir.'

'Slump, eh?' As though he had never heard of it. 'I don't want to know about that. What I want to know, Obermann, is this. What I want to know is — why didn't you go to the wife about it? Eh?'

Saying it, he looked very smart, most triumphant, as though he had heard, at some time, that there is always a woman in the case. He smiled with beautiful bitterness, with nice cruelty, as though to say: 'That's got you, Obermann. *Cherchez la femme.* You can't get away from that, Obermann, my friend.'

And strangely, Oscar had nothing to say. He stood staring, not so much at a loss as like a man who realizes, suddenly, that the end has come. He stood like that all the time his solicitor was making his plea.

It was a short plea, a mere formality. There was something in it about Oscar's being a good father and a good husband and something else about Oscar being sorry. I forget what else. There was nothing about fascism or communism or Germany or beating up or hatred or intrigue or politics or deportation. Nothing at all.

And if the magistrate heard it he did not show it. He sat like a man carved out of pink lard, a man without feeling. He sat like that until there was silence. Then, as though his mind had been made up from the very beginning and as though all the rest had really been silence, he said:

'I have no option, Obermann, but to send you to prison. You must pay the penalty. You will go to the second division for twelve months. You must pay the penalty. Take him away.'

They took him away. Oscar did not look at me. He did not look at anyone. And I saw him, in that moment, not as a man wanted by the factions of two countries and hated by both, but as a man apart from us, a man of no country at all.